Thanks for ~

Pete Andresen

"To John Mahoney" —

THE PYRE

I'm interested in your thoughts!

A novel of the Great 2022 Earthquake, the
Breaking Apart Of the United States of America,
And
the Creation of the People's
Republic of California

By
— Peter G. Andresen —

TIMEWALKER
PRESS

Salinas, California

The Pyre
A novel by Peter G. Andresen

Copyright © 2020 by Peter G. Andresen

Timewalker Press
P.O. Box 1434
Salinas, California, 93902

Printed in the United States of America

Publisher's Cataloging-in-Publication Data
Andresen, Peter Garth

ISBN: 978-0-9854285-5-6 (paperback book)
ISBN: 978-0-9854285-6-3 (iBook)

Library of Congress Control Number: 2018902093

Disclaimers, Groveling, and Lawyer–Speak

This novel intentionally contains genuine places, because part of the fun of reading should be the retracing of events as they happen in the novel. If you visit these places, please consider that you do so at your own risk, although in truth millions of people have toured these locations without mishap.

There is racial, sexual, emotional, and physical violence in this novel, including descriptions of horrendous behaviors, brutality, rape, nudity, sex, gore, gender-shaming, racial misidentification and stereotyping, use of guns, cannibalism, Vienna sausages, carnivorous diets, and books. The author and the publisher do not advocate any of these politically incorrect attitudes or actions. In fact, this novel was written in large part to warn against them. The actions of governments described herein are intended as warnings, not prophecies.

The author has gone to great lengths to create characters in this novel who are unlike any real people, although archetypes of human behavior are certainly here. If you perceive that you identify with, say, one of the 'Eat The Rich' crew then please deeply examine how that might be so.

Likewise, the novel contains no incidents which really occurred in history, except those which are generally acknowledged, for example, the Battle of The Rosebud, or the history of Nazi Germany. When people in this novel make political statements, many of those are intentionally plagiarized from public comments made by well-known people, to highlight the statements' absurdity. Some political statements in this book do not convey the beliefs of the author in the slightest. In fact, they are described to emphasize their repugnance.

Likewise, any social or political attitudes or opinions in this novel are not those of the publisher and anyone involved in the selling or distribution of this book.

For additional reading and information concerning sources, a short bibliography follows the novel.

It's all made up.

"The 'common good' of a collective—a race, a class, a state—was the claim and justification of every tyranny ever established over men. Every major horror in history was committed in the name of an altruistic motive. Has any act of selfishness ever equaled the carnage perpetrated by disciples of altruism?" Ayn Rand, **The Fountainhead**

Democide = genocide and mass murder of unarmed non-combatants by governments.
The term was created by R.J. Rummel, who wrote:

"The total victims of democide in the 20th Century:
262,000,000.

"Just to give perspective on this incredible murder by government, if all these bodies were laid head to toe, with the average height being 5', then they would circle the earth ten times. Also, this democide murdered 6 times more people than died in combat in all the foreign and internal wars of the century. Finally, given popular estimates of the dead in a major nuclear war, this total democide is as though such a war did occur, but with its dead spread over a century." R.J. Rummel, **Power Kills: Democracy As A Method Of Nonviolence**

Peter G. Andresen

"Socialism fails because while most individuals don't want others to have more than they have, few are averse to having more than others." Gary Bernhard, Ed.D. and Kalman Glantz, PhD. **Psychology Today**, January 2020.

Salinas, Republic of California
April 18th, 2054

The feeling, when it came, was shocking. Today was the day, the anniversary of the day. Thirty-two years ago, today. April 18th, 2022. It had been a Saturday, a lifetime and an entirely different world ago.

Back then, he, Garth Ericson, had roared like a lion. Back then. Now he simply stayed alive at age 99 and enjoyed life, to piss them off. That also explained why he had buried the last of his guns under the old, abandoned sewage cast iron pipes deep in his backyard, rather than surrender them. It paid to live in the older part of town, after all.

He thought of the guns often, waiting in their water-proof plastic tubes. Mosin Nagants, Enfields, 1911 pistols. Stainless steel revolvers. Waiting for what? He wondered. Better than surrendering them to the chopper. Besides, his very existence was an irritant to the Republic of California. His ancestry. His language. His culture. All wrong. All officially the attributes which reminded the Republic of the former oppressors.

He looked up, at the crisp, cool blue sky framed by the tops of the buildings around him. Framed by the street side new-leafed trees. Old town Main Street, Salinas, California, mostly the same as it had been for all one hundred years of his existence. And for the eight generations of his ancestors before him

A few new tasteful buildings had been built here since the earthquake, and after the war. He had to admit that the new buildings were nicely done, with appropriate commercial zoning at ground level and residences above, mostly now intended for the new arrivals. It dawned on him that he could actually remember the original owners, long since fled or deceased. The wealth and inheritance taxes had taken their toll, of course.

Now these buildings were mostly owned by the Republic of California, or by large distant megacorporations, mostly in China, which somehow made the buildings less substantial. As though the bricks and cement cared who owned them.

Down the street, where there had once been the Dick Brown clothing store in his youth, was an entirely new building, eight stories tall, a condominium complex for the new arrivals. There was a large sign on the roof:

"吉祥新生活大厦"

Garth Ericson had been told that this meant "Good Fortune New Life", although it may well have read "Water Bug Convention Center" or "Wow Did We Screw Up", since his skill at reading Chinese was imperfect at best.

He watched the sign gleaming in the brilliant sunlight, and the similar sign on the new building next door to it. He had to admit, the new arrivals, the Chinese who had arrived since the earthquake and secession, were mostly wonderful people. They embraced local life with gusto. By law, they had automatic dual citizenship in the Republic of California and in China.

By law, the new arrivals had a monopoly on jobs in the sciences and medicine. But they did it well. Garth's health care was free, largely automated. His medical liaison, a young new arrival who had been born here, spoke to him in English, which was a major condescension on her part. Most of them used translating software. After all, English was the language of the former oppressors. They discussed artichokes, and Big Sur. The good stuff. Smiles.

Garth turned and looked down the street. The solar panel driving surface which had replaced asphalt was shiny and clean-looking, and new arrivals were well-known for their fastidious habits. The ubiquitous cameras would instantly identify anyone who littered or mistreated the area. After that, the police, and reeducation, and processing.

Here was the place where there had been a coffee shop before the earthquake, where the skateboard groupies had hung out smoking each night, leaving cigarette butts and half-consumed beer bottles to face the sunrise. Now it was all new. The entire building had been knocked down.

Across the street, an original brick facade building remained. That was the store where Dina Montero's bookstore had been, and where she had printed the Salinas Index Journal, one of the last paper newspapers in the state. It had mostly been an affectation, he thought. Yet, it had been one of his favorite haunts before the earthquake, where a person could go inside and inhale and actually smell real printed books. Such memories.

Now the venue was a methadone and marijuana clinic, owned by the local elites, the Johnson family, and much-used by the descendants of pre-earthquake families. The new arrivals didn't use drugs like that. The Johnson family owned most of the legal drug trade in Monterey County, and a substantial portion of the buildings on this street, and throughout the town. It paid to be on the winning side.

At the head of the street the University Buildings, formerly repurposed for re-education and processing, now reimagined yet again as an ethnic studies hub. The abuses of the prior regime, the United States, were taught there. The hard sciences, with the blessing of the natives, had become the legally exclusive expertise of the new Chinese immigrants or their descendants. The remaining pre-earthquake descendants were welcome to take degrees in counselling and soft arts, such as racial grievance, to become prosecutors for the social crimes of the new Republic of California. Such prosecutions were reserved for only the pre-quakers. The new arrivals had their own courts, their own justice.

So few pre-earthquake natives now. Many had fled to the United States, over to East California or Nevada, across the San Joaquin River, to the heartland where most of his surviving children lived these days. He wondered how they were, this morning. The new great grandchildren. It was a rougher and more rewarding world over there.

Most of the native-born who remained here were in the labor barracks. That was one benefit of the new regime: no homeless sleeping on the streets. They were all in the system or processed. No more shit on the front porch.

He contemplated that he was fortunate that he was still in his own home. He was aware that he was still here only because of the influence of his family, there in the United States. Good publicity. The Republic of California needed that.

Inevitably, though, publicity had its limits. Small as it was, his home was too attractive for new arrivals, too useful. The knock summoning him for processing would come any day now. When that happened, he would have his son's electric car drive him over the East California border, to Modesto. To freedom.

Cars were not allowed to anyone but the new arrivals here in the Republic of California, to lessen congestion. Yet because of his family over in the United States, because of his son, he had the car, waiting just for him and for that moment. But oh, such a loss when that happened. So much finally surrendered.

Today, here and now, was a beautiful sunny day. And in a few months, he would be 100 years old.

The service bot in the wall facing him intoned some phrases in Chinese. There were service bots on every wall, moving to keep up with him, always muttering suggestions and advice. He did not respond, on principal. Then the bot spoke in Spanish. Beautiful voice, really. As though it was a 25-year-old young woman. They knew how to program these machines. Then the voice repeated, in English, "Please look at the facial recognition sensor".

He turned and faced the wall of the convenience store. His account still had a few of the new dollars. Just numbers, really. He hadn't even seen cash...public cash, bills or coins, outside of the collectibles in his own home...for twenty years. Why he should shop himself, why he should not simply tell the automated assistant in his home to fetch what he needed, was another act of life force. He was here because he knew it pissed them off. An unreconstructed United States citizen, still living here. It pissed them off.

The fisheye lens moving on the wall examined him as he faced it. It seemed to focus, intently. It blinked, artificially, simulating life. A yellow light blinked below the lens. "Low Social Credit" blinked in yellow below the light. Then yellow text appeared in Spanish below that, and below that another line of yellow Chinese script appeared.

"Access denied".

Ah.

It was a beautiful day.

So many memories.

Capitol and Central Streets, Salinas, State of California April 18th, 2022 5:52 AM

The woman lying on the ambulance stretcher, itself resting on the lawn in front of her home....she was brave. But too badly stabbed, thought Wallace Ericson. Ambulance EMT's preparing to transport, two other police officers, Mickey and

Hugh, managing traffic, the IV's in her arms, and the kids and the husband, African Americans, middle class, standing about five yards away on their own lawn, in front of their own old well-kept Victorian home. She had gone to take out the trash before the morning pickup and a lurking homeless man had stabbed her. Now the flashing lights of emergency vehicles lit up the predawn darkness, and they were preparing to transport.

The senior EMT was nodding to him. Negative. Blood pressure was plummeting. Internal bleeding. She probably wasn't going to make it. Lifting her up on the ambulance gurney. She was speaking a few quiet words with her husband now. So brave.

You would think I would be used to this by now, thought Wallace. I'm not.

The husband stepped back as the EMT's began to move her gurney. The husband...Mike Rogers, Wallace remembered, her name was Lacy Rogers. Kids Sherry and Raz, eight and seven years old, now standing up by the home's porch watching wide-eyed, frightened, hugged from behind by the Hispanic neighbor in a bathrobe. All of them dressed for sleeping.

The husband, Mike Rogers, walked a few steps to where Wallace stood, shaking his head angrily. "That homeless guy. Ronny Reynolds. He's been shitting on our doorstep and threatening us for five years! Stealing the ladders and tools out of my work truck. More than that! We've asked the city to do something about it and you didn't do anything. Now my wife may die and you helped make it happen!"

Wallace stepped closer in the darkness, to speak quietly. "You know I've arrested him at least ten times. Theft. Vandalism. Threats. Defecation. Trespassing."

"And somebody always lets him go, and he always comes back. Always. Your zero bail policy, and that priest...that pastor's constant demand to the city that the homeless are more important than the people who actually live here. You haven't defended us. You haven't done ANYTHING!," said Mike Rogers, his anger rising.

Of course the man was right, thought Wallace. State law. City law. All biased against people who just wanted to live their lives. Wallace's father's home was one block away, on the other side of Roosevelt Elementary School, on Gabilan Street. Wallace had grown up there. His own family had struggled with vandals, petty crime, and especially Ronny Reynolds, for years.

A bright red Mercedes sedan pulled up, coming to a stop athwart the ambulance's path, blocking its departure. Oh, great, thought Wallace. Here's the mayor. Happy Johnson. And he's here to help. As always.

From the car emerged a large, red-haired man, at least 6 foot 3 inches tall and somewhat overweight, concern written across his pale face. Green eyes. Dark red Elvis hair. The effect was always a bit shocking.

"I came as SOON AS I HEARD!", the mayor said emotively, looking at them both. Turning to Mike Rogers, he said, "You must be THE HUSBAND!"

As soon as he spoke, he embraced Mike Rogers in an enfolding hug.

The mayor smelled mildly of marijuana, thought Wallace. The mayor had helped bring that industry to town, advocated making it legal in the state, and then he had profited from it when a major distributor had made him a partner. Natural that he should sample the product.

"TERRIBLE! TERRIBLE!" said the mayor.

Behind, in the street, Wallace could see Mitchell "Mickey" Ramirez, nicknamed "Mouse" although he was tall and fit, one of the shift's police officers, guiding the ambulance to back up over the lawn. They knew from experience that the mayor was not going to move his car, he thought. And here came another car, a dark blue BMW, black in the near-darkness of the inadequate street lights. That would be the city manager, Causwell Dubbers. Oh great. A circus.

My shift is going to run late again, thought Wallace, to entertain these two. Not to fight crime. Not to help Mike Rogers. To participate in this dog and pony show of virtue signaling which is about to engulf us all. As it has before. Again and again. For your pleasure, a retinue of dancing monkeys, and all of them have ingested LSD.

"You met me two weeks ago, Mr. Mayor. Mr. Johnson," said Mike Rogers. "At the big conference on the homeless at the YMCA. I was the painting contractor. The guy whose ladders were stolen by Ronny Reynolds right in the middle of a big job. I spoke at the podium..."

"Of COURSE! Of COURSE!" said Mayor Johnson. "I didn't recognize you in this light."

"It's Ronny Reynolds who did this, Mr. Mayor. Ronny Reynolds stabbed my wife," said Mike, breaking down. "Lacy.

Lacy. Stabbed her! Stabbed her! Remember I stood up there in front of everyone at that meeting and I TOLD you he was bad news? Stalking and ruining everything in our neighborhood."

"Now, now, we don't know he did that. Did you actually see him do it?" said a voice behind Wallace. Wallace turned. There stood the pastor of the Day of Blessings Church, the nearby congregation which had elected to turn itself into a homeless shelter and feeding area, thus attracting the homeless from all over the city of Salinas. Wallace tried to remember his name. Ah...Pastor Paco. Paco Mayweather. Blonde. Looked like a bearded aging surfer, with a protruding stomach. Preferred to speak Spanish and affected an Hispanic connection. 'Paco' looked more like 'Sven'.

"You shouldn't accuse people of crimes you aren't sure they committed," said the pastor, his clerical collar reflecting the streetlight. "If you didn't see him do it, you shouldn't make allegations."

"Yes, I sure DID see him stab her. I was talking through the open front door to my beautiful wife...my beautiful wife...". Mike Rogers began to cry. "And he just came out of the shrubs with this great big knife and stuck her. And stuck her again. And she was screaming, and pushing at him, and I came outside, and he stepped back, and he shouted, and then he just ran off."

"Oh, dear, how terrible," said Mayor Johnson, hugging Mike Rogers again. "Terrible. It's OK if you want to cry. Let those feelings out. After all, African Americans like you have been marginalized for centuries. Centuries!"

Mike was struggling to free himself from the mayor.

"What did the attacker shout? Words?" said a strong woman's voice from the darkness. Wallace recognized it and winced inside. Dina Montero, local one-woman bookstore owner and sole reporter and editor for the city paper, a clinging vestige of its former self, the Salinas Index Journal. The Salinas city paper, as was the case with most newspapers, was these days not big enough to wrap a salmon. Sometimes Dina was a gadfly. Sometimes an illuminator.

Wallace thought to himself that all this had already been recorded by his officers. Dina Montero should be waiting for his report. The big question now was to somehow keep Lacy Rogers alive. If that was possible. In the distance, in the dawn, there was a siren. The ambulance. Heading for the trauma center at Natividad.

When nobody answered her, Dina Montero grumbled. "Yep, I know, out on bail, homeless, insane, more crime, nothing changes," as though to herself.

"Oh, no, as I said at our meeting at the YMCA several weeks ago, things WILL change!" said Mayor Happy Johnson. "Definitely, things WILL change! We will BUY a hotel and put them all there! And our Pastor Paco will be in charge!"

"Yes! Things ARE getting better!" said Pastor Paco.

Things don't look better for the Rogers family, thought Wallace. Things don't look better at all. That meeting two weeks ago was just more virtue signaling, more of the Kabuki of California promise-based politics. Let the people holler. Then enact taxes from on high.

But he, himself, was the beneficiary of those taxes. His pension in only twelve more years would be the envy of many.

Twelve more years. Just get through this for twelve more years. Then he would do what almost all Salinas police department officers did when they retired. He would move far, far away, perhaps to Georgia or to Idaho as his older friends had.

Wallace had a sudden surge of recollection of skiing... Nordic skiing...a few weeks back, before he put his wife and their two children on a plane to visit her relatives in Denmark. To be precise, to visit the beautiful little rural town of her family, Aabenraa, set among farm fields.

The ski trip had been with his father, Garth, and Garth's Filipina wife Dove, and Wallace's much younger sisters Francesca and Akemi. Oh, damn, that adventure had been beautiful. Brilliant blue sky, magnificent white snow, the ski lift at China Peak taking them up to the snack bar on top of the mountain, even the children, even his little six year old daughter, so brave on the chair lift, and then skiing down through the trees with glacial slowness, stopping for a picnic of jerky and chips and hot chocolate while they watched the panorama of Lake Huntington spread out far below them. Oh, so beautiful. How he missed his family. How horrible... unthinkable...to be in Mike Roger's situation. Denmark was far away but at least his family was safe.

"How are things going to change?" said Dina Montero, a bit snidely. "Seems to me things haven't improved for the Rogers family. Your hotel will just give them a base of operations."

She was writing on an old-fashioned stenographic pad with a thick four-color pen, squinting down at the page in the feeble illumination of the street lights.

"Oh, yes, Mr. Mayor," said Causwell Dubbers, the city manager. "How do you want things to change?"

Wallace looked at Causwell Dubbers in the half-light. Dawn was just beginning. Causwell Dubbers was looking up at the large mayor, at the mayors' groomed sweeping dark red hair, the color almost burgundy, with apparent reverence. Recently revealed by the minimalist Salinas Index Journal to be receiving a city-paid salary of $500,000 a year, a medium level of compensation for a city manager in California, Causwell Dubbers seemed to be a small wizened mole rat in a suit, glasses reflecting the streetlight as he spoke. Causwell Dubbers, thought Wallace, made a great sidekick to the Mayor. He lined up the business opportunities, and the mayor brought them into actuality. After getting a partnership in whatever was happening.

"WELL!" said Mayor Johnson, "We're going to have a big CONFERENCE! Another conference about the homeless at the YMCA!"

"Another big discussion! With dry erase boards," said Pastor Paco, enthusiastically.

"Didn't you already do this?" said Dina Montero.

"If you'll excuse me, I need to be with my kids," said Mike Rogers. "This is just more bullshit. Another shovel full of the same old manure. Meanwhile my wife is fighting for her life."

Mike Rogers stepped back and turned up the walkway of his front door. Wallace noticed he was still wearing his bathrobe. With his wife's bloodstains. Behind him loomed the giant bulk of Hugh "Tiny" Tupuola. Samoan. Well over six feet. Weightlifter, his muscles straining against his blue uniform almost comically. Tiny reached out sorrowfully. Mike Rogers acquiesced reluctantly with a small hand tap as he walked into his home. Wallace corrected himself. Hugh hated to be called 'Tiny'. Always Hugh.

"You're serious, Happy? Really? How does this help the homeless, I mean, really solve the problem?" asked Dina Montero, ignoring Mike Roger's departure.

"Oh, we will solve the problem, Dina! God has blessed us! We feed the homeless every day!" said Pastor Paco excitedly. "We have a grant for millions of dollars from the state! Mayor Johnson got that grant for us!"

In return for undying loyalty, a hefty salary paid to the pastor, and campaign contributions kicked back, thought Wallace. Jeez. I need to leave before I vomit.

"But why was Ronnie Reynolds on the street anyway?" asked Dina Montero. "I mean, he was so mentally ill he couldn't wipe his own butt when he shat in people's driveways. He's threatened people here for years. He even killed that family's dog a few years back." she motioned at the home next door. An elderly Hispanic woman, white hair stark in the dim light, standing stooped, was gripping the bannister of the porch and watching them from there.

"So why not find him a nice safe place? Keep him out of the way?" Dina continued.

"There's not funding for that!" said Causwell Dubbers. "No, no! He's a victim of the system! Discrimination against the homeless! Don't you talk down to the underprivileged! And Ronny Reynolds is Hispanic! Hispanic people have been oppressed by discrimination for centuries! Downtrodden for centuries!"

"Seems to me a lot of people are benefiting from the system as it is now," said Dina. "Except homeless people."

Wallace made a note to talk with Dina Montero sometime in the future. After all, their families knew each other. He had attended Salinas High School with her daughter, Zejaica. Wallace turned and looked as Mike Rogers shepherded his children back inside their home and shut the door. Wallace scanned the lawn, and the neighborhood. The morning daylight was definitely growing brighter.

"Why Dina, how can you say that?" Happy Johnson was saying. "That's cruel and unfair, and untrue. We need another meeting so people can express themselves, you know, grieve. Vent. Audience participation! Clarify this victimization and illuminate the discrimination against the homeless."

Dina began to respond but Wallace was distracted. Hugh's K-9 police dog, in the back seat of the police cruiser with the window rolled half-down, began to howl. Never seen that before, thought Wallace. Dog must be sick? Get it out of there before it panics.

San Antonio Mission, State of California
April 18th, 2022
5:52 AM

Crickets. Crickets chirping, somewhere out in the waning darkness. In the river, about a quarter of a mile away, frogs.

Or were they toads, making all that noise? Perhaps they were calling out for love, thought Raley.

The night was chill, and her 1840's coat was barely adequate. Above her loomed the sprawling milky way, stars strewn across the sky, and north and south the horizons lit up with the inexorable glow of distant cities. The cities were like hives, she thought. Never sleeping. Over the mountains to the east the dawn was lighting the dark sky pink.

Here, though, at the San Antonio de Padua Mission, at 5 AM, everything was quite dark. She could barely see, and if she stepped on a wayward branch, or tripped over a tent line and went sprawling...well, her light-sleeping grandfather Poppa would be up from his pioneer plow point tent and that would be that.

Or, worse yet, she could trip over Hero the Service Dog. Seriously. What qualified Hero as a Service Dog was a mystery. What motivated Hero's owners to let him roam was a still greater mystery.

As was that boy, the boy of tonight, Terp Taylor. Nineteen years old. He was always grinning at her. Always looking. So, she had made the decision, last month. He was her first. Just for the experience. She was seventeen years old. That wasn't too young, was it? Her mother had told her that a woman had to practice pleasing a man. Had to learn. The thought made her smile. Boys were such idiots. Slaves to their hormones.

Raley moved through the darkness very cautiously until she came to her own tent, the modern tent. It was mostly screen and nylon. In the old-fashioned canvas tent nearby, she could hear her grandfather snoring.

There was a noise across the yard. In the distance, Raley could see Mrs. Ericson, all 102 years old, moving with her walker very slowly down the tiled walkway along the mission, illuminated by a bare lightbulb on the wall. Going, as she always did, to the bathroom and then back to her tent. How Mrs. Ericson was moving at all was a miracle. It was insane that the old woman was here, in this place full of dirt and boring old people. Mrs. Ericson was 102 years old. That meant that this mission, this old pile, was only about 140 years old when Mrs. Ericson was born, in 1920. Both had gotten old together.

She felt with her hands for the zipper to the door. Through the screen she could see the light of several cell phones. Her sisters, up all night playing digital games and talking with distant friends. At least she and her sisters had that. At least, somewhere out there, were her friends. Not this boring stick Francesca who actually thought that living history...pretending to be back in the 1860's... was any fun at all.

"Quiet!" whispered her sister Hillary "Don't wake up Francesca and Akemi! They'll rat you out!"

"Quiet yourself," came the voice of Ophelia, her other sister, "I'm talking with a very nice young man at home in Hollister."

"It's 4 AM. What's he doing up?" came a sleepy voice. That would be Francesca, their friend from Salinas, daughter of that professorial earnest old fud Garth Ericson.

"You're supposed to be asleep, Francesca!" whispered Ophelia, laughing.

"So you know what's going on?" Hillary asked Francesca.

"Yep, Raley's having sex with Terp," replied Francesca wearily. "And it's supposed to be a secret."

"How did you find out?" said Raley, whispering. "Oh my fracking God!"

"It's all you talk about, you three. When you think I'm not listening or you think I'm asleep," replied Francesca in the dark. "It's like you're the first person to ever have sex."

"Well have YOU had sex?" asked Raley.

"No, and until I'm about to be married I don't WANT to have sex," whispered Francesca. "We're too young, and I want to go to college. Believe it or not, there's a lot of life beyond mating. Consider that flatworms and nudibranchs and earthworms have sex."

"That's not what those toads out there are sayin,'" whispered Raley, laughter in her tone. "They sayin' it's the season for LUUUVE!"

"What you are hearing is mostly Pacific tree frogs, Pseudacris regilla, and they have the brains of a dung beetle," answered Francesca. "They're really stupid. Hopping little rocks, really. And they eat bugs."

"Oh, you and your rocks and your geology and your stars and astronomy," mocked Ophelia. "Francesca, you have your nose stuck so deep in a book you'll never have sex."

"Better than a sexual disease or a pregnancy when we're underage," replied Francesca. "Better with a man who doesn't leave. Besides, the less I have in common with a beetle who pushes crap around all his life, the better. Genus Scarabaeinae, by the way, in case you were wondering. So you don't stay awake wondering. By the way the common factor of all these brainless poop pushers is that the male always leaves."

"Terp doesn't leave me, I leave him," said Raley. "He's just practice. Besides, I'll bet I could frack any man in this camp. Any man, by nightfall. You couldn't do that, Ophelia. Your boobs aren't big enough."

"Why would you WANT to?" whispered Francesca. "Speaking of which, what are you doing about pregnancy? Are you thinking about THAT at all?"

"Oh...I push him away," said Raley. "You should see, like, when, you know...when we're...and I push him away, he's sad like his dog died. Mom's right. I'm totally in charge. You'll see."

Raley laughed quietly.

"Oh my freaking God, too much information!" whispered Hillary. "I DON'T WANT to see."

"I'm in a tent full of idiots," said Francesca. "Just don't copy the praying mantis. Messy."

Hillary laughed, embarrassed. "Poppa's gonna wack your fanny, Raley."

"Poppa's gonna bust Terp's head. Seriously," added Ophelia. "He's gonna kill him!"

"No he won't. Poppa's too busy pretending he's in the cavalry in 1863," said Ophelia. "Strutting about in his blue pants with the yellow stripes at age 75. Like there were ever 75 year olds in the cavalry. It's the Walker Brigade, with Mrs. Ericson in charge. Seriously, we teenagers are the adults here, the adults are like small children, and they're all playing pretend. I wonder why they do that."

"'Cause their lives are boring as dirt," said Francesca. "Their real lives, back in the world. Paying mortgages. Making families. Work. Nothing worth doing is easy, my father says. Boring."

"Speak for yourself, Francesca. My parents' lives are a little TOO interesting," said Ophelia.

"It's why we live with Poppa instead of our parents," added Hillary.

"So where are your parents right now?" asked Francesca.

"They're divorced, they hate each other's guts, and right now, our father is using cocaine in his low-income housing in San Jose. He hasn't gone to sleep yet," said Ophelia. "I just texted him. He's got a new girlfriend and a new tattoo, and it hurts. Plus his arm is getting crowded. All those names."

"Our mom isn't answering messages this weekend," said Hillary.

"That means she's drunk and she's under some retired sailor she met at the American Legion," said Ophelia.

"Seriously?" said Francesca.

"Oh, yah, she told us that men are a woman's super-power," said Raley. "She used to bring one home all the time. One reason the court moved us to live with Poppa."

"That, and the hitting," added Ophelia.

"All I hear back home is STUFF, not drama," said Francesca. "Knowledge about stuff. Stories about the good old days, and schoolwork. And ballet. And voice lessons, and competitive shooting, and camping, and... that's how my parents live too. My God they even watch science and history on TV. We ARE different! Anyway, boring."

"All stuff, no passion," said Hillary, "and we're passion, no stuff. We're just different."

"Yep, and we're stuck in a camp full of geezers who don't know what century it is. Today is going to be EPIC boredom!" said Raley.

"It's as boring as you want to make it," replied Francesca. "Last week my grandmother gave me her geology rock hammer from her adventurous days in World War II. I don't have a choice. Enjoy or not, I'm stuck here. So I'll make the best of it."

"I'm going to sleep all day," added Hillary. "I'll just tell Poppa I'm sick. Act like a kid. He'll buy it. He always does."

"The adults are such idiots," said Ophelia.

"At least we're not boring like them," added Hillary.

The ground began to move.

Garth Ericson woke up. Morning semi darkness. In a tent nearby, a dog...that detestable aging Hero the Service Dog... was howling insanely. All the dogs were howling. Beyond, coyotes were howling, and there were bird sounds in the sky. Far off, wild turkeys chortling. In the corral beyond the canvas walls of his tent, the horses were neighing and screaming. Surely it must be a mountain lion. Why were animals so far away reacting to a mountain lion here? He sat up, reached for his pants, and then reached for the thick black leather belt with the brown flap holster, in which rode an unloaded Remington 1858 Civil War percussion military pistol.

Which was instinct, he imagined, since at this living history event, here at San Antonio Mission in central California, any ammunition was forbidden. In real world terms, that meant that Garth and his friends kept their ammunition in the cars parked out of sight. Useless pistol. He was going to have to confront the mountain lion in the dark with an axe. As he pulled on his 1863 regulation cavalry pants, he remembered his deceased sister, so long dead, who had battled a mountain lion with her sheep dogs and a lariat and stones, and won. Let me be courageous like her. And let me hurry. So much noise out there. Something terrible must be happening. The lion must be among us. Visions of a bleeding horse in the corral, terribly ripped.

His Filipina wife, Dove, could sleep through anything, but she stirred now, and groggily reached out a bare brown arm for him from the warmth of the joined sleeping bags.

"What happens?" she asked.

Garth didn't know what to say.

"I don't know," he responded.

In nearby tents, other people were now awake, and he heard his friend Paul "Poppa Bear" Singleton yell, "What's going on?" and then there was a sound like a train was rolling through the camp, a giant rattling breaking sound, and then the ground jumped beneath him and he fell onto their sleeping pad, barely missing Dove. Confusion. Had he fainted? No... as a California native, he knew an earthquake when he felt it.

At least, he thought, he was wearing his pants. Instinctively he looked at his watch: 6:23 AM. He looked at Dove, and she was fully awake now, lying alongside him, staring at him wide-eyed in the semi-darkness. She was from Mindanao. She, too, knew an earthquake when she felt it.

The rolling was strong. Chaotic. Noisy: like a locomotive, or a low-flying jet. It threw him slightly into the air. Unwilling to move, he stared into the half-lit canvas of the tent ceiling, which was flapping and cracking as though in a strong wind.

His mother, his 102-year-old mother, was sleeping in her own tent nearby, and he had not heard a sound from her. In a new nylon tent, out in the open under the sunrise, she was as safe as she was going to be. With her hearing aids out she wasn't going to hear him anyway. If only she would stay down. A fall could be catastrophic.

He called out to his fourteen-year-old daughter who was sleeping in the modern screen tent alongside. He called her name, Francesca, as the ground rose and fell below him, bouncing him on his foam pad. Fear began to rise. How long could this go on? He checked his watch: 6:24. One minute and it had felt like an hour.

Unseen beyond the canvas, fourteen-year-old Francesca let out an answering yelp. She sounded incongruously happy. One of her teen friends, Raley, a particularly daring girl, began to laugh and another girl whooped, and it came to Garth that they couldn't be any safer, out in the open, away from the trees under the sky, in a rural pasture. Just ride it. Just relax.

There was a crash of metalware from the direction of the mission's cafeteria, beyond the tents, and Garth imagined the institutional pan racks next to the stoves coming down. Big metal pots. Probably nobody was there at this dawn hour.

There was a loud ripping and a thumping sound from a nearby California oak tree, probably shedding a giant limb, as sometimes happened. Wait it out. So noisy. The mission's bells were ringing now, in a disorganized, chaotic jumble of sound. The ground kept rolling. 6:25 AM. He mindlessly cursed those arrhythmic clanging bells. It had been like this forever, it seemed.

People in the other tents around him were calling out, alarmed. He recognized the voices. No screams of complete terror or agony. Just ride it. Just relax.

6:26 AM. Those bells. So disorganized, so clanging. Discord. Next to him, Dove was simply laying there rolling with the ground, looking up at the flapping white canvas above them. Anxiety. He must do something.

Garth low-crawled to the door of his tent as the ground kept rolling and bucking and roaring. The sod punched him in the chest, then hard in the stomach, as though he was on a trampoline surrounded by jumping children. Noise like a nearby locomotive, but all around him. He looked out the door in the scant light of first dawn: the sky seemed normal. How odd. The girl's modern nylon tent: whipping and bending, orange jello in a hurricane, with a battery lantern illuminating. Inside he could hear shouts and laughter as the teenage girls rode it out. Nearby he could see other people, Bear and Hopi Jack and Randall, also on the ground, also peeking out the doors of their tents. Watch: 6:27 AM. Four minutes. He'd never experienced an earthquake which lasted this long before.

Salinas, California
6:21 AM

Wallace heard other dogs all over the neighborhood begin howling. Wallace's adrenaline kicked in, and instinctively he turned away from the clot of people, the mayor, the city manager, and Dina, and looked around. Birds...many birds flying in the dawn light. Even seagulls, as though there would be a storm out in the Pacific Ocean, beyond Monterey twelve miles west. Yet the air was very still.

A small shout and Wallace turned to the other policeman, Mickey.

"What the hell?" said Mickey, pointing his flashlight downwards. It was still dark enough that a flashlight could illuminate the three gophers which had left their holes in the lawn and were running blindly, frantically, in circles. Another shout from Mickey, while all the dogs in the neighborhood were howling, loudly. Now even the mayor and the others were noticing, and looking around, and Wallace saw three racoons, two adults and a kit, emerge blinking from a nearby storm drain.

His cell phone vibrated. Everyone's cell phone vibrated. From the OES. The Office of Emergency Services. The text: "Our sensors indicate that an earthquake is imminent. Prepare for a large-magnitude earthquake within the next five minutes."

"WE HAVE TO WARN PEOPLE!" shouted Dina, alarmed.

There was a rumbling noise, like a train, in the north, towards San Jose. It seemed to be approaching.

Wallace could see Mike Rogers looking out his front door.
"GET THE KIDS AND GET OUT HERE! AWAY FROM THE HOUSE!" Hugh shouted at him, reaching over and lifting the daughter, Sherry.

Wallace looked at his watch. 6:22 AM.

"NO! Don't say anything! No sense in just panicking them!" said the Mayor. He looked terrified, thought Wallace.

Mike Rogers came running out of the house onto the lawn, pushing his small son Raz, both of them in bathrobes, the Hispanic neighbors also outside, looking around.

There was a louder approaching noise like rumbling trains, and a jolt as the ground suddenly moved beneath them. Causwell Dubbers cried out and went down on his hands and knees. The ground jolted again, and now the motion was constant, and it sounded...loud, loud like a passenger jet flying just overhead with the dogs howling and the power lines began to sparkle, flash and snap, and Wallace thought, Damn we're gonna get fried out here or get crushed if we go inside. Dina was on her knees holding up her phone, filming. Video, I hope, thought Wallace. With that in mind he reached up and turned on his own vest-mounted police camera. The motion felt insecure, since the earth was still moving. Thank God my family is in Denmark, thought Wallace.

Another sharp large jolt and the brick chimney in the house across the way snapped off and fell with a ground-shaking thump onto the lawn, half-buried. The shaking was worse now, and Wallace braced himself as though on a ship in a storm, and he saw that almost everyone was down on their hands and knees, and Dina, still holding up one arm with her phone, looked poised to run a sprint, as though she was about to run a track competition, which somehow seemed wildly hilarious, and then Wallace realized that he felt nauseous, and then a small ball of light, glowing, the size of a tennis ball, seemed to rise out of a gopher hole in the lawn, and it rose up. Wallace now could barely see clearly due to the shaking, and he thought, my God the power mains have ruptured and the electricity is in the ground. Or, perhaps aliens are invading?

The small glowing ball floated into the sky like a wayward balloon, and then there was another great crash and another old Victorian home down Capitol street fell off its foundation and the ground underneath it slumped down about six to ten feet. All the houses were losing parts, or sliding off their foundations, thought Wallace.

Loud, so loud. Car alarms going off everywhere, it seemed. The rolling went on, and Wallace reluctantly went down on hands and knees as nausea and fear overtook him, and he vomited onto the lawn. Oh so embarrassing. But others were vomiting too, surely. He could hear gagging in the cacophony of noise. Children wailing.

There was a greater crashing noise now, as the shaking continued, and a seam opened up alongside the house which had already collapsed, across Capitol Street and the Monterey County parking lot, about six feet deep, about the same width, like a canal, and Wallace looked over and saw the four story Monterey County building tilt sideways, incongruously, just a few feet, and several people and some parked cars fell into the new ravine.

Wallace looked around him, amazed. It was hard to see clearly. He realized that the windows in the houses were blowing in and out like soap bubbles, like they were liquid, so much flexibility! And some were breaking, shattering, exploding, and broken glass was everywhere. Amidst the noise, Wallace heard a man scream a few houses down, and Happy Johnson, and Causwell, and Dina moaning, and Mike Rogers crouching near him looking around silently as the ground bounced him up and down, holding his crying children, and the Hispanic woman neighbor hugging the entire Rogers family.

The shaking continued. It had been going on for hours. It would never end. The power went out and the crackling and sparking of the power lines stopped, and there was dust in the air, like smoke, and noise. Crashing, banging, car alarms. A nearby large tree shed a large branch which came down and crushed a car beneath it, and Wallace thought, there are going to be many, many casualties. Another crash and the house next door shifted with a giant ripping sound and slumped.

Down the street there was a pop and then a whomping noise, not really an explosion, and the back of a house began to burn effusively, flames shooting from the windows. Gas line, thought Wallace. Hot burner, making breakfast, broken gas line. Casualties. He tried to stand up, but the ground was shaking too hard. People, he could see, were running, stumbling, falling, out of the front of the home. Hopefully they would be OK.

Mickey was crawling past him now, heading to the burning home, and Mickey put his hand in Wallace's vomit and let out a yell and hollered over the noise, "Aye Sergeant! That got in my glove!"

They both laughed, and Mickey crawled on, wiping his gloved hand on the grass as he went, and the ground bucked beneath them.

Next to him, Sherry Rogers, all of 8 years old, was now standing up, supported by Hugh, and like Dina was still taking video on her phone.

Wallace began crawling, following Mickey, the shaking making him unsteady, so that a few times he fell over on his shoulders, but the shaking was lessening now, quickly subsiding.

Cars were hopping like they were on springs, and a few had drifted into the center of the road, and there was a loud distant boom, and Wallace realized it was something in the antique part of town, Old Town, and a loud cloud of what seemed to be dust was rising over there. A dust column in a dusty dawn sky. The shaking was lessening. Wallace stood up. Time to get to that house fire. As he began walking unsteadily away from the group, following Mickey, still queasy, so unbalanced, he pulled his protective medical paper mask from his hip pocket and slipped it over his mouth. Dust and smoke. He heard Happy Johnson shout at him,

"Hey, police people! Stick around! Your job is to protect ME!"

San Antonio Mission, California

The ground was quieting, still bizarrely quivering like a shivering horse. Garth attempted to stand up, tried to put on his high black leather boots, and fell over. He was too emotionally unsettled to stand on one foot. Equilibrium impaired. He sat on his sleeping bag, pulled on each boot, buttoned his blue wool cavalry tunic, strapped on his pistol belt, finally. Grabbing his broad dark blue cowboy hat, he stood up and ducked through the door flap.

The half-risen sun was bright in a dark sky, a few inches above the mountainous horizon to the east, over the buildings of the Fort Hunter Liggett Army Base. At first there was silence, immense quiet, the bells quiet. Crows overhead, cawing, a few shouts from other living history volunteers, then Garth could hear vehicle engines turning over out on the Army motor pool, a few miles down the road. That base was supposed to be closing down this year so only a minimum military staff was left over there. He stood quietly, waiting for the ground to move again. Nothing.

Closer, there were voices in all the 19th Century living history tents, which were all still standing. His own group's tents were still upright in their Civil War military order. McClellan saddles piled outside each door. Beyond, in the horse corrals, the animals were spooking, stomping and neighing, and he could vaguely see a cloud of dust rising over them. No horses screaming. Apparently, none badly injured.

Beyond the base, over by the creek that comprised the San Antonio River, there was a large cloud of dust. Garth watched it carefully. Dust, light brown, not smoke. Still too early in the year for a wildfire. Probably a landslide.

People were emerging from their tents, into the crisp air of an early morning. Excited conversations, which he ignored as he turned to seek out his mother. As he approached her tent, she opened the flaps and peered out smiling, leaning over her walker. "Oooowee we haven't had a shaker like that in decades!" she said, smiling. "Good thing I went to the bathroom at 5 AM. I move like a turtle these days and it's great to not have to worry about the line."

Garth pondered that random comment. She seemed fine. "Mom, let me check everyone else and I'll get back to you."

She waved him away, smiling, nudging her walker onto the grass, looking around with interest. "Look!" she commented, pointing. "The mission is still standing!"

Following her gaze, he turned to inspect the nearby mission. Built in 1812, it had for the entire last decade undergone a rigorous earthquake retrofit. That had involved carefully concealed steel beams and gallons of epoxy pumped into the adobe walls. In the sunlight he could see that at least from the outside the large old church was still standing. He could see cracks, and some of the cracks were large enough to look through. But the building itself was still standing.

"Praise God," he said.

"If we hadn't done that retrofit it would be a pile of rubble," she added.

He turned. Across the lawn he could see the downed oak limb. He wondered if any more branches were about to break off: best keep the people clear. By the light green new foliage of the downed limb he could see a large snake gliding smoothly, straight. A large kingsnake, disturbed from its squirrel hole nest. Best keep the girls away from it.

That caused him to turn back and look at the girls' tent. They were all outside, with Dove, wearing their long 19th Century dresses. Francesca, 15, slender and blonde, was wearing her long blue cloak with her hood pulled up. Akemi, dark haired, part Filipina, the youngest at 12, had merely wrapped a blanket around her head and shoulders. That made Garth realize that it was slightly cold. Still chill in the early morning. The girls were poking with small oak tree twigs at a small moving pile by their tent. He heard Bear, grandfather to the girls and putative Troop Sergeant, shout to them, "Leave those ants alone!"

Curious, Garth stepped closer to observe. Yes, astonishingly, an entire ant nest had stampeded up from underground, larvae, ant queen, everything. "Just step back and watch. Everyone OK?"

Francesca looked up and grinned. "That was something! I thought the ground was going to toss us."

Raley grinned even more broadly. "And I thought Hillary was going to toss herself! Seasick on flat ground!"

Her sister Hillary turned, scowling and indignant, and said emphatically, "I WAS NOT!"

"Were too!" added the third sister, Ophelia.

Bear was standing behind him. Garth turned. "Nothing but pots fell down in the cafeteria. A few dents. Everybody was scared but OK. They're all going to the bathrooms now."

He laughed. "And most importantly, the toilets still flush. So we're in good shape whatever happens next."

Garth silently pondered the accidental good fortune of his own unhurried 5AM visit.

"Scared the pee out of em!" Bear added, laughing more broadly.

"Horses?" asked Garth.

"Hopi Jack's with 'em now" said Bear.

"And?" Garth asked.

"Hopi's right behind you." said Bear. "I'll let him tell you".

Garth swiveled. There stood Hopi Jack, small, wiry, be-spectacled, in a 1860's regulation long sleeve undershirt, suspenders, regulation trousers, and boots. The regulation pistol, in the regulation flap holster, worn on the left side. Period correct. Why the pistol? It was empty. Phallic symbol for them all, maybe, he thought. Something for the fear.

"All good" said Hopi Jack. "It's a miracle. Not one injured. There was a squirrel hole what collapsed underneath 'em, but the horses are all sound. All sound. And Randall beelined to the water system, and the spring is still flowing and the water tank is full. No leaks. Astonishing."

"Anything you need to do for the horses?" asked Garth. Bear was circling around to stand by Hopi Jack, and Garth could see he was wearing his Colt Single Action pistol as well. All empty.

"Feed 'em," snorted Hopi Jack. "And I did that already. And they got water. Hell, it's all good. The hoss don't care."

Garth watched Hopi Jack and Bear carefully, and looked

over the camp. A small surge of pride and adrenaline swept over him as he watched Larry in his late 70's in his civilian 1840's clothing silently splitting firewood. Then he watched a crew of the men in their antique attire retightening the lines on all the tents, and the women gathering together with baskets around the horno, the traditional brick oven, which someone had lit before the quake. A small scarcely visible plume of smoke rose into the increasingly blue sky. Bright sunlight now. Like an antique classic pastoral painting. Everyone was instinctively falling into their living history roles without missing a step.

On the far side of the yard, the Spanish Colonial Lancers, a six-person living history group representing the Catalonian Volunteers of the 1790's, were tending to their own camp. Garth remembered that they were from someplace south. Mission San Miguel? The smoke of their newly kindled campfire was already rising thinly into the air.

Then there was Bat, the solitary black man in his seventies who was here representing a "Buffalo Soldier", the famous 9th Cavalry, with his wife Belinda. Replete with 1873 Winchester rifle, which Garth had never seen used in the military. Anyway, there was Bat, suspenders and undershirt, apparently frying bacon over his own little campfire. Food. Ten minutes after an earthquake and the man had a fire going. That was a good idea. Garth felt his stomach rumble, although his own repast would regrettably consist of a banana, oatmeal, and walnuts. Anything for fitness.

"We may as well make breakfast. If you'll please round up the girls, I'll go take a walk around the mission and the cars and meet you back here." Garth smiled, adjusted his service hat, and turned to go.

"Ahhhh Garth?" asked Bear behind him.

Garth turned. Bear was looking at him sheepishly.

"Could you grab a box of ammo out of the car while you're down there? Ya know. Snakes. I've got a feeling law enforcement is gonna be pretty thin on the ground," said Bear. "I know, I'm being a bit paranoid, but..."

Suddenly the ground shook again, simply one solid jolt. But it almost knocked Garth down. More rumbling. Garth noticed that over by the creek bed there were sudden squirts of dust, straight up, as tall as 30 feet. Too wet for a fire. Erupting volcanoes? No: no heat, no brightness. The situation was very strange.

"What caliber?" asked Garth. It passed through his mind that what Bear was suggesting was against the rules of the gathering, and probably illegal. But none of the organizers were here at the mission. Everyone was merely a volunteer.

"All of 'em. Any of 'em. Just something. Ya never know." replied Bear. "Grab your lever action while you are down there."

"I'll just go get the ammo, and come right back," replied Garth. "Why don't we just eat breakfast and then, let's walk the horses out. Take them for a ride. With the girls. Might as well see all this together."

Thinking about the implications of what Bear had said made him nervous.

His thought was disrupted by the sight of Hero the Service Dog, his rear end covered in ants, yowling loudly and racing through camp. Apparently, Garth guessed, he had tried to defecate on the ant nest, and it hadn't gone well. Ah, well, there was a silver lining in all this.

Salinas, California

Wallace pretended he hadn't heard, wondering if the mayor was going to chase after him. Ahead, the house was almost fully engulfed in flames. Beyond, in the distance, he could see other smoke columns rising, on other streets. Other homes were burning. But no massive block-long fires. The full light of day. Wallace realized that he wasn't going to go off shift for hours, if not days. Thank God that his family was in Denmark.

An elderly Hispanic man on the front lawn of the burning home, on Central Street, in his underwear. Red blotches from 1st degree burns...no apparent blisters...on his right side, arms and legs. Crying. Not apparently from pain. They were only a few blocks from the fire station. Wallace could hear sirens. Looking down Central Street, then Capitol Street, Wallace could see that both streets were blocked. Cars had bounced into the center of the road, tree limbs and power poles were down. A few electrical wires, but thank God the electricity appeared to be off, system wide. Most houses were damaged but few were crumpled or down. The nearby apartment buildings were sagging, but Wallace couldn't see any which were completely collapsed. Even Roosevelt Elementary School, built in 1920, was cracked and battered, with many broken windows, but still upright. The school's tile roof had shattered and partially slid off in a few places. As Wallace looked around, a bit stunned, he saw a crowd of neighbors, mostly talking in Spanish, dressed in bedclothes and Hawaiian shirts and old tee shirts, a wild assortment of hastily chosen clothing, surrounding the burning home, moving furniture and clothing out onto the front lawn through the broken front window, while another crew was spraying the fire with water from garden hoses. The fire began to diminish, and Wallace saw a man in a polka dot bathrobe with a shining crescent wrench step back from the gas shutoff valve on the side of the home. Mickey and Hugh were both involved now, organizing, shepherding the children of the home onto the school lawn across the street.

"What the hell is THAT?" said a voice behind him. Causwell Dubbers.

Apparently they had followed him over here. Causwell Dubbers was pointing down Capitol Street at the massive fissure across the street, and the tilted yet intact Monterey County building.

"THAT, my friend, is REDEVELOPMENT DOLLARS! Yes, redevelopment dollars! Sure to come from the state AND federal governments. At last we'll be done with these old firetraps, and we can have the modern city of our dreams," said Happy Johnson.

"Actually, it's the slough," said Dina Montero behind them. "100 years ago, when they filled in the creek, they used landfill, then built on it. Apparently, we got some liquefaction. The landfill turned to jelly in the earthquake."

"So this crack is all over town?" said Wallace. "Is it dangerous?"

"I'm guessing. It's not going to close back up or anything, as far as I know," said Dina. "But you're going to find more damage down the length of where the slough used to be. Towards the community college, I'm guessing."

"That's going to limit our ability to use emergency vehicles," said Wallace.

There was a collective moan behind them. Wallace turned back and saw that the water hoses had run dry. The fire was growing again. Reluctantly, driven back by the heat, the crowd stepped back, moving the furniture, the scattered household goods, to the neighbor's front lawn.

Wallace saw the stooped elderly woman with a cloth shopping bag full of plastic water bottles. She was walking through the crowd giving one to anyone who would accept. She approached Wallace and spoke in Spanish.

"Dear Sir, are you thirsty?"

"No," replied Wallace. Then he realized he should accept. After vomiting earlier, he was sure to become dehydrated later. Today would be long.

"Yes," he said again, and reached down and took a bottle. *"Thank you deeply."*

"My neighbor, she is dead," said the elderly woman. Mexican, apparently. *"She was in the back, where the fire started, cooking, and the home collapsed on her, and then there was the fire."*

Sweet Jesus, thought Wallace. I hope she was dead when the fire started.

"That is her son in his underwear there, the man crying," the old woman pointed.

The whole house was burning now. Wallace felt the pressure to be more places, to do more. This sort of thing must be happening all over Salinas. So much need. How to organize that. The mayor. We need strong leadership this instant.

Wallace looked around. Dusty bright morning. The house was completely burning now, flames roaring perhaps twenty feet into the sky. No fire department, although there were some distant sirens. Strange moment of calm.

There were about thirty or forty people out in the street now, talking mostly in Spanish, already cleaning, tidying, comforting. About five of them were taking phone videos of the damage. Wallace heard the buzz of a chainsaw, looked down Central Avenue towards the old part of Main Street, and saw a crew of young men sawing a large limb which had fallen across the street, crumpling several cars. That limb was massive, perhaps two feet across, with leafy branches covering the entire street, yet here they were, in their shorts and flip flops, cutting away. No city employees in sight. City employees probably couldn't get through the rubble.

There was shouting, and the homeless man accused of murder, Ronny Reynolds, came racing down the sidewalk, pursued by a squad of young people, his hands cuffed in front. "Suspect has escaped from the squad car." crackled Wallace's shoulder mounted mike. Hugh's voice.

"Pastor Paco turned him loose." added the voice.

Ronny came dodging and twisting across the street, running fast, his long dark snarled hair swaying as he twisted and turned. Barefoot. More shouts. Angry now. Ronny had been tormenting the police with impunity for years. He was smirking as he ran, as though he was confident in his ability to outrun them all. Then a young boy, black hair crew-cut, rode his bike hard into Ronny, intentionally, and they both went sprawling, the boy flat on his back, and as Ronny sat up, someone...Wallace could not see who it was in the crowd... smashed Ronny in the face with the edge of a shovel, and Ronny fell back spitting teeth, his mouth transmogrified into an angry blood-pulsing gash which reached from ear to ear, eyes wide with astonishment. Nobody had ever done that to him before.

At that moment someone else smashed Ronny in the stomach with an axe and Wallace stepped forward and shouted "Stop this! Deja de hacerlo!"

People cleared away, and there was Ronny lying sideways, fetal position, curled up on the street, red wet joker grin wide and flapping, with all his front teeth missing, his mouth pulsing blood, and he slurred, "A la mierda con tu madre," and clutched his abdomen as he stared up at Wallace, half afraid. The fire nearby heated the side of Wallace's face, and now the entire home was burning, with a roaring, crackling noise.

Dark purple blood poured out between Ronny's fingers. Ronny was panting now, his eyes screwed shut, head down on the asphalt. So much blood. Hepatic?

"Who the hell did this?" shouted Mickey.

"You are all ANIMALS! MONKEYS!" shouted Pastor Paco at the crowd, standing behind Wallace.

Wallace turned and stood up, enraged at the man.

"Why did you turn him loose?" Wallace asked Pastor Paco tightly.

"I thought it was inhumane, to keep him locked in that car. He was overheating. Ronny has always been our free spirit. Free people like Ronny deserve freedom. Free people should stay free as is their right. The right to roam is sacred. Frack the police, anyway."

"Ronny has always been our parasito, our enfermedad. Siempre ha sido nuestra castigo," said a voice. Wallace turned, and looked down, and there was that small stooped elderly woman, white hair hastily pulled back, with her basket of water bottles, looking up at him steadily. There was no anger at the police at all, Wallace noticed.

At their feet, Hugh, wearing blue gloves and a facemask, was attempting to deliver first aid, trying to uncurl Ronny enough to examine the wound. Whatever it was, it was bad. Bad. The fire was louder now. Wallace remembered that he, too, was wearing his mask, as a dust filter. He pulled it down to his neck.

Wallace looked up and noticed several people taking photos or video with their cell phones. Evidence. Good. He looked over and there was Dina taking notes on her old-fashioned steno pad, and the mayor and the city manager standing close together, looking fearful and disgusted.

Down on the pavement, Ronny made a gagging noise, and vomited an immense gush of blood, emptying out, and relaxed. Hugh unfolded him. He looked up at Wallace. "Dead," he said.

"Aye, eso es asqueroso," said a young girl's voice.

It IS gross, thought Wallace. He saw the young mani-cured feminine hand extended through the crowd, slender, bejeweled, and beautiful, filming Ronny's corpse. And then Hugh reached up as he rose and lightly snatched the phone from those well-kept fingers. Someone laughed. She was diminutive, and Hugh was gigantic.

The young woman was very attractive, Wallace saw. Dressed with a bare midriff pullover sleeveless knit, and a tight pair of jeans. Anger flashing in her eyes, she leapt for-ward and attempted to grab the phone away from Hugh, and for an instant it all looked like a game. From the side, Mickey said, smiling slightly, "Excuse me, ma'am, evidence!"

Another voice in the crowd said good-naturedly, "Be nice to him. They are here to help us."

Wallace felt a surge of joy hearing that.

"Besides, he's guapo!" shouted another young woman's voice, and there was more laughter.

Another voice: "Es un toro más grande de lo que una va-quilla pequeña puede acomodar!" He's a big bull for such a small heifer.

More laughter amidst the sorrow.

"You...ALL of you... know not God!" said Pastor Paco bitterly.

Wallace's shoulder mike crackled again, "All units, the Brown building on the second block of Main Street has col-lapsed. Casualties. We can't get anyone else over there because the streets are blocked. Anyone in vicinity please respond."

"Mickey! Hugh!" said Wallace. "Stay here and do what

you can. I'm not sure forensics can arrive on-scene. Get whatever evidence is available, especially the cell phones. Soon as you can, get over to Main Street and join me."

"You got it, Boss!" said Hugh. "I don't think you can drive the cruiser across all those cracks. Better hoof it."

"Good thought. I'll take the shotgun just in case," replied Wallace. "And a backpack."

The old woman approached, wobbling, small. Wallace noticed that in the full light of the morning she was dressed in an antique style blue paisley long dress. Wordlessly she pressed another water bottle into his hands.

"Gracias por su servicio a nosotros," said the old woman. "Será un día largo. Ven a comer con nosotros más tarde, por favor." It's going to be a long day. Come back for food.

"It's very kind of you," said Wallace. "I will try to come by later. I'm sure I'll be hungry."

"Hey Mouse! Hey Tiny! I'm headin' uptown and I got the scatter!" he yelled to the two other policemen in the distance. Might as well yell. Save the batteries on his talkie. He shook the shotgun above his head, and they waved back.

"If we can, sunset, at the new police station. If we don't have the street cleared, sunset back here to remove these cars!" He yelled again.

They waved and turned their attention back to the people who surrounded them.

As he walked down the center of the street, a silver pump-action Remington 870 12 gauge shotgun slung over his shoulder and a forty pound "go-bag" backpack from the police cruiser pressing him down, Wallace could see that the streets were impassible for most vehicles. Not irreparably. Not even catastrophically. But most, if not all of the emergency vehicles of Salinas would be unable to travel easily here. Some cracks in the pavement, a few enough to forestall a motorcycle. If Dina was right then some of these crevices would deserve careful repair, to mitigate the continuing effects of one hundred-year-old landfill.

But for the most part, the majority of obstacles were downed tree limbs, a few downed power lines, broken glass from large plate glass windows, clumps of down brickwork from older buildings. Wallace paced as he walked, measuring distances. There was a meaningful obstacle which could block traffic perhaps every six feet. Cleanup would take days before emergency traffic could return, and weeks before routine transportation could return. But, as he had seen before, the inhabitants were already all outside, stacking, lifting, raking, cleaning up the damage, calling to each other in Spanish and English.

He noticed one young Hispanic woman, slender and surprisingly beautiful in plastic sandals, pajama pants and a pink sleeveless tank top which read, "I'm Your Bitch". Nothing underneath. She was standing in the street with her arm in a makeshift sling created from a man's long sleeve dress shirt, talking happily in Spanish with two other women who were lifting a chainsawed tree limb out of the street. There was a red-stoned wedding ring on her left hand.

She was the only injured person he could see, so he stopped and asked her if she needed help. Her shoulder was just strained, she said in Spanish. Her husband was a nurse, and he said she would be OK. The husband was now walking to Memorial hospital, to help. It hurt, but it was not too much. Their house had lost its windows and the chimney had cracked but was otherwise still on its foundations and safe. Their two young children were even now playing with the neighborhood children in a nearby backyard. They were blessed.

"Este es un día de milagros," she concluded.

Yes, indeed, it was a day of miracles, thought Wallace. He suppressed the urge to talk with her more. She seemed so beautiful, so...God bless him, thought Wallace. Fertile. Sexual. How incongruous to have such feelings with his wife in Denmark and the world shaken apart. So much wiser to simply admire this beautiful creation of God and go to the Brown building where he was needed. A surge of guilt and a self-directed silent rebuke.

"Vaya con Dios," he said gently.

"También vas con Dios," she replied, as he turned and walked on.

Everyone seemingly in a surprisingly good mood. Aside from the home which had ignited, the rest of the residences seemed to be damaged but repairable. Homes made of wood, he thought, stood up to earthquakes surprisingly well, and resisted fire terribly. But there were no other residential fires on this street, although columns of smoke in the distance indicated that some other buildings were burning somewhere in the town.

Wallace stopped, and shifted. The buttstock of the shotgun was clacking against the grips of his holstered 1911 .45

pistol, so he moved it to his left side as he continued walking. The dust was settling, and it was looking like another beautiful California day. Thank God, he thought. Thank God the kids weren't in school. Thank God this didn't happen during a workday commute. Thank God his family was in Denmark.

He walked down Central Street in the sunlight, and crossed Salinas Street, where a broken water hydrant had spewed water over the intersection before it ran dry. Someone had already put up a sign, hand-printed in spray paint, "Free Carwash: Park here and wait." That made Wallace smile involuntarily.

He entered the city's social hub of the antique Main Street of Salinas. Lots of brickwork was down in the street here, from the antique buildings. The recent remodeling of the street, to convert the street to two way traffic, had removed all the trees, so most of the damage was cracking, and brickwork, and stunningly several large old brick buildings had slumped almost entirely apart. It looked like a photo of the London blitz, thought Wallace, except that the more modern buildings, the Taylor building, the Steinbeck Center, the Maya Cinema, all built within the past few decades to revitalize the downtown, were cracked but otherwise entirely undamaged. Broken windows. Surprising. Several large cracks running across the street, barriers to any wheeled vehicles.

Almost no people, thought Wallace. This time of day on a Sunday, the people were all home. Truly, this was a day of miracles.

He stood in front of Dina's bookstore. Apparently, she lived upstairs and published the Salinas Index Journal in the basement. Wallace wondered if she owned the building. If so, she was relatively lucky. The windows of the bookstore had shattered, and the marvelous trove of books was exposed. That would be a looting hazard later.

Large clumps of bricks, some of the masses as big as refrigerators, had fallen from the second story and the roofline. Otherwise, the building seemed intact, with the ubiquitous structural cracks, but still upright and whole. Patch up the cracks, turn on the lights, and if the pipes were sound, the building might be livable. Amazing.

But there, a few blocks down, was the Brown building, entirely collapsed. No fire. Some dust in the air. He made his way there cautiously, picking over the rubble and around crevices.

None of the street crevices were particularly deep. He could see the bottom of all of them, and the greatest was perhaps as deep as he was tall. A rising stench from a few indicated broken sewer lines.

Surprising how few people were here. The shotgun... that obsolete Remington Mariner 870...hung heavily on his shoulder and felt unnecessary. He had only twelve buckshot rounds for it anyway, six in the magazine, and six more on the sidesaddle cartridge carrier on the side of the gun. Which only seemed to make it more lopsided, and more heavy. Four copper slug sabot rounds in his backpack. Not ready to fight a war. As though any kind of shooting would be needed anyway. He wished he could just stash the shotgun under some rubble and come back for it later.

Suddenly there was a jolting noise, as though a train was

coupling its cars, a clashing jolt, and the earth shook beneath him again, and he braced, then automatically moved into the center of Main Street and crouched as the earth shook. I'm not far enough from the buildings, he thought. Some bricks fell from facades, and already-broken windows fractured again with a clatter. Noise. Then it all passed, and there was silence. Far away a siren wailed, and he could hear voices from people he could not see. A small drone passed overhead as he stood up to continue walking to the Brown building. Good: somebody was seeing the damage from a bird's eye view. Better allocation of resources.

As he approached the Brown building, he could see a captain in the fire department, whom he recognized. Wallace struggled to remember his name.... Richard.... the man was not Dick, he kept insisting that people call him Richard during their emergency planning conferences. So of course, someone in the police department had taken to calling him "Penis" when nobody from the fire department was listening. Richard.... a vision of golfing, which Wallace never did. Richard Green.

"Hey, ahhhh...Richard, what's going on?" said Wallace. "I got the word I was needed over here."

"Oh, Wallace, I'm Captain Green, please. Well we didn't need you here. You probably got sent here by the mayor, and the city manager. I tell you, I think this is the least of our worries. The building is down but aside from two homeless people who were squatting in the basement, I don't think anyone was inside. We've got bigger issues elsewhere," said Captain Green. "I think we'll just tag it and go help people who are hurting."

"Who were the people inside?" asked Wallace.

"Oh, you know, that guy with his shopping cart packed full of trash and his girlfriend. The guy who kept stealing out of people's cars," said Captain Green.

"Um...let me remember.... Boogie, he called himself," Wallace searched his mind. Memories of Boogie breaking car windows. Boogie defecating in the planters on Main Street and wiping with his tee shirt, which he would then leave behind. Boogie incessantly smoking non-profit-supplied marijuana, medical marijuana supplied by Pastor Paco and his band of anarchistic do-gooders. Marijuana. Marijuana.

A vision of a film star. Memories of many written citations.

"Bogart," he said. "His girlfriend's last name is Blessing."

"Well, they're squashed-like-bugs Bogart and Blessing, then," said Captain Green. "Serves 'em right. Like lice, they were. Live like parasites, die like parasites."

Wallace felt repulsed. Yes, these two had been homeless, mentally ill, panhandling, relentless scavengers. But they had been people. Human beings. Wallace could see them in his memory. We should have taken better care of them.

"We're not getting cell," said Captain Green. "And we can't get the trucks through the streets. Too many cracks, too much debris. Power out. It's gonna be a mess."

There was a small aftershock beneath them. A clattering, and shiver, and they both braced.

A helicopter passed low overhead.

"There's your answer," said Wallace. "Air mobile."

Both their shoulder walkie talkies erupted at once. "Anyone who can hear me, Sargent or above in fire and police, report to the parking lot behind Patria's on Salinas Street. Meeting with Happy at the old Armory."

"Meeting with the MAYOR," corrected Captain Green. "Gotta show a little respect around here."

Happy's probably pretty unhappy, thought Wallace. "Let's get over there," he said.

San Antonio Mission

There was the crushed car, a vintage pastel blue and white Volkswagen van, and the smell of gasoline, and the buzzing of flies. A hive of bees? And there were several lancers in their 18th Century Spanish clothes and flat broad brimmed hats... lancer re-enactors, Garth reminded himself....leaning over the crushed car, and a young teenage boy in bright black, red and white lancer clothing standing apart, apparently stricken by grief, and an older man in similar clothing hugging him. Garth stepped closer. There was a bare foot...a bare man's foot, pale white with short sparse black hair growing on top... protruding from the crushed van's rear window. It looked boney, and bluish white, and the toenails were misshapen by fungus and untrimmed. Disregarding the strong smell of gasoline, Garth stepped closer and looked through the collapsed and broken windshield.

The sightless eyes of a woman, an apparently dead naked woman, looked up at him. Fully dilated dead-deer eyes, which made her look sleepy. Bright red blood and pink lung tissue protruded from her wide open mouth. It looked as though she was screaming, and yet bored. Vomiting up her own lungs. Her head hung down from the seat to the floorboard. The floorboard was covered in smooth pooled blackening blood which had soaked into her long brunette hair.

Garth was stunned at the sight, and then he recoiled with the remembrance: the boy was this woman's son, and the man comforting the boy was this woman's husband.

The words just came out of his mouth, "Oh damn. Oh damn."

"Maybe they are, maybe they aren't", said the man beside him, dressed in a vaquero outfit. Ah, yes, the Caballeros Vistadores, the riding group from Santa Barbara, representing 1820's cowboys. They were also here camped behind the lancers. Garth couldn't remember his name. That could wait.

"They?" asked Garth.

"Yep, that young idiot Lucky, that's Lucky Martin, is crushed on top of her, towards the back. He's one of ours. He's naked too. He was.... anyway they were together" the man said.

"Sure he's dead?" asked Garth.

"Well, the oak tree smashed his head through her pelvis, so that's a "yes". At least he'd better be. Stupid fool. Always messing around."

Garth didn't know what to say. They stood in silence, watching the other men lifting oak branches away from the car. In the distance, Garth could see Bat and Bear walking down to them from the mission. Probably wondering what was taking him so long.

"They weren't married, right?" asked Garth. He felt somehow paralyzed.

"Nope, that's her husband and son, over there. Paul Desault, the husband, and that young beanpole all shook up is Freddy Desault. I think he's fourteen years old. Terrible way to see your mom, ain't it? The dead woman there was, or is, Kathleen Desault, 40 something and Lucky, that's the man, he was about 30, maybe less, always kidding around, and they flirted but nobody thought this would happen. His wife and son and daughter are all up at our camp and don't know yet. Now what are we going to do?" said the man. He removed his flat black Spanish hat and mopped his brow and gray crew cut scalp. It was still slightly cool.

"Well, it's a crime scene, right?" asked Garth.

"Seems pretty obvious that it's not murder," said the man. "People have consensual sex, the universe...in the form of an oak tree, disagrees. It's like Steinbeck or DH Lawrence. You know that Steinbeck book? "To A God Unknown?"

Garth reviewed the book in his mind. He couldn't remember any adultery.

"Did you call for a sheriff?" asked Garth. A large fly had landed on the woman's open eye and was scuttling across it. Appalling. Someone cover her. Garth reached through the crushed windscreen and brushed the fly away.

"No cell service. All the landlines down too." replied the man.

"Well we've got to do something", said Garth. As though they were discussing a ruptured pipe or a leaking ceiling.

Bat and Bear were walking around the van, helping the

other men slightly, and eying the van in disbelief. Suddenly they swarmed the husband, and forced his hand up, and Garth saw a cheap plastic cigarette lighter, unlit as yet, resting in his palm.

"Burn 'em! Burn 'em both in hell for what they did! Burn em!" screamed the man. Then he began sobbing. Bat twisted the lighter out of the man's hand.

Garth realized that the gasoline-soaked grass and the entire van could go up in a fireball. Not safe. He began backing away.

The son reached through the group and hugged the father tightly and shouted as well, "Stop it! Stop it!"

That calmed the father, Paul Desault, Garth remembered, the newly widowed husband, who collapsed into sobbing and allowed himself to be led away. As they left, Garth turned back to the man who had explained the situation. "Excuse me, but what is your name? Sad time for this, but..."

"I'm Mike", said the man. "Red Mike Robinson, count'a my red hair. Well, used to be red. Helluva mess."

The hair or the deaths? Wondered Garth. What's he talking about? Speak. Say anything.

"Too right," replied Garth. "Now what do we need to do? I agree, we have to do something."

"You've got that retired CSI guy, what's his name?"

"Ah, yes, Steve Sanchez. He's not retired. Still at it".

"Let's give this to him. Make it a crime scene but clean it up. God knows we can't leave them here. Not like this", said Mike.

"Good plan for now. I have a satellite phone and that's

sure to work. Then I'll drive over the Army. They'll have a way to call. We'll get law enforcement and the coroner here in a few hours anyway", replied Garth.

Salinas, California

The helicopter was a National Guard Blackhawk, and it had seen much use. Conveniently it had been refueling at the Salinas Municipal Airport at the time of the quake. There was a small hydraulic leak in the ceiling of the passenger cabin.... that was the engine up there, wasn't it? Wallace watched as a droplet of clear viscous fluid...oil? Hydraulic fluid?...collected and fell onto the greasy slick pooling on the metal cabin floor. Slippery, thought Wallace. Flammable.

A shudder of turbulence rocked the craft. They were flying at about 1,000 feet, heading out towards the Pacific Ocean over the Salinas River, the river a meandering corridor of green trees and brown water below them. Thank God he had gotten a window seat, thought Wallace, nervously. Even in the Air Force he hadn't enjoyed helicopters, and this specimen looked like it had done a few years in the war on terror. No wings. Think of something else. Apparently, according to Mayor Johnson, they were here to observe and report, so he should do exactly that, and consider the law enforcement requirements.

Next to him, Fire Captain Richard Green was energetically vomiting into an airsickness bag, eyes screwed shut and sweat beading his face. They had been aloft five minutes, pondered Wallace. Probably stress. Captain Green was looking rather green. Thank God the airflow was intense....the door was shut but a window was slid open...and due to the intense noise they were all wearing headphones. Wallace checked his seatbelt. The 870 Mariner was in a convenient gun rack, chamber empty. Across from him, Happy Johnson in his window seat was intoning a description of what he was seeing to Causwell Dubbers who was craning across him, attempting to look out the window. Next to them sat Supervisor Mercurio Dimmick, an Hispanic man with superb black hair combed back. Wallace recalled that Supervisor Dimmick was immensely proud of his Tejano heritage. He should meet Wallace's father, Garth, since they were both history nuts.

The mild turbulence caused the aircraft to shake, which caused Wallace to tense, and compelled Captain Green to heave into the bag yet again.

"It's gonna be great," Mayor Johnson was saying, "The redevelopment funding is going to be astonishing. Look, the bridge to the Monterey Peninsula is down. We're gonna get big bucks for that. Extra if there's dead people."

Wallace looked down as the helicopter tilted precariously and saw that yes, indeed, Salinas was cut off from the nearby coastal city of Marina. The bridge had been isolated by a crack in the road on the Salinas side, although it was eminently reparable, still standing. More landfill failure, thought Wallace.

The voice of the pilot interrupted, "Ah...we have a tsunami inbound, now,"

"NOW?" shouted the voice of Supervisor Dimmick in the earphones. "How?"

"The only way that could happen would be a landslide in the submarine canyon out in the ocean," said a woman's voice. United States Geological Survey. She had been visiting OES...Office of Emergency Services...in Salinas when the earthquake occurred. She was seated opposite the Supervisor. Small, blond, slender to the point of thinness, intense looking, the Chihuahua vibes of a constant startle condition. When they had boarded, there had been no chance of introductions, and she had eyed the shotgun with noticeable alarm. Wallace guessed that she secretly smoked.

"In Monterey Bay, deep in the ocean," the woman's voice continued. "A gigantic slide would push a bolus of water ashore with little notice. Otherwise the bay is too deep for seismic effects by themselves. That's why it didn't happen with the quake itself."

Wallace looked down, and he saw a surge of dirty brown water, rushing up the Salinas River. A moderate-sized wave, yet it overflowed the banks of the river and overtopped the bridge below and spread like an overflowing syrup across the lettuce fields alongside the river.

"Will it strike Salinas?" asked Causwell Dubbers.

"We don't know," replied the woman's voice. "It's very unexpected. Keep flying out to the coast."

In a few minutes they were at the Salinas River mouth, where it normally entered the ocean, and dirty seawater had covered all the farms below them. Here and there were a few intact roofs which rose above the tide with little or no damage, so the surge could not have been a classic crushing wave. Yet there were homes underwater there as well.

"Ground subsidence," said the woman's voice. "Like the Japanese quake at Fukushima. Ground level seems to have dropped a bit. The ocean's already as far as Castroville."

Castroville was a small village between Salinas and the ocean. Wallace had a sinking feeling in his guts. He pondered his rising nausea. People were dying down there. As he tried to focus his attention outwards, he noticed that Captain Richard Green was no longer vomiting, but instead was staring intently out the window. The helicopter entered a slow wide circle, 1,000 feet up. There was the river, flooded. There were some sand dunes rising out of the surrounding flood, where the coast had been. Beyond, there were lines in the ocean, waves, which didn't seem very large.

The helicopter continued to circle, and the view changed beneath them. The Mariposa Dunes development of luxury homes, famous for its magnificent coastline, was....simply gone. There was wreckage down there, shattered beachfront villas now washing in the turbulence, and a few small moving figures, some wearing bright clothes, some wearing nothing, or next to nothing. Now they were all in the water, moving, struggling, waving, swept along. Wallace had the incredible, horrible sensation that the people looked like ants in a flowerbed which was being watered. The helicopter continued to circle. No voices in the headphones. Moss Landing, the small seaside settlement nearest Salinas, was utterly submerged except the power plant, which had somehow escaped major inundation due to its flood barriers. The barriers, designed for rising sea levels, had worked as designed, thought Wallace. In the Moss Landing harbor, mid sized fishing boats were all tipped and askew. Some still afloat, some sunken, some floating untethered towards destinations inland.

"So much underwater," said a voice. The woman. "Moss Landing is devastated."

The helicopter turned and headed back towards Salinas.

"Shouldn't we go farther down the coast and check out Monterey?" said Causwell Dubbers' voice in the headphones. "They've got a bigger harbor. They've probably had more damage."

"They've got someone checking them out now," said the pilot's voice. "Our mission is the Salinas area."

"Shouldn't we help them? Those people down there?" asked another voice. Captain Richard Green.

Good thought, considered Wallace. Admiration for Captain Green.

"Let's see where the need is greatest first," replied a voice. Mayor Johnson. "Damn, if Monterey got clobbered by that wave, they're gonna suck up all our funding."

"I tell you, we should help them," said Captain Richard Green emphatically.

"Ahhh we got some of the smaller helicopters from that helicopter school, several of the instructors are up. And some of the cropdusters. We'll get them over here. They're smaller, they can help here. More nimble."

Voices on the headset as the pilot called the other helicopters. Eager sounds of multiple helicopter pilot voices, heading to the coast.

Meanwhile Wallace felt their own helicopter turn inland.

Flying over Castroville. "Miracle of miracles. It's an island, but it's still above the flood," said Supervisor Dimmick's voice.

Looking down. Yes, there it was, the tiny town of Castroville, now, temporarily, beachfront property.

"We've got a report of a fire inland, by the mountains, by Toro Park," said the pilot's voice. "Heading there now."

"Negative," said the commanding voice of the mayor, "Head east a bit and let's see how north Salinas and east Salinas are doing. Then we'll check out Toro Park. If we need assistance, can you move fire crews in this aircraft?"

"Ah, roger, we're at your command," came the pilot's voice.

"Well, OK, but Toro Park is in my district too," came the voice of Supervisor Dimmick.

They turned east, and through the windows of the helicopter Wallace could see a pillar of smoke rising out by the canyons of San Benancio, nestled in the hills which bound the Salinas Valley where Salinas itself was located.

Technically San Benancio was outside of Salinas city limits. By now they were over Boronda, a suburb of Salinas, and looking down Wallace could see dozens of small vertical columns of smoke rising from individual structure fires, the same as he had seen when the earthquake had happened. Dense, black columns rising almost straight into the sky. Bending inland a bit. The Salinas malls: remarkably intact. A few slumped roofs. Older subdivisions: more homes collapsed off their foundations, many shed chimneys, a few fires. The new Salinas Creekbridge subdivision, and its mall: remarkably intact, with some slumps, landslides, and broken roads in the hilly areas.

As they flew past, Wallace saw a life alert helicopter coming in for a landing at one of two local hospitals, the Natividad Trauma Center. Already in operation. Amazing.

East Salinas. The lower-income part of town. More land slumps, more cracked streets, more landfill failures, but overall, astonishingly little damage. More smoke plumes from individual structure fires.

A flyover of the World War II era runways of the Salinas Airport: cracked, but not apparently irreparable. Small planes might still land now. Helicopters could certainly operate. As they flew over, Wallace could hear a CDF fire delivery helicopter from the nearby town of Hollister talking with the pilot. Ready to siphon water. Ready to fight fire.

Now west towards the adjoining small town of Spreckels. Old homes down. Riverside homes flooded by the tsunami, but beyond the riparian corridor of the Salinas river, there was no damage. There was a major fire developing in the hills of Corral de Tierra, Wallace could see a massive smoke column rising. But the Salinas River bridge connecting Salinas to Toro Park with the elite subdivisions of the Toro Park area was apparently unusable, with tsunami flooding across the road and the approaches washed out. Not catastrophic, Wallace saw. The cracks in the roadbed filled approaches were extreme, but the standing water itself had already subsided to about the level of the axles of the cars which had been caught on the highway. One or two cars on their backs, off the road, still immersed, Wallace saw. There would be casualties there. But most of the big trucks and the SUV's were still upright. Below, people were wading in the water, helping, surrounding a capsized smaller sedan which was mostly underwater. As Wallace watched, a door was pulled open, and living, moving people were emerging under their own power.

More talk by the pilot, as he directed the smaller helicopters to the scene.

"OK, Salinas Rural Fire will have to fight that monster fire on their own," said Captain Green, looking intently out the window. "We can't get equipment across the river to them anyway. We're going to focus on Salinas itself. We should be able to handle this, with helicopters to get us over damaged streets."

As they watched the growing massive fire engulfing the hills on the other side of the Salinas River, a dayglow green aerial firefighting tanker aircraft flew low over the flames and they saw a distant bright plume of pink as liquid fire retardant streamed from its bomb bays.

Wallace agreed. "Send law enforcement with the fire crews to patrol via helicopter, and apply resources as needed. Right now getting all hands on deck is the first priority," he added. "Mr. Mayor can you call everyone in the police department onto duty?"

"Already done," said the voice of Causwell Dubbers on the headset, "The chief has issued instructions for all officers to establish a presence wherever they are, and if available, they are to go to the new police station on East Alisal for assignment. All hands on deck."

"I'm astonished that we escaped more damage," muttered Captain Green.

"The police chief agrees with you," said the Mayor's voice in the headset. "She says that it's a tragedy, but it could have been much worse."

Amen, thought Wallace.

"Este es un día de milagros," said Supervisor Dimmick.

Near San Antonio Mission, California

Cell phones were down. Power to the mission was off, although several of the living history crew were working on solar power and gasoline-powered generators. Wireless internet was down.

Yet Garth's satellite phone, which he carried for business emergencies, was still operational. Garth stood in the grass apart from the others as the sun rose in the sky and made calls to the Sheriff's office, his son Wallace in Salinas, Wallace's wife in Salinas, his ex-wife in Salinas, his co-worker Lanie at the office, and two friends in San Francisco. All the calls were answered with a robotic voice that "All Circuits Are Busy. Please call again at another time."

But his son Ernst, who now lived in Brooklyn, New York, across the continent, working as an investment advisor in the family firm, answered on the first ring.

"Dad! How are you?" Ernst was almost shouting.

"Everybody in the family is wonderful. A little shook up. Amma's good. We all send our love," said Garth.

"Love you too!" answered Ernst. He sounded far away. "We are worried! Wallace and his family are in Salinas. No contact with them yet," responded Ernst.

"Damn. I hope they're OK. Have you heard from your mom?" asked Garth.

"Oh, she's fine. She's visiting Michigan. So she's good," responded Ernst. "Is everyone else OK?"

"Two of the people in our group died in the earthquake. That was terrible. Not our family though. I can't talk for long because I want to save battery on this phone. Can you tell me what's happening, please? What kind of earthquake was this? On our end it felt huge."

"You got that right. It was really big," responded Ernst. "At least a 9. Centered just south of San Francisco, like San Mateo. Bridges down all over. Highways pretty much out of operation. They've shut down the power."

"Shut down the power?" asked Garth

"Because of wildfires. They are afraid of wildfires," responded Ernst. "There's a big one burning from a downed power line in the Santa Cruz mountains.

"Oh, OK. What about help?" asked Garth.

"Army, National Guard. There's social unrest. The Federal government has declared a State of Emergency from San Francisco to Los Angeles," said Ernst. "The aqueducts into San Francisco and Los Angeles are shattered, so water is an issue.

"Anything else?" asked Garth.

"I'm worried about Wallace and his family. It feels nuts."

"I'd better save this battery. Can you please let everyone know that we're shook up but OK? Please call the Monterey County Sheriff if you can. Our plan is to drive out somehow tonight. Keep the phone close. I'll be back in touch. I love you," said Garth, feeling his voice beginning to break.

There was no reason for the emotion, he thought. Just the surge of uncontrollable events, and the shock of the day overwhelming him. Time to sign off.

"I love you too, Dad," said Ernst.

"Oh! Oh wait!" added Garth "About the business."

"Dow futures down about 2,500," responded Ernst. Voice full of gravity now.

"Not bad, when you consider the situation. For the time being, take over the business entirely, as per our emergency plan, and do what you think is best," said Garth.

"OK," came Ernst's business voice, now cautious. "Until we're back to normal. Just stay safe, and stay healthy, and give everyone our love," said Ernst. We love you lots and we're fine on this end. I'll call everyone and I'll call the Sheriff."

Garth pushed the button on his satellite phone and hung up. And turned to see Bear, Poppy Roswell, and Hopi Jack in Bear's 4x4 Toyota truck, driving towards him on the dirt access road, dust billowing behind.

"No way to get out!" shouted Poppy Roswell out of the front passenger window. "We got a new Grand Canyon between us and the Army base!"

"If there's an inch of you NOT covered in mud, I can't see it," said Beeston Bragg to Paolo Archuleta. Young men, working hard on the water system. Pickaxes, shovels, no shirts. And there was Terp, thought Raley. He compared favorably. Flat stomach.

"Clay. We could make pots out of this. Or adobe. Adobe bricks," said Francesca.

Francesca was almost as muddy as the boys. She was looking at the mud, avidly.

"See, there's where the earthquake broke the plastic pipe. Quick fix," she said, reaching down into the hole.

"My kind of girl," said Paolo.

"Who has the joint and the glue?" responded Francesca, in the hole, water from the uphill pipe spraying into her eyes. Covering, soaking her. So muddy. All the boys were watching. Smiling.

A flash of jealousy. Two could play at that game, thought Raley, jumping into the hole.

"Turn off the water, at the valve uphill," said Francesca, squinting her eyes against the spray. "Can't miss it. Just walk uphill."

The water diminished to a trickle.

"Terp...Terp you do the repair, and Francesca and I will bail," said Raley.

"Crushed like a bug, I tell you! Smashed. I mean, her eyes were popping out of her head and her guts were SQUISHED OUT HER MOUTH! Imagine Freddy, he's fourteen or whatever and there's your mom! Naked! With her guts squished out her mouth and some naked dude still in her. Crushed like a bug. Damn that's embarrassing! I can't imagine what he must be feeling," came Ophelia's voice from under a nearby tree.

"I still can't get any bars," came Hillary's voice.

"I imagine he feels pretty badly," said Paolo softly, turning and looking towards the tree.

"I took photos of everything but I can't get any bars. Can't send anything," said Hillary's voice.

"Jeeze. Just fix the frackin' pipe," muttered Francesca to herself, bailing with a plastic bucket. "Talk after we get water."

Terp, shirtless, bent over the repair as he and Paolo discussed the work. Apparently Terp had done this before, with his grandfather. Lean, muscles rippling. Raley felt herself hypnotized, watching him. It isn't supposed to be like this, she thought. I'm supposed to be in control. Don't blow it.

"Just let the repair rest in the heat of the sun for a few hours. We'll turn on the water then," said Terp to Paolo.

"This is a naturally sunny place, isn't it?" asked Francesca, looking into the distance. "Max exposure."

"No internet. The mission internet is down," said Hillary's distant voice. "It's unnatural, being cut off like this. It's scary. I mean, I can't reach Dad, up there in San Jose. He's probably still sleeping."

"Haven't seen him in six months anyway," said Ophelia's distant voice. "When you DO reach him, it'll be the same old stuff. New tattoo. New love of his life."

Raley looked over at them, slightly embarrassed. The

entire camp was working and these two were sitting under a tree working their cell phones. Like Hero the Service Dog chewing a stick, she thought. Useless.

"What's important about the sun?" said Beeston to Francesca.

"Look over there," said Francesca, pointing.

Up here on the hill they could look down the long green ridgeline a mile or so to the Army base, beyond the raw new zig zag canyon which ripped across the valley floor. There was an equipment dump shining in the sunlight.

"No internet," said Hillary, furiously working her phone. "No cell."

"It's outside that barbed wire. They must not care who gets them," said Francesca.

"Gets what?" said Terp.

"Ahhhh," said Beeston. "Solar panels, I think. Discarded solar panels."

"Yep," said Francesca. "Probably degraded but good enough for us."

"What are you talking about solar panels for? We'll be outta here in a day or two," said Paolo. "We just needed to repair the water line."

"Still, it's good to know," said Francesca. "Never can tell. Like this clay here. Nope, you never can tell."

"What now?" said Beeston. "I'm gonna go look for sand blows in the creek. Supposed to happen after earthquakes."

"Wow, great idea!" said Francesca. "I hear my dad's gonna ride out to the Army base. Let me grab a rifle, just in case."

Raley turned to Terp and spoke softly, still unexpectedly moved by the sight of him.

"Let's go to the creek too," she said, almost whispering. "Let's go wash up."

The horses were skittish. But they calmed quickly, after the soothing effect of grooming, after saddling, after a few hundred yards of being bridle-led, and now people were riding at a walk. Garth's own mount, a thick large gelding named "Dogfood", seemed to be scanning around looking for an excuse to act out. He had found a few terrifying twigs waving in the light breeze, and a horned lizard which skittered away across the sand, and those made him skip nervously, but that was all. Dogfood seemed disappointed that he could find nothing to send himself into a bucking frenzy. Now apparently bored, the horse was rolling his bit in his mouth and tossing his head.

The group walked on, fourteen together, in a traditional column of twos. At the rear was Terry Taylor, a genuine octogenarian, on his crow-hopping giant black gelding named Alastor. Garth considered what would happen to Terry, who was already frail, if Alastor decided to bolt for the nearest town. Catastrophe. But in reality, Alastor was more interested in cropping the volunteer alfalfa which grew amongst the river cobbles.

With Terry was his son Barry, who as always looked like a disheveled middle-aged stoner on a middle aged, disheveled stoner horse, despite his 1850's garb which was entirely hand-me-downs from Terry. Somehow the son had never gotten traction, thought Garth.

Then at the rear was Terry's grandson on an appaloosa mare, with Bear's granddaughter Raley Singleton riding alongside. Raley, seventeen, slender, blonde, smiling radiantly, as though infatuated. Garth couldn't remember Terry's grandson's name, but he seemed bright enough. Those two were certainly grinning at each other.

They rode around the mission buildings. Some large cracks, as they had seen before, but all astonishingly upright and reparable. The heavy tile roofs gleamed red in the sun, all still intact. It was astonishing. As they left the mission behind, the river valley flattened before them.

"And here's the new Grand Canyon," announced Bear as they rode up to a crevasse.

Garth, involuntarily puled Dogfood back from the edge. "Don't get too close! This bank might collapse!"

He watched as the young people pulled their horses to a stop. His daughter Francesca was riding her pinto Arion, next to Bear's granddaughters Hillary and Ophelia on their horses. All blond, smiling. To them this was all a great adventure.

"Only about 20 feet deep but all that water will make it deeper soon. And what? About 100 yards across?" asked Hopi Jack.

"More like about 75," responded the horseman next to him, Fred Paxley. Fred reeked of booze this morning, after an apparent bender last night. Garth had seen him vomiting in the grass earlier. He would probably be dehydrated and in bad condition now.

"Frackin' earthquake," added Fred, talking to himself.

Garth wondered with irritation if Fred was still drunk. It seemed that Fred was always complaining.

"You say we can't get to the Army gate in a car?" asked Garth

"Nope, the cracks are too big between us and the base," replied Bear. "That's why Hopi and I had to turn around."

"Did you try going up the hill and around the back?" asked Garth.

"Didn't see the point," responded Hopi Jack. "They've got fifteen foot high concertina back there and the horses needed a walk anyway. Just follow this canyon up a ways and we'll try to get across wit' the caballos."

With that, Hopi Jack turned his horse left and began a slow walk towards the Army base. As they rode their horses into column, the noise of the chainsaw cutting a tree limb off the van behind the mission could be heard above the sounds of the rippling water.

"You know we've got to tell the Army, right? We need someone from the coroner's office or the sheriff's office so we can send the remains out," said Garth.

The ground was full of round river stones, and the shod horse hooves made a clacking metal-scraping sound as they walked along. The adults were all silent as they rode. In back of the column the four girls, Terry's grandson, and 19 year old Stan Sanchez, Steve Sanchez' son, were chatting happily and quietly. Garth considered that Steve Sanchez, as a crime scene investigator, was probably not having a good morning caring for those rapidly aging corpses.

Around them were wildflowers in clumps amidst the

stones, and mule-fat bushes standing tall and green. Cottonwood and willow and sycamore trees, a few with broken limbs. There was a new waist deep crack running down the side hill, now filled with a steady stream of clouded liquid. So they couldn't drive a car out that way. The tire tracks of Bear's earlier reconnaissance were plain on the dirt. The day was heating up, and the familiar good smells of sycamore and sand and creek water brought back a swarm of delightful childhood memories to Garth. Soothing. Everything was fine.

As they came through the cottonwood trees to the boundary of the mission property, Garth could see a series of sand cones rising from the creek bed, like man-high volcanoes, all in a row along the creek bank. On Army land.

"Sand blows," said Bear from just behind him. "I've only read about them. Never seen one before. The earthquake made them."

"Well we gotta go look," replied Garth, as the column of horses crossed onto Army land. "The Army's OK with it, don't you think? Let's investigate as soon as we find someone we can talk with. Let's get the sheriffs onto our two dead people. It's their mess, unfortunately."

"I'm thinking we're screwed whatever happens," said Fred Paxley's voice behind him. "Can't even get a car to us. Garth, did you really call for help or are you lying? You're probably lying to us. Finally you get to control us. For real, instead of pretend."

Garth suppressed his anger and pushed down the urge to shout back. Instead he said nothing. He reminded himself again that it was possible that Fred was still drunk, or perhaps dehydrated.

"Hey, Fred, perhaps we should go back," came Terry's voice. I notice you aren't feeling so well this morning. Just let's get back to the mission and rest up. We'll be OK soon."

Soothing words.

"I'll take 'im," came the voice of Barry, Terry's son. "You all go on."

Ahead, Hopi Jack pulled back on his reins and the column stopped. "OK, anyone want to go, head back now, before we cross this crevasse."

They waited. Garth pondered his situation. He had hurriedly retrieved five plastic handloader's boxes of ammunition: two boxes of .45-70 carbine handloads for their Springfield trapdoor carbine rifles, two boxes of light .45 colt cartridges for their pistols, one box of modern 12 gauge buckshot for the two shotguns, and a cigarette tin box of hand-rolled paper .44 lead ball cartridges for his own gun. Now all that ammo rode unseen in Garth's saddlebags. Unseen, but heavy on his mind.

Garth had already loaded his cap and ball percussion 1858 revolver, carefully leaving a chamber empty for safety's sake. Garth was aware he was breaking the rules for the mission, and certainly the law once they crossed over onto Army ground. Now he had second thoughts. No sense getting everyone else arrested.

"I'm thinking I need to go visit the Army alone," said Garth.

He passed Bear the saddlebags. Bear's eyes widened at the weight, and he understood.

"I'm thinking Garth's got a point. We've had a good outing, but they probably need us back at camp. Almost lunch time anyway and we gotta eat up the refrigerated food before it goes bad."

Bear stared meaningfully at Hopi Jack and hoisted the saddlebags up and down several times. Hopi Jack seemed clueless. Then acceptance spread across his face.

"Agreed. Let's just turn this around now. Garth, see you back at camp," said Hopi Jack.

Jack, Terry, and the boys rode back to the mission far ahead of the girls. Raley watched her grandfather Bear gesticulating, pointing all around him, caught up in some discussion with Terry.

"My God, we're stuck with a bunch of senile creepers," she said aloud.

Francesca, riding alongside her, laughed.

"I'm not so sure about that," said Francesca. "Think about it, most of these guys are war veterans. Old, yes, but experienced. We're with some of the most self-reliant people anywhere. Give most people a hammer and they'll hurt themselves."

"Oh, don't bet on these antiques knowing what day it is," answered Raley. "They're fat old little boys, and the religion that made this mission is false. Combine the two, as they have here at this living history event, and you have a delusional gaggle of geezers playing pretend, with a big imaginary friend in the sky to top it off. Terry Taylor says God has a plan. I haven't seen it yet."

"I wonder about that myself," said Francesca as the horses walked beneath them. "I mean, perhaps we're not realizing that God speaks in everyday life. Maybe back when people didn't have science to explain everything, they were more aware of God. That might be what we're missing."

Raley looked over her shoulder. Behind them, Ophelia and Hillary were riding along, oblivious to the world, obsessing over their cell phones.

"No bars. No bars," she heard one of them say.

"What if all our stuff distracts us from what is sacred?" asked Francesca. "I've been thinking about that...since the earthquake. What if this day itself is the voice of God?"

"So everything is sacred? Taking a poop is sacred?" said Raley.

"What would happen if you couldn't poop?" said Francesca. "Maybe the ability to poop is more valuable than we know."

"The outhouse as a place of worship," said Raley. "Never thought of it like that."

"Organ music," said Francesca.

"Colonic symphonies," said Raley.

They laughed.

"Seriously. Let's shut up and let the day happen. Listen and look," said Francesca. "Maybe God will tell us something."

They rode for a few minutes in silence. Warm perfect day. Wildflowers and green wild grasses spread before them. As they watched, a few contrails of high-up aircraft crossed the sky, heading out over the Pacific Ocean. A circling hawk.

Distantly they could hear the chuckling of an acorn wood-pecker family in the sycamore trees of the creek bed.

"I tell you, it's unnatural," said Ophelia's voice behind them. "No cell service. It's unnatural."

Raley laughed.

"Ok," she said. "I see your point. But I still say that the religious part is fake."

"Hi ladies," said a voice nearby. Fred Paxley.

"Hello, Mr. Paxley," said Francesca.

"I'm just here to see if I can give you anything," said Fred Paxley.

"Nope, we're good," said Raley.

"I'm hoping we can get to know each other," said Fred. "I mean, you're both lookin' so pretty riding back here, and I'm so lonely up there with those idiots. Discussing the Fetterman Massacre or some such fantasy. More fun back here with the pretty girls. We should spend more time to-gether, ladies. What are you discussing?"

Raley realized that Mr. Paxley really DID reek, of old booze and vomit and more. Almost as smelly as Hero the Service Dog.

"Mr. Paxley, we are discussin' God," said Raley. "God in his majesty."

Fred Paxley pulled up his horse, feigning distaste.

"Damn, that's even more boring than talking about the Sioux," said Fred Paxley. "Let's talk about you two. Do you ever skinny-dip?"

"If we do, Mr. Paxley, we're sure to do it alone," said Francesca, hesitantly. "It's a secret of the sisterhood."

"Next time you should invite me," said Fred Paxley. "I'm fun, you know. You're young. You're healthy. You gotta wash. Why not?" said Fred Paxley.

Raley saw the shock on Francesca's face.

"See what I mean?" Raley said to Francesca. "All men are pigs. My mother's boyfriends talk to me like this all the time."

"I'm not a pig. Just a man who appreciates," said Fred Paxley. "I can look, can't I?"

"You know I'm fifteen, and Raley is seventeen?" said Francesca softly. "And you are what? Sixty? Why would you talk like that to us?"

"Because I can," said Mr. Paxley firmly. "Those pretend heroes ridin' up front won't do a thing. This earthquake, you know? I realize that the rules have changed. Nobody's gonna do nothin'. We're fracked. It's all bullshit. Might as well get what I can."

"Mr. Paxley," said Francesca. "It's only been a few hours since the quake, and if the world has changed, I don't know it. But if the rules really HAVE changed, then that means the rules have changed for us, as well as for you."

"True, true," said Fred Paxley enthusiastically. "What ya got in mind?"

"I expect you to leave us alone, Mr. Paxley," said Francesca. "Any more talk like this and who knows? You might fall down an outhouse and drown. We're young, and there's a lot of us. We ladies gotta stick together, and we're surrounded by our families. Like you just said, if this lasts very long, then the rules have changed."

The Army Colonel: young man, perhaps 45, soft billed Army hat, harness, SIG military plastic pistol in a classic World War II black leather pistol holster and matching World War II web pistol belt. Unique, thought Garth. He's making a statement of some kind. Looking carefully, Garth could see the gaping back of the pistol and realized that it had no magazine. Two canteens, which hung full and heavy on the belt. The Colonel stood, preoccupied, tense, no ballistic armor, slender in brown operational camouflage uniform, leaning against an armored Humvee. He was rattling orders to subordinates and examining an iPad.

"What do YOU want?" he snapped at Garth, setting the iPad onto the Humvee's hood and turning to face Garth squarely.

Aviator sunglasses. Rapid breathing. Sweat. Stress.

"I assume the Major has filled you in, Sir?" Garth answered. Then, automatically, unexpectedly, he saluted, and was instantly filled with embarrassment and concern, and even a little fear. He was standing before a bird Colonel of the U.S. Army dressed like an 1863 Captain of U.S. Volunteer Cavalry, and he was a total fraud, and he had a loaded 1858 Remington Single Action Army revolver in his brown military flap holster. Empty chamber under the hammer, and if they bothered to see that gun, unregistered on a U.S. Army base, they would arrest his ass and lock him up for the rest of his life. Ridiculous.

"Oh, DAMN!" the colonel said, and laughed. "We got the world on the brink of an imaginary war and a frackin' earthquake and some married woman gets drunk in a hippie van and she and the hookup boyfriend get crushed by a TREE? And you are dressed up like the student prince or something. Cosplay, right? E Clampus Vitus? Some sort of initiation? Should I fracking GUESS?"

Garth pondered. The Colonel was clueless, and disinterested. He restrained himself from discussing those details. Clearly the Colonel had a lot on his mind. A small bark of anger deep inside. "So you've got it handled?" he asked.

"Nobody is answering at the Sheriff's office. Dead people all over out in the real world. Even more hurt living people everywhere," the Colonel replied, looking at his iPad and waving dismissively. "We've got enough problems. Most of these problems are fantasies in civilian minds. We'll try to get you someone. Meanwhile, deal with it. Ya know this base got closed by our loving Congress last year. We're the last ones here and we're supposed to turn out the lights as we leave. So adios. Your state government and all your greenies don't want us here, so we don't want to be here. Good luck!"

The silent major standing next to the Colonel began moving towards Garth, to usher him away.

"Thanks Sir. If I could ask, brink of war? How...how bad was the earthquake?" asked Garth hurriedly, intentionally sounding a bit clueless.

Before he could be escorted out. Beyond stupidity. He should not have said a word, he thought to himself. God, don't let them notice the pistol.

"We're being moved out, the whole unit, to San Francisco. Nothing behind, and no supplies, only a few facilities guards.

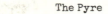

The Army has already removed the hardware, the equipment. Hell, we've been living off field kitchens and MRE's for three weeks as it is. Today we turned off most of the plumbing.

"Meanwhile this earthquake apparently knocked the crap outta that area up north. Apparently unzipped all the way up to Vancouver." said the Colonel. He picked up the iPad and punched a screen. An image of a smoking, wrecked city.

"Looks horrible," replied Garth, trying to say as little as possible.

"Don't sweat it, it's not as bad as it looks. They're saying 9, but they're exaggerating. Remember 1989? This is a bit worse, but not catastrophic." said the Colonel.

"Brink of war?" Garth repeated.

"Oh, that. That's the Chinese. You know their drought is drivin' 'em nuts, and their tungro rice blight, and their recession is worse than ours. Somebody in the beltway got scared."

"They've got too much debt," answered Garth.

"Well, that premier's gotta do something to take their mind off of all that. So he's telling them that they need to take back Taiwan, now. Something about ancestral land, blah blah. Same old game as Argentina with the Falklands back in 1980." said the Colonel.

"Sounds like your plate is more than full," said Garth, soothingly.

He thought to himself that he needed to get out before anyone noticed the pistol.

"Look," replied the Colonel. "San Francisco isn't as bad as it looks. We aren't getting any big reports of casualties.

And China...well, you know, China, they threaten about every six weeks. So just go back to your fellow play-actors and tell them to stay calm and go home. We've got everything handled. Everything. You got fairies and goblins dressed up over there? Got any Game of Thrones characters? Pretend fires?"

With that, the Colonel laughed harshly, saluted, and motioned to the major to take Garth away. He grimaced an attempted smile, nodded, and returned to his iPad.

After the Major escorted Garth back to his horse, Dogfood, Garth mounted and began to gently canter down the dirt track to the mission. Get as far away as possible before they notice the pistol. Turbulent emotions, fighting to keep from shouting. Reconsidering his panic, he held Dogfood back to a walk. No sense attracting attention.

The sat phone in his breast pocket buzzed. It was his oldest daughter, Sarah, who was living and working with her husband Osten in Oslo, Norway. A call from Norway while he was riding a horse in rural California. Amazing world.

He reined Dogfood to a stop, looked behind him, saw nobody, and swept the phone up and answered it.

"I saw you had an earthquake!" said Sarah's voice on the phone. "How are you all?"

"We're all just fine. Ernst can tell you more. I need to save battery. How are you, and what are you hearing on the news?" asked Garth

"Copacetic here," reported Sarah. "Nobody in Salinas is answering the phone, which has me worried."

Garth felt his world spinning as Dogfood plodded along.

Astonishing. Thank God that he and his family were here. But so many families and so many friends!

"Casualties?" he asked.

"Unknown, but big," replied Sarah's voice.

"Tell me more and I'll let you go," said Sarah. "You know Osten is curious. No earthquakes here."

Garth explained everything. "I think we're good," he concluded.

"Terrible about that couple in the car," said Sarah's voice. "Shocking"

"Yes. But I'm sure the sheriffs will handle it," replied Garth.

"I'll keep trying Wallace in Salinas. We love you. Stay in touch, OK?" said Sarah.

Back to reality. Dogfood was walking slowly on the dirt roadside trail back to the mission. Definitely, Garth felt, he was overreacting. Yes, those two people had been crushed. Awful. Yes, there had been a terrifying earthquake. But the world was intact. It was a sunny day, and there were poppies and lupine blooming in the green meadows. Beyond, the dome of the beautiful old Spanish mission loomed up, intact. The two people were dead. But the world would go on, in beauty and in peace. Prayers.

Dogfood plodded on. Garth checked his sat phone. 32% battery. He should conserve. He took a photo of the vista of the approaching mission, went to his Facebook page, posted the photo, and commented, "Big shaker! We're good!" Might as well not spread the news of the deaths to the world until the relatives were notified. It was their business, after all.

A quick check of Wallace's Facebook, and Wallace's wife's Facebook. Nothing posted. His page was full of people marking themselves "safe" from the earthquake. Most of those posting were Los Angeles friends. Nothing from Monterey County, or San Francisco. He didn't scroll down farther to see what was happening elsewhere, because he didn't want to drain his battery.

Then he turned his sat phone off, put it back into his blue Civil War uniform breast pocket and forced himself to admire the beautiful morning. It was warm. He felt sweat trickling under his shirt. Most of that was from stress, from his meeting with the Colonel.

As he passed the boundary of mission property, he felt a gust of relief. All would be well. The best of life continues in the worst of times.

Bear, Hopi Jack, Francesca, Akemi, and Raley came galloping up to meet him, their horses dry. That dryness was good: they hadn't been exerting the mounts riding excitedly in circles. As they rode up, Hopi Jack pointed wordlessly into the clear blue sky. Garth looked up.

Thin white contrails. Perhaps a hundred. Many jets, very high up, heading out to the Pacific Ocean over the mountains. Towards Hawaii. Towards China? Adrenaline. Were they under attack? Was this entire experience an act of war, somehow?

"What are they?" asked Garth, mostly to himself.

"Missiles?" said Bear.

"Maybe drones." responded Hopi Jack. "I don't think we got that many planes."

"Fast." Garth said. "Really moving."

"And this is the second wave!" said Akemi.

She seemed rather happy and excited about it.

"What's happening with Kathy and Lucky?" Garth asked. "I mean, their remains."

"Not a thing," said Hopi Jack, "Steve Sanchez did his investigation, and took some photos. Now Terry Taylor and his grandson are watchin' over 'em. The remains are still in the van but the tree's off 'em and they got a poncho over the whole mess. No sense letting the sun beat down."

"So now we just wait for the sheriff and hope they come soon. The heat's gonna mess with the bodies," added Bear.

There was a loud increase of engine noise from the army base on the road behind, and they turned on their horses. A convoy of armored Humvees began to roll out the gate where Garth had met the Colonel, heading away, down towards the Salinas Valley. Towards King City and Soledad. Nobody in the gun turrets, and guns not mounted. There wasn't going to be a war today, praise God. No alien airborne troops. No Red Dawn.

They all watched the convoy roll out. Everything...almost everything...remaining on the base. In the distance, off the airfield, they could see several scout helicopters rising into the sky to accompany them. Overwatch. No guns evident.

And below those helicopters, on the dirt road to the mission, driving in the opposite direction of the convoy, came a little black quad all-terrain vehicle, with a large antenna, from which flapped a yellow banner. "Sheriff" was stenciled in black letters on the little yellow flag. Law Enforcement, at last.

The Sheriff's Deputy was a young man, neat, close-cut hair visible as he removed his wraparound helmet, wearing aviator sunglasses and, beneath his uniform shirt, body armor. As he stepped off the ATV, Garth noticed that his name tag said "Davis". Once again Garth was deeply conscious of his own pistol in its holster on his old fashioned left side flap holster. He wished he hadn't loaded it, so long ago this morning. Leave it alone, he thought. Reaching for it now will only attract attention.

"Good morning, I'm here because somebody from New York reported a homicide?" Deputy Davis said quietly. "I don't really understand how that happened, but I'm here anyway."

"Good morning. Sir!" said Bear, "It's more of accidental death, we're guessing. May we dismount from our horses?"

Notepads. Explanations. Pointing and a map. Deputy Davis returned to his ATV and called his headquarters. They all waited, holding their drowsy horses. A few flies. It was spring. The day was warming.

"Can someone take me to the crime scene?' asked Deputy Davis. "Base is a bit crazy. They are overwhelmed and their comm is going in and out."

Garth raised his hand. "May we lead the way? You'll want to see everything."

Garth looked around the grassy camping area, which had a scattering of green valley oak leaves, oak bark, and sawdust.

Everyone, perhaps thirty people, had gathered around Deputy Davis, amidst the tents. The deputy addressed them all.

"Thanks for helping me today. I can't do more than a preliminary investigation. What you may not know is that it's a mess out there. I don't know what's going on: I'm based out of Jolon, which like you is a small community. We got shook up pretty badly. Some injuries, no fatalities. The towns down in the valley got hurt much worse, and there's word that social unrest is spreading. The Army and the National Guard are heading towards the big cities, and we in the Sheriff's Department are left with the smaller towns."

"How about Salinas?" asked Larry.

"Hit hard," replied Deputy Davis. "I don't know much, but here's what I've heard. All the bridges are down over the Salinas River, and there are big new fissures. The highway is closed, there's no water, no power, no groceries. There's a fire in the Santa Cruz Mountains so air quality is marginal. You can get there now by ATV or by horse, but if you don't need to go there, I recommend that you don't. They've got some looting and some rioting going on as well."

Garth saw Akemi gasp. Like him, she was probably thinking of her older brother Wallace and his family. Dove and Francesca looked stoic.

"How about Hollister?" asked Bear.

"I'm sorry, I don't know anything else. Except the Monterey Peninsula is worse. They had a tsunami. I know that they got smacked pretty badly," replied Deputy Davis.

"So what do we do?" asked a woman's voice. "My husband is laying over there dead. When will you take him away?"

That would be Patty Martin. Her husband...her dead cheating husband...was Lucky Martin.

"Ma'am...everybody...I'm sorry," said Deputy Davis. "The station is so overwhelmed, and reception is so bad that they really didn't tell me what's going to happen. I get the impression that there's a lot of dead people out there. Mr. Sanchez has completed his investigation. Ma'am, I'm deeply sorry, but the best option may be to lay your deceased husband to rest here."

He gestured towards the old cemetery beyond the mission.

"That hasn't been used for a century," came Poppy Roswell's voice. "Maybe longer."

Garth turned to look at Poppy. Poppy, slender and wrinkled in his 1850's clothing, looked all of his 70 plus years, sweaty and worn, as he stood next to his equally disheveled wife Samantha. They had been working all day to restore the area, to repair, to cook, and to comfort. Garth realized that Poppy and Samantha knew both the Martins and the Desaults quite well, were history, horse and music friends with both families. This day must be very hard for them, Garth realized.

"All I can tell you is that I'd be surprised if anyone came, for weeks," said Deputy Davis.

"Well then," answered Poppy. "Who will help me? We have graves to dig."

"And after that?" came a loud hard voice. "What have you geniuses got planned for our next adventure?"

That would be Jonathan Sanchez, Steve's cousin, a lawyer. Garth remembered that he'd been whining all week.

About fifty, balding, red-faced, a touch overweight. Wearing Hollywood Hills western with crinkled woven hat and aviator sunglasses. Pointy little pimp cowboy boots.

"At this point I can't really advise you," replied Deputy Davis calmly. "I don't really know what's going on out there, except for a general feeling that it's a big mess. For example, headquarters is telling me that they can't evacuate or investigate your incident. What does that tell you?"

"Deputy, what's your first name?" asked Jonathan.

"Sir, it's Pike. Pike, like the fish," replied Deputy Davis.

"Well, Pike like the fish," said Jonathan, "Don't you feel that you, and your whole sheriff's office, might be a little incompetent here? I mean, are you THAT clueless? Or do you actually KNOW what is happening and you are just hiding it? I say we should leave."

"Who are you?" asked Deputy Davis.

"You don't know who I am? You REALLY don't know?" responded Jonathan Sanchez loudly "I'm famous, if you paid attention, and I'm a tort attorney, and a good one. Stanford Law School. Stanford Law School. You probably have seen my TV advertisements. In fact I'm contemplating a lawsuit right now, against your agency, against anyone who stands in our way. I'm already gonna sue this mission for the earthquake."

A moment of silence. Garth could feel attitudes hardening against Jonathan within the circle. A threat of a lawsuit doesn't make friends, thought Garth.

"You can't get your car out of here, Sir," replied Deputy Davis. "Even if you CAN get a vehicle out, I can't really tell you what's happening. All I know is between here and Jolon. Beyond that, it sounds like chaos and combat."

"All exaggerations, no doubt," replied Jonathan. "Overreactions. I checked into my Facebook and my friends at home are marking themselves safe."

"Where is home?" asked a voice. Poppy.

"Mulholland Drive, in Los Angeles," replied a younger shapely red haired Hispanic woman standing next to Jonathan.

That would be his wife, Sierra, thought Garth. Very very tight neon blue pants. Nice to watch. Long fingernails. She probably couldn't do much work or household chores with nails like that. Garth remembered that the teenaged girls had been calling her "Squirm-era."

"It might be best to stay here a few days and let the situation clarify itself," replied Deputy Davis.

"Pike like the fish, I should point out that Los Angeles is south of us. You DO know that LA is to the south, right? Should I get out a map for you, deputy? I was only able to get cell service for a few minutes. But the Internet says they're looting in San Francisco. Otherwise no other news. I'm assuming that you and your agency don't know shit. On threat of a lawsuit, can you promise me that I can't get out of here?" said Jonathan.

"No, Sir," replied Deputy Davis, subdued.

"I've got big business waiting for me at home. It's costing me tens of thousands of dollars an hour to not get it done. I've also got a great four wheel drive truck. I know it's good, I paid $120,000 for it, and it's the best. The best. The absolute bigliest. So I'm getting out of here. I'm going back to my air-conditioned home overlooking LA, and I'm gonna swim in my pool with my beautiful wife in her tiny bikini. Don't try to stop us. I'm used to being right. WE'RE used to being right. We have our brilliant minds and we have the law."

Hopi Jack was fidgeting. Garth recalled that Hopi was a retired judge.

"I'm a lawyer too, so I guess you could say I also have my mind and the law. Perhaps my family would debate the 'mind' part. Anyway I'm not seeing the wisdom here," said Hopi Jack. "Can't you wait a day? Until you know more about what's going on out there?"

"Some of us have places to go home to, and things to do," said Jonathan Sanchez. "Did you know that I have $500,000 in gold coins in a fireproof safe in my basement, back in LA? This quake's gonna make them EVEN MORE VALUABLE! What do you think of THAT?"

Everyone was silent. Then Hopi Jack spoke up. "Did you know that I have an entire green winged teal, you know, a small duck, feathers, guts, and all, in my freezer back in Salinas? I shot it dead last November, during duck season, with my ol' Brown Bess."

A few subdued chuckles from the group.

"Not so sure about it with the power out, though," Hopi continued, as though to himself.

"WHAT THE HELL DOES THAT HAVE TO DO WITH ANYTHING?" shouted Jonathan Sanchez. "You mocking me? I can make you regret it."

"Here's the point," said Hopi Jack. "Gold doesn't rot,

unlike my duck. It doesn't burn. The Fort Knox in your basement should be waiting for you if you delay a day. Wait until
we know more."

"No guts no glory," said Jonathan Sanchez. "I went to the
big time, you stayed in a hick town. Nice chatting. We gotta
blow. We have room for a few more passengers in the back.
Who wants to go? Anyone who stays one extra minute in this
dump is a loser. Gotta move. Move or lose. Your choice.
I'm guessing you're a loser, deputy. That's why you are standing there in your loser uniform and your loser gun, and I'm
outta here. Winners don't need guns."

Hero the service dog had been rolling in horse manure. Or
something worse. That explained his horrendous smell,
which in a way was helpful, since it masked any odors coming from the coffins. There was a slight smell of rotting meat
and a whiff of gasoline. Those coffins were quite well made,
thought Garth. Made by some of the younger people with
Poppy's supervision. Beeston Bragg and Paolo Archuletta,
from the 1st Volunteer Cavalry, two young men who seemed
to have joined the unit as a sort of Boy Scout experience.
Unpainted sun-bleached boards and nails from the empty
old storage shack behind the mission, which had sagged during the earthquake, not completely down but tipped over so
that its boards and frame were now mostly useless. It was a
great use of the boards, thought Garth.

They had dug the holes side by side, which appeared to
have silently offended both families. The river cobbles which
infested the soil had made excavation terribly difficult. That

young grandson of Terry Taylor's had been incredibly helpful. Then they had of course found human remains. Of course, it was an old cemetery after all. Half a skull here, a tibia there. All these had gone back in the holes, under the coffins. The coffins had been lowered into the holes with ropes, and they had forgotten to put any risers on the coffins so the ropes required tugging and jerking to save them for later use. Almost comical, thought Garth. Almost and not at all.

"Anyone want to say a few words?" said Tiger Tanaka.

Tiger was a Buddhist, from Salinas.

In the distance, Jonathan Sanchez was revving his giant 4 x 4 truck. He was anxious to leave. Waiting on Deputy Davis.

"Isn't anyone here a minister? A pastor? Anything religious?" asked Fred Paxley. Fred looked sallow, shook up. "Frack, this is embarrassing."

"That scumbag revving his truck over there should stop it. I told him it wasn't seemly, and it isn't safe," added Gritz Garwood, who was swaying a bit.

"I reach up to the universe for consolation and healing," said a young woman in a flowery summer dress, reaching skywards. She was the journalist from Los Angeles, here to write about the living history event.

Another woman in a colorful serape and very large round sunglasses began to do an interpretive dance, waving her arms and humming. "Ahhhhh. Ahhhhh. Ahhhh, WE WILL ALL MEET AGAIN ON THE RAINBOW BRIDGE! Ahhhh, Ahhhh, Ahhhh!"

Garth contemplated where that rainbow bridge might be, exactly. These women did not believe in Christianity. Their beliefs seemed diffuse. This gathering was rapidly losing its focus. Garth's mind wandered. It had been a big day and he was exhausted. Confused. Hero the service dog, who was now urinating on a dusty shovel stuck upright in the soil, certainly DID reek. Perhaps he had dug down into one of the old outhouses. They had those old wooden outhouses on the far side of the campground, and they had cement slabs around them, Garth remembered. So that couldn't be why Hero smelled like that.

Kathy Desault's son, Freddy, began to cry gently over her open grave. Garth considered that Freddy was young, perhaps 14. Too young for this. Any attempt at a funeral seemed to be coming apart. Belinda Jefferson reached out and hugged him. Where was Kathy's husband, Paul? Who this morning had tried to torch the crushed and bloody van and everything in it? Not present, Garth realized. But there was Patty Martin, Lucky's widow, silent, tears streaming down her face, holding her two small crying children tight. All of them silent.

"Ummm, I have this," said Terry Taylor, in his blue 1861 cavalry uniform.

He produced a small black leather-bound book.

"It's the Book of Common Prayer, and there's a service for burial in here," said Terry, thumbing through the pages.

He began to read. In the distance, Jonathan Sanchez spoke over a loudspeaker, apparently built into his truck. "If the Thomas family and Sheila Celaya really want to leave, instead of dicking about, get over here now. We're out of here."

"Dicking around, dicking around. Who's the dickwad?" muttered Gritz Garwood. "I told him. Stay here, I told him.

No, he says, he's a genius, he'll be home by tomorrow night, sitting by the pool, laughing at us stuck here in the dirt."

Salinas, California

Sunset, Mickey Ramirez was looking grimly into the ruins of the burned building, a charred ruin, the chimney standing up redly above their heads, and the rest black, flattened, and still smoking a bit. Wallace was stepped up behind him. Mickey had an AR-15 slung over his shoulder, and a backpack similar to that which Wallace was wearing. What they carried when they had to abandon a squad car due to impassable streets.

"Well, I guess they gave him a Viking funeral," said Mickey.

Wallace looked, and immediately felt the urge to vomit. There in the steaming charred flatness of what had once been the living room was a shriveled cremated corpse.

"Oh my God, it's not the old man, is it?" asked Wallace. "The one who lived here? His mother died here, right?"

His comments were drowned out by three helicopters flying noisily in loose formation, low to the ground, small civilian aircraft, now ferrying firefighters and police all over town. Noise. Este es un día de milagros, thought Wallace. When they passed, he repeated his words.

"Oh, nope, that's Ronny Reynolds," said Mickey. "Guess they didn't feel like hauling him away."

"Damn," said Wallace.

"The woman whom everyone thought deceased turned

up later at a neighbor's home. Turns out she'd been cooking in her underwear when the earthquake hit, so when the place lit up, she scampered over there. Didn't want to be seen in her scanties. Nobody died here," said Mickey.

"'Cept Ronnie," said Wallace.

"Gotta admit, not gonna miss him," responded Mickey. "Kinda glad that eighty year old woman beat feet to the neighbors when the house lit up. I've got enough to erase from my brain."

At that point they saw the old woman walking towards them, carrying a basket. Hunched. Walking slowly in the dusk.

"Ven conmigo, por favor" she said, and turned away.

"Porque?" asked Mickey.

But she didn't answer.

Up a driveway into a backyard of an intact home, the secret was revealed. There were both squad cars, parked on the back lawn. Pristine.

Wallace felt a surge of embarrassment. He hadn't even thought to check out his car. There was another roar in the sky as several small light helicopters flew over in the darkness, lights flashing. Off to help someone else, thought Wallace. This was really working out. The backyard was lit with several large electric lights, and Wallace could hear a generator, and at the far end of the darkened back yard, out of the light, the glow of a barbecue pit and delicious smells. The smells weakened him. He realized that he hadn't eaten in twelve hours. There must be twenty people here, he thought. All speaking Spanish, quietly. No raised voices.

Out of the back door of the house came Hugh "Tiny" Tupuola, with his K-9. The dog, Diablo, a large Alsatian, had a pink bow on his head. Clearly there were children in the home. Behind them came the diminutive highly attractive woman who had tried to take the cell phone video of Ronny's final moment. Disgusting, thought Wallace. The lights illuminated her near-perfect figure and dark lustrous hair. Next to Tiny, she looked like a half-sized doll.

"Hey Sergeant. I just got back here myself," reported Tiny.

A water bottle was pressed into Wallace's hand. He looked down. The old woman looked up at him.

"Hidratación, hijo mío. Luego comida," said the old woman quietly.

What I would really like, thought Wallace, is a gallon of tequila and twelve hours' sleep. Instead he opened the plastic water bottle and took a long drink.

"I was over at University Park. Surprisingly good over there. Just like the rest of town, people pulling together. Cracks, homes off foundations, broken windows, yada yada," said Tiny. "I checked on your home. A few broken windows. The neighbors taped cardboard over them. The chimney's down."

"All the chimneys are down. Damn near all the chimneys are down," added Mickey.

"I gotta tell you, this place rocks," said Wallace.

The girl covered her face with her hand and laughed silently.

"Oh, Margarita...." Tiny motioned an introduction of the young woman at Wallace.

"Margarita Sanchez," said the tiny woman, white teeth glistening. She WAS very attractive, thought Wallace.

They shook hands lightly. After the Coronavirus in 2020, this was seldom done.

"Nice to meet you, Miss Sanchez. Um, Margarita," replied Wallace. "Thanks for your hospitality. Thanks for watching over our police cars. We can't drive them anyway. But still, your hospitality is most appreciated."

"It's this way all over town. It's astonishing," said Mickey. "There's an old packing shed down over on East Market, I mean, flattened, and there were six people killed, and a whole bunch more injured, trapped, and, I mean..."

At this point Mickey's eyes filled with tears and he wiped his eyes with his fingers.

"Terrible," said Margarita, and her voice was filled with compassion.

"Well, yes, of course, but what happened was this crowd of people just ripped that old wooden building apart, it was amazing, and there was Jesus Garcia and his bag of cholos...

"Jesus Garcia? As in, 'I just got out of Soledad State Prison for murder' Jesus Garcia?" asked Tiny.

'Yep, the very same," said Mickey. "Anyway the crowd just rescued everyone. The gang members were right in there with the rest. They just got everyone out of that wreck and onto the helicopters. It was beautiful, guys."

"Amazing," said Mickey. "Everyone was great with me too. A little light looting over by the mall, at Northridge, but volunteers came over from Boronda."

Margarita reached up and put her hand on Tiny's massive

well-muscled forearm. Well, he IS single, Wallace thought. In a few days, when this all clears up, those two should see each other.

The back door opened above them and the single light bulb on the steps illuminated a vision. There stood a woman...a very very beautiful woman, Wallace thought. Dressed like Margarita in form fitting clothing. She looked oddly familiar. In her thirties, about Wallace's age. Ah...she looked like that old-time actress, Sophia Loren. Italian. Very very beautiful.

Then he saw the sling supporting her arm, and he remembered. The woman on the front lawn, utterly transformed by a change of clothes and hair combing. Now she was carrying a bowl, a large metal bowl, and she came lightly down the stairs and stood next to them, almost as tall as Wallace.

"Nice to see you again, Sergeant," she said quietly. English.

Oh, my she was beautiful.

"Oh, meet my older sister Katerina. Katerina Sanchez," said Margarita.

"Katy will do. Just call me Katy," smiled the beautiful woman. The same white teeth as Margarita. She was about nine inches taller than her sister. And married. Very married, Wallace reminded himself.

Greetings from everyone.

From the metal bowl, Katy produced foil-wrapped cylinders.

"Burritos. Left-over chili verde. Please sit down and eat. We'll also have some asada at any moment. They are just finishing up over there. And, if you need them, we've got washing water and an outhouse set up over behind the garage. You guys have flashlights?'

Wallace was too smitten to answer. He stammered an answer which may have been positive. Smitten by his hunger. Smitten by his fatigue. Smitten by her. It was all very confusing. Somehow, he found himself sitting in a plastic lawn chair, at a table, shotgun propped alongside, eating under the night sky with the two policemen and the women.

Wallace unwrapped the foil from the burrito and the scent-laden moisture rose up into his face. The flour tortilla was soaked in the chili verde juices. That first soft bite, the tortilla giving way to the saltiness of the meat within. Hints of cilantro. Whisps of green chili and onions and garlic. Wallace looked across the table at Mickey and Tiny, who were also eating.

"Would you like to rest here for the night?" asked Margarita, eying Tiny.

Oh my, thought Wallace.

"I think we're still on duty," responded Wallace. "I'll check in and if we're good, we can nap in the patrol cars, even if we can't drive them away."

"The streets are still much too littered and broken," said Tiny evenly through his burrito. "This is superb. Who made this?"

"Oh, I did," responded Margarita, gazing wide eyed up at Tiny.

Wallace remembered Tiny's former girlfriend. A banking executive who couldn't bake a frozen pizza. More importantly, she wouldn't. At first Tiny's awesome physique had kept her enthralled. Then the long hours of his work and her need for an societally provocative man on her arm at important corporate events had led to their breakup. Wallace wondered where that woman was now.

The conversation swirled around him. Wallace realized that he hadn't thought about his family all day. He had been swept from one small incident to the next. He hadn't called his wife and children in Denmark. In Aabenraa. It was morning there now. He hadn't called his father and the rest of the family down at Mission San Antonio. He pulled out his cell phone and turned it on. No signal. Not a bar. No internet, because there was no power.

Based on what he had seen here in Salinas, he was guessing that everyone was OK. This was a wonderful town, thought Wallace. Yes, they had been hit hard, but the people had responded beautifully. They would remember this day forever. Truly, it was a day of miracles.

San Antonio Mission, California

Around 10 PM. Dark. A full moon rising to the east. Garth was brushing his teeth at the outdoor faucet. The water came from a spring up the hill, and it was delicious. The group had been discussing what they would do if Jonathan Sanchez could find or make a way out. Alternatively, they had discussed what to do if the effort somehow failed. That would be indicated if they returned to camp. Now there was a commotion, raised voices, fast movement, out towards the road. Garth looked up.

Fred Paxley was drunk again, with Barry Taylor, and Gritz Garwood. They seemed to be the source of the noise. Patiently, Garth spat, rinsed his mouth, and walked through the rising moonlight in the cool evening towards the noise.

"I tell ya, we're all gonna die. I mean, look at her! LOOK AT HER!" shouted Gritz.

Damn near useless, he is, thought Garth.

Then he saw that Fred was holding and shaking, the small sobbing form of Tabetha Thomas, the six-year-old daughter of Merry and Zachary Thomas. The last time Garth had seen the Thomas family, they had all been riding in the back of Jonathan Sanchez's monster truck, all headed to freedom and Los Angeles. He reached out and gripped Fred Paxley's hands as hard as he could, and he said quietly, "Let go of her now."

There was a lethal feeling in him. The pulse in his ears. He felt Fred letting go, and instantly Belinda Jefferson and all the teenage girls were there, and they were hugging and touching the small sobbing child in the darkness.

"She is covered in blood, but I don't think it's her blood," said Dove. "She won't really say what happened, except that she hid in the bushes. She's too frightened to talk."

"Sentries out now," he said, to Terry and to Bear who had just walked up. "Live ammo, empty chambers. Let's be safe."

"Already in place. Tiger and Hopi Jack," said Bear.

"It's a full moon, so we'll be able to track," said Garth.

"Who's going?" asked Terry.

"We need some younger eyes for night vision. So, your grandson for eyes. Me, Dove because she's a nurse, Sally Beth Sanders because she's young and tough, Randall because he knows the ground." replied Garth. "Bear, you come too, please. Terry, please take care of security here. Let's leave in five minutes, with the calmest horses. Water and gear for overnight. Let's assume we're gonna have casualties, we'll need a medical kit."

A few feet away, in the half-light, Gritz Garwood tripped over Hero the Service Dog and went sprawling, rolling drunkenly on the ground, unable or unwilling to rise. He lolled there, slurring loudly, "Playin' soulder again. You people just don't listen!"

When they saw Deputy Davis, they thought he was a log, or perhaps an animal, laying still in the moonlight. Then he moved, a little, and they realized he was alive, and they dismounted their horses quickly and surrounded him. With his motorcycle helmet on, the deputy's facial expressions were hidden.

"Security out," said Garth, quietly. "Randall, and you, young man, please stand watch."

As those two faced outwards into the moonlight, Randall, an Army veteran, sat down with his trapdoor Springfield carbine, looking intently away as a slight breeze moved the dark brown hair which cascaded from under his cavalry hat. The younger man remained standing holding the horses.

Garth said to the young man, Terry's grandson, "What's your name, please? I've forgotten."

"Terry Taylor like my grandpa but everyone calls me Terp."

"Well Terp, you might want to get down. Whoever is out there can see us too."

Terp sat down abruptly with the horses looming over him and swiveled until he too faced outboard. He also had a trap-door Springfield carbine, undoubtedly from his grandfather.

Bear, Sally Beth and Dove were evaluating Deputy Davis, who remained laying in the dirt on his back with a saddlebag under his head. Dove examined busily while Deputy Davis moved slightly, apparently very much alive. With an affirmative nod from Dove, Bear gently and slowly removed Deputy Davis's copper wrap-around motorcycle helmet. Deputy Davis was talking to them very quietly, but Garth could not understand his words. He'd better take his own advice, thought Garth, as he crouched down. The horses were of course standing tall, but they weren't people.

Dove crept over to him and spoke. "His ballistic vest stopped two bullets, which means they didn't shoot rifles at him. However, he is shot through the thigh muscle, although the femoral artery is not hit, and he has another bullet through his hand, which broke the bones. His pulse is regular and he has not bled to a critical degree, but he is barely conscious from shock."

"No femur fracture?" asked Garth.

"No, if we get him back to the mission he will probably live, if there is no infection."

Garth crept alongside Deputy Davis.

"Hello again, deputy. Sorry to meet like this. Can you tell me anything?"

The deputy looked him in the moonlight and began to speak, haltingly, quietly.

"That canyon can't be crossed by any normal car, but we winched the truck over, using the power winch, tied it to a down sycamore on the far bank."

"Yes," interrupted Garth. "How did you get shot?"

"Oh. I'm not sure," responded Deputy Davis.

"Not sure?"

"We got across the canyon, and onto the road, and we were driving very fast. I mean, I was on the quad and Jonathan was driving ahead, too fast. That truck was so loud. He kept going out ahead until he'd hit another break in the pavement, then he'd slow down to cross and I'd catch up.

"Anyway, there were headlights on the road, and I was riding up...catching up in my quad, and I stopped because those headlights were strange, like a roadblock. Two sets, pointing towards us. And then I heard Jonathan say, 'You can't do that!' very loudly. I accelerated to draw abreast of them, to see what was going on. There were about ten shots, two or three pistols...perhaps. I couldn't tell what was happening. Muzzle flashes. Then I was hit in the hand, and that hurt a lot. I couldn't control the quad, I couldn't slow down, then something hit me in the leg and I think I went over the top when I hit some dirt."

"Did you see who did this?" asked Sally Beth Sanders.

"No... I fell off into a hole, a little creek or something, or a crack, and it knocked the wind out of me. I was laying there, and I heard shooting, and more screams from the women, and more shooting, individual shots. I couldn't find my Glock. It fell out of my holster when I hit the ground, I think. I gotta admit, I didn't know what to do, and I just laid there in the dark. I heard them take my ATV. I played dead."

"That's probably why you're still alive," said Bear. "How did you get here?"

"I heard them drive their cars away, and that big loud truck behind them, and I heard the ATV. Then I got up and limped and crawled away from the moonrise, and here I am," said Deputy Davis. "I...I didn't protect anyone."

He grimaced and let out a small sob.

Bear leaned over, and said quietly, "Enough of that. If you weren't alive, we wouldn't know what had happened. Your being alive might keep the rest of us alive as well, if they're still waiting out there."

"What do you mean?" asked Deputy Davis weakly.

"Now we know we have enemies," replied Garth.

Salinas, California

The mic on his radio woke him up, in the early morning darkness, at the same time that Mickey shook him.

"Any station this net, respond."

Wallace shook himself awake. He sat up from his reclined squad car seat and looked around. The electric lights were off: saving gasoline for the generators. Mickey's flashlight was lighting the area intermittently. Save the batteries.

He reached for the mike. "Whiskey Six Delta, go." he said.

Where was his shotgun? He wondered. Reached out and groped until he found it. Check the load: nothing in the chamber, praise God. Loaded magazine, with a full side-saddle of slugs on the side. All in all, I'd rather have a rifle. A real rifle. All in all, I'd rather be in Maui. Napili. Blue sky. Wife and the kids. A bottle of super-chilled Old Rasputin in hand.

"Ah, Whiskey Six Delta, good to hear from you. Report of rioting at the new police station. All units pull back to defend the station," said the voice.

"At five in the morning? That ain't right," said Mickey, off-mic, standing outside of the squad car. "Got my spidey sense tingling."

Wallace checked the squad car's screen: no internet. GPS. No cell. He checked his own phone. No bars. The utilities were taking longer to restore service than he had expected.

Wallace noticed Tiny looming in the darkness be-hind Mickey. Alongside Tiny there was the small figure of Margarita. Behind her, Katy. Katy's hair was disheveled from sleep, and she was wearing pajama pants and a rough jean jacket. Carrying a bag.

Oh my goodness his mouth tasted terrible. His breath must be awful. Wallace remembered that as always he had a toothbrush in his go-pack. He needed to use the outhouse. First he would respond to the radio.

"Whiskey Six Delta, question, what's the status of the riot? We want to position ourselves before we move, over."

"Ahhhh looks like about ten protestors and a kazoo, over," said the voice.

"Say again?" Wallace responded.

"Some people with a trumpet. Or a loudspeaker. Anyway, at this time we don't seem to be in imminent danger. We don't know the cause.," said the voice.

"Why are they doing this? Isn't the whole town still in ruins?" asked Wallace into the mic. "Streets aren't clear yet, are they?

"Roger that. Streets aren't clear yet. Anyway Mayor Happy wants everyone here. The rioters are throwing firebombs but half of them aren't working and the rest are burning the concrete on the outer walls. Perhaps ten protestors. Loud and lit up. They are holding up banners saying, 'Venganza por nuestras hijas asesinadas'.

"Vengeance for our murdered children?" asked Wallace into the radio "Who got murdered? Anyone kill anyone overnight?"

"Not that we know of, Whiskey Six Delta," responded the voice on the radio. "We can't figure it out either."

All in the vicinity of East Alisal Street, thought Wallace.

"Air support?" asked Wallace.

"Due to coastal marine layer fog, not at this time," said the voice.

"Drone up?" asked Wallace.

"The mayor feels that would be inflammatory. The police chief told him that they're already throwing Molotov cocktails at us," said the voice. "They seem pretty inflamed."

"Roger that, we are about a mile out," said Wallace. "Streets are blocked. Three of us will walk in via Alisal Street."

"See you soon," said the voice.

Dawn was approaching. Dim pink light in the sky beyond Fremont's Peak.

"Let's take a few minutes to compose ourselves, gentlemen," said Wallace.

"I'm already composed," said Tiny.

"You may be composed but I'm indisposed," said Mickey. "Hold my rifle."

"I'm remembering the Three Stooges now," laughed Katy, passing Mickey the large plastic bag. "We don't have refrigeration, so we are cooking all our food. We brought you breakfast and lunch. For all three of you."

Conscious of his breath, Wallace spoke. "Have you heard from your husband?"

"No," responded Katy, "But I wouldn't expect it. Our cell phones aren't working. Are yours?"

"No bars," replied Wallace.

"He'll come home when his shift is over, when he can. Meanwhile I'll keep the neighborhood going. We've got a lot of food, and we've got a lot to clean up," said Katy.

Her husband is a lucky man, thought Wallace. She looks even better with sleep in her eyes. Then he stifled the thought. He was married. She was married. He should brush his teeth.

San Antonio Mission

"That Poppy. Sure as hell he coulda' shot better than this," said Raley. "Why'd he have to shoot that doe in the first place? It's not like we're starving."

"The deer just wandered into camp. He says he couldn't resist," replied Francesca. "All he could grab was his horse pistol. Flintlock horse pistol."

"It's like this earthquake gave people permission to do anything. Especially men. Men are dogs, I tell ya," said Raley. "Watch your step. This grass is slippery."

"What's that the Bible says? 'Like a dog eating it's own vomit, so a fool repeats his folly.' I think that's it," said Francesca, as they approached the ridgeline and got down on hands and knees.

"Yep, that's men," said Raley, giggling. "Always suckin' their own puke."

They crept together over the crest of the hill in the tall grass.

"A red ribbon blood trail," added Francesca. "At least Poppy used enough gun for that."

"You can track this?" asked Raley.

"Oh, yeah, Dad taught me," said Francesca. "And there it is. It's a buck, not a doe. See, under that oak? Range about 200 yards."

Francesca rose into a sitting position and brought her scoped rifle up to her eye.

"That your rifle?" asked Raley. "All modern and everything. How did you bring that here?"

"It's my older sister's gun. My sister's name is Sarah.
She's 32. Lives in Oslo. Anyway this is her long range competition rifle." Francesca said, raising the rifle and looking
through the scope. "Thousand yard gun. .30-06, so she
could compete in the vintage sniper matches. She couldn't
bring it when she moved there. We were gonna take it to the
range on our way home."

"I have no idea what that means, Brainiac. Let me look,"
said Raley, reaching for the rifle.

"Look under that big valley oak," said Francesca, passing
the rifle.

Raley squinted through the scope, moving the rifle back
and forth.

"It helps if you sit with your knees up. Rest your elbows
on your knees," said Francesca.

"Ah. There's the buck," said Raley. "Poor thing. Look at
that hole in him. Poppy didn't need to shoot him. We'll be
back home eatin' beef burgers in a few days."

She passed the rifle back.

"Venison tonight, before we go home," said Francesca. "It's
not even deer season. Daddy says the world is made up of a few
people who can pull the trigger, and lots of people who can't."

She worked the bolt, chambering a round.

"Hold on, where are the other people?" asked Raley.
"The people who went out to see what happened to Tabetha
Thomas's family. We don't want to shoot at them."

"They're behind us, south of us. They went south and
east, we're going north and west," said Francesca. "Miles
away. I hope they're OK."

"Oh, they're fine. We'll get back to camp and Jonathan will be there with his truck yellin' at us. My bet is that Tabetha fell out of the back of the truck in the rough country."

"Hope you're right," said Francesca, squinting through the scope.

She fired.

"It's down. Head shot," said Francesca, peering through the scope.

"Damn. The slayer," said Raley. "Have you named the rifle yet?"

"Named the rifle?" said Francesca.

"All the superheroes with guns name their firearms," said Raley.

"Ummm. Not yet. Not really my rifle. Anyway, like you said, all this will be over tomorrow," replied Francesca.

"Now we gotta gut this deer, and clean it. The hard work," said Raley. "You know how to do that, right?"

"Hey let's have the boys do it. No crevasses over here. They can drive a pickup right up to that buck," said Francesca. "You said before, men are your superpower. Just blink at them, and they'll get this done."

In the darkness, Bear and Sally Beth had hoisted Deputy Davis up on a horse, painfully, and headed back to the mission. Garth, Terp, Dove, and Randall had carefully reconnoitered the surrounding hills on foot, leaving the horses tied in a gully. The horses were left unguarded, which meant they might be stolen or injured. Now, in full daylight, Garth, Terp, Dove, and Randall were under a spread of oak trees on a hill, looking down on what seemed to be the ambush site, where the truck had been taken. Below them were a mash of tracks and two bodies.

Garth could see those two bodies by the road below him. A sick feeling. This wasn't good at all. Perhaps those people down there were playing dead. Deputy Davis had done that, after all.

Garth nodded, and Randall slipped and crawled his way towards the site. In half a minute, Garth began to follow him. Terp and Dove, as arranged, would stay in hiding as over-watch. Terp had his hard-hitting but slow-to-fire trapdoor Springfield. Garth considered that Terp was probably not a good shot, if he had any experience at all. Garth should have asked Terp that question before leaving him up there exposed to God and evil-doers. And Dove had a double barreled 12 gauge hammered shotgun with a short barrel, useless at anything beyond fifty yards, which she had used in Cowboy Action Shooting competitions briefly a few years ago. She wasn't any kind of gunfighter.

A sensation of extreme unreality. Surely he was dream-ing this. Surely this was a mistake: he needed to wake up in case he hurt someone accidentally. Surely the world had not changed so greatly in one day...since yesterday's dawn, when the earthquake hit. He...none of them...probably had any business chasing after the truck. In fact, they should wait, and call the Sheriff, and demand that law enforcement do something. Garth kept down, now walking in a crouch, careful to follow Randall's path. As they approached the first body...apparently a man, apparently Jonathan...Randall veered off and stopped short. Garth guessed that he didn't want to disturb any sign. The sun was beating down.

"He's still dressed," Randall said quietly.

"Sure he's dead?" Garth asked.

"Look at his back. I'm guessing he's dead," said Randall.

There was a large fist sized bloody hole cratered into the back of the still form of Jonathan. Bits of unidentifiable viscera, probably lung and arteries, and bone. Many buzzing flies. No other noise. Jonathan seemed awfully still, and awfully white.

Garth stood up. "We have to check. We...we have to be sure."

He gingerly approached the body, careful not to step in any tracks. He knelt down and felt the hard stiff neck for a pulse. Nothing. Cool. Face down in the loose sand. Jonathan would have suffocated if nothing else. The slight wind ruffled the carefully coiffed hair on the back of Jonathan's head.

Six feet away was the staring body of Zachary Thomas, the father of the small girl, Tabetha Thomas, who had come into camp covered in blood the night before. That explained the blood which had covered her. He was face up, eyes wide. He had been shot directly through the right lens of his glasses which had destroyed his eye and killed him, probably instantly. He looked surprised. Flies were crawling on his gray tongue in his wide open mouth. The body was spread eagled. Surely quite dead. The sun would not be his friend.

Zachary was one of their own, one of their own cavalry living history unit. He hadn't owned a horse. He had been a social worker in Santa Barbara, with a thriving practice doing marital therapy for the troubled affluent. He had loved his life, always laughing. And he had had a family, most of which was now gone.

"Brass, all nine millimeter and forty," said Randall. He had been moving around behind Garth while Garth looked at Zachary. "About 14 shots. I'm sure there's more brass hidden in the grass. Range ten feet. Two cars, apparently not four bye's, just normal road tires."

Garth's tired mind attempted to focus.

"Who is missing? Who was on that truck who is missing?"

"Well, there is Zachary, and Tabetha is at the mission. So that leaves the mom, Merry. She's missing. Then there's Jonathan's wife, Sierra. And there's that young reporter, I can't remember her name. And there's Marco, that dancer. Great guy. Four people missing."

"Ok, now what?" asked Garth.

"We don't bury the body, in case they come back," said Randall. "Besides we don't have time. I'll have Terp go get the horses. If there's any of our people left alive we don't want to linger over Jonathan and Zachary here. Just in case."

Randall stood up, looked at where Terp and Dove would be hiding, and made a sweeping motion with his arms. Plains Indian sign, thought Garth. Who would think it would be useful in this modern era?

"Keep your head on a swivel, we still don't know what's going on," said Garth. "Let's find where Deputy Davis ditched."

"Stay in the grass, no tracks on the road," said Randall. "It looks like they all went that way, and it looks like they're gone now, back towards town. When you get done, we need to decide what we'll do next."

"Follow me," replied Garth

He reached down and held up a Glock pistol. He removed the magazine and pulled back the slide to remove the chambered round.

"All safe now"

"The tracks check out," added Randall, "and here's Terp and Dove."

They looked up in the now-brilliant sunlight as the young man and the woman on horseback led the other two mounts to them perfectly. How odd to be living this, thought Garth. The two riders and their horses were beautiful in the sunlit pasture. As Terp pulled up to them, he pointed away, down the road.

"Vultures forming over there."

They mounted and rode into the sheltering trees in the nearby meadows, and shadowed the road as they watched the great black birds gathering and wheeling in the clear blue sky. Two of the largest birds were wearing yellow plastic tabs, thought Garth. Endangered California condors. As they approached, they saw another corpse, another man, the dancer, face down in the road. What was his name? Garth couldn't remember.

Quick review by Randall. "Shot in the back of the head," he said, as he remounted.

"Executed?" asked Terp.

The kid is catching on, thought Garth.

"They've killed all the men," said Dove. "I worry for the women."

"Let's go down the road a bit," said Randall. "They might not go far."

"Any guns we don't know about?" asked Garth.

"Two nines and a forty," replied Randall. "I'm seeing four tracks. Let's go up the road a bit before we give up."

"What'll we do if we catch them?" asked Terp in a small voice as they rode on.

"Let's see when we get there," responded Garth. "Terp, you hang back. Dove, you hang back even farther. You're my wife and a nurse, you are here to provide medical care, and this isn't your fight, and you don't know what you're doing."

"You DO know what you are doing?" asked Dove.

"Honestly? Not really. I'm hoping we won't have to do anything. But Randall and I have shot firearms more. And we were in the military. So let us handle whatever happens."

Randall was riding ahead of them, and he dismounted abruptly and crouched, making signs that the rest should do the same. Leaving Terp to hold all four horses, Randall led Garth and Dove forward.

The two cars were small Japanese sedans, with the truck, and they were in a circle under the trees, and there was a man with his pants down on top of one of the women, and his white bare buttocks were rising and falling. With a plunging feeling Garth recognized the woman beneath the man as Merry Thomas, the wife of the dead Zachary Thomas they had left behind. She had her eyes shut and her face was a grimace, and her open mouth was bloody. He could see another man standing, laughing, apparently talking to a third man sitting in the grass.

Shock. He turned to face Randall. "What should we do?"

Randall was preoccupied by Dove, who was crawling rapidly ahead of them through the grass. Garth hastened to catch her, but she was slithering along quickly on her hands and knees. Just as Garth reached out, Dove stood up straight, the shotgun in her hands. She raised up the double barreled gun as the standing man turned and there was an explosive blast and the man, smiling, came apart into red mist and crumpled over backwards.

That third man stood up with a small black pistol in his hand. One hand. He shot once, and Dove fired again, and his face turned to a red mass and he went backwards.

Dove levered open the short shotgun and jerked it backwards, which caused the two empty old fashioned brass cases to fall out, and she quickly, smoothly, forked two fresh twelve gauge shotgun shells into the gun, snapped the action closed, and cocked the gun. A shot from a pistol. Garth felt the bullet blast past them, and Dove fired again at the rapist, the man who had stood up over Merry with his pants around his ankles. He was naked from the waist down, fully exposed, and the nine pellets of double ought buckshot blew his groin into bloody hamburger and he screamed and sat down hard and rolled into a fetal position, wailing.

Garth rushed forward to the campsite with his Marlin rifle, levering a cartridge as he ran. There was Merry, curled up, crying, naked except for her dirty shirt, there was Sierra Sanchez, on her back, sightless eyes staring upwards and a dark bloody bullet hole between her eyes, and there was the young woman journalist, cowering behind a tree, face bruised.

That man's screaming was so loud. What would make him stop?

There was a deep throaty engine roar from Jonathan's truck in front of them, and it lurched forward and past Dove and Garth. Apparently a fourth man, someone they hadn't noticed, was driving. The truck ran over the shattered body of the man who had been standing, and the truck bounced high off the body and the body spun, limp arms flailing and the truck sped down the dirt road towards Terp and the horses.

Garth saw Randall stand up and yell to Terp, "Don't shoot the truck! Don't hurt the engine! We need it!"

There was a single shot and Garth saw Terp, standing straight up with his trapdoor Springfield carbine and a plume of black powder smoke, and a sheet metal bang as the bullet hit the truck and a large dark hole appeared in the driver's door, and the truck spun sideways and stopped with its nose in an large elderberry bush, and the four horses which Terp had been holding shied a little and then resumed nosing the grass.

Terp looked with satisfaction at the truck lodged in the elderberry, and he yelled back, "Just like shootin' trap!"

The rapist on the ground was still wailing loudly, curled, clutching his groin, dark blood pouring from between his fingers, sobbing. Dove turned to Garth and said, "Have we rope?"

"Back with the horses, maybe," Garth said. "Perhaps there's some in these cars, or in the truck. I can check."

His mind was reeling. So much, so strange. Were there any other people in the cars?

Dove looked at him stonily. She leaned over the man's head, put the barrels up against his hair, and pulled the trigger.

After the shot, it was very quiet. Bits of the man's head were all over Garth, and Dove, and the campsite. Garth's ears were ringing.

"Now we don't have to hang him," said Dove, walking away.

Salinas, California

Tiny was walking in front, and there was no way to hide him. He was simply large. He was wearing his dark blue uniform field jacket, which helped. Behind Tiny were Mickey and the dog Diablo, who was noticeably skittish. Smart dog, thought Wallace. Diablo clearly preferred to be with Tiny. Diablo was straining at the leash, pulling, agitated.

They were coming down a side street, spread out, column formation. They had picked their way through the shattered Highway 101 overpass, partially collapsed, rebar poking from the shattered cement like blackberry brambles, crossed over shattered streets and stepped gingerly over scattered downed power lines. And now, they were approaching the police station from the back, cautiously. They could hear noise around the front of the building.

As they watched, a group of people were stacking what seemed to be bags of potting soil, or fifty pound bags of rice, against the back wall.

"Ah, station, Whiskey Six Delta, we are observing people stacking bags of something against the wall of the maintenance bay, over. Advise action," said Wallace into his handset.

The voice of the police chief came back at him, surprisingly feminine through the radio.

"The mayor is on the other line screaming at us to avoid confrontation so we're letting them stack it. We think it's sandbags to gain access to the roof, and we have officers up there."

"Can you gas them?" said Wallace. "This isn't looking normal. Something's up. Those sacks are too big for sandbags, over."

"The officers on the roof dropped a bit of tear gas on them already, then the mayor advised us to stop," she said. "Apparently the media is out there filming all this. We want to avoid police brutality,"

"Roger that," said Wallace. "We will stay concealed and advise."

"Hey, look they are all wearing black," added Mickey. "This ain't right. Nobody gets dressed up like that for a riot."

"They have gas masks," said Tiny. "Stranger and stranger."

"Not as strange as a bunch of bluebells hiding in broad daylight. It's not even time for a decent breakfast," said a new voice behind them.

Wallace turned. Jesus Garcia, local gang leader, late of San Quentin and Soledad prison.

Diablo strained on his leash, leaning towards Jesus Garcia. No barking, yet. The dog seemed very very agitated.

"Jesus reincarnated. Welcome back. Hopefully you are a changed man," said Wallace.

Jeez that sounded sanctimonious, he thought. And how the hell did Jesus sneak up on us? While we had a dog?

"Time will tell," said Jesus Garcia slowly. "Look, Gringo, we're all bein' played. That's what's pissing me off."

"OK. Why?" said Tiny, cautiously.

"Nobody's angry, nobody's looting, then these naco pendejos show up, somehow. They runnin' around breaking windows and telling us the border patrol shot up a bunch of kids, down on the frontera, just executed a bunch of kids, they say. We're too busy cleaning up broken glass from the earthquake to riot. Things are cool on the street. Hell, I'm just happy being out, broken glass and all. Anyway these people speak espanol muy malo and they are trying to make us fight, and now they are here at this police station. I tell you, we bein' played."

Wallace considered that. Something definitely wasn't right. Those people in black had to know they were here but they were ignoring Wallace and his crew. The dog was leaping around like a hooked trout, and despite their attempts at concealment, he and Tiny and Mickey were in a street carrying guns. These people were too organized not to notice. Something was wrong.

Diablo spun and began barking at the building. The people in black were leaving, running around to the front.

"Oh, that ain't right at all," said Mickey.

The blast knocked them all to the ground, flat, in a sudden punch with a ear-rending blast. One second standing up, the next flat. Wallace lay there, struggling for breath. It felt like his ears were blown out in a stab of sound and pain, and for some reason he couldn't see, blinded by the sudden brain-dazzling brilliance of the blast.

Move, he told himself. At first, nothing. He couldn't move. Then he felt his legs kicking in the dirt of the landscaping, and he moved his arms. All there. There was a shot, somewhere. Wallace rolled over and sat up, and his core muscles screamed, wrenched.

"Ammonium nitrate," whispered Wallace to himself.

"Field expedient fertilizer bomb," said Tiny quietly, laying next to Wallace. "I should'a remembered that from the Army. How'd we miss that?"

Another shot, and more shots, some fully automatic, and Wallace's eyes cleared enough for him to see the police station, with one half of the building crushed now, and people in black with masks coming back around the side of the building, where they had taken shelter. Guns. They had guns. Shots. The people in black were shooting into the exposed interior of the building. There must be survivors in the interior.

Wallace cursed to himself. He had a shotgun and the range was perhaps 70 yards. Too far. He felt mildly dizzy. That would be from the blast., he told himself. Probably not badly hurt. Courage. He breathed a whiff of pepper spray and fought against coughing. Focus. He looked. The people in black were still shooting into the exposed interior of the police station. He must do something.

He heard a shot and saw Mickey prone behind a cement block in an open area of the parking lot. Prone, and shooting at the people in black. Good plan. Move forward.

He jacked a cartridge from the magazine into the chamber and took aim. The shotgun sights consisted of a bead and a rear peep. Double ought buckshot, which meant he would be shooting eight thirty caliber lead balls at the people in black, which would spread out into a pattern about five feet wide at seventy yards. He might not hit anything even if he aimed right at it.

There was a hesitation. You own your bullets forever, his father had said. Yes. When he fired, he was going to kick loose a cascade of consequences. But people...his people... were probably dying inside the police station. Certainly dying.

He lined up the sights on a distant figure in black, which was running around the gaping hole in the building. Pulled the trigger, and everything was jounced as the gun recoiled. Work the slide, back on target...the target was swatting at his arm as though stung by a bee. Still up and moving.

"Body armor, dude," said Jesus, alongside him. "They got body armor. Got any slugs?"

"Rioters with body armor?" said Wallace.

"Told ya, dude," said Jesus, who was crouched behind him. "These people ain't from roun' here."

Wallace removed a slug cartridge, a solid copper sabot which, unlike shot cartridges, put all its energy into one stabilized copper projectile. It could go through a car. Powerful. But one big slug from a smooth bore barrel meant that a miss was more likely. He lined up the bead on the target, that person in black who was now resuming shooting into the gaping hole in the police headquarters building. That person seemed to be using a Russian AK-47 assault rifle. Rather sophisticated, thought Wallace as he pulled the trigger. Recoil. Everything out of kilter, then a return to sight alignment and the target was down. People in black now running around downrange, more agitated, angry ants, and shots snapping over his head. Instinctively he ducked down below the parking stanchion in the parking space. The stanchion was about six inches tall, he realized. He wasn't ducking successfully behind that. His shot and its impact had attracted the attention of the people in black.

"Good shot, good shot," came a voice above him. Jesus. "Buen tiro!"

Lucky shot, thought Wallace. He looked up, and there was Jesus, standing relaxed as though he was watching fut-bol, bullets from the people in black snapping past. Standing right next to him, looming tall above him, apparently completely unconcerned. Jesus' loose baby blue shirt flapped in the slight breeze. Jesus looked as though he was about to go bowling.

"Get down! You're drawing fire!" said Wallace, feeling slightly embarrassed.

"Ellas no pueden golpear a un elefante a esta distancia,' muttered Jesus reflectively, as though talking to himself as the bullets snapped past. "They can't hit a thing. See what I mean? Not from around here."

"Whatever you say. Now get down," said Wallace.

"I got my people, they be here soon," said Jesus, again seeming to talk to himself.

The people in black were leaving now, moving away down East Market to some rally point to the south. The shooting into the building had ceased. Quiet.

"Whiskey Six Delta," said Wallace into his mic.

No answer. Only static.

Wallace stood. He felt bruised. Sore everywhere. The world was going to hell, he thought. God he wanted to take a dump. He felt tired, 100 years old, and it wasn't even 9 AM.

A vision flashed in his mind of the mission, Mission San Antonio De Padua, where his father and family was participating in a living history event this weekend. Nothing happening down there, thought Wallace. There's a shitshow here, but down there, they are sitting around the campfire cooking breakfast. The remembered sensation of fresh, moist, soft breakfast tortillas. Wonderful down there. Wonderful in Aabenraa. Anywhere but here.

Jesus was now walking across the parking lot, towards the sundered building, as though he was walking to greet friends. Astonishing. Insane. From the interior a dusty figure in a police uniform, an overweight red-haired man, who Wallace recognized as Sergeant Wright, emerged, saw Jesus, and drew his sidearm.

"YOU'RE UNDER ARREST, YOU GREASER SON OF A BITCH!" he shouted, pointing the pistol at Jesus.

"Jesus H. Christ," said a voice from the dark interior. "Racist dumbass. The man is standing there without a gun. Put the goddamn pistol down or you're toast with this department. If we didn't have to deal with this goddamn earthquake, I'd fire you right now."

That would be the chief, Wallace realized. Bettina Jefferson. Good to know she was still alive.

Jesus turned and looked at Wallace. Jesus looked as though he was about to take a nap. Incredibly calm.

"Same old, same old," Jesus said to Wallace. "Snafu, you know? Situation normal..."

Jesus looked at the crumpled body of the black clad person sprawled over a large chunk of concrete wall.

"I dunno. Looks like he's beyond help. Let's check, though, then we'll see if anyone in there is hurt," he said.

Wallace reached out and pulled the black balaclava from the head of the person he had shot. Blond hair. Blue eyes half open. Very pale. Clearly deceased. Wallace carefully took a carotid pulse to make sure, moving his fingers, seeking any sign of life. Nothing.

"Dead as my aunty's parrot after it met the fan," said Jesus. "She doesn't look like a local to me. Ella no es de por aquí."

She. Wallace studied the pallid face of the corpse. Little silver studs in the pierced ears. Perhaps a woman. Slender. Small. Wallace ran his hands around the corpse's collar. Looking for dog tags, instinctively, like the tags he still wore from the United States Army. Nothing. The corpse had very straight teeth, white teeth, he noticed. Braces, at some point in its life. Her life. His life.

"Hey! Gimme some help here!" came a shout from inside the building.

Wallace turned. In the dim dusty interior, he could make out the looming form of Tiny, carrying someone. Someone in blue. Wallace leapt over the rubble of the collapsed wall, following Jesus.

"More in there," said Tiny. "Damn half the department's dead in there."

As he entered the building, Wallace could see that most of the structure had collapsed. The ceiling of the first floor, which was the floor of the second level, had partially disintegrated straight down, crushing many. There were injured and dead, he could see, but not recognize, and he felt a stab of horror and apprehension. If he had followed his normal shift schedule he would easily have been in this building, right here, he realized.

"Sergeant Wallace." came an authoritarian woman's voice.

"Yes, Chief Jefferson?" Wallace answered.

He didn't necessarily care for the lady, he realized. She seemed a bit of a pest with her emphasis on the details, constant nitpicking about safety and perp's rights and the eternally changing budget. Right now, he realized, he felt glad, as though a burden had been lifted from his shoulders. Why was that?

"Check that scattergun. Is it safe?" she said.

"Oh, sure, as always, Chief," answered Wallace.

God she was a pest.

"Check it again. Right now. All of us are rattled and we don't need an A.D." said the chief, stepping closer. "Once upon a time, I myself reloaded without thinking, after a shooting, back in the day."

She was a tyrant, thought Wallace. The chief was a

small African American woman, slender, and right now, in the gloom and debris, she looked like a dusty blue elf. Hair pulled back in a bun, covered in dust. Even her eyebrows were dusty. Here they were, all in a crisis, and she was obsessed with range safety. A total waste of time. A surge of anger. Wallace bit back an angry retort, unslung the shotgun, and pumped back the action.

A bright red buckshot cartridge, copper rim gleaming, sprang out of the gun. Chief Jefferson caught it deftly and handed it back to Wallace without a word.

"Thanks, Chief," he said.

Wordless. Say nothing. Oh my goodness she was right.

Chief Jefferson spoke first, "This is gonna be a goddamn bitch. Half our friends are dead. I need you strong, for a bit longer," she paused, a tear appearing in the corner of her eye. She turned and walked back into the darkness of the smoking, half-demolished building.

In the distance a string of shots began, which became a cascade of battle noise.

"What's that?" said Mickey, looking up. He was carrying out another crushed, dusty dead corpse, the remains of a Salinas Police officer, holding the arms of the limp form while Jesus lifted the feet. Wallace looked down, recognized the dead man, said nothing. The dead man had been young. Wife. Two small children. The officer had known Jesus as a street criminal and now his corpse was being carried by him.

Jesus continued to awkwardly lift the dead man, speaking matter of factly. "Oh, those are my friends. I called them earlier on the walkie talkie. As I said earlier, those people in black, they weren't from around here."

San Antonio Mission, California

"I think God saved me," said Terp. "God saved me."

He was sitting in church with his carefully cleaned trap-door Springfield carbine between his knees, in his soiled 1863 cavalry uniform. He was shaking. Clearly almost overcome with emotion. The ancient carved wood saints looked down from behind the altar. Clearly, unlike Terp, they were not overcome with emotion. In a variety of poses of hand painted Catholic agony, they remained frozen and silent.

"Ummm, well, OK, did God speak to you?" asked Raley.

She was sitting next to Terp, so close that their legs were touching through the fabric of their 1850's clothing. Despite her comforting posture, she was inwardly repelled by him. He seemed to be so emotional, not fun at all. She wanted to back away and go see what the girls were doing. More fun out there. But she did not leave. For some reason she was compelled to be with him. She didn't understand him, or her own feelings. Confusion.

"No, no, it's not that simple. It's like when everything busted loose, God just took over. I mean, I've never seen anything like it. I was terrified, then something happened and I got really calm, and everything got slow, and I was, like,

I can do this. Like when I'm cutting wood, or feeding horses. I was hyper alert. Completely alive."

"But did God speak to you?" asked Raley. "I mean, did he come out of a cloud or something?"

"You should'a seen that little Dove. She is always so meek and friendly. But when the shooting started it was like she was fearless. Every shot of hers hit. And she's hardly fired a gun, I think," said Terp. "She just ran at them shooting."

Raley could feel his trembling through his leg. Impulsively she reached out and hugged him tightly. Oh this boy is crazy. He's mentally ill. At some point he'll be talkin' to barn owls. How do I get out of this?

"Did God do any miracles or not?" asked Raley quietly. "How do you know he saved you?"

Might as well talk him down, before he gets religion. He IS very cute, he's the only man....boy...I've ever slept with, and it was GOOD, too. So I owe him this. He smells terrible though. Sweat. Fear?

"The whole thing was a miracle. The whole thing was a salvation," said Terp, shaking so hard that it seemed his jaws would clack. "Miracle."

"It's terrible what happened to those people," said Raley. "That's no miracle."

"The earthquake has changed everything," said Terp. "That Jonathan Sanchez. He shoulda' waited. They told him not to go."

Terp seemed to need to talk on, stream of consciousness. Shivering as though he was cold.

"The miracle was that once we got in that fight, it was

like they couldn't touch us. Like God was with us," Terp continued.

"Wasn't that about shooting?" said Raley. "You had Garth and Randall there, and they did the shooting, right?"

"No, it was Dove, and it was me," said Terp. "I saw Dove and she was just chargin' at 'em, and then I had to shoot that guy in the truck and two shots went snappin' right over me...I mean I could FEEL the air from 'em, and then I just got all calm, and I stood up, and it was like it was all automatic. I just shot, and I hit that guy who was drivin' away in Jonathan's truck dead center, in the ten ring."

"Good job, I guess," said Raley.

So that's it, she thought. He's feelin' guilty.

"It wasn't me," said Terp. "I literally swear to God, somethin' took me over, and I stood up and I made that shot, but it wasn't me. It musta' been God."

The boy was hunched over his carbine, shaking. Staring down at his scuffed unpolished cavalry boots. Oh, thought Raley, he's close to madness.

"Then it was as you say. It was God. He did that. Silent, like," said Raley.

"I know you don't believe, and I don't either, not really. But watch. I dare you. I dare us both. Watch. He's gonna make a miracle here. My Gramps has always told me that God is real, but I didn't believe. Today I felt it, for the first time, and I felt his hand. This,"

He gestured around the room.

"This gonna get hard, like in the Bible, and it's gonna beat us all down like grass. Hard times. Harder than those people out there know. But he'll deliver you and me, together. He's promised me, out there in that field today. Otherwise I'd be dead, out there," said Terp.

She needed to calm him, she realized. The two of them, together. Insane. She felt claustrophobic as the relationship closed around her. A reptilian spasm of panic.

I don't deserve this, she thought. All I did was sleep with him. Mom does that with men all the time and nothing comes of it. Yet here I am. No way back.

"Oh," Terp sobbed. "The reapin' will be terrible. God's will."

"Easy, Trooper," said Raley. "One step at a time. Right now, let's get you washed."

Salinas, California

"Water," said the Mayor to the assembled group. 'WATER! AND FOOD!"

The group of about ten looked at the mayor expectantly. Happy Johnson's tone had been declarative and confident. When he didn't say anything more, the stillness hung in the air until Dina Montero spoke up,

"Water and food?" she asked.

"We haven't got any," the mayor grunted.

Wallace was taken aback.

The mayor's long sweeping auburn Elvis hair was very groomed. And the mayor had shaved, his face smooth, shining, and florid this morning. Clearly, he had access to water.

"Where is it?" asked a voice behind him. Dina Montero. Ever questioning. "Where is the water, and where's the food?"

"It's not here," replied the city manager, Causwell Dubbers. He looked more like an emaciated rat than ever, thought Wallace. Pallid as that corpse this morning, that dead person in black utilities. Black body armor, even. Memories. He looked over at Chief Jefferson. She had dusted herself off but seemed distracted. Wallace's head hurt. His ears still rang from the blast at the Police Department Headquarters. Plus, he realized, he was hungry. Starving.

Thoughts of his wife in Denmark, at the farm in Aabenraa, missing her and the children deeply, then thoughts of his wife's mothers' cooking, Stegt flæsk med persillesovs, crispy pork with parsley. The thought of that food shocked him with its intensity, filled his mouth with saliva so suddenly that he almost drooled. He caught himself, took a drink from his water bottle to hide his embarrassment.

"When may we expect food and water supplies?" asked Dina.

"Don't know, really. We'll scrounge up something," replied Happy Johnson evasively. "Causwell, when are we getting resupplied?"

"I.....I don't know! I really can't say. Perhaps in a few days," replied Causwell.

"No clue, right?" said Dina to Causwell. "What's the state saying?"

"The state has its hands full," said Chief Jefferson. "We

have a HAM radio link as well as the standard California OES link, and we get the same answer everywhere. It's much rougher in the bigger cities. More damage, more unrest already, more looting. We lost half our police force in this morning's attack, and we've asked for the National Guard. Unobtanium."

"Hold on, I already know about the attack, but have we figured out who is responsible?" asked Dina.

"Badges and ideology found on the one casualty they left behind, a young transgender Caucasian male, indicates that the group is Reconquista, an Hispanic liberation group seeking to reunify California to Mexico, but that doesn't add up," said Chief Jefferson. "Except for a few tweets and a Facebook page, this group is a non-violent tiny gaggle of about ten young Hispanic activists sitting in grandma's basement in Los Angeles. Virtually no indications of violence or militarism. Then this."

"And also the casualty, that young personex they left behind, is a blond blue eyed gringex," added Gillian McTavish, the County's state liaison.

"Gringex? Personex?" asked a gentle looking blue-eyed Caucasian man, grey hair, grey beard, sitting at the back of the room.

Mark Lockhart, owner of a giant vegetable farm near the Salinas River, thought Wallace. Friend of my father. Fellow history buff. About half his Salinas River row crop acreage was inundated by the ocean. Many acres. Years to desalinate. Here's someone who has really been hurt by this earthquake and knows it. But here he is, being altruistic.

"A person of multiple yet unknown gender identification. A white person of unknown gender identification," said a stern female voice. Gillian McTavish, state liaison to the county. "This is a public meeting, so such terms are required. Let's all keep that in mind."

Wallace looked back and saw a puzzled look on the bearded face of Mark Lockhart.

'Aren't they just people?" asked the man, quietly.

"No, they are unique legally because failure to address them properly is a hate crime," said Gillian McTavish, loudly. "A HATE CRIME!"

"Fortunately, this personex won't be offended because this personex is extremely dead," said Chief Jefferson.

"Like an ex-parrot?" said a voice. "A parrot-ex?"

Wallace had to control his laughter. It had been a long and stressful day already.

"Water," said Happy Johnson, changing the subject emphatically. "Many broken water mains so running water is temporarily out. But about a third of our wells are operating, on a boil-as-needed basis. People will just have to walk to the wells. The other two thirds are either off-line due to sea-water intrusion or other breakage. But it should be enough."

"What's the state doing?" asked Dina. "What about the Feds?"

"State's got its hands full, Feds are flying in a major FEMA operation based out of San Jose. Runways are cracked so they're bringing in heavy lift to Stockton, which is intact, then helicopter to wherever it's needed. A full war-level response."

"Food?" asked a voice. Wallace turned to look. Bettina

Ayala, one of the city's council-people. A Puerto Rican-American, owner of a successful Monterey Peninsula restaurant and a famous food truck, the Platinum Platano, her recipes were legendary. She certainly could make a meal. Wallace was ruminating on his hunger. Oh, for a tripleta sandwich, right now.

"We have a problem," said Causwell Dubbers," We're gonna burn through whatever food supplies we've got quickly. The State can't help, and the Feds will take about a week to really get rolling. I'm afraid we're looking at hunger until we can get our transportation infrastructure back up."

"Well, that transportation infrastructure failure is actually a great opportunity for the farming community to step in," said Mark Lockhart. "Look, financially the farmers are gonna take it in the shorts for a little while. We can't harvest and we can't ship, but we sure as heck have food, although it will fade fast when we can't irrigate. For the moment, we've got vegetables and plenty of 'em. All we have to do is get them out of the ground. One of my fields is just due west of Star Market, and it's full of broccoli waiting to be picked. Someone should organize the harvest and go pick it. Free food. I'll help with the access."

"The Lord provides!" said Bettina Ayala, "I'll work with you."

"Ma'am, we can work out security," said Wallace. "It should be easy."

The Chief nodded affirmatively towards him.

"God almighty, it's a blessing," said Mark Lockhart.

"WE DO NOT RECOGNIZE RELIGION OR THE

PATRIARCHY IN PUBLIC MEETINGS!" roared Gillian McTavish. "NO SAYING MA'AM! NO SAYING SIR! NO REFERENCE TO CHRISTIANITY! YOU ARE VIOLATING STATE LAW WHEN YOU ENGAGE IN THESE FORBIDDEN BEHAVIORS!"

"Um...thank you Zumu the sacred culebra?" said Bettina Ayala, wryly. "A mí, plín."

"You, you, you as a femanex of color should KNOW BETTER than to evoke the white patriarchy in a government meeting!" said Gillian McTavish.

Silence.

"Aren't we just talking about feeding hungry people?" said Mark Lockhart quietly.

"Race and gender awareness MUST come first!" said Gillian McTavish.

"What about infrastructure inside the city?" said Dina Montoya, changing the subject.

"It's astonishing how lucky we've been," said Chief Jefferson. "Locals are cleaning up their own streets. Looting is minimal. We're really coming together as a community. Except for the attack on the police station, and the apparent gang intervention when the people in black, the alleged Reconquista, were retreating towards the airport, violence has actually gone DOWN."

"That police station attack was a major event. It's newsworthy by itself. Someone attacked the City of Salinas. Premeditated. And we don't know who did it," said Dina.

"Half," the Chief's voice broke," half of the police force died or was wounded or injured in that event this morning."

That was sobering, thought Wallace. As though he needed reminding. Someone was out to get them. Someone was taking action to hunt and kill police officers.

"Perhaps the police department should have been more culturally aware," intoned Gillian McTavish. "Perhaps they brought this upon themselves."

"Hey! Phone service is up!" said a voice at the back of the room.

Instinctively the people in the room spread out, moving into the hallways and outer offices for privacy. Wallace opened his phone and automatically dialed his wife. Her phone was set to receive international calls. As he listened to his wife's ringtone he walked as far down the hallway as he could, the cool linoleum stretching before him, until he reached the brilliant light beyond the swinging doors.

"Wallace! How are you? It is 3 AM here and I've been so worried!" said his wife's voice.

"I'm good, I'm good," replied Wallace. "We had a big shaker."

No kidding, he thought.

"Oh, I saw it in the news. It looked terrible," said his wife's voice. "How's the house?"

"I don't know yet," replied Wallace. "But Tiny went by yesterday. He said it was shaken and cracked but mostly intact. Not looted. Really, sweetheart, we've been very lucky. The whole town's been really fortunate."

"Not like those poor children down on the Mexican border. So terrible! The Danish government has filed a protest," said his wife's voice.

"What?" said Wallace. "What is that about? I don't know what you are talking about, darling, how are the kids? How is your fam...."

The line went dead.

"All circuits are busy," intoned a woman's computer voice.

Wallace dialed his brother Ernst's phone number. "All circuits are busy," intoned the voice.

He dialed the phone number of his entire family, one at a time. All circuits were busy. Then the entire phone system went down again. No more bars. Wallace collected himself, struggling with his feelings of aloneness and panic. He really should return to work.

Through a broken glass window, Wallace could see a reporter from a bay area TV station standing outside the building, looking disheveled and lost. On her belt was a satellite phone, large and boxy.

"Hi, Ma'am," Wallace said to her.

"I'm not a ma'am," said the girl, apparently angry. "You heard the Commissioner. I'm a femanex."

"Of course you are," said Wallace. How would you like to be addressed?"

"Mx. Call me Mx," said the young woman, brushing her hair back.

"Yes Mx. How can I help you?" said Wallace.

"Were you at the police station today? When those freedom fighters blew it up?" said the girl.

Wallace stifled his anger.

"Not sure who they were," he answered.

"Oh, the talk around is that they were cancelling the police. Taking back the community," said the young woman.

"Yes. Yes, I was there," said Wallace.

"Can you tell me about it?" said the young woman, smiling attractively. Flirtatiously.

"I see that's a sat phone," said Wallace. "Let's make a deal. I tell you about the attack today. And you let me make one call. One call. That's all I ask."

San Antonio Mission, California

"The news is, they just executed those Latin American children. It's genocide," said Sarah's speaker-amplified voice over the sat phone.

"Tell us more, from the beginning," said Bear, alongside Garth. "WHAT happened?"

Garth was feeling panic rising within him. He fought to control his breathing. Jesus Christ, he thought, what a mess. He had spent the week convinced that at any moment, sheriff's deputies would arrive to arrest them for killing those rapists, who were now buried in the old cemetery.

Since they had arrived back at the mission a week ago, they had eaten all the formerly refrigerated food, as well as the deer which Francesca had killed. They had existed in a sort of time-out, he realized, none of them accepting what they had experienced. Dove had spent most of her time caring for the injured, Deputy Davis and the women, and she had been absolutely silent, and dour, and she had unzipped her sleeping bag from Garth's and slept with her face away from him. No contact from outside, until this. It felt like the whole world was going insane.

He looked around the mission church, lit by candles. In the past week, hard work had stabilized the walls and the roof, despite the aftershocks, although some of the cracks were still gaping. Now they were holding a community meeting. Garth looked around the candlelit room at the stunned faces, young and old. Horrified.

Sarah's voice from Norway echoed through the church. "There was a riot on the Mexican-California border, and the mob was about to free two thousand detained illegal immigrant children, and the US border security guards executed all those children."

"Bullshit," said a voice standing in the darkness behind Garth. Randall Smith. "Aside from the obvious fact that our people wouldn't do such a thing, someone in the Border Patrol would have fought that kind of insanity. They aren't Nazi's regardless of what people say."

"There is a video," continued Sarah. "It's bad quality, but it shows them shooting the little children! The children are screaming and shouting in Spanish in the video. And then the rioters got in and took video of the bodies."

"What's the source of the video?" asked Garth.

"An independent news source," responded Sarah. "Nobody we know. But the video has been distributed by all the major news sources. And the world is taking it seriously. The United States has been condemned in the United

Nations. There is talk of sanctions. Mexico has withdrawn its ambassador."

"And the denial of service? Is that part of this?" asked Garth, feeling nauseated.

"Denial of service? You mean why our phones don't work?" asked Hillary Singleton.

At 19, Hillary Singleton was going through definite technology withdrawal, thought Garth. Since the earthquake, she had been examining her disconnected iPhone at least ten times each day, as though she could bring it back to functionality. Now she was obviously losing weight, pale, blond, and withdrawn.

Out beyond the mission walls, through the stabilized cracks, Garth could hear Gritz Garwood and Fred Paxley singing. Drunk again. Garth wondered if Hopi Jack and his security team would silence them.

"You don't have power yet, do you?" asked Sarah over the sat phone.

"Hi Sarah, this is Paolo Archuleta, I'm a friend of Ernst. Remember me?" said a young orange-haired man in a cavalry uniform next to Garth. "The short answer is, we have several solar panels scrounged from nearby road signs and from a solar power dump at the army base so we can recharge devices such as this sat phone, and we have a gasoline generator but since we can't get gasoline yet, we aren't using any electronics unless necessary."

"Hi Paolo! Long time no high school!" came Sarah's laughing voice over the phone. A pause, then, more seriously, "Nobody in California has power reliably. Power is out because there's that denial of service. Someone is hacking the internet so that it's down. Phone service is down. Water is disrupted. It's bad out there."

"Water is disrupted?" asked Garth.

"Dad, it's really bad in the big cities. LA is rioting over the Mexicali Massacre. That's what they're calling it. There's no water in LA anyway. Apparently, the Koreans are killing any Hispanic they see, so the Hispanics are killing any Asian they see. There's a rumor that the whites are harvesting black people for organs and sending those organs to the east coast. So the blacks are rioting too, and they are avoiding using the hospitals. The injured and the sick are being treated, or not treated, at home. There's widespread looting and burning."

"Oh my god!" said Merry Thomas from across the room. Only eight days ago, her husband's body had been brought back in the truck, all the bodies stacked like dead deer or firewood, and all of them laid to rest in the cemetery where there were now nine fresh graves, all in a row. It felt like five years ago. Garth was still not sleeping soundly.

Merry was acting much stronger than she probably felt, pretending that what had happened had not occurred, as she devoted herself to her young daughter Tabetha, who was remarkably beginning to smile again in these past few days. How remarkable is the human spirit, thought Garth.

There was a loud wail from the young journalist, who had almost secluded herself since being brought back to the mission. "The poor children! The poor children! How could they do it?"

"I'm sorry," said Sarah's voice. "I'm really sorry."

"Curse the United States! Damn them to hell, and damn President Price to hell as well!" shouted the young woman. "Damn the white pigs who did this! I hope that deputy...I hope that deputy in our clinic DIES!!!!"

"Any news from Wallace and his family in Salinas?" interrupted Garth. "I haven't heard a thing."

"Number one son called me!" replied Sarah, "He borrowed a sat phone from a reporter. Apparently, he's well, and the family is in Denmark, so they're well. Wallace is working 24/7 at the police station. Apparently about half of the department was killed in some sort of gang attack. There's rioting and looting in Salinas, too, because of the Mexicali Massacre, and they've heard that the US government will deport all people of Hispanic people back to Mexico even if they are citizens!"

"That's absurd!" replied Garth. "That's unconstitutional! It's not going to happen."

"That's what they're hearing," responded Sarah. "The President is apparently tweeting that, so people are believing it."

"I don't believe it," said Steve Sanchez. "I think we're all being tooled."

"I find it dubious also," said Garth's mother. "This sounds like the disinformation the Nazis used before they invaded Poland. Someone is doing this."

Garth turned and looked. Sure enough, his mother was seated behind him on her walker. Beyond her, in almost complete darkness, Garth could see Terp Taylor hugging Raley Singleton. Those two had become inseparable since last week. Always hugging, sneaking kisses. Life finds a way, thought Garth. Terp and Raley were both too young. Grandpa Bear would have to get involved somehow.

"Hi Grandma!" came Sarah's voice. "The rest of the world is believing it. I don't know what to say."

"How's Norway? How's Oslo?" asked Garth's mother.

"I'm not telling anyone I'm an American," responded Sarah. "There are big protests outside the US embassy, and the Norwegian government has joined most other governments in demanding an investigation and condemning the actions of the United States. So I'm just going to work and keeping my head down."

"Sounds wise," replied Garth. "Obviously we're just going to stay here. We're all well. I think we're all ready for hot showers and the internet, but we're alive and healthy."

"Those people who were injured in the earthquake and the fighting are all healing," added Dove into the phone. "No infection yet."

Garth looked at her alongside him. She had resisted any attempt to discuss what had happened when she had shot those men. He had asked, and she had said a few words, such as 'They needed it' or 'you don't get it' or 'It was a good thing.' Dove had stoically helped the women, gotten them onto horses, since the truck was filled with dead, returned to her medical care. He had cleaned the shotgun. Now it was slung over her shoulder unloaded on a canvas Mosin Nagant sling.

Bear nudged him and pointed to the battery. Running down.

"Sarah, we have to go. Our battery is almost gone. I love you. Given my best wishes to Osten," said Garth.

"Osten's in the other room, Dad," came Sarah's voice. "I think he's feeling that all Americans are animals. He's not happy about this whole thing."

"He wasn't a big fan of the United States before this," replied Garth. Still, give him our love."

"Will do! All's well in Norway. Stay safe. We love you," came Sarah's voice.

The line went dead. People looked at each other, silent. Uncertain.

Terry Taylor stepped into the candlelight. He was holding his book of prayer.

"If anyone wants to join me, I'm going to stay here and talk with God," said Terry. "Me and the church cat. We're doin' all we can to get by, and a little prayer can only help, including our prayers for those caught up in all the insanity outside."

Terp nudged Raley, and they both stepped forward, and then Ophelia, and Francesca, Garth's own daughter, and they each carried one of the large candles up towards the font of the building.

He was left in darkness as the candles were carried away towards the remarkably untouched altar. Looking around, he could see his mother gently pushing her walker forward. Almost all of the people were staying to pray.

The next morning Garth was feeding Dogfood in the horse corral, carefully stepping around the droppings and keeping the horses focused on their own feeding. He was eyeing the haypile, on the other side of the green metal fencing. Thank God the mission had purchased a year's supply for all their expected community events. Bless the people who built this small corral. All that meant that now there was a decent hay supply, and good lodging for the livestock. Perhaps they had another month of hay, and then they would be forced to gather forage. In fact, they probably wanted to start gathering now, so they could save some of this hay for tough times.

As he pondered this, his daughter Francesca walked up to the corral smiling. Garth noticed she was a bit thinner. A bit more browned by the sun. Her fingernails were trimmed and clean. Skin clear, which for a sixteen year old girl was an accomplishment. Apparently, living at the mission was agreeing with her. But too much had happened to the young people and the children psychologically, thought Garth. Too much.

Then he realized that while he had been with the horses, he hadn't worried about being arrested. He hadn't thought of the men they had killed. He hadn't thought of the financial markets, or wealth. Not once. Apparently living here with these horses was good for him too.

"I'm here to invite you to a group meeting, now, in the mission," said Francesca.

"OK, let's go right over. I'll stop and wash my hands. Let's walk together. How have you been?" asked Garth.

As he spoke, he worked the latch on the green metal gate and they both walked through.

"Oh, you know, I'm good," said Francesca. "It seems to

be a big mess out in the world. I miss Mom. But I'm glad she's not here. And the girls are good. Hillary's still dealing with no internet in her life."

"How are you feeling?" persisted Garth.

"Well, you know, it's shocking. I've never seen any of this before, really. It's like it's not real. I mean, dead bodies. And rape. And graves. And blood, and people crying from pain," said Francesca.

"I'm sorry," replied Garth, "If I was able to do it, I'd keep it all away from us."

Feelings of loss. Dread. Guilt. Garth struggled to stay focused.

"That's the thing," answered Francesca, as they walked together across the grassy plaza to the mission. "I went through my whole life not knowing what people would do for me. Now I know. I eat food that people cook for me, and I sleep safely because you and your friends are guarding us, and all I have is because of my family and my people."

"Yes," answered Garth. "It's different."

"I've never lived like this before," added Francesca as they approached the mission door. "Everybody here has faults, like that Gritz Garwood and Fred, they're always drunk. But the whole group...I mean, you know, we're all in this together. I trust them, because I don't have a choice."

Inside the mission, Garth and Francesca took a seat close to his mother's unoccupied walker, in the front battered wooden pew. He noticed with surprise that there seemed to be a woman's committee sitting along a table up by the altar, up where a priest would usually be. Another surprise: his mother was seated there, along with the usually silent Katrina Paxley, wife of Fred, Merry Thomas, his wife Dove, Belinda Jefferson, Samantha Roswell, Poppy's wife, and Patty Martin, widow of Lucky. It felt like a third of their entire group was up there. Garth turned to look at the people sitting behind him.

"This is our informal inventory committee," announced Katrina. "We women were talking, and we decided that we should take our situation seriously. We've been here awhile, and we don't know how much longer we should expect to be here."

"If we don't know, I'm thinking we should expect, and plan, to be here indefinitely," quavered the voice of Garth's mother. "History tells us that big events sometimes take a while to sort out. Like the dust bowl. Like the San Francisco earthquake in 1906."

"So this is what you've been doing, woman!" announced Fred Paxley from behind Garth. "Feminists! Hate sex! Counting beans instead of pleasure. What a waste. It doesn't matter what you count. We're all fracked anyway."

"Would you just SHUT UP?" roared Bear at Fred. "These people 'r right. Let's hear their thoughts."

I would have said more, thought Garth. Fred is a drunken abuser.

"Anyway we did an informal inventory, and here's what we found," said Katrina, visibly shaken by her husband's outburst. "Merry? Please fill us in on food supplies."

Merry seemed distracted, as was to be expected, Garth thought. But she seemed to rally, visibly shook her head, and spoke. "We have basic supplies in terms of food for about a month. We don't have much butane for the kitchen, not enough electricity for refrigeration, so after a few weeks we will need to rely on fresh foods which we gather by hunting and foraging for fruits and vegetables. What canned goods we have now should go into reserve for hard times. We'll need to ask the Army if they have anything on their base, although it's mostly closed now. We need to establish a food team, a cooking group, and that can include the young people. Also we need hunters and gatherers who go out from the mission area, which as we all saw last week, might be dangerous."

Garth spoke, "We could combine security patrols with scouting for food and hunting."

Katrina answered, "We can get to the details later. Dove, what about medical?"

Dove was alert, and formal, and referred to papers which she held before her. "I am a nurse. We have no other trained medical people except for first aid. Our first step is to recruit some of the young people to learn. Also we have limited medications including no more antibiotics. We have used them for Deputy Davis and...for other injuries."

Here Merry Thomas looked at the table stonily.

Dove continued, "We need to go out and find more medical supplies. Right now, we have Deputy Davis and he will take weeks for his hand to heal but he can stand watches now. He can observe. We need to go out to get medical supplies. That is all.

"Belinda will now talk about the mission buildings and

how we can make use of them," said Katrina Paxley. "The facilities."

"Oh! Facilities! Think I'll go use them! I'll do my part by inspecting the shitters. We're all fracked anyway," muttered Fred Paxley.

He stood up and staggered out as people glared at him.

Belinda stood and faced the sitting group. "I checked on the state of the mission and the camp. We have some broken windows we can nail sheets over to keep out vermin. The cracks in the walls are repairable. Our cemetery is already in use. We have water via one spring on the hill behind us, and it's still flowing quite nicely, and the plastic water tank is in good shape. We have three solar panels which Paolo Archuleta," here she smiled and pointed at the orange haired young man, who smiled from the back of the room, "and Beeston Bragg," she moved her pointing hand to the other young man, "have amazingly assembled to provide a little consistent electricity for charging devices, and for a few lights. We don't intend to use that source very much as yet. Bottom line, we need to create a team to repair the cracks and maintain the panels but essentially, we're good. Also, after what happened last week, we need a security unit which is dedicated for the safety of this area itself."

Belinda sat down.

Katrina spoke, "And now education."

"We need education?" asked Randall Smith.

"Why not assume we'll be here for awhile?" said Garth's mother. "We don't know what is going on, and this may be an opportunity. For example, Poppy Roswell plays both the violin and the bagpipes. You, sir, are a genuine descendant of the Esselen people who were here before us, while Mr. Grainger is of the Hopi people. Terry Taylor has a book of prayer. Samantha Roswell sings. And I know history."

"I see your point," said Tiger Tanaka. "I can teach Buddhism and some Japanese and some shodo and some cooking."

"What's shodo?" asked Deputy Davis from the back of the room. He had hobbled in on the shoulder of Ophelia, Jack's granddaughter.

"It's Japanese calligraphy," replied Tiger.

"Anyway we all have skills and we all can teach each other," interjected Katrina.

"Brilliant, actually," added Bear.

"Samantha Roswell will plan this aspect of our lives," Katrina added formally. "And now for Patty Martin."

Samantha Roswell laughed and smiled, having not said a word the entire time. She looked at Patty Martin.

"I'm a psychologist," said Patty Martin very quietly. "While obviously I'm not in the best place right now emotionally, I have to be concerned about my daughter and about the rest of our young people and about the rest of us. So Katrina has put me at least temporarily in charge of wellness."

"Wellness?" asked Bear.

"Yes, my job will eventually segue into governance and justice and thriving. This isn't some power grab we women have done. We just want to get the ball rolling on some organization. Are we ready to plan more?

"Actually I'm ready to split some wood," responded Larry.

"No wood, no fires. No fires, no eat. Can we postpone this for another time?"

"Seems reasonable," said Katrina.

"This works great for me," said Bear. "Less time worryin'. More time on the horse."

"For anyone who is interested, the first history lesson will be tonight, around the campfire, at 7 PM," said Garth's mother, standing up and grasping her walker.

"Please plan on more organizing," added Katrina. "We're a work in progress."

Garth and Bear were at the gate of the Army base, holding their horses. The horses were bored, rolling their bits in their mouths. While thousands of acres of training areas surrounded them, mostly beautiful oak meadows and hills, the buildings of the base were almost entirely encompassed in a gleaming double chain link barrier, with the fences about twenty feet from each other, in a giant circular enclosure about the size of a football stadium. The effusive rows of shining concertina on top of the fences gave the entire facility the air of a prison.

Now the welded metal gates were shut and locked, and crash barriers had been placed across the two lane main access road. Garth was pushing the button of the metal intercom box bolted to the gate. It buzzed.

They waited. No response. Garth looked up. A beautiful blue sky. Around them, beyond the wire, meadows of lupine, poppies, and mustard were blooming. Garth noticed that inside the wire enclosure was mostly asphalt, pavement, lawn, and buildings. The lawn was overgrown. Between the two rows of fences, about twenty feet high, Garth noticed, was a ribbon of dirt. He pointed at it and spoke to Bear.

"They must use pesticide on that."

Bear studied the fence. "Absolutely. And look at those flood-lights. They still go on every night. The place lights up like maximum security around 8 PM. So somebody's got to be here."

"Or they have the lights on a timer," responded Garth.

"If we don't have power, what's their supply?" asked Bear. "Oh, there you are."

He waved his arm at the solar panels which were slightly visible in a parking lot between the buildings.

They both saw one person walk from amidst those buildings and approach them. As the person approached they could see that she was obviously an African-American woman in a camouflage Army combat uniform, with a soft billed hat of the same fabric, a riot shotgun slung over one shoulder and a pistol holster on her belt. Garth was acutely aware that this time he had placed his own percussion pistol, about 130 years more antique a design than the gun the woman carried, in his own saddlebags. The Master Sargent...Garth could see the rank insignia on her shirt now...wasn't smiling as she walked down the abandoned road towards them. She stopped short about twenty feet from the gate.

"Excuse me, gentlemen, this base is closed, and we aren't supposed to talk to anyone. Not even if you need help. I'm sorry but we're closed, and unable to assist, by order of higher command," she said in a brisk military voice, looking stern in the sunlight. She began to turn to go.

"We're from the mission right down the road," said Bear loudly. "We're checking in as neighbors. Obviously, we're also looking for food and anything else."

"News would be good," added Garth. "We don't really know what is going on."

"From your hill here you can see the mission, so you know what we're doing," added Bear. "You know we've buried a few folks and we're fixin' the place up. You know we don't have much power. And you might'a heard some shooting. We lost a few people.

The Master Sergeant turned back to them. "I'm really very sorry, but I am ordered to not talk to anyone, and not to help anyone. You have to know by now that the situation is very confused. So I can't help you. I'm sorry."

Garth felt anger surge inside him. "You mean you won't help us at all, even if you could? I mean, antibiotics? Food? It's like you aren't here? Isn't it your mission to help the American people?"

She had a conflicted, sad feeling on her face, and Garth felt sorry for shouting at her.

"The thing is, we've been told to evacuate the entire base and close it down, and lock it up," said the Master Sergeant. "I've been told to abandon it when we get the command. The whole unit lit out of here, and my little group is left over, and we have been ordered to let nobody in, and talk with no one, and help no one. Those are my explicit orders."

"Can you come over for dinner and meet our people?" asked Bear.

"Nobody in here is allowed to go outside the wire until

relieved by higher authority or we are ordered to leave," replied the Master Sergeant.

She had a slight southern accent, Garth noticed, and she seemed exasperated by her situation.

"We've got lots of raw food, like flour, we've got some medication in the clinic, and we've got three trucks and three Humvees and we can't haul all that away," said the young woman in uniform. "And I'm not supposed to tell you that, but it seems senseless. Last I heard they wanted me to burn or destroy or bury any supplies I can't transport. Doesn't that beat all?"

She looked well-groomed, with her long black hair in a neat bun, and tired.

"Have you asked a higher command if you can help us?" asked Garth. "Or at least meet us?"

"We really can't get through to higher headquarters very well. There's a denial of service on the internet. When we DO get through, we are told to just wait for orders. Just wait for orders, and don't go outside the wire, and don't let anyone in for any reason whatsoever. I already asked and they said not to share anything. So here we sit. Frankly it seems more interesting out there."

"Well, it's been interesting. That's true," said Bear.

"You're right, we've been watching you, and we even can identify you individually by now. But we can't go out," responded the Master Sergeant. "I'm sorry."

"Any news from outside?" asked Garth.

"We were told to begin keeping the lights off at night," responded the young woman. "Russians and Chinese have reconnaissance satellites up, although why that matters is beyond my pay grade. Now someone is ordering us to sit here and keep the gates locked, which makes no sense at all to me."

"How many people do you have now?" asked Garth.

"I can't tell you," said the Master Sergeant.

"Makes sense," responded Garth. "How's your unit doing?"

"I can't tell you that, either," replied the Master Sergeant. "But I can tell you that the cities are pretty rough. I'm guessing that wherever the U.S. Army is, it's working hard for its money. Everywhere except here. Here we just sit."

"You are always welcome to visit," said Bear, soothingly.

"I'll look forward to it," said the Master Sergeant. "Now, since we're being filmed, I suggest we all go back to where we are from. No sense getting the brass' panties in a bunch. They can see us and hear us, wherever they are watching us from."

Near Salinas, California

"I tell you, they got a real inferno going over there in the Santa Cruz mountains," said Richard Green, the fire captain. "They got another big burn going over by Toro Park, still, the one we saw from the chopper. But it's not burning so many homes."

Richard Green was standing next to Wallace in a farm field just outside of Salinas, towards the Salinas River, waiting for the citizens' broccoli harvesting to begin. Three days since the shake, thought Wallace. Tiny, his gigantic form unmistakable, was a Greek god in blue uniform about five hundred yards away, across the field, forming people into queues. There seemed to be about two hundred people lining up. The air was smokey.

"Can't see it from here," replied Wallace absently. "Air quality's too bad. How big?"

"Something like eight hundred homes, they say, and still burning through Santa Cruz. They don't have water. Roads blocked just like ours but worse. Redwoods are big trees. When they block a road, it stays blocked."

"How are we doing here in Salinas?" asked Wallace.

"All the house fires in Salinas are put out, or burned out," said Richard Green. "The fire crews are mostly focusing on community search and rescue."

"Can you roll trucks any distance yet?" asked Wallace. "We can't really go far in our squad car, but the streets are clearing fast. It's astonishing. People are really coming together."

"No trucks yet. All on foot. I gotta tell you, I'm amazed. We've had a total of like one hundred fifty structure fires, and one hundred twenty-five more structures burned over by the Toro Park wildfire, but they were all contained. The structure fires mostly didn't spread."

"What's the count?" asked Wallace.

"I tell you, it's remarkable. In the city of Salinas, we have maybe fifty people dead, maybe three thousand injured. For a quake they are now calling a magnitude 8.5? Amazing," Richard Green gushed.

There was a disturbance at the far end of the field. Someone was waving a sign which read, "Justice For The Murdered Children". Then another sign. "We Remember The Murdered Innocents."

"I tell you, the Border Patrol sure made us a mess, didn't they?" said Richard Green.

Wallace felt hot. The air seemed smokey and thick. He saw Mayor Happy Johnson, Causwell Dubbers, and the field's owner, Mark Lockhart, driving in a jeep towards the other side of the field. As the open-topped jeep approached, the noise from the crowd increased, and someone threw a water bottle at the vehicle. Wallace and Captain Green began to walk towards the crowd.

There were a few more signs. Perhaps five in all, in a sea of about 500 people. One: "We Not Gonna Pick Yo Cotton," large, bright red, held by a young blonde white man who seemed angry. Pastor Paco stepped out to the front, the wind whipping his beard. He looked like a patriarch. He raised his hands. He shouted, "Share our anger! These are your pobres! Estos son sus hermanos! Yo! Yo! Yo! Why don't you join us and get down wit' us?"

"Ever heard that fool talk like a black person?" said a voice. "He's adopting the accent of the moment. Gaslighting."

Wallace turned and saw Mike Rogers walking alongside them.

The young blonde man with the large red sign saw Mike Rogers, and shouted, "Yo! Don't pick their cotton! Resist for the sake of the slaughtered innocents!"

The young blonde man was wearing a woven hoodie, with

some sort of indigenous design, and carrying a yard-long skateboard with his sign. That young guy certainly has his hands full, thought Wallace.

Mike Rogers shouted back, "I'm not going to join you because this is not cotton, this is broccoli, and you're not Black, not a single one of you, and I NEED TO FEED MY FAMILY! LET ME FEED MY FAMILY!"

The young blonde man shouted, "NO! WE CAN'T LET YOU ENSLAVE YOURSELF TO THE MAN!", dropped his sign, and ran at Mike, raising his skateboard to strike him.

Wallace reached up, grabbed the young man, and flipped him and his skateboard into the green broccoli. The man lay among the plants, sputtering, the breath knocked out of him, and there was a shout, "Look out!" from Richard Green, and a sharpened spear of rebar steel skewered into the dirt at Mike Roger's feet.

Mike Rogers picked it up and faced the crowd, as fighting, shoving, and pushing erupted in the midst of the packed people. Screams, panicked flight by many, some falling underfoot. Wallace prepared to fight, looked around and saw Tiny running into the mob, reaching for the individuals who were violent. He was at least two feet higher than the people surrounding him.

"POLICE! STAND DOWN! GET BACK! LET THE RIGHTEOUS ANGER OF THE PEOPLE BE SEEN!" came a voice on the loudspeaker. Gillian McTavish, the county liaison.

"Mike and Richard, you pick, I'll guard, "said Wallace, stepping back slightly. "Here, let me hold this,"

He reached out and took the rebar spike from Mike.

"You'll need both hands," he said.

"LET THIS BE A DAY OF FASTING! LET THIS BE A DAY OF SOLIDARITY! LET THE POWER BE IN THE HANDS OF THE PEOPLE! OUT OF REVERENCE, LET NOBODY ENTER THIS FIELD!" came the loudspeakered voice of Gillian McTavish.

"WE KNEEL BEFORE THE HONEST GRIEF OF THE PEOPLE!" she continued. LAW ENFORCEMENT PLEASE LEAVE! PEOPLE'S GUARDS, PLEASE TAKE OVER!"

"What in the name of Jesus is this?" said Bettina Ayala. "People's guards?"

She had come over to stand next to them. The crowd was now being shepherded by a few who had stepped out of the crowd. Tiny, bleeding from the head, walked over to join them.

"They brought sharpened rebar," he said, holding one of the sharpened metal spears. "They were looking for a fight."

"I'm counting like ten of them. Max. More like six, not counting the pastor. Five hundred of us and six of the violent ones, "said Bettina.

"Damn it people! This is about FOOD!" yelled Wallace.

"Calm down, cowboy" said Bettina, "Let's get as much as we can.

"HEY! HEY! WAIT A MOMENT! HERE'S THE FOOD RIGHT HERE. AT LEAST LET THE PEOPLE PICK IT," shouted Mark Lockhart, exiting the jeep and walking towards Gillian MacTavish.

As he walked, two of the young people ran to Mark

Lockhart from the crowd, one with a baseball bat, and they began to beat him savagely. He fell. They kept hitting him as he lay in the green vegetables, as Gillian McTavish watched silently, loudspeaker poised, from several yards away. There was a look of distaste on her face.

Tiny covered the distance to the scene in perhaps five seconds, and smashed into the two young people, sending them sprawling, as two more young people left the mob and threw rebar metal spears at him. They missed. Wallace brought up his shotgun and pumped a round into the chamber. How to stop them without accidentally shooting into the innocent crowd? He began to run towards Tiny.

"IN THE NAME OF THE PEOPLE, STOP!" commanded the loudspeaker voice of Gillian McTavish. Wallace saw that the mayor, Happy Johnson, was standing next to her. Mayor Johnson reached out and took the loudspeaker from her.

"SALINAS POLICE WITHDRAW!" said the mayor. "RETREAT!"

Wallace was dumbfounded. He stopped halfway between his group and Tiny.

"Hey! Hey everybody!" came a loud voice behind him and Wallace turned, the broccoli crunching beneath his feet.

Mike Rogers was standing holding the rebar spear to the young blonde man's throat. He yelled, "I'm sorry the children were murdered. It was terrible. How does THIS RIOT feed my children?"

"YOUNG MAN! YOU WILL PUT THAT DOWN THIS INSTANT, came the loudspeaker voice of Gillian McTavish, scolding.

Scattered laughter in the crowd.

Tiny picked up one of the two young people who had attacked him and held him by the throat. The other scrambled away, tripping over broccoli stalks. Causwell Dubbers was kneeling next to Mark Lockhart, who was still on the ground.

"Anyone else notice that all these people talking for black people are white?" shouted Mike Rogers. "White people making us fight! So I'm gonna stay here and everybody pick all the broccoli you need, and maybe a little extra, and if anyone makes a fuss this fella's gonna have a spear stickin' out of the top of his little white head! Any questions?"

"YOU SERVE THE CAUSE OF INJUSTICE!" said Gillian McTavish through the loudspeaker.

"I don't care! I don't care! I'm just trying to feed my family!" shouted Mike Rogers.

"SALINAS POLICE! ARREST THAT MAN!" said Gillian McTavish.

"Hey Sargent, don't we take orders from the city, not the county?" asked Tiny loudly, shaking the young man like a rattle. The young man seemed terrified.

"Last I heard," said Wallace.

He checked the safety on his 870 shotgun. As an afterthought, he added one more buckshot cartridge to the tube magazine. Nice loud sliding sound.

"WE KNEEL TO THE POWER OF THE PEOPLE!" said the loudspeakered voice of the mayor.

There was Happy Johnson, on his knees in his suit and dress pants, in the broccoli. A short distance away, Causwell Dubbers was helping the bleeding Mark Lockhart step into

coming, that it would change everything, and that made him realize that this was probably a dream. A surge of remembrance: the feelings of love, the passion, the brilliant smiles, the all-enveloping lovemaking when new life was the result. All memories. Where did the time go? What had happened? He should warn them, warn everyone, that the hijacked airliners and the flames and the chaos and the darkness were coming. The evil would win, even by losing. Yes, it would win.

There was a knock on the door and it became an insistent pounding, and he got up, wrapped himself in his bathrobe, but they had bashed the door open and there were explosions and noise outside, and they were streaming in, policemen and firemen and Marines and Army, in dusty turndowns and combat gear, down the hallway of his home, yelling, The twin towers, in Manhattan, was collapsing just outside, in screams and fire and waves of dust.

He incongruously thought, they'll wake the children. Then he thought, I should get my pistol, I should get my AR, I should help them. He was standing there in his bathrobe and his underwear, barefoot on the hardwood sunlit floor, as the sweaty dirty men pushed past him, down the hall and into the back yard, on an insistent mission he did not know, dozens of men, and he looked back into the bedroom, incongruously alarmed that someone might wake the young children, and he saw his beautiful wife sleeping despite the noise in her red negligee and he realized he would never see her again.

Garth woke up. He lay on his back in his warm sleeping bag in the tent, his face chill in the dawn air, looking up at the canvas lit only slightly from the outside. Re-orienting himself. All that was a dream, and he was here now. Some quick thoughts about his current life: the earthquake, where his pistol was located now. There were no alarming sounds outside. He needed to use the restroom. His digital watch still worked: 5:14 AM. Dove. He was now married to Dove. She was a good woman, a good person, although the dream had left his mind canted to his past life.

He looked over in the darkness. Dove was enveloped in her sleeping bag, facing away from him. In some ways her behavior since the earthquake was astonishing to him. If anyone ever looked deeply into her actions when they had found the women, her execution of the rapist would possibly result in a murder charge. His silence would have to be absolute.

The cool dawn air was crisp on his face. Steeling himself, like a hermit crab changing shells, he levered his legs from the snugness of the warm sleeping bag into his cold cavalry pants. Boots. Stand up, buckle on pistol, coat, hat, saddlebags with razor and toothbrush, step outside.

There was a small dim light in his saddlebags. He groped inside. His satellite phone was cabled to his cellphone, and astonishingly the sat system was accessing the internet. This was rare and unexpected. He looked up. Beyond, he could see Steve Sanchez and his son Stan, both coming off guard duty, and he was filled with the thought that he should tell them that the internet was available. But then he realized that it might not last long, so he sat down immediately on a flat broad oak tree stump and opened up his CNN app, and there was a headline, "President Price Tells California To Go Sink". Apparently the President had been at his Twitter account again. Farther down the page, "California Declares Open Borders, Expropriates Medical System" subheading, "Medical Personnel Flee State Under Threat Of Arrest". Behind him he heard noises and felt Steve and Stan gathering behind him, looking over his shoulders. He could hear their sharp intake of breath as they read the tiny headlines on his phone.

"So the state has nationalized the health care system?" said Steve very quietly. Almost a whisper.

"Looks like it," Garth replied very quietly.

"What else could they do?" said Stan.

Afraid that the satellite internet would cease, Garth scrolled down the phone screen.

Headline: "Death Toll In Western U.S. Quake Is Set Above 250,000 As Riots And Violence Continue" Garth felt the air leave his body.

"Holy shit! I don't understand, what killed those people?" asked Stan.

"I don't know. But look, they're killing each other!" replied Steve.

No water in Los Angeles. Video of people standing in lines to get bottled water. Smoke from the fires of riots rising over the Los Angeles basin. Korean Americans with rifles guarding their grocery stores. A Hispanic man pulled from his truck and beaten to death by an angry mostly black crowd. Looting. And more looting.

Video. The entire San Francisco Bay Area was down and burning. But worst apparently were the mass slayings of gays by homophobic straight whites, which had led to riots led by a group known as the Gay Allied Youth, which had been burning entire affluent sections of San Francisco itself. There was a video of them kicking a young pregnant Asian woman to death along with her unborn child.

"Jesus," whispered Steve.

"If it's real," said Stan.

There was a security camera video of a car bomb ammonium nitrate explosion...they watched the obviously white young people leave the rented van in the parking garage...and it had wrecked the capitol building in Sacramento, which had killed hundreds, and that act of terrorism had been claimed by Christians United, a group seeking a theocracy in Northern California.

If it was real, thought Garth.

As a result, the governor of California, Carson Grantham, had nationalized all health care and mobilized the National Guard. The state government was now relocated to San Francisco, and there was a video of the governor standing in shirtsleeves, with white shirt and a red tie, declaring that California would rise from the rubble with absolutely open borders and a new non-racist green society. Stroking his lush combed-back hair in the sunlight, the governor cursed the "depraved" national government, "evil President Price", white privilege "the secret force behind all this", religion, and guns "in the hands of yokel rural terrorists determined to decimate the rightful people of this state". He then announced that more emergency executive action was pending, especially the possibility of a state wealth tax which would access IRA's, bank accounts, and brokerages. Capital was apparently fleeing California by the millions of dollars daily.

Not so much was said about the mechanics of emergency relief. There were cholera and typhus epidemics spreading from the homeless populations into wider communities in all large urban areas. Los Angeles and San Francisco were without water and people were rioting, looting, and fleeing.

The governor had issued an executive order making it illegal to travel. If you were in LA or San Francisco, you were commanded to shelter in place under threat of arrest and incarceration in relocation camps. At some point soon, complete aid would be brought to the cities.

The Federal Government's response to Governor Grantham's actions had been to move ICE checkpoints to the Nevada border crossings and denounce the autocratic actions of the state governor. And then had come the President's tweets. "Fake news! Fake news! Loser criminal Grantham should be careful what he wishes for!" and "See? The animals who crossed the border illegally are TAKING OVER!!! RAPISTS!!!"

Garth contemplated that the rapists he had met were white. All white. So far.

Breaking news: The Chinese government had discovered a U.S.-led revolution against the Chinese nation plotted from Hong Kong and Taiwan. Pending.

At that point the internet died, and the screen went dark.

"Things aren't so bad here at the mission after all," said Stan.

"I am reminded of the invasion of Poland in 1939," said Garth's mother. She was sitting in the church at mid-morning, sitting on her walker with a worn pink and yellow blanket over her shoulders. Today was clear but crisp.

"How so?" asked Belinda Jefferson.

"Remember how Hitler invaded Poland? He dressed up a few prisoners in Polish uniforms and shot them on German soil, just across the border from Poland, and then claimed that the Polish had attacked Germany. That excused his start for World War II."

"But this was an earthquake," said Fred Paxley morosely.

His wife Katrina eyed him with no expression. Apparently Fred was not drunk, or hungover, and had not been seen or heard to vomit this morning. It was a good day in the Paxley family.

There was a honking sound from the back of the room. Eyes turned. Hero the Service Dog had farted, loud as a goose.

"Oh, bad dog," whispered Samantha Roswell, chuckling. "Go, bad dog. Go outside."

Garth could barely hear her. There was a growing rank smell. He rose and opened a side door. Several church cats, which had been in hiding, scrambled towards the outdoors.

"But with 250,000 dead?" asked Terp Taylor. Garth watched him. This morning Terp was wearing a pistol, a Colt Single Action from his grandfather by the look of it. Terp was entitled to that. Based on the truck incident, Garth thought, Terp was both competent and reliably calm.

"That death toll seems rather high to me as well," opined Terp's grandfather Terry, who was seated next to him. "250,000 dead from what? From the actual earthquake? I know it was bad, but it wasn't THAT bad. Riots? I'm not sure I understand."

Garth realized that Terry had worn a full clean Civil War uniform since they had been stuck here. Garth wondered how Terry was able to do that, since most others had lapsed into a combination of modern and antique style clothing as wear and dirt had taken their toll. At the moment Garth's own replica wool cavalry coat was immersed in a bucket of cold water, soaking away the blood from this morning's deer carcass. Whatever the cause, Terry looked great.

"I have to agree, Terry," said Garth's mother. "And the Chinese government finding a U.S. plot for a Chinese revolution seems to be an excuse for an action of their own."

There was a scraping flatulent sound. Everyone looked. Hero the Service Dog was hunched, defecating upon the 200 year old tile floor, feces flooding steamily out of the dog's rectum to plop wetly upon the floor. God damned dog, thought Garth. Poppy and Samantha need to clean that up.

"Never let a good crisis go to waste," smiled Garth's mother. "I believe that Obama's chief of staff said that, but it could have been anyone in politics. The factions and entities are sure to jockey for advantage as this disaster plays out."

"Let's see if our beloved president can get his head out of his own ass for ten minutes and create a decent response to that," added Poppy Roswell. "He's an idiot."

"Idiot? That Governor New-planet is the idiot. The President is doing a tough job right now, and he's doing it well," bristled Gritz Garwood, loudly.

"President Price is a butt head," said Poppy, standing. "He's a bully, and he doesn't GIVE A DAMN ABOUT US! HE'S A CRIMINAL! Every night I pray that he's dead before morning."

Across the circle of people, Gritz stood and shouted back, "I'M GETTING PRETTY DAMN TIRED OF YOUR MOUTH AND YOUR DOG! NOW CLEAN UP AFTER YOUR GODDAMNED DOG!"

BANG! There was a loud crash and the chairs near Garth's mother toppled over. Everyone stared. Had the old woman fallen? Was she injured?

Garth's mother pulled herself upright over her walker and eyed them scowling. "Disinformation! DISINFORMATION AND CONTROL! Whoever they are, they WANT US TO FIGHT, THEY WANT US TO HATE, AND THEY WANT US TO NEGLECT THE BEST QUALITIES OF OUR NATURE!"

She stopped, panting with the effort. She seemed spent and disoriented for a few moments.

Poppy seemed contrite. Gritz seemed to be fighting for self-control, stifling the urge to scream.

"Listen, please, I'm 102 years old, and I've seen this before," said Garth's mother. "If we fight amongst ourselves, we lose."

Later in the evening, after everyone had left, Francesca and Raley finished their mopping. The church smelled delightfully of mint and alcohol. Fresh. No more fecal odors.

"Thanks for cleaning that up." said a voice from the darkness, across the sanctuary.

"Oh...oh you startled us, Poppy," said Francesca, jerking. "Is there anyone back there with you?"

"Only my wonderful Hero," replied Poppy's tired voice. "We're just sitting here enjoying the quiet."

"Your wife Samantha did most of the cleaning. We just mopped a little," added Raley, peering into the darkness. "She picks up after that dog a lot."

"Yes. We've had Hero now for twelve years. He's not a young dog," said Poppy's voice. "He's an attention-getter."

"Well, since you're sayin' that, yes," said Raley. "Seems like he's always bitin' or barfin' or poopin.'"

"Or tripping someone. Or stealing food," added Francesca.

"He's really quite intelligent, you know," said Poppy. "All that is just his way of communicating."

"He communicates by bitin' children?" said Raley. "He really chomped that kindergartener a few months back."

"Ah, well. I retired from teaching about the same time we got Hero. All my life, I've been ignored. All my life, I did whatever anyone told me. Samantha didn't want to have kids. Bad for the planet, we were told. So we didn't have children. The school district told me to teach sixth grade, then fourth grade, and then second grade, and they moved me from school to school whenever they wanted. I was not an impressive student, not an impressive teacher, not an impressive husband. Nobody ever bragged about old Poppy. But I always showed up for work. Always. Forty-two years of work. Always at the back of the room. I always did whatever

I was told to do. Then this other retired teacher, she gave me Hero, and she showed me, make him a service dog," said Poppy, as though to himself.

"What's he do for service?" asked Francesca.

"Ha ha! That teacher taught me what to do. I just invented his job," replied Poppy. "He's...he's my spokesman to the world."

"Isn't a service dog supposed to do something?" asked Francesca.

"Oh, but he does, he does," said Poppy. "That's the thing. They may ignore me, but nobody ignores Hero. What a scamp!"

"Well, that's true," said Raley, softly.

"So, the result is, nobody ignores me anymore," said Poppy.

"No they don't," said Raley. "Well, goodnight, Mr. Roswell. Sleep well."

She and Francesca lifted their bucket and mop and began to leave.

"Oh, before you go, here's something else," said Poppy. "Something from Terp's grandfather."

He held up something which glittered faintly. The girls looked at it, uncertainly.

"It's a little pistol, a derringer, a .44 Magnum," said Poppy.

".44 Magnum?" said Raley. "Isn't that like an elephant gun?"

"I don't think it would stay in your hand if you fired it," added Francesca.

"Oh, that's not the point," said Poppy, holding out the gun. "Careful, it's loaded. That little spring-loaded safety's in place, but don't cock it."

"If I'm not supposed to shoot it, what's it good for?" asked Raley.

"Oh, it's to keep Fred away. Just scare him a twinkle. I've known Fred for decades. Maybe forty years. We were teachers together. We were in the socialist club together, and the teacher's union. Anyway, after his son decided to be patriotic and go off and get killed in Iraq, Fred's been insane. An insane drunk."

"We've noticed," said Francesca. "Should we do something?"

"Mostly watch out," said Poppy. "Terry gave me that because ol' Fred is a bit too interested in you. It's a recent fixation. Fascinated by you, Raley. Somehow the sight of you takes him back to his boyhood days. Anyway, when he's drunk, he talks of you and nothing else."

"I'm not gonna shoot him," said Raley. "Poor geezer. You know my grandpa's gonna kill Mr. Paxley if he gets near me. But he won't. Mr. Paxley barely has the strength to puke."

"Poor Mrs. Paxley," said Francesca.

"You won't have to do anything," said Poppy. "Just hide that somewhere and if Fred gets out of line, stick it up one of his nostrils. It will calm him right down. Call it a tranquilizer gun."

Salinas, California

Sitting around a campfire in a backyard, stars overhead. Mickey was on one side with Diablo the police dog, who looked intelligently about him as though he understood the discussion. Tiny and Margarita were across the flames, and near them Katy, sitting alone. Katy was looking good, Wallace saw. Cozy in a cloth stadium coat.

Mike Rogers and his kids sat with them. Dinner...Wallace was astonished at the neighborhood's ability to scrounge. Fresh tortillas, beans, broccoli, and a little spam. Delicious. The women were now refilling water plastic single use water bottles from boiled water from the local wells. They had been waiting all day to get that water, he realized.

His walkie-talkie was silent. Let it stay that way. Today had been one long mundane foot patrol after another. Infrastructure was being repaired, but cars still couldn't travel more than 500 yards. So they had done it on foot. Questions everywhere they went. When will the power return? When will my cell phone work? Where is our missing cat? When will there be food, most of all. Wallace's Spanish had gotten a workout.

"Think the mayor and that county administrator hates us?" asked Tiny. "Think we're gonna get fired?"

"Well, they haven't fired anyone yet, and it's been two days since the world's first Broccoli Bowl." said Mickey. "Still haven't found the football."

Diablo seemed to be pondering that comment. Perhaps, if Mickey was fired, he'd find a new partner.

"Guess they need police," said Tiny.

"Somebody out there needs goons. I keep thinking about that whole mess. The riot was organized. That pastor was out in front and he knew that those kids with the rebar had his back," said Mike.

"Hey Mike! Think that kid you grabbed expected to have his own spear held to his throat?" asked Mickey.

"Shaka Zulu, man!" laughed Tiny. "Kid needs therapy after that."

"Whatever you say, Maui," giggled Margarita.

Margarita really WAS miniscule sitting next to Tiny. Intimate thoughts flashed into Wallace's mind, which he quickly intentionally replaced with thoughts of his own family, there at the Danish farm at Aabenraa. Tranquility. A little of that would go a long way right now. Wonderful to be part of this community.

There was a shuffling and the sound of women, and there were two, speaking in Spanish, calling Margareta and Katy away to private discussions in the dark. The sound of Margareta suddenly loud, suddenly shouting in Spanish, then grief, spreading to all the women, and Wallace's walkie talkie, on his shoulder, suddenly shrilled with a voice,

"Whiskey Six Delta, immediate action, violent disturbance at the mall. Looting and burning. Shots fired," came the voice.

"Roger that," replied Wallace. "We're on foot so we may take an hour, but we'll get there."

"Understand," came the tired voice from the handset.

"Hey, man, what happened to the women?" said Wallace to Mike. "They're upset!"

"Oh, oh they just found out that Katy's husband was murdered...." Mike's voice broke, "Murdered like my Lacy, stabbed by some drug-addicted goon, while the husband was at work at the hospital. Word is, the county's pulled your police back."

"They've done WHAT?" said Tiny.

"Yep, it's a health facility and the county felt that the presence of police would frighten illegals, keep them from coming to get health care," said Mike.

"Un-fracking-believable." said Mickey.

"Speaking of which, we got something for you guys," said Mike, his voice still quavering. "This will help you get to the mall, and you won't come back so wiped out."

He led them around the building and into a neighbor's garage. With no electricity there were only a few flashlights illuminating the five lightweight dirt motorcycles, which looked trim, beat-up but in good repair. Someone had obviously tended them. The old woman was there, wearing a headlamp, with her old style dress and a sweater. She turned to look at them and the light from her forehead was blinding.

"Estos serán buenos caballos para ustedes, hijos míos," she said quietly.

"We have helmets!" said Mike.

He was strapping a helmet on his head as he spoke.

"Wait. You're going?" said Tiny

"Who else here has ridden or serviced a dirt bike?" said Mike.

A chorus of voices.

"Right. Nobody," said Mike. "Somebody's gotta give you a lesson as we go. So me and ol' Tigre here are coming along. We spend a lot of time on dirt bikes over at Hollister Hills."

'El Tigre," seemed to be about sixteen, dark, with pimples and long black curly hair, slender to the point of frailty and about five feet tall. Some tiger, thought Wallace. El Tigre was wearing his hat backwards.

"Who is El Tigre?" asked Tiny. "I mean, who are his relations around here?"

"Oh, he's Margarita's nephew, from Oaxaca, up here visiting. Not a word of English. He's learning Spanish as we go. He sure speaks dirt bike, though! Got wrenches in his fingers."

Mike was distributing the helmets, ignoring the confused looks of the officers.

"Wallace, you got the Red Rocket. Tiny, you get this BSA," here Mike motioned to a larger motocross machine. "Oh, and Mickey, you get this beat up Bultaco. It's my camping bike and it has a cargo carrier. Diablo can ride there."

"WHAT THE HECK WAS THAT?" shouted Tiny at the top of his lungs. The noise made the tent shake. 'YOU KEPT US GOING FROM PLACE TO PLACE FOR FOUR DAYS! WE WERE NEVER NEVER ALLOWED TO ENGAGE! THIS TOWN HAS BEEN LOOTED AND BURNED FROM NORTH TO SOUTH AND WE DID NOTHING! NOTHING!"

Mayor Happy Johnson stood at the head of a folding table, with a new preoccupied look in his eyes. He wouldn't look at the police officers. He wouldn't look at anyone, except Causwell Dubbers and Gillian McTavish. Ms. McTavish seemed empowered and defiant. The mayor said nothing.

Bettina Ayala, at the other end of the table, spoke up, more quietly. "I'm up for some answers myself, Mister Mayor. It seems to me that this town was doing rather well, until that broccoli field, and then the widespread looting. What set everyone off? And why won't you let the police do their jobs?"

"Latinx lives matter," said Gillian McTavish emphatically.

"That's it? That's all you've got?" said Wallace. "If that's true, then why did you abandon so many Hispanic communities and Hispanic small businesses to the mobs? And why did you let the gangs take over as the de-facto police in East Salinas?"

"Remember the children in cages," replied Gillian McTavish.

"We wanted to respect the rage of the people over the Mexicali Massacre," said Happy Johnson, sullenly. "The last thing we needed was more police brutality."

Thanks for the love, Mr. Mayor, thought Wallace. THAT was insulting.

"By letting mobs burn people's communities to the ground?" asked a young police officer, angrily.

Wallace looked at the young man who had spoken. The young man was Hispanic himself. He was so young. Must be early twenties. Feeling insulted like Wallace, certainly.

"Oh, the Latinx were in solidarity with the protestors," said Gillian McTavish.

"Well, actually, that's not entirely the case," said Dina

Montero, who had been standing in the back of the room. "I was out looking around. We're still printing a two-page Salinas Index Journal on a solar-powered laptop and printer. Anyway, the people who were doing the burning, or at least leading the burning and the looting, seem to have been white. Nobody knew who they were. After they stirred everyone up and the locals got into it, then these white people seem to have left. That's what I'm hearing, anyway."

The same as the broccoli field, thought Wallace.

"The gangs started it all," said Gillian McTavish.

"No. No, the gangs didn't, so far as I can determine," said Dina Montero, looking aggressive. "They got into it to STOP the looting. In fact, they acted when the police didn't act. Ericson, I saw you there, watching. You didn't do anything."

Wallace felt a punch of adrenaline coursing through his body. Shame.

"Yep, you're right, Dina. We were ordered to stand to the side and watch," he replied.

"WE DIDN'T WANT ANY MORE VIDEOS OF MILITARIZED POLICE KILLING CHILDREN!" shouted Happy Johnson, his face reddening.

"We should defund the police. Tell them to stand down," said Pastor Paco, who had entered through the cloth panels at the back of the tent. "We have to let Latinx take charge of their own lives."

"I'm not Latino?" asked the young officer.

"You're a white Latinx," replied Pastor Paco. "You're a coconut. As a police person you conform to the oppression of the overlords."

The young officer was taking a deep breath, ready to say something belligerent, when Chief Jefferson spoke. "Cool it, Mendoza, we got a bigger problem."

"Candida?" said Dina. "I heard."

"Candida?" said Tiny. "Isn't that a song from the 1970's? I think Tony Gourrmando and The Sunrise."

"That too. We have another pandemic starting," said Chief Jefferson. "It started in the Midwest, apparently in a beef packing plant. That seems strange, but that's the story, anyway. It's much more lethal than COVID 19, fatality rates up to 30%, very necrotic, long recovery times, and it's spreading fast. It doesn't show symptoms for two weeks and the infected individuals are contagious for about a week before symptoms appear."

"The perfect weaponized agent," said Dina, under her breath. "Cows my ass."

"Any near us?" said Tiny.

"No, no, but we're going to take precautions," said Gillian McTavish. "The state is sending strike teams to help us out, to prepare. They are young idealistic individuals who are fully trained in social justice and are fully aware of how to combat the virus. Everyone still got their COVID masks somewhere?"

"In my sock drawer," said Mendoza.

"Are the socks clean, Junior?" said Tiny. Some laughter.

"This is the first I've heard of the strike teams," responded Chief Jefferson. "Who are they, and when do they arrive?"

"Idealistic young college students recruited from the sciences, fully aware of the challenges faced by every community in the state," said Gillian McTavish. "Listen up, folks.

Let's get real. We've been dealt a bad hand of cards here, and it's going to get rougher. Now we have three issues: the earthquake, the social unrest, and now this Candida. We need your best game."

"We're already playing our best game," said Officer Mendoza.

"You may think so, but we need more," said Happy Johnson. "We need your complete conformity to our agenda. When we say go, go. When we say stop, stop. The reasons why we do what we do may not be clear to you, but we need you to follow our orders without question. Our wonderful governor, working together with our wonderful state government, is doing everything for us, so we need to do everything for them. When those state strike teams get here, they're in charge. They know how to beat Candida and we don't. They're in charge. Everybody got that?"

Los Padres National Forest, California

Another dawn, and Garth was seated on a steep hillside under an oak tree watching the sunrise while Dogfood and a pack horse cropped grass nearby. The grass was annual oats and brome, invasive and introduced from Europe perhaps 200 years ago. It was still green, barely. In a few weeks all the grass would be brown, and much less nutritious for the horses to eat. Garth contemplated that the pack horse, normally Sally Beth Saunders' saddle horse, was named "Lucy" because she was red-haired like Sally Beth, and prone to getting into trouble.

Garth had removed the horses' bridles and left them on long-lead halters for better grazing while he waited for the hunters. He was hoping for the sounds of distant shots. Better to leave the apparently skittish pack horse Lucy undisturbed by loud noises. Nothing so far. Garth watched the horses eat with apparent happiness. So quiet. There was the sound of a nesting acorn woodpecker in a nearby tree. Probably babies, already. A solitary honeybee buzzed past and settled on a lupine, frantically gathering pollen. Hard work, if you can get it, thought Garth.

Then Garth watched the magnificent sunrise to the east, towards the Salinas Valley. There were giant columns of smoke rising in the red haze beyond the nearby mountains. Something in the valley was burning, perhaps something all the way across the valley, in the Gabilan Mountains. Perhaps sage brush, or chemise. Perhaps more. But despite those smoke columns, Garth thought, it was a peaceful day. Warming by the minute.

Should he try the satellite phone, he wondered? There had been almost no reception for the past two weeks. A few times he had gotten a mere glimpse of internet, and he'd heard Sarah's voice or Ernst's voices a few times for an instant, but then the connections had dropped and the static sound of nothing would fill his ears. He'd learned to not perseverate, not keep trying, because that could waste time, as well as the battery.

Garth contemplated that except for perhaps his 102 year

old mother, they were all going through an electronics withdrawal, himself included. He worried about his investment advising business often, although he told himself over and over that Ernst in New York had it all under control. He hoped. The clients knew Ernst, and they trusted him. But still, he didn't know, and his clients paid him to know.

He remembered that Hillary Singleton, Bear's granddaughter, had refused to participate in chores around the mission for several weeks, remaining in a priest's unlit empty cell with her defunct iPhone, until finally Bear had taken it and hidden it while she was in the bathroom. Panic, tantrums, and depression had followed until Hillary, now pallid, underweight, and listless, was supervised by Dove and the volunteers such as Merry who worked in the medical team. Hillary needed outside care, and that was yet another reason to go out into the wider world. They needed to go out. It had been weeks. Deputy Davis was healing well, except that his hand would need surgery, and was a bit inflamed. Deputy Davis could go out with them. As an ambassador, or as an escort.

Garth was disturbed from his thoughts by the sight of Bear Singleton and Hopi Jack on horseback, riding slowly up towards him on the slender dirt cow trail from the Big Sur seaward mountains to the west. He watched them ride towards him looking stolid, mildly disappointed. Full 1860's clothing.

Ostensibly Garth, Bear, and Hopi Jack were out hunting, while Katrina Paxley and Belinda Jefferson managed a well-guarded expedition to unharvested local fields, to harvest raw wheat. That would be a first: harvest their own grain, make their own flour, make their own bread. More of an experiment, really, in case they couldn't get resupply somehow. Much discussion about the morality of thieving from the farmer who had done the planting. Consensus: they weren't going to be here much longer. They could pay the farmers when things returned to normal.

"Nothin' but cattle," said Bear as he reined in close by. "No wild hogs, no deer."

"Slow elk, s'more like it!" laughed Hopi Jack. "Seriously, there's meat on the hoof all around us, and today's task is hunting. So let's hunt. Slow elk. The kind that moo."

"That might be a good plan but how much longer do you expect we'll be here?" Bear asked Hopi Jack, both of them sitting their horses side by side. "I'm bettin' we'll be outa here any day. Then we'll have to pay for any cattle we plug. Perhaps we'll even get arrested for rustlin'. I mean, those cattle are property."

"And I say we should eat them now and pay for them later. The courts and the government will understand," said Hopi Jack.

Garth finished bridling Dogfood, who was tossing his head, resisting the bit. "I vote that we shoot one steer. That's food for about two days. That way we aren't just killing for nothing," said Garth. "And if we CAN pay, we SHOULD pay, when we find the rancher. Let's make sure we keep the hide with the brand on it. Look upon this as a drive-in grocery."

With that, he pulled himself into the saddle, and followed the other two, who were already walking their horses towards the location of the livestock.

The steer had fallen with one shot from Garth's .45-70 Marlin, tumbling into the tall mottled grass of a side hill, without running or struggling. They had then slid the carcass downhill to a tree, hoisted it by the heels with a rope, gutted it, skinned it, quartered it, wrapped the meat in the fresh steer skin and in the canvas which had been brought for the purpose. Three quarters of beef were now tied to Lucy the pack horse, and one quarter tied behind Bear's saddle, and they were riding home single file. Garth looked back. Bear was tugging the recalcitrant Lucy by the halter. Lucy didn't like the smell of it, apparently. Nostrils flaring, she braced like a mule against the lead. Bear wrapped the halter lead around the horn of his saddle and pulled the reluctant Lucy forward.

Then Garth looked forward to Hopi Jack, who had halted at the bend of the trail, outlined by oak leaves, leaning from his saddle to observe something in the dirt. He was frozen. Seeing something remarkably interesting. Garth rode up behind Hopi Jack, careful not to crowd Hopi's horse, which might cause it to kick. Garth was aware of the hot sun on his back. A bold clear day. He looked down.

There in the dirt were fresh tracks made by unknown people. Athletic shoe tracks.

"How many?" asked Garth.

"At least three individuals," answered Hopi Jack. "But if more than one of them have the same kind of shoes, I'm screwed."

"What else can you tell us?" asked Bear, who was now sitting on his horse just behind Garth.

"I'm guessing three, all men, very recently, heading for the creek. Heading for the mission. Not carrying a lot. Walking, not running. Nobody's bleeding. Nobody's in a hurry. Just saunterin' down the trail."

"Any guess about intent?" asked Bear, talking past Garth.

"Not a clue. Just standard athletic shoes," replied Hopi Jack.

"Why men?" asked Garth.

"Feet are big. If they're women they're big too. Probably men," answered Hopi Jack.

"Let's go down the trail until we meet them," replied Garth. "Hopi, you please lead out, I'll follow at a fifty yard interval. Stop when we get to the San Antonio River."

"The San Antonio River. In Arkansas that isn't big enough for a gutter runoff," responded Hopi Jack, turning his horse down the trail.

"We find our pride where we can," smiled Garth, "and it's all we've got."

Hopi Jack was right, Garth reflected. They were now sitting silently on horseback looking below them, down into the riverbed. The small cobbled river stretched before them, a silver water ribbon under the blue sky, transparent, smooth, and idyllic, with banks lined deeply with the yellow greens of a deep riparian forest, in a band about two hundred meters wide.

Downhill from Garth, Hopi Jack, and Bear, peeking around a sycamore tree, facing away from them, were three young men, all wearing brown hoodies, all unaware that they had been seen. They were watching something in the river, intently. It was a beautiful day, thought Garth. About seventy-five degrees. Scarcely a cloud in the sky. Those men below them, so preoccupied, didn't appear to have any firearms. They seemed, oddly, to be out for a walk. Garth considered that it was reasonable to move on soon, to keep that precious newly killed meat fresh. No time to be stalking three tourists, no matter how out of place they might be.

Garth looked beyond the young men to the sunlit river. It sparkled smooth in the sun, emerald riparian walls of willow and cottonwood and sycamore trees. So many birds. In fact, the young men appeared to be watching merganser ducks. There was a mother duck with babies clustered on her back, a swarm of them, small fluffy brown and yellow puff balls, all apparently quite content with life. It was a good day to be content.

Then, beyond them, Raley waded into view. She appeared to be naked, laughing, looking behind her, water up to her knees. For an instant Garth watched, aware that she was angelic, beautiful, apparently a part of this environment like the trees and the deer, and then the enormity of what he was seeing...a seventeen year old girl wading nude in a wilderness creek...shocked him suddenly, and he averted his eyes. And then there was movement near her, and there was Terp. Terp? Newly-twenty-year old truck-shooting Terp! And Terp was naked too. And laughing. And he was very very happy. Very happy. The source of his happiness appeared to be Raley. There was something natural and good in what was happening. Something healing. Something he should not be watching at all.

There was a bellow above and behind them, as Bear rode out of the trees and could look down. "WHAT IN HELL YA DOIN' DOWN THERE? What in Hell? What in Hell?"

The three young men down behind the sycamore made no attempt to run. They thought Bear was yelling at them. They simply turned, and raised their hands in surrender, with fearful looks on their faces. They were terrified. Garth watched carefully to see if they would brandish weapons, but they stood still.

Farther beyond, Raley yelled "frack!", laughed, and sank down to her chin in the water, followed shortly thereafter by Terp, gradually ducking so that only their heads were bobbing disembodied on the surface of the creek. Raley was smiling. Terp appeared horrified.

"YA THINK THIS IS A JOKE, YOUNG LADY?" yelled Bear.

Raley began to laugh, gently, and submerged completely. After several seconds her head rose again, blond hair slicked back, and she began to swim carefully to the opposite bank, her beautiful bare back barely surfacing as she swam.

Bear pulled his horse up abreast of Garth and Hopi Jack.

Terp remained in the river, submerged to his chin, watching them cautiously.

"It's OK, Terp," shouted Garth, "I'll keep him from shooting you. Go get dressed and we'll meet you both by the trail across the ford,"

Then Garth couldn't control himself and he began to laugh.

"What's so goddamned funny?" asked Bear. "I'm RESPONSIBLE!"

"Ya know, Bear, I might take that anger down a notch," said Hopi Jack, smiling broadly. "Seems to me these young people have a better idea of what to do on a sunny summer day than you or I do. I think they know exactly what they're doin'. I mean, what did YOU DO when you were that age? Both of them are doing as much work as anyone, and more. And they are actually acting like a couple, instead of just gettin' down with casual strangers. Besides, they don't drink or do drugs, do they? And better him than some jackass tattooed techno geek with a goatee."

"Who smokes dope, who vapes, who lives on a sofa," added Garth. "Terp's about the best we've got, when you think about it."

"Hmmmm. Maybe you're right," responded Bear. "He DOES split firewood like a demon. He's not hibernatin' in a dark room back at the mission, trying to get a cellphone to work."

"What about these three?" asked Hopi. "Seems they got an earful and an eyeful!"

"Who the heck are you, anyway?" shouted Bear towards the young men.

"We're Catholic monks from the Carmelite Monastery at Big Sur!" replied the oldest, loudly. He seemed more courageous. He had gray in his beard. Apparently not as young as he had seemed.

"The three of you are MONKS?" asked Hopi, half shouting. "That's about fifteen miles due west of the mission! Long walk! And you're monks, you say?"

"Catholic monks," replied the man. "I'm Hugh. I'm a

master vintner. This young fellow is Mike, and he's a mason. That gentleman is Chuck, and he's a chorist."

"What's a chorist?" asked Bear.

"He's a choir monk, a chorister," replied Hugh.

Garth, Bear, and Hopi Jack stared at him blankly.

"He's a priest. He can provide the Eucharist," added Hugh

"That means he sings?" added Garth.

"He's a priest. The rest of us are skilled monks," replied Hugh. "Artisans"

"Why were you watching my granddaughter?" asked Bear gruffly.

"Because we didn't expect to see her," replied the young-est, Mike.

"We REALLY didn't expect to see her. She's really rather beautiful and Biblical," added Hugh, the vintner.

"The young man seems rather David-like, actually. Classic. Sculpted," chimed Chuck.

"But you're monks!" replied Hopi Jack, smiling. He seemed to be stifling laughter.

"We're monks but we're not dead, praise God," returned the chorister, Chuck.

At this Garth began laughing again. Deep, satisfying, healing laughter.

"Why did you leave your own place?" Bear asked.

"You mean our monastery? It got hit hard in the quake. But nobody was hurt. The water system went down, and no power, and no phone. Some wooden apartments are cracked open. Then the tsunami came in."

"Tsunami?" blurted Garth.

"It looked like lines in the ocean, one wave after another. I'm guessing the highest was ten feet tall. It smashed the cliffs down on the seafront, and probably destroyed Lime Kiln State Park, and Andrew Molera State Park, but it didn't kill anyone that we know of," said Chuck.

"So what was the problem?" asked Garth.

"The problem is the roads. Our monastery road down to the highway was taken out in a landslide," said Mike "And the highway, Highway One, fell into the ocean in several places. We could see the dust clouds south of us at that whole weak area, you know the place that went into the ocean a few years ago, after the big forest fire?"

"Mud Creek?" said Hopi Jack.

"I think that's it," said Mike. "Anyway, Highway One is cut in several places. People probably got killed in that. And there's people trapped in each little section, isolated.

"Who's helping them?" asked Bear.

"So far as we know, nobody is helping them," replied Chuck. "That's why we're here. There are refugees coming to our monastery, about twenty-five so far. There's only about that many monks! We are running out of supplies, and since prayer didn't seem to be the only answer, I'm acting. This is faster than hiking up Highway One, especially since there are rumors of crime north of us, near Carmel, on the highway. Some sort of group took control up there. We went out to get help, over the Nacimiento Road, but there's too many trees down so we took the trail around Cone Peak, and here we are. I hope you have food. We haven't eaten in two days."

"Glad to have you. We've got to get this beef to the mission, which is only a few miles away. People will welcome you. Especially you, the mason!" said Hopi Jack loudly.

The mason raised his hand, smiling, "I'm Mike, and I can't wait to see it."

"Well, follow us, then. Welcome.," replied Bear. "Beef for dinner."

"BEEF FOR DINNER!" laughed Mike. "I'll build you a house for a good meal."

There was a call from down the hill, across the river. The small forms of Raley and Terp were standing there. They were dressed now. Raley was lifting something that looked like a short thick rope.

"BEEF?" came Raley's distant voice. "Did I hear beef? Better than this big 'ol rattlesnake I just kilt. Oh, well, guess we'll just have it for lunch."

San Antonio Mission, California

Some people might have slept late, after a delightful barbecue dinner, but for the distant sounds of morning reveille playing on the Army base several miles away. The tinny recorded sounds of a bugle echoed in the distance. Immediately there came an unending blast of bagpipes closer by.

Holy Sacred Relics of Mary, thought Garth as he scrambled to his feet and buckled on his now-loaded 1858 cap and ball percussion revolver. What the hell? Boots on and outside, leaving behind the still-sleeping Dove in her own sleeping bag. She had moved her cot to the opposite side of the tent. Garth missed her nearness, he thought fleetingly as he ducked through the canvas into the brilliant sunlight.

There, in front of the church, stood Poppy and Gritz with their bagpipes, hooting away somewhat incoherently, smiling with the chanters in their mouths. Very loud. Relentless. Somehow Garth's mother had maneuvered her walker to sit near the pipes. A bit of deafness was an asset in this situation. Others were coming out of their tents now. There was Tiger Tanaka, there was Terry Taylor. And more. There were the three monks, who had slept on benches alongside the galleria. Wide awake now, and a bit startled by this sudden wailing sound. They were well fed, though. Garth finished buttoning his white cotton cavalry shirt as he walked over to the pipers. It was going to be warm by noon.

"I thought since it was going to be a busy day, we could start with some music," shouted his mother over the noise. "Don't blame them."

Garth had to laugh.

Poppy and Gritz ended their tune and let the bagpipes deflate, smiling broadly.

In the distance, the Army base began reveille a second time.

After a communal breakfast of yesterday's homemade bread...quite delicious...and leftover beef, they celebrated their first church service, a thanksgiving, with Chuck the priest in charge. Eager hands found all the equipment and even the vestments, and most of the people were there, with newly contrite Terp and Raley in the front row, sitting together while Bear glared at them.

Fred Paxley, sitting with his wife, looked even grayer than usual, unshaven, and reeking of old alcohol and urine. Gritz Gresham also looked disheveled and distracted, as did Barry Taylor. Terry Taylor sat behind them, gray, old, and dapper in his uniform, complete with sword.

The group celebrated their first full communion since the earthquake, with the sunlight streaming in through partially repaired cracks. Singing, led by the monks, and Terry, and the girls, so many of them. Guitar by Hopi Jack, beautifully done, bagpipe by Poppy Roswell, organ...a genuine pump organ which had survived the earthquake...by that young journalist, who seemed so emotionally damaged. What was her name? Garth couldn't remember.

Little Tally Martin, who had been bitten badly on the hand by Hero the Service Dog earlier that week, seemed engrossed in the music, and filled with a silent radiance, next to her mother Patty, who now held her close and smiled at some secret reverie. A moment of peace, Garth thought.

Garth noticed Tiger Tanaka entering at the end of the service. A Buddhist in a Catholic community. What was that experience like? Was Tiger alienated from them in some way? Garth considered that he should ask, privately.

After the service, more people joined them in the coolness of the church and once again the women sat at a table before the gathering, with the three monks sitting off to the side. Belinda Jefferson was wearing a blue Victorian dress of about 1870's design. She began the meeting, as always, with news. There was no internet, media, or phone connection, the same as for the past few weeks. The monks relayed their news of their Big Sur experience and their travels, just as they had over dinner last night.

The women at the table then discussed the plan for the day.

Wood cutters including Paul Desault, and "Red Mike" Robinson, would cut up an already-down dry oak tree. There was some discussion about using precious gasoline for a chainsaw. The group's decision, reached by a hand vote, was to save the gasoline. They would keep using the antique two man crosscut saw which had been liberated and repurposed from the mission's ramshackle museum room. Some of the young men groaned and laughed when that decision was reached. The woodcutters were also the repair team, and they welcomed the mason Mike eagerly. He was young, and he seemed strong and healthy. That would be a good match, thought Garth. Also, he could teach.

Chuck the chorister monk was entrusted with the mission's church sanctuary, religious issues, and music. That would be interesting, thought Garth. Music. Organized music. The group agreed that the church services in the future might be conducted in Latin, as was traditional in the original mission days.

The group also decided that the kitchen crew would rotate out a few members to the medical team, headed by Dove, to alleviate boredom and share knowledge. Hugh the vintner eagerly joined the cooking staff with hopes of beginning some fermentation in the mission's old barrels. That brightened up the men considerably, Garth saw.

The teenagers, such as Akemi, thirteen years old and somewhat left out of the recent drama, Francesca, Ophelia, who wanted to spend all her time in the medical team, Hillary, who was still pining for her electronics, and who looked puffy and pale, Freddy Desault who was still grieving for his crushed mother, and Raley, who was definitely pining for Terp, would continue with their studies with Merry Thomas and Garth's mother from nine to two daily, as would the younger children such as Tally Martin. Then they would do chores with assigned work crews until after the evening meal, as would everyone else. Poppy Roswell asked Garth's mom to continue her after dinner history stories, which were becoming a favorite of everyone. That was possibly due to the absence of television, thought Garth. Several others murmured assent. Garth's mother asked Hillary to join her as an educator, to which Hillary grudgingly agreed. Typical teenage slouch, thought Garth.

Steve Sanchez, his son Stan Sanchez, Paolo Archuleta, and Beeston Brag were the technology team, and they reported that the solar panels were delivering consistent but limited power, enough to provide lights every night for the entire mission and charge most devices. They looked forward to establishing an internet system within the mission area, and computers could now be used locally. Smart phones could be used as self-sustaining devices as well. The problem was that there was very little connection to the outside world, and what tidbits they had received indicated dire conditions in the state.

"I want to thank you all for caring for me," said Deputy

Davis. Pike Davis, Garth remembered. Pike was a bit pale. He'd been working with the kitchen crew, on light duty.

"It was our honor," said Dove. Garth was startled to see that there was a hint of passion in her expression. Passion which was utterly absent when she looked at him, her husband. Best to do nothing, he thought.

"It's time for me to go," said Deputy Davis, "I'm healed enough to ride one of your horses and I need to report in."

"Your hand still doesn't work," replied Patty Martin. She also seemed very drawn to the young deputy, Garth saw.

"I still have to report in. I'm surprised nobody has come here yet," said Deputy Davis. "I'm slow. I'm still not 100%. But that's not an excuse. I need to go in."

"I'll visit the Army. Perhaps they'll pass on a message for you," said Garth.

Dove spoke up, "We need medical supplies anyway. We were low on antibiotics from the beginning. If Deputy Davis had gotten gangrene, then he probably would have lost his hand or his life. When Tally was bitten by the dog last week, I expected an infection but we were lucky and there was none. Therefore, I'd like more supplies, if we can get to a hospital."

"I'd like more news, plain and simple," added Bat Jefferson. "We really don't know what's going on out there, and we need to let somebody know we're here. Heck, maybe we can all just go home. Although I've learned a lot here, that would be for the best."

"So you're getting tired of us?" joked Katrina Paxley, who was on the cooking team.

Bat laughed, "Oh, no, I just miss my home, same as

everyone. I miss hot water. I admit it, I miss Netflix. We're all going to get tired of this campout soon enough."

"Then it's agreed? Garth goes to the Army, then we send out a large group to find someone outside?" Belinda Jefferson asked the group. "And if we can, we wind this up and head to our homes. But that comes later. All in favor of sending out a team, show me."

Almost all of the hands went up.

Garth looked: his daughter Francesca had kept her hand down. Raley had not raised an arm. Hopi Jack hadn't raised his hand. And his own mother had kept her hand down.

"Why? Why don't you want to go?" demanded Merry Thomas, apparently angry at the thought that someone might like their current situation. "I love you all, but I can't be quit of this place and its memories soon enough. I'd like to go away and never come back."

"Yes! YES!" said a small woman's voice from the back of the group. Garth looked. There was the young newscaster, now helping with teaching, and she was in tears.

"I want my phone back," said Hillary. "I'm sick of being stuck here in the dark."

"But why doesn't EVERYONE want to go?" asked Merry. "It's just common sense."

"Freedom," answered Francesca. "Freedom from style, freedom from all that stuff coming at us all day long. 'Buy this, like that, she's FAMOUS!' she mimicked. "Also I'm on a semi-permanent camping trip, I don't worry about makeup, and I'm healthy. No SAT tests. No grumpy school officials. It's better here than there."

"But our choices here are SO RESTRICTED!" replied Hillary. Out there in the world we have so much more!"

"And most of it we can't have, they just dangle it in front of us like a carrot in front of a mule," replied Francesca. "I know it's better to have good medicine, and dentists, and I know we need more. But here...here is better, day to day."

"Here is NOT BETTER!" shouted Fred Paxley, clearly drunk. "It's global warming here, just as much as there, so WE'RE ALL fracked!"

At this, Tiger Tanaka and Hopi Jack burst out laughing. The others had to join.

"Really people work like dogs all their lives so they can retire as we are living now," said Bear. "I know it's going to end. And yes, we'll need modern medicine and computers and the internet soon enough. But it's been good, and you've all been wonderful. We've got plenty of slow elk..."

Here people began to laugh again.

"But those men! What they did to us! What they did to me! I'll never forget, and never forgive," said the young newscaster, crying. "How can you ignore that?"

"Did we ignore it?" responded Terp, from near the back.

Garth turned and looked. Terp seemed to be a young, completely grown man, resplendent in his fullness.

"No, I mean that was as ugly as anything anywhere!" cried the young woman. "Murder and rape and violence! You mean that you LIKE IT? Did you LIKE killing them? Are you all insane?"

"What would you feel if that had happened with no earthquake?" responded Belinda.

"I would know that those men were safe behind bars, where they deserve to be!" shouted the young woman. "Not dead, murdered by...by...by vigilantes! Bodies buried out in the dirt!"

Silence. Nobody had any response to that.

Finally Garth's mother spoke. "Well, my dear, you are most welcome to go out to the world with whatever group makes the journey. I intend to stay here and savor for as long as possible."

"Savor what?" asked Terry Taylor, dapper in his cavalry uniform. How did he find the time to wash it? Garth wondered.

"Savor you all. Savor each day. I'm 102 years old and I lived alone back in Salinas, and let me tell you, it's a prison like that. Here, I'm free, and you are all stuck with me," said Garth's mother.

"There's a point there," said Francesca. "You are my grandmother but back in Salinas I barely saw you. School. Life. Now I feel free too."

"Seriously. Here I am with you, and you are with me, and we are all forced to live together," said Garth's mother. "Of all of us, I'm the one most likely to need medical and dental help, and it takes me all morning to walk to the bathroom and back."

Laughter. Garth's mother smiled and waited until it quieted.

"Let me clue you in, we are living in historic times, and I feel blessed to be here, and I rejoice in our togetherness. So let Garth go to the Army, and then whoever wishes will go out into the world, and I will stay here until I have to leave. Until they evict me. I suppose going back to our former homes is what we will need to do. Until then, like my granddaughter, I'm free."

Fort Hunter Liggett, California

Garth stood by the chain link fence. Inside, the base looked abandoned. He pushed the button. Nothing. He spoke into the intercom. No response. Time to wait for an answer. He turned and looked around the gate. Here was this base, surrounded by this double layer chain link and barbed wire, and the Army owned all this land, but the area inside the giant double fence encompassed an area only the size of a shopping mall. Big, but not even the size of a football stadium. Yet it looked abandoned. No helicopters going in or out. No people moving. Someone must be in residence because there had been a response to the bagpipes. But why was there no sign of life?

All around him, the dry landscape of summer lay baking in the sun. It would be ninety degrees today. His horse, Dogfood, looked sullen and overheated. It was time to ride back to the mission and begin the day.

Once in the saddle he realized that he had been able to get a good signal from near the base during his last visit, so he brought out his fully charged sat phone, and dialed Ernst in New York. There was a dial tone, and after two rings Ernst picked up the phone.

"Dad! Dad, my God it's great to hear from you!" said Ernst. He sounded far away.

"It's great to talk to you too!" said Garth loudly. "I love you and I hope everyone's well."

"Oh, well, lots is going on," said Ernst, somewhat hurriedly. "We are well. How are you?"

"We're surprisingly good. I think we're ready for this to be over, but after what happened we've been nervous about going out."

"Nobody's hurt?" said Ernst. "Great news. We didn't hear and we didn't know, so we were worried."

"We haven't been able to call, and we haven't had any outside contact for the past two weeks, since my last call. I just visited the U.S. Army base here, you know that one with the fences? Nobody's talking. It's like it's deserted. Can you tell me the news?"

"Lots is happening. Look, there's a denial of service all over the nation right now. Sporadic, but it's intentional. But we may not be able to talk long," said Ernst, talking rapidly.

"Holy Christ, what happened to the financial markets?" blurted Garth.

"Oh, it's a wipeout. Down about 15,000 points on the Dow. Down about 65%," replied Ernst.

"The clients..." responded Garth automatically.

"Calm down, Dad," said Ernst. "Look, ah, yes, it's down lots, and you haven't been in touch for some time, so I knew something was really wrong. It wasn't the quake that did the damage to the financial markets, it was the denial of service, and the yeast. And you DID give me control of the company, right?"

"Yeast? What did you do?" asked Garth coldly. Terrified to hear the answer.

"Well, after I took over management, I liquidated, then I shorted. Shorted big the morning of the first DOS. I bought inverse ETF's, exchange traded funds, big time."

"DOS?" responded Garth.

"Denial of Service," responded Ernst.

Reception was getting weaker. Garth pulled Dogfood to a halt. Hopefully he could stay in touch by staying close to the Army base. He said nothing.

"I can't hear you, Dad. I hope you are still there. Anyway I bought a bunch of those inverse triple leverage ETF's. And then a disease broke out in the Midwest, it started in Saint Louis. It's a yeast, actually, it's called something like Candida, and it kills about 30% of everyone who gets it. Loves hospitals and water and it's weaponized."

"You mean it's intentional," replied Garth.

"Absolutely. They don't know who turned it loose, but it's resistant to everything, and it's killing people, so the Feds have cut the nation in half in eastern Kansas. Second roadblocks at eastern Colorado. Nobody gets in or out."

"Jesus," replied Garth.

"I'd say that's right," replied Eric. There was a lot of static on the line. "Anyway that's when the stock market and the bond market really came unglued. We made millions of dollars on the short side."

"Bond market?" asked Garth.

"It crashed too. The supply of new debt is going to overwhelm the economy," replied Ernst.

"What now?" said Garth "Obviously you need to stay in control of this."

"Well, the state of California opened its border to Mexico, to compensate for the children being allegedly slaughtered. Still a lot of unrest. Rioting. Big cities are in big trouble. Big fires. Water supplies gone. Food shortages. The state government tried to arrest and evict the border patrol after that mass shooting of children. But here's the thing: those were doctored tapes. There was no mass murder of children."

"It didn't happen?" asked Garth.

"Didn't happen! Fake news! Computer graphics tape from a shoot 'em up video game, improved and enhanced. But that was after California declared open borders," replied Ernst.

"Open borders?" responded Garth, incredulously. "Who would want to come in?"

"Anyway the President responded by putting border patrol on the border between Nevada and California. And he tweeted..."

"Tweeted?" asked Garth.

"Social media. Anyway he tweeted something like, 'California and that rat Grantham can just slide into the ocean!' and then "Beach front property in Las Vegas!" said Ernst.

Ernst's voice was distorted and distant. It sounded like he was talking through a long plastic pipe.

"Is the President insane?" asked Garth.

"That's when Governor Grantham activated the National Guard in California and declared himself in charge and tried to take over all U.S. military bases inside California. He said that because of the emergency they were now under state control," added Ernst.

"That didn't go well," muttered Garth.

"Oh, no, the Governor announced that Federal troops represented the oppressive white patriarchy and that they should turn over all their gear for use by the enlightened state of California. He also declared a state of emergency and martial law, enforced by the National Guard."

"You've got the state versus the feds?" asked Garth incredulously. As an afterthought he added, "But Grantham's white!"

"That's when the financial markets really lost it. The California municipal bond market is down about 70%, depending upon the kind of bond," said Ernst's distant voice. "I'm afraid we got a bit burned on that one. We didn't get entirely out in time."

"What are we buying instead?" asked Garth.

"We're in cash, we are short bonds and the dollar, and we're into Euros and the Swiss Franc," responded Ernst.

"God, I'm glad you had the balls to take over," said Garth quietly. Below him, Dogfood shifted, bored. "Anyway that explains the Army. They're in hiding. No help to anyone, as ordered."

"Correctomundo! The President ordered all U.S. military forces to stand back and not engage, and let the state handle it all. They aren't supposed to help anyone so that explains that," responded Ernst.

"I guess we'll go out into the Salinas Valley tomorrow, or

the next day. Once we figure out who's going, and why," said Garth. "We're calling it 'the world" like it's different or some-thing. I expect it will be just fine. No big cities near us. Hey how about Wallace and the family? How are they?"

"Wallace? Oh, shit, Dad, Salinas is a mess, but Wallace and the family are apparently OK so far. The family is in Denmark, and life is normal there. I talked to Wallace last week and he's in a mess because..."

The line went silent. Static. Garth attempted to redial. No reception at all.

San Antonio Mission, California

Raley walked into the darkness of the old church and paused. Midday, and while the heat was building outside, the mission nave itself was cool. Still a hint of disinfectant, and a whiff of the candles they had burned earlier.

She walked quietly to a pew and sat down. Impulsively, she pulled down the kneeling bar from the pew in front of her, and she knelt. There was a scraping sound behind her, and she turned in disappointment. Somehow, she was hungry for solitude. She saw Francesca, walking up the aisle, carrying a book. An old book. Francesca nodded, smiled, and knelt beside her. Disappointment turned to a quiet completeness. Uncertain good feelings.

Francesca turned her attention towards the altar, and Raley looked there as well. She watched the dust in the beams of mid-morning light through the windows and the few unrepaired cracks. The altar: three statues, and four if you counted the avenging angel on top. She looked at Francesca, kneeling alongside. Francesca had her eyes closed, chin down, hands clasped, praying. A perfect picture of repose. Raley tried that. Nothing. A slight urge to fidget.

"Are you feeling anything?" whispered Francesca.

"Just that damn little pistol Poppy gave me. I've got it in my panties. Feels like I'm carrying an orange between my legs," said Raley.

Francesca's face worked as she tried to stifle her laughter. "That's not what I meant!" she whispered.

Both girls resumed their attempts at serenity.

Francesca began to snort quietly...." But....but carrying an orange between your knees WILL keep you safe!"

Now both girls struggled to avoid laughing.

"Look at that angel up there. The one on top. I mean, he's pissed. Feel like he's gonna come down here and spear me," said Raley.

Francesca kept her head down. Eyes closed. An attitude of contemplation. Then her face contorted with laughter.

"Wouldn't...be the first time," whispered Francesca.

"No...no...I mean...are you feelin' anything when you pray?" asked Raley.

"It's like talking to a frog," replied Francesca quietly. "Easy to do. The miracle's gonna be if the frog talks back."

"It gets easier the more you do it," said a small quiet voice behind them.

Raley turned and saw into the dark corner of the opposite

pew. There sat Mrs. Ericson, Francesca's grandmother, Garth's mother.

Francesca stood up and walked over, sat down alongside Mrs. Ericson.

"Grandma, can you get good at prayer, really?" asked Francesca.

"Can't say if God talks back. But yes, if you practice, it gets better. Perhaps it's like meditation," said Mrs. Ericson. "Why are you praying? What's on your mind?"

"Hmmm. Why am I praying? Can someone tell me why we're here? I didn't sign up for this earthquake n' stuff," said Raley. "The whole world is nuts."

"Nobody signs up for it, child. But what we do with it is all ours," said Mrs. Ericson.

"I'm praying because I'm afraid," said Francesca simply.

"Oh, we're all afraid," said Mrs. Ericson. "I'm 102 years old, and I'm still afraid. That's a bit surprising. I thought I'd be fearless by now. But here I am, still a child deep inside. And I know that life is just performance art anyway. Yes, I'm stuck here in this aging body in this aging building in a universe gone mad. I will die soon whatever happens, I know that. All I can do is face life with creativity and courage. It's all I've got. That, and love."

"What if everything we do is pointless?" said Francesca.

"That's the amazing part," said Mrs. Ericson. "It's surprising how much of life has meaning. That's where God DOES speak to us, I think. I've been surprised how the tiny little choices I made fifty years ago still have impact. Like there's a plan after all."

"So there's a plan," said Francesca. "We'll all be safe?"

"I wish I could say that's so, but the plan is much bigger than us, whatever it is," said Mrs. Ericson. "Some of us die young, and some later. The point is that while we're alive, we have the ability to create, to make something bigger than ourselves, at least to admire the momentary beauty of the world."

"What do I do with Terp?" said Raley. "I'm in over my head. I don't want to love him. I want to be free."

She felt surprised. The words had just fallen out of her. Unexpected.

"I keep thinking about those decisions I made sixty, fifty, forty years ago," said Mrs. Ericson. "I keep feeling regret for making selfish, momentary decisions, and I feel good about decisions I made which caused the world to be better. The lesson for me is that most of the time I could tell even back then what the right choice would be."

"You mean follow my heart?" said Raley.

"Raley, if I had followed my heart, I would have shot my husband ten times, abandoned the kids, run off to Kona with the handsome milkman, and I'd be dead thirty years ago from alcohol poisoning," said Mrs. Ericson. "No, don't follow your heart. Follow your soul. Follow your goodness. What's the best choice for the next thirty years?"

Francesca laughed, "So I can't shove Fred Paxley head-first into the shitters?"

Mrs. Ericson laughed, "Is 'shitter' the most lady-like term?"

Francesca raised the old book she was carrying. "I found this in the library."

"The Gallant Gallstone," read Mrs. Ericson. She laughed. "The author was a fascist named Ellsworth Toohey, I think. Back in the 1930's."

"It's the story of a gallstone who tries to be independent," said Francesca. "But he can't because he's still part of the body. I think the point is that we're trapped inside society."

"Nice parable," said Mrs. Ericson. "Evil message."

"Why evil?" asked Francesca.

"It's the same evil we're facing now, the same evil we've faced all my life," said Mrs. Ericson. "Think it over."

"I don't have time to think about what to do wit' Terp," said Raley. "It's all happening too fast. I never have time to think. I just respond."

"That, my dear, is why I sense greatness in both of you. Yes, we're stuck in a society of humanity. That's just the way it is. And yet, inside that society, the world is better when we dare to be ourselves, when we have the courage to act," said Mrs. Ericson. "You two have the courage to do the right thing."

"I'll know?" said Raley. "I'll know when the time is right?"

"No, no, it's not that simple. If you are like me you'll always be a bit confused," said Mrs. Ericson. "Just think of what is best for the next century. Best for you. Best for yours. Best for the world. Then do it with courage and grace."

"But how do you learn what's right?" asked Francesca.

"That's why I pray," replied Mrs. Ericson.

"We gotta get Fred back on the horse," said Hopi Jack. "He's crashing. Since his son died he hasn't been good, but now he's worse. Get him back on the horse. That's what my Grandmother would say, and she knew her stuff."

Garth looked at the campfire. It was getting late. They would have a big day tomorrow.

"Literally, back on a horse?" said Bear. "Where'd that idea come from?"

"See, my grandmother, back on'a Hopi Rez, she was a tribal elder. And she used to say you can be good on a horse or a drunk, but you can't be both. If we wanna get Fred off that hootch he's drinkin' we need to get him back onna horse," said Hopi Jack.

"I'd be tempted to be a drunk too, if my son was blown up in a friendly fire incident in Iraq. And I was career military. I gotta ask, for what?" said Bat tiredly. "My daughter's the police chief in Salinas and I worry about her every day. My God, if something were to happen to her, I'd probably just give it all up. But of course, nothing's going to happen, thank God."

"It's a scary time," said Bear. "It was scary before all this happened, but now it's worse."

"So, Hopi, have your ever seen a person get over alcoholism on a horse?"

"Well, there's me," said Hopi Jack. "I was getting started, as a teenager. Then my grandmother got involved and got me up every day at 4 AM regardless of how I felt, and put me on a horse. I used to get on the horse, and vomit, and she'd hand me lunch, and send me out after the sheep. Came a time when I woke up and didn't vomit and that was that."

"Followed by law school?" asked Bat.

"Well, that came a bit later. Thing is, my parents, pa was

Hopi, ma was white, you know, one of those women who thinks that everything Native American is mystical, until they don't have plumbing. Anyway, they got divorced, and they both moved away when I was, like, two. All I had were my clan, my grandparents," said Hopi. "After the horse I learned that the modern path of the warrior is education. So, yes, the horse led me to law school."

"So you talk like you are kickin' horseshit just for us uneducated types?" laughed Bear. "Good of you."

"Hey, when in Rome..' said Hopi Jack. "Just get Fred on a horse. He'll get better. Without a horse, he's doomed."

Salinas, California

"I HAVE WONDERFUL NEWS! WONDERFUL NEWS!" shouted Gillian McTavish from the stage.

Her amplified voice reverberated through the auditorium of the Salinas Cultural Center. Standing next to Gillian McTavish, a man translated her words into American Sign Language, gesticulating wildly. Wallace pondered that none of the emergency service workers, elected officials, and government employees called to this meeting had hearing impairments.

"Well, at least the translator is enthusiastic," muttered Bettina Ayala, sitting next to Wallace. "Perhaps there's a gymnastics show afterwards."

"Interpretive dance," replied Mickey, quietly. "By city officials."

"We're Fracked. The musical," said Tiny.

"A local politician's kazoo band, maybe?" whispered Dina Montero, sitting behind them.

"Shhhh. We've had a catastrophic earthquake, the US is going broke, and we've got ten thousand refugees from San Jose starving in strawberry fields north of town, quarantined because of the threat of Candida. I'm ready for good news," said Wallace.

"Don't forget, we're all still shitting in buckets," replied Bettina Ayala.

"You have a bucket? I don't have a bucket," said Tiny quietly. "When do I get a bucket?"

Wallace began to laugh silently. Calm it down, he thought.

"WONDERFUL WONDERFUL NEWS!" Gillian McTavish repeated on stage. "You already know how tough things are. You already know that your...our...pensions and social security are suspended. You've got all the bad news. It's time things turned around. And here it is: after weeks, MONTHS, of neglect by the shameful racist United States government, after decades of white privilege, California has finally had enough. To paraphrase our former President Obama in the 2020 Democratic National Convention, WE ALL KNOW HOW FAR THE DREADFUL REALITY OF LIFE IN THE UNITED STATES HAS STRAYED FROM THE MYTH! So now the United States is broken, defeated, the tired era of deception is over, and it is time for action!"

A pause. Silence. Wallace looked quickly around the dark auditorium. Shocked faces reflecting the stage light.

"Under the enlightened hand of our tireless Governor

Grantham, California declared its independence last night. WE ARE NOW OFFICIALLY PROUD CITIZENS OF THE REPUBLIC OF CALIFORNIA! WE ARE FREE!"

Scattered clapping. A few affirming shouts. A boo. Someone shouted, "What the frack?".

Mostly silence.

"NOW WE ARE FREE TO ASK THE REST OF THE WORLD FOR AID!" shouted Gillian McTavish.

Her amplified words echoed through the hall. The slender young man translating into American Sign Language was gesticulating wildly, his motions frenzied, struggling to translate all that had been said.

"Kid's gonna start breakdancing in a moment," muttered Bettina Ayala.

Wallace was stunned. The news seemed insane.

"THE PEOPLE'S REPUBLIC OF CHINA HAS PLEDGED WHATEVER IT TAKES TO HELP US! THEY WILL SEND EXPERTS TO GUIDE US IN THE NEW WAY OF LIVING, BEYOND CAPITALISM! WHATEVER IT TAKES! WE WILL RISE AGAIN! AND THERE WILL BE FOOD! AND OUR PENSIONS RESTORED!" shouted Gillian McTavish.

Noise now began to fill the cavernous theater. Gillian McTavish passed the microphone to Mayor Johnson.

"REDEVELOPMENT DOLLARS! PICTURE OUR WONDERFUL CITY, PART OF A GREATER REPUBLIC OF CALIFORNIA, SHINING, REBUILT, AND LARGER THAN EVER BEFORE, WITH NEW TALL BUILDINGS SHINING IN THE SUN!" shouted Happy Johnson, standing alongside Gillian McTavish on the stage. "A NEW BETTER

IMPROVED SALINAS! THE YOUNG FRESH VOICE OF THE COURAGEOUS FREE NEW ERA!"

People were too busy talking and shouting to notice him. Wallace saw that Happy Johnson was piqued by the crowd ignoring him. Mayor Johnson scanned the darkness beyond the spotlights, as though searching for affirmation.

"That's a stunner," said Bettina Ayala. "How do normal people who are already living here play a role in this brave new world?"

"Not sure I feel good about this," replied Wallace. "There's too much we don't know. The police are already marginalized. A new republic? I'm not sure that's legal or necessary."

"ATTENTION! ATTENTION!" shouted Happy Johnson. "We have to work out some details about how we're going to handle the transition!"

His amplified voice echoed in the hall and the American Sign Language translator vigorously translated, his face wearing an expression of magisterial indignation.

A giant image of a new flag appeared on the stage-wide screen behind Happy Johnson. It was the California state flag, with the bear removed and the red star made large and central, with the 'California Republic' made larger over the red stripe at the bottom of the flag.

"This is turning into a shit show," muttered Bettina Ayala. She began to rise.

People were getting up to leave, apparently repelled.

"Not so fast," said Happy Johnson from the stage.

"We now control your pensions and your paychecks and

the titles to your homes. Your compliance will ensure that we can keep the transition of your...our.... financial futures running smoothly," intoned Mayor Johnson. "Seriously, most of you have known me for decades. I'm a stand-up guy. I'll look after you. But you have to look after me. Us."

"Now the gloves come off," said Dina quietly.

"Until now we've been tolerant," said Happy Johnson. "The State...the Republic...has looked the other way while you've opposed the inevitable triumph of the people. But now, now that our redevelopment dollars are on the way from our benefactors, you WILL serve the people. Everybody, the time for doing your own thing has ended."

"We've been doing our own thing?" muttered Tiny.

"The police will be delegated to the role of community facilitators," said Happy Johnson. "There is too much bad blood in the community, too much anger over past police transgressions against people of color. So police, you will keep all your gear, keep your organization, but stay in the background to avoid community unrest. In your place, we are bringing in more young strike team personnel from outside to interact directly with the people. Members of the police force, these strike teams will have COMPLETE policing authority, and you WILL NOT INTERVENE regardless of whatever takes place, unless I or Gillian McTavish orders your involvement. Am I clear?"

Wallace could see Chief Jefferson in the front row, looking unhappy, saying nothing.

"The laws are going to change! Candida is already here, in the refugee camp in Prunedale, ten miles away from us! The

Republic of California has declared Martial Law. Chinese assistance will be arriving shortly, and they'll bring us food, but in the meantime, we're in lockdown. There is a curfew from 9 PM to 7 AM, and commerce is forbidden. New currency will be issued shortly. In the meantime, to smooth the flow of genuine information, the internet and cell phone systems will remain temporarily offline."

"They've been jammed?" said Mickey, quietly.

"If you have not yet moved your family to safekeeping with us, please do so immediately," said Happy Johnson. "Your family will be much safer with us at our new residential facility at Hartnell College. This Candida will hit the community hard, and your families will be safer in quarantine at Hartnell."

"THIS IS BULLSHIT! THIS IS ALL BULLSHIT!" shouted a young voice from the darkened stands.

"WHO SAID THAT?" shouted Gillian McTavish. "WHO SAID THAT? WHO IS SO REACTIONARY AS TO DRAG US DOWN JUST WHEN WE NEED SOLIDARITY?"

A figure stood. The spotlight swung and illuminated the solitary slender young police officer.

"Oh, frack, Mendoza," said Mickey. "Kid's too young to know when to shut up."

"Kid's got more guts than all of us put together," said Dina Montoya, quietly.

Chief Jefferson stood up and turned to face the young officer.

"OFFICER MENDOZA! SIT DOWN AND SHUT UP!" shouted Chief Jefferson, and she turned and faced the stage.

"My apologies, ma'am. And Sir," said Chief Jefferson deferentially, to the stage, bowing her head.

"Good for her," said Bettina Ayala. "A little groveling to placate the crazies."

"YOU WILL NOT ADDRESS ANYONE BY THOSE TERMS AGAIN!" bellowed Gillian McTavish, her amplified voice reverberating. "The Republic of California has decreed that henceforth we will use the gender-neutral term 'Mix' as a salutation. Got that everyone? Mix. Plural 'Mix-eye.' Now, Chief Jefferson, we forgive you, as you are a person of color. Now address us properly."

"Anyone else notice that these are white people on the stage? Talking down to a black woman?" muttered Dina Montero.

"Yes, Mix-eye," said Chief Jefferson, looking up to Gillian McTavish. "I'll take care of this young and misinformed officer, Mix-eye. He doesn't realize what he is saying."

"You do that, Chief Jefferson," said Happy Johnson from the stage. "And, Officer Mendoza, keep in mind that your pay, your pension, and your future are all with us. Officer Mendoza, your family is already with us at the rodeo ground stadium quarantine center. We are your future. Keep that in mind."

Near Jolon, California

They came up alongside the Jolon Road in a classic cavalry column of twos, with the Santa Barbara Lancers scattered up forward as scouts and the 1st Volunteers and then the Caballeros Visitadores in the main body. All in a column, as though they were on parade. After much discussion, they were armed, and after much discussion they were dressed in their historic finery and in their historic uniforms, as though to make a joke of their weaponry.

If anyone sees us, they'll think they ate some LSD with breakfast, Gritz Garwood had joked. He would know, thought Garth.

About half the people of the Mission had stayed behind, including most of the women and children and certainly Garth's mother, who could barely sit a horse. They had left a crew to guard the mission, but only just. Most of the able bodied were in this parade, mostly out of curiosity.

Since leaving the mission, they had encountered many cracks and crevasses in the roadbed and the surrounding hills, some perhaps 20 feet deep, even across the San Antonio River, utterly impossible for normal motorized vehicles. Somehow, though, the US Army convoy which had departed the base weeks ago had gotten across or around the earthquake-created ravines, leaving tracks in the freshly torn earth. Certainly no normal vehicles, except the most extreme four wheel drive machines, could travel here. To protect their horses' hooves, they rode alongside the shattered asphalt roads, in the dirt.

Garth's hopes for an easy journey were throttled by now, on this unseasonably hot day. They rode on dourly, red and perspiring, the horses' sweat foaming beneath the leather tack, while fatigue, ennui, and discouragement built within them and stilled their chatter. As they rode, Garth watched the people around him. The teenagers were all thriving, while Deputy Davis looked hot and pale and not at all as robust as he was pretending to be.

They saw that the highway bridges into King City were toppled down, giant concrete slabs of the overpass, black asphalt still incongruously sporting lane stripes, jumbled down into the river bed. The Salinas River and the Arroyo Seco River had liquefied in the earthquakes, leaving sandblows, ten foot high cones of sand, like giant ant nests in rows in the river bed, surrounded by impassable mud. Islands of brown reeds and trees rose above the quagmire and the river flowed cleanly in places. Garth wondered if the dams upstream had broken. There seemed to be more water in the riverbed than before. And beyond were huge columns of smoke, apparently wildfires burning in the mountains in the distance, and perhaps in the towns as well. Garth counted four giant pillars of smoke, far ahead.

The column halted as the mounted lancers began to ride down into the river bottom. As much from show as from any sense of need, they were incongruously carrying their lances, sticking straight up like great bamboo skewers, beflagged near the tips with small streaming gold and red Spanish pennants snapping in the mild wind, silver spear points gleaming.

With them, wearing modern clothing, was Hugh the vintner, along on a borrowed horse to send messages about his monastery and apparently unskilled at riding. He would be sore tonight, thought Garth. Alongside Hugh was Poppy Roswell, cartoonish in his Spanish Colonial finery. He was along to discover what had become of his home in the Santa Cruz mountains, and he had brought with him, incongruously, a four gauge flintlock blunderbuss, which Garth imagined was as effective as a slingshot, even loaded. But it was part of the costume.

"You've got to admit that's a sight you don't see every day," said Terry Taylor, behind Garth.

Garth pulled Dogfood to a recalcitrant stop in the bright warm sun. Dogfood wasn't happy about that: he could probably smell the water on the warm breeze out of the south. Garth swiveled in his saddle and looked back at his sweating and weary comrades.

"Think of what it must have been like, in 1846," added Terry Taylor. "Riding out to meet the Gringo Americans with knives tied to poles."

Garth studied Terry Taylor. He must be 85 years old, a riding accident ready to happen. This morning in the bright sunlight he looked extra damp and pallid. Yet his horse, Alastor, a gigantic black gelding, seemed unfazed, eager to move on. As Garth watched, Alastor seemed to look around Garth at the distant lancers. There was a light popping in the riverbed, like far off firecrackers.

"That's shooting!" shouted Bat Jefferson from somewhere in the back of the column. A Vietnam veteran. He should know, thought Garth.

"Let's pull back," said Garth to the group. "Let's wait for law enforcement. We don't know what we're getting into."

Deputy Davis began to ride forward. He didn't have a gun of any kind, since his hand was still disabled.

"Stay back, Pike," shouted Garth. "You can't do anything but make the situation worse if you go down. Stay BACK!"

Pike reined his horse and halted.

Garth looked down at the riverbed. A riderless lancer horse was running back towards them from behind a stand of reeds, splashing across the wet gray river cobbles and sand in the bright sunlight.

"I'd guess that our choices just got ree-duced," said Bear. "This thing's goin' to hell fast. Whoever that is, we have to go get him. Or her. Probably some idiot crazy dope grower with a .22 rifle."

Garth considered that silently. Beneath him Dogfood was nervous, shifting and swaying.

"Go go go!" came a shout from behind, and three brightly clad Caballeros Visitadores came racing past, their horses at a dead run, lances tilting down into the ready.

"STOP!" shouted Garth.

The Caballeros ignored him and continued to gallop full tilt down into the creek bed.

"We don't want this," said Garth to himself.

"Looks like we don't have a choice," said Bear. "We can't abandon whoever that is down there. You know we're pretty much all fake, right? Pretend warriors. Except for the veterans, we don't know shit."

Bat Jefferson bounced up on his galloping horse, with his wife Belinda riding close behind. "At the very least we can set up a base of fire," he said sharply. "In case we need it."

"Yes," said Garth. "Anything long range. The escopetas won't do. Get the cartridge guns forward."

"You three Taylors, you five ladies, Desault, follow me at the gallop. Garth, you go in and see what's going on," commanded Bat.

"I don't have any ammunition! Where's my ammo?" shouted a Caballero Visitadore somewhere in the column behind.

Bat reined his horse apart from the group and spurred it into a run, followed by a swarm of riders. Most of the women, Garth noticed. His daughters Francesca, with her older sister's scoped .30-06 rifle slung diagonally across her back, and Akemi with her .22 rifle. The other girls. How were they that eager? Certainly more people than Bat had expected. The group's speed increased as they rode away up the bluffs along the river to the north at a dead run.

Garth watched them go in their dust, distractedly, aware that he'd never seen anyone ride that rapidly before. He contemplated that the girls and the women were not only staying on their horses, but they seemed to be thriving. It was a relatively safe adventure to them. Bat and his wife Belinda would keep them from shooting anyone, and they were safer up there on the bluff than in the river bed. What the hell was going on down there in those reeds?

"Well Garth?" said Bear. "I'd rather chase Bat and Belinda's dust but we might as well see what's happening".

"Tiger, you have the Garand rifle, you cover 100 yards behind. Any kids left, stay here, dismount, take cover, form a circle with Tiger, Caballeros Visitadores stay as security for them. The rest, you are with me. Let's go," said Garth.

"I'm going with you," said Deputy Davis.

"Please stay here and provide a patrol base. Stand by to receive wounded and injured and anyone who gets confused. I'm probably overreacting. Just take care of everyone else and keep them out of the way."

"I guess you're right. Better safe than sorry," responded Deputy Davis, looking downcast. "If you contact any law enforcement, bring them here."

Garth nodded his agreement, and neck-reined Dogfood towards the riverbed. There were more shots, all from the reeds. Another lancer horse was down, motionless, in the water, and the rider was collapsed and still as well.

"Don't go straight at that down lancer, the shooters are off in those reeds to the right," said Bear. "They're using him as bait."

Bear sounded calm as glass. Like they were out on a leisurely pleasure ride, watching frogs. Are things that bad? Garth wondered as he led the column to the place Bear had indicated, away from the shooting, as an unseen bullet snapped over their heads. A few horses crow hopped nervously. Down into the water, about two feet deep. The reeds ahead were like an island, brown, about twenty feet tall. There was a sense of unreality.

A man dressed entirely in orange coveralls stepped rapidly around to the left of the reed island, wading in the water up to his knees, entirely bald, tattoos on his neck, and he pointed a pistol directly at Garth. Garth sat shocked into paralysis on his horse, about 50 yards distant from the man, and contemplated that the bore on that pistol looked gigantic, like a grenade launcher. Garth should move. He should do something. Yet he was frozen.

There was a shot, a snapping bullet from behind, and the man jerked over backwards and landed on his back in the water and began floating slowly away. Towards Salinas, to the north. Garth looked carefully at the man who had been shot: orange prisoner's pullover. Heavy set physique, not yet fat. Heavily tattooed face and arms, and a shaved head. The man's eyes were unnaturally bulging out, pushed out by the impact of the rifle bullet, which had left a crater about three inches wide in the center of his forehead. Around the man's waist was an old US military web pistol belt, with a black leather holster flapping empty in the river current.

Garth turned in the saddle and looked behind. There was Tiger Tanaka, dismounted, behind a downed cottonwood log, with the barrel of the M-1 Garand rifle sticking up. Tiger waved.

Garth turned in time to see a lancer...without a lance, for once...detach from the group on the opposite bluff, and gallop headlong down the steep slope into the river bed, hallooing and cheering as he came.

"Oh my God," said Bear, "That's Barry Taylor. Must be drunk again. Look at that fool wave that old flintlock horse pistol. Hope it's unloaded so he don't hurt himself."

Not much firepower there, Garth contemplated.

Hopi Jack had ridden up behind them. "I'm thinkin' we should wait for the sheriff. This is turning into one big-assed mess. Maybe we SHOULDN'T be here."

Garth pondered that this was wisdom. They could just ride away. But what about the downed lancers? And Tiger had just shot that man, and apparently killed him. They were committed. They were probably all going to prison.

Someone on the other side of the reeds shot the onrushing horse, and it, and Barry Taylor, twisted headlong into the river bed with a giant splash.

Garth had a sensation of extreme disconnection, extreme tiredness, extreme overheating. He was soaked with his own sweat. Dogfood was shifting his hooves beneath him, as though anxious. It was as though Garth was hearing everything through a paper tube. A shot came straight through the reeds, just ahead of him, fired from the other side of the reed island. There was another shot, and someone yelled behind him, "They grazed me! When are we going to stop messin' around?"

Somehow the words came into Garth's mouth, as though they had willed themselves. "Light up these reeds, the wind's at our back. Who's got a match?"

Hopi Jack leaned over his horse's neck and stuffed his bandana into the dry reed stems. Then he pulled his percussion Smith carbine out of its socket, gleaming in the bright sunlight. "You all's might want to back up for this".

Garth wheeled his horse back about ten feet, careful not to expose himself to more of the ongoing shooting from the other side of the reed island. Hopi Jack adjusted his percussion carbine on its across-the-chest sling in one hand, leaning again to poke the barrel deep into the dry reeds, which reached at least ten feet above him. There was a loud low thump, and a cloud of pungent sulfurous smoke. As the smoke cleared Garth heard a crackling and saw the glowing red of a rapidly leaping fire enveloping the reeds. A sensation of heat. Dense dark smoke rising. The horses began to shear away, and their riders fought to keep them concealed from the shooters beyond.

"Oh and here comes Paul Desault. It just gets better," muttered Bear. Garth looked up as the lancer on his distinctive cream-colored horse plunged down the distant slope, raising dust as he went, waving a giant flintlock pistol.

"He's tryin' to get to Barry," said a voice...Grits Garwood, a lancer. Grits should be in the rear, yet here he was. Out in the riverbed, Barry was sitting up, reaching down into the shallow water to attempt to stand.

"Just lay back down, Barry, and they maybe won't shoot you dead," muttered a young girl's voice. Sally-Beth Sanders.

Paul came charging on, his horse galloping, and a bullet took him in the chest and knocked him end over end out of the saddle, crashing into the rocks of the riverbed. The horse continued to run mindlessly across the wet riverbed.

"Paul's dead, or he's going to be dead. Maybe drown" said a woman's voice behind.

"The next fool down that hill's gonna be swinging a cutlass, or maybe a frackin' banjo, or a squirt gun," commented another voice.

Garth turned in the saddle and looked. There were about ten horse-mounted people behind him, men and women, and there was his own wife, Dove. Sweaty but alert. She was supposed to be on the bluff with Bat and Belinda. Say nothing. Do something.

It was like watching a football game, thought Garth, oddly detached. "Well, that's that. In for a penny, in for a pound," he muttered mostly to himself, and spurred Dogfood around the burning pyre of reeds. At that, he drew his percussion revolver, and prayed that it wouldn't misfire.

Dense smoke. As they cleared the heat of the burning vegetation, Garth was aware of another island of reeds, and it too was a conflagration, flames reaching up thirty feet. The fire had spread in the wind. Dogfood startled then moved off, and as he did, a man clad in orange came looming from the smoke, carrying a small Ruger Mini 14 rifle, and Hopi Jack cleanly shot him in the face with his single action pistol, and the horses jumped and skittered as the man fell limply, and Garth heard Gritz yell "Get his gun! Get his ammo! Get it all!" and they moved beyond the second stand of burning reeds. Confusion. Noise. Cloying smell of burning foliage. Garth could see only thirty yards ahead in the smoke.

Ahead in the grey haze there was a gaudily dressed Californio on horseback, clad completely in the old style with a bright red bandana under his black flat hat, holding a large flintlock blunderbuss. How had he gotten ahead of them? Could they be circling in the smoke? "It won't shoot, it won't shoot," said the man, and Garth recognized him as Poppy Roswell, holstered his unfired revolver, and said, "Aren't you supposed to be with the lancers?"

Poppy made a gesture of helplessness, frustration playing across his wrinkled face, and he said, "Gaucho just ran away with me!" and Garth reached out for the blunderbuss. Incongruous weapon. Ridiculous.

"Here, you've got it on half-cock" said Garth, cocking the hammer back and beginning to hand it to Poppy. There was a motion to Garth's left and a bang and a bullet snapped past his ear. Garth turned in his saddle, instinctively leveled the blunderbuss at the onrushing orange clad man and jerked the trigger. There was a flash next to his face as the priming ignited and an explosion of flame beyond the barrel and a blizzard of smoke and a punch of recoil. As the smoke cleared Garth could see the orange clad man stretched half in the water of the river bed, shredded and bleeding and completely still.

"What did you load this with?" asked Garth, astounded by the gigantic effect.

"Empty brass .22 casings and marbles," responded Poppy. "You know, non-lead, hunting legal. For the squirrels in the garden!"

Garth had no idea what to say. It dawned on him that he had just killed a man.

"Reload," he said, and handed the blunderbuss back to Poppy.

Poppy slung the blunderbuss, looked at the tattered orange-clothed man below them in the water, and shrugged. "No, I'm just done. I'm done with this. You fight. I'm done."

A group...three figures in camouflage Army uniforms, complete with helmets, came running at them through the smoke, arms upraised. "Don't shoot! Don't shoot! We're friendlies! U.S. Army! Please don't shoot!" A woman's voice.

Through the haze just behind the soldiers rushed two men in orange. No apparent weapons on them. Garth saw the rifles and pistols of his own group come up and point.

"Don't shoot them! Don't shoot them!" shouted one of the uniforms. "They're with us! They're on our side!"

Garth turned to his group. He realized it was all mixed up. People who weren't supposed to be there. "Gritz, Sally Beth, take four of your lancers and get these people to the rear, back to Deputy Davis. Search them first. The rest, follow me to flank this row of reeds so we can get Barry and Paul out of there, and recover anyone else who is down."

He wasn't even sure he was in charge, Garth thought. But someone needed to make a decision.

There was a "BUMP BUMP BUMP....BUMP BUMP BUMP" somewhere ahead and Bear yelled, "That's a fifty! That's a FIFTY MACHINE GUN!"

"What's going on?" Hopi Jack said from the saddle to one of the uniforms, a woman, standing below him. "What the hell is going on?"

"The earthquake, it went straight through the high-security prison in Soledad and broke it open like an egg. Most of the prisoners are just trying to stay alive, but some have rioted and taken the place over. Terrible. Only a few but they're ruthless," said the woman from under her Army helmet, looking up at him. Her face was dirty.

"How did you come to be here? Talk fast, then we'll deal with that fifty. Fast, please," said Hopi Jack.

"I'm Specialist Munz," said the woman. "I am in charge... was in charge...of a medical Humvee, a special medical supply truck. We were ambushed when we stopped for what we thought was a casualty on the road. The highway's ruined, and so we were on a side road. The prisoners killed two of us, and got our Humvee."

Garth was about to ask about that last comment when

the sound of the fifty machine gun filled the air, apparently shooting elsewhere. No bullets snapping overhead. "BUMP BUMP BUMP....BUMP BUMP BUMP" Shooting at the group on the bluff? The kids were in danger. A surge of adrenaline hit Garth and he forced himself to stay calm and focus.

"Specialist Munz, I'm Garth Ericson. I'm sorry. No time. Speak clearly. What's the armament?" asked Garth. He could see Bear and Dove gathering close. Bear's granddaughters, Garth's daughters, were up on that bluff.

Specialist Munz stared at him evenly. "M-2 on the turret. 300 rounds. Four M-4's, Four mags each. 2 M-9's. They've also got two Mini-14's from the prison guards."

She knelt on the sand and scraped up a mound. "We are here," she said and she put down a stick

"The Humvee is here and the last I saw, it's pointed that way," she put down several more sticks and drew a small arrow in the sand.

"If we don't get that gun we're all toast" said a voice from around him.

Garth pondered that they were already too damn close to that gun. They would have to go in on foot. He found himself dismounting, distracted, wondering "Why am I here?" pulling his .45-70 Marlin rifle from the saddle holster, feeling the sand crunch under his feet as he stepped down.

"Have we got any supporting arms? Any comm? Air? Any friendlies? Law enforcement? Anything?" asked Garth.

Specialist Munz shook her head. No. Then we'll need to move fast, thought Garth. "BUMP BUMP BUMP....BUMP

BUMP BUMP" in the distance. Garth noticed the others dismounting as well. He had forgotten to order that.

"The bad guys know what they're doing?" asked Bear.

"Aside from surprising us, they don't have a clue," responded Specialist Munz. "The military veterans in the prison population won't help them. Some of the convict veterans have been killed by the radicals for resisting. It's like a civil war there."

Garth, Bear and others knelt around the sand map. "We'll go around and catch them from the rear," said Garth, drawing in the sand. He felt terrified for the first time. Must keep moving.

"If you've got weapons, my Army team will go in around the other side, in front, and draw their fire. Time to get our damn fifty gun back," said Specialist Munz.

Garth drew that on the sand. It made sense. Someone handed Specialist Munz the M-4 taken from a convict earlier. She instantly checked the chamber and the magazine, and flipped on the safety. Garth could see the others arming as well. One young girl in Army uniform, looking like a young teenager with her helmet too big, was in tears, standing back.

"She holds the horses with my crew," Garth motioned at the sobbing girl.

Specialist Munz nodded, turned, and walked into the smoke with three other soldiers, muttering, "Let's kick some ass. Payback's a bitch."

Garth stood, holding his Marlin .45-70. Quickly he selected four of the closest 1st volunteers and they walked together around the flaming reeds. Suddenly the "BUMP

BUMP BUMP BUMP BUMP BUMP "BUMP BUMP BUMP BUMP BUMP BUMP"" of the fifty caliber machine gun became one long roar, and Garth began to run. In the smoke he saw a man in orange, kneeling, facing him about 10 feet away, bringing up an M-4, and Dove, his wife... Dove? Why was she there...fired her double barreled shotgun, both barrels, and the man's body jerked and there was a mist of red behind him as he clutched at the side of the Humvee, and they rushed on, and there was the Humvee, and the man in the turret was swiveling it towards them, still firing in great gouts of red flame and the muzzle blast he could feel in his chest, oh so terrifying, and then there was a shot from a gun next to him and the man ducked down inside the turret as it moved. The man in the turret stood up again and someone from the side...Specialist Munz?...shot him in the head, and there was sudden silence, and the man's head tilted sideways as he sank back down inside the Humvee, and another man in orange stood up alongside the Humvee in surrender, and suddenly a lance erupted from the front of his chest, incongruously, Garth thought, and there was a lancer on horseback behind screaming "Santiago! Santiago!" as the man writhed screaming impaled on the lance, and then blood was pouring from the man's mouth as he clutched at his chest, and the lancer behind, backing his horse, pulled the lance back and out the man's chest. The shining lance head seemed to disappear and made a slight pop and the man was on his knees coughing blood, and there was Specialist Munz looming over him, and she said, "Hurts, doesn't it?" and he died.

Silence. Silence. One more shot. No more.

The smoke was so thick. It felt suffocating, and hot. Garth looked up and saw that there was blue sky directly above. Over the distant town of Soledad there rose a plume of smoke as big as a wildfire, at least a mile wide. Suddenly he felt very very tired.

Salinas, California

"The elites always look after themselves," Katy Martinez said across the fire pit. The stars were brilliant overhead. No rain tonight, apparently. Wallace was feeling the shock of the earlier announcement, and he had described it to Katy. Voice low. Late at night, everyone else asleep.

"Do you think it was a good idea? The Republic of California? What does your family think? What do you think?" said Wallace.

"What do you know about me?" responded Katy.

"I know you are strong. You are courageous. You are extremely giving. You are intelligent. You didn't have to give Tiny, Mickey, or me a patch in the back yard for our tent, the ability to stay clean, and the food has been exceptional. I can't thank you enough." said Wallace.

"That all?" asked Katy, her voice breaking. "Tiny and Margarita seem to have found more."

She smiled widely, and it was a rich, warm, promising smile in the firelight. Wallace saw with surprise that there were tears in her eyes.

"You must have tremendous organizational skills to keep all these people fed, and watered, and sheltered," said Wallace.

"Oh that," she said, wiping a tear away. "This wonderful community."

"Why the tears?" asked Wallace. "What's up?"

""I'm thinking of my husband's corpse and it's more than I can stand. Where is it? Where is HE? In heaven, in hell, or nowhere, just gone? And you know, my babies, they are three and five years old, and they ask, and I don't have answers."

"We've seen enough death, haven't we?" replied Wallace.

"I mean, I'm about to have a mental breakdown. My husband died for what? So a governor could become a dictator?" she said.

"I don't know what to think about it. I'm afraid to even guess," he replied.

They stared silently at the fire for some time. Then she began to look at him, staring across the flames. She was too beautiful, he thought.

"Where did you go to college?" she asked.

"Oh, political science, a BA, at UC Davis. I think my father thought it was a useless degree," replied Wallace. "After the Army. GI bill. Then the police department."

"I went to UC San Diego, Public Policy, with my MBA from UCLA," she replied.

"What...what are you doing here?" he asked.

"I was the Chief Financial Officer for that little startup bank in Monterey, you know, Central Coast Western Bank. I was bilingual, I loved numbers, so I got in on the startup," she replied, staring at the fire. "Before that I worked in San Francisco, for Global Bank. But I wanted to be with my family, closer to home, so I moved here, and met Fernando."

"Fernando was your husband?" asked Wallace. "How did you come to be here, on this street, during the earthquake?"

"Ahhh, well, Fernando, God bless that wonderful man. A blessing. A perfect husband. He and I, we were a power couple. Rotary, Chamber of Commerce. All those made-up fundraisers and awards. But when I had the babies, I wanted to be near my parents, for some childcare, for some love. Some tradition. Spanish language in the home, you know? And then COVID shut everything down, and I decided I would just work from home. A little less pay, a little more joy."

"Wow. I had no idea," said Wallace.

He was surprised by mild feelings of jealousy. Towards Fernando or towards their past life together?

"Thought I was just a little chica-mommacita?" she said, smiling.

"Ummmm," said Wallace.

"Actually this has been the most rewarding time of my life, in some ways," said Katy. "You're right, we've done a lot. Nobody messes around with us. They are afraid of you, I think."

"Mostly afraid of Tiny and Diablo, maybe," said Wallace.

They both watched the fire for a moment.

"Here's the thing. I still have my contacts, in the community, and around," said Katy.

"What are they telling you?" asked Wallace, now on guard.

"I know that there is no Candida in California. Oh, it's

quite real in the Midwest, but the nearest case is in Elko. That's in Nevada," she said.

"Ahuh. You got this from?" said Wallace

"The head of the hospital where Fernando worked. I went there seeking Fernando's remains, but they were already gone. I gave the man a burrito. He was grateful."

"You make great burritos," said Wallace quietly. His mind was spinning.

"I know that they don't know where the internet denial of service attacks are originating. But the attacks have been successful for whoever is doing them. They've shut down most of the nation's power and communications. Lights out!" said Katy.

"We are under attack but we don't know who that enemy is," said Wallace.

Katy continued, "Also Candida is kicking the hell out of the Midwest. It might be killing more people than the earthquake killed here. Candida makes COVID look like a summer cold. It's got to be a weaponized agent. Like it was designed for this."

"Jeez," said Wallace. "That gave the California government the reason to make their move. But who would slaughter people intentionally with a weapon like Candida? I mean, men, women, kids?"

"The Chinese dumped their U.S. Treasuries, crashed the bond market, and then offered to bail out California, so how's THAT for intent?" she said. "California will be part of China's 'belt and road" initiative. As far as I know, nobody knows enough to accuse anyone."

"It begins to make sense, from a crazy perspective," said Wallace. "But what should we do? What should I do?"

Silence. Wallace considered that she probably didn't know what to say.

"You should want me," she responded quietly, and laughed dismissively.

Wallace looked at her. Then he looked at the fire and said, "I have a family in Denmark."

"I see it in your eyes, Wallace," she said. "I'm not blind. But I need to move forward. Every day I'm more desperate, more tired, more discouraged. I'm not strong enough for this. Soon I'm gonna collapse. If I do that, it's not gonna be good for anyone, especially my children. I HAVE to start living again, to keep the kids alive. I need you to want me. Even if we don't do anything about it. Please. Even if we fake it."

Wallace stared at the fire. Turbulent mixed feelings.

She poked the fire and went on, "If I seduce you, if we simply have sex, that isn't love, that's only my own need. I know I'm crazy now, with my husband dead and my life in ruins. But I can't let this terrible experience consume me, I can't permit myself to give up, and I can't allow myself to consume anyone else. Real love is to send you back to your family alive, healthy, well-fed, with honor. We both have to get through this. Together, and apart."

"Yes," said Wallace. "Together, and apart."

His own need, his own emptiness was sweeping over him, rendering him almost immobile, almost speechless.

"I love that you care for me like you do. With you I'm not just serving people. I like the way you look at me," Katy said. "I love the way we talk each night. Like you're coming home from work. I crave it. Let's just agree: during this crisis, we need each other. That's good. That will also keep us away from anyone else, and give us both a dream. Need but don't touch. We can be a power couple, in our own way, if we go forward with honor. When all this is over, we can go apart and send each other postcards at Christmas."

"When this is over we can friend each other on Facebook," laughed Wallace.

"You see, there it is, right now in this dung heap we've found something to laugh about," she said. "Let us help each other to think of beautiful things. Beautiful possibilities."

"Can we do that?" asked Wallace. "And stay respectful?"

"It will be our project," she said, and she laughed. "I will dream of a golden future, even if it can never be real. The prospect will keep us sane."

"What about the Republic of California?" asked Wallace.

"My grandparents came here in 1920 to escape the political chaos in Zacatecas," said Katy. "If I wanted to be Mexican, I'd live there. "'Mi patria', as you say, is the United States. For me, the Spanish language is the language of Los Estados Unidos and it always has been. Many of us Hispanics here feel the same. Don't forget that."

San Antonio Mission, California

Garth awoke to the sound of retching, and the excited talk of the girls. In the darkness he took time to orient himself, as he sat up. Dove was in her own cot, in her own sleeping bag, pushed against the other wall of the tent. Garth swung his legs into his cavalry boots. The full force of summer had arrived. It would be hot again today, perhaps 100 degrees, so an early rise was a good thing anyway. He checked his wristwatch, which was solar powered: 3:40 AM. Might as well get up.

Somehow he was conscious of his need for uniform correctness. That had become a habit: to dress like an Army officer in the 1870's. Why that was important was uncertain to him, but there it was. Shirt on, he stepped out into the darkness.

Garth contemplated that in a few months, everybody would be moving into the priests' cells in the mission, each to their own room, with running water and electric lights, thanks to the solar panels and the plumbing crew. Putting the tents away in time for winter. That would be very different. His mother was already ensconced in such a room, nearer the bathroom. Garth felt a surge of gratitude to all the people who had been working so hard to repair the building. Steve Sanchez. Paolo. Poppy. So many others.

And of course they might also leave at any moment, when the situation outside stabilized. They would all go back to their homes, their internet, their lawns. Someday that would happen. Meanwhile they were here.

The girls were gathered in the darkness between the tents around Raley, who was bent over at the waist, a pool of pale vomit between her feet. She looked up at Garth and smiled wanly. The girls chattered among themselves, expressing their concern to Raley. Did she need anything? Did she need water? Did she need to lie down?

"Food poisoning? The flu?" asked Bear, behind Garth.

Specialist Munz, first name Renalyn, Garth remembered, came out of the darkness wrapped in an Army blanket and extended an electronic thermometer to Raley's forehead.

"96.8," she reported. "No fever. Did you eat anything unusual last night?"

Raley shook her head negatively, "I'm fine, guys, really."

Then she vomited again, with liquid splashing sounds in the darkness, directly between her feet.

"Good aim," said Francesca. The other girls laughed. Behind them the youngest GI, the teen girl who had been so overwhelmed in the river fight, stood smiling. Annie, Garth recalled. Annie Camacho. 19. She had been just out of boot camp at the river fight. She seemed more at home with the girls than the adults. She slept with the girls in their modern tent, and Garth had heard them all talking late into the night. She was a hard worker and she fit right in.

"When was your last period?" asked Dove's voice, behind Garth.

Silence all around. Raley smiled ruefully towards Dove, who responded with a half-smile of her own. She took some time to look around at everyone. By now, Belinda and Bat Jefferson had joined the group. In the distance, Garth could hear Hero the service dog howling, off chasing something in the night, and he could hear others waking in their tents, the daily ablutions of an early morning.

"Three months ago. I thought I missed my period from stress," replied Raley.

"Oh shit!" said Hillary.

"NOT SHIT!" said Raley angrily. "If I'm pregnant then BRING IT! BRING IT ON! Five dead in that goddamned river fight, and Mr. Desault is in the medical ward dying, and it's the fracking end of the world. I'm scared. Terp's the best thing."

Garth realized that Freddy Desault, age fourteen, who deeply loved his father and was in complete shock over his wounding, was standing there next to the girls, holding both his hands over both eyes, suddenly beginning to sob. Ophelia and Patty Martin were moving to comfort him. Meanwhile, Raley began to cry as well.

"And...and I don't know if Terp wants this baby or not. I'm seventeen and he's nineteen, and dammit, it's been so much."

Patty Martin was reaching for her as well. Raley gently fended off her attempted hug by grabbing her hand, holding it, and talking directly to her.

"I know. I know it's been hard," said Patty Martin. "But a baby?"

"Terp is wonderful, and he's strong," replied Raley, "and the only hope I've had on this earth has been in his eyes. If I'm pregnant then maybe this baby is here to save us all."

"Well," said Patty Martin, looking imploringly at the group.

"Young lady," began Bear. "As your grandfather, I feel..."

"Young lady my ass," responded Raley. "Somebody's gotta live around here. I made a choice and I loved every second with Terp. You people all rattle on about history. Well this, right here, right now, is history. I don't know if Terp wants this baby or not...I don't even know if he loves me."

"I do," came a voice behind them all. Heads turned.

There was Terp, with his father Barry, who still had a bandage from the river fight wrapped around his head, and grandfather Terry. Terp was dressed incongruously in large Star Trek pajamas, with flip flop plastic sandals on his feet.

"I do want this baby. I DO! I want you, even if you aren't pregnant, and I want to marry you," said Terp, as though nobody else was there.

"Terp, you are a dumbass," said Terp's father Barry, standing next to him. "You don't have to do this. Just let her have her baby and we'll work this out later."

"Now, Barry, let's think this through," said Terry Taylor, reaching and touching his son's shoulder.

Francesca handed a tin cup of liquid to Raley, who rinsed out her mouth, leaned over, and spat.

"Too young to marry, in my book," said Bear, looking at Terp. "What the frack were you doing with my granddaughter?"

"That seems obvious and self-explanatory," said Renalyn Munz.

"I love you," said Bear abruptly to Raley. "Listen anyway. I'll support you in this. I'd rather you had waited. I'd rather you were both more educated. I'd rather the earthquake hadn't happened at all."

"She should get an abortion," said another voice, harshly. Garth looked. Fred Paxley.

"The world's going to hell. Global warming. Seriously, anyone who has a baby in this giant shitstorm of a world deserves whatever happens to them," said Fred.

"An abortion is not what I want," said Raley.

"That's because you're young and ignorant," said Fred. "Seriously, the most educated women, celebrities even, now realize that having a child in this era is a disaster. They just aren't having any kids at all. So if anyone's got a way to end this pregnancy right now, I say we end it."

"I wasn't aware we were voting," said another voice. Hopi Jack.

"I don't think we have the medical skills to do an abortion safely, even if you could find someone do it. I won't," added Dove. "The parents are two healthy young people. They love each other. Why not leave it alone?"

"We should vote. Another mouth to feed. Another muling little grub. You can squirt it out, but we're all going to have to feed it," said Fred.

"Mister Paxley," responded Raley, "Thanks for your advice, but we don't even know if I'm pregnant, really."

At this point, Hero the service dog threaded his way between the people and began lapping the vomit between Raley's feet.

"Ewwww!" said Hillary, and pulled Hero away roughly by his collar.

"Hey! Be nice to Hero! He's only trying to clean up. You can see how much he wants to be included in this discussion," said Poppy Roswell. "And by the way, my two cents is that it would be nuts to bring a baby into this world after what's happened. It's better to end the child right now instead of bringing the little soul into this world of pain."

"See? Global warming," replied Fred Paxley. "We're all

fracked. We don't need another mouth to feed. I say flush it. And I thank Gaia that my wife and I had only one child."

"If your ancestors were as reluctant to have babies as you are, you wouldn't be here," said Bat to Fred. "What if my African American ancestors had given in to despair through centuries of slavery and bigotry?"

"No personal attacks, please," said Patty Martin.

"Yeah, Bat, maybe we need a talking stick or something," laughed Steve Sanchez.

"Patty, who made you frackin' God?" said another slurred voice. Gritz Garwood.

Drunk again, Garth thought. Where in hell were they getting the alcohol? He thought. And why the hell weren't they sharing?

"Hey, tone it down!" said another. Pike Davis. "Let's be kind."

"We're talking about the marriage of two children here," said Poppy Roswell.

You know seventeen and nineteen is very young for marriage and a child," said Terry Taylor. "But it's been done. I mean, in the past people have married at that age, routinely. And we seem to be living in a new era."

"Patty, you are a psychologist yet you married a cheater. Like you can help anyone," muttered Gritz.

Garth saw Freddy glaring in the darkness at the man who had just insulted his mother.

"Gritz, you drunk-ass turd, you shut up. Don't ruin it for these good folk," said a voice. Sally Beth Sanders. "Besides we're all screwed up. Jus' some of us know it."

"Marriage my ass. It's all about sex, lust, two kids with out of control hormones making the two headed beast," said Fred. "Naked in the creek fornicating like bunnies."

"Fred, perhaps we should have spent a little more time naked in the creek like bunnies ourselves," said a voice. Katrina Paxley, Fred's wife. "Perhaps then you wouldn't be as you are."

"Please, please, stay on topic," came the voice of Patty Martin.

"All I know is that I have big regrets, and I don't like what's happening here, but I wish I had more children," said Katrina, who began to sob.

"Do we have anything to discuss?" said Hopi Jack. "Seems to me this is between Terp and Raley, and they seem to have decided."

"So, what, we just sprout bastard babies like growing weeds? Everybody screwing in the shrubs?" said Poppy Roswell. "We don't need babies around here!"

"Actually it's a natural response to death and crisis," said Terry Taylor. "More natural and less neurotic than getting drunk. These young people are actually healthier and braver than many of the rest of us."

"I can marry them," came a new voice in the darkness. Chuck, Garth realized. The chorister. A genuine priest.

"It's an opportunity for hope. Why not have a genuine wedding?" said Chuck.

"Oh, that's disgusting," responded Fred Paxley, moving away from Katrina through the crowd. He stood next to Garth, and Garth realized that once again, Fred reeked of old sweat and booze. Where were they getting the alcohol?

"Terp, young fella, you should make this official, before our judgmental friends ruin the moment," said Terry Taylor.

Terp walked through the people until he reached Raley, who, lifting the hem of her bathrobe, stepped over the pool of vomit to meet him.

"Please marry me," said Terp. "I love you."

Garth waited for him to say more. Nothing. Then he was aware of Katrina Paxley, standing next to Terp, taking his hand. "I don't have any more children, my husband's a drunk, and right now you are as close to a son as I've got. Here's my engagement ring. Put it to good use."

Terp held up the ring. A sapphire. It sparkled briefly in the half light. He hesitated, looking at it.

"Do it," said Katrina Paxley. "Do it in the name of my lost son."

Terp took Raley's left hand in both of his and held the ring poised before her finger.

"Please marry me," he said again.

"Yes. As soon as possible," responded Raley, beaming in the sparse light of the few battery powered light bulbs.

"God, what a circus," mumbled Gritz. "I can't wait to get out of here."

"Gritz, just shut the frack up," responded Sally Beth Sanders "Ya' all ruinin' the moment. My God, you'd fart in church."

The group began to break up, with a few chuckles at that last comment. Gritz probably WOULD fart in church, thought Garth.

Suddenly, there was a flash in the sky, far to the north, as if a meteor had fallen to earth, and for an instant the world was bright as daylight again, and Garth could see everyone's expressions turn from delight or puzzlement to horror as the sky to the north blinked into daylight, and then the light went out as people shouted in fear. As the light extinguished, Garth could see Raley holding on to Terp, hugging Terp, and then there was a distant crack and boom like thunder, and everyone stood frozen, too uncertain to move.

"WHAT THE HELL WAS THAT?" shouted Poppy Roswell in the darkness.

There was a rumble in the ground and the earth shook slightly beneath their feet.

"Another earthquake?" asked Katrina Paxley.

Another great flash, this time to the south, and suddenly it was almost daylight again, almost as bright as before, and again Garth could see everyone, everything, the mission beyond the gathering, the oak tree, and Hero the service dog once again, unnoticed, lapping up the vomit. There was less shouting after the second flash.

Garth heard Dove say, "Oh my!" and Francesca clutched his arm, and Tiger Tanaka hollered "Everyone stand still!"

Then darkness flooded back in, and again there was a crack and a boom like another thunderbolt, this time coming out of the south, and again the earth moved, a small earthquake beneath their feet.

"Those were explosions," said Bat Jefferson.

"Agreed. Big," said Renalyn Munz.

"Anyone got cell? Satellite?" asked Merry Thomas.

Nobody had a device with them.

"Those were explosions, and one was to the north of us, and one was to the south of us," said Bat. "Coordinated. LA and San Francisco."

"But we don't know what they were," responded Poppy. "I've heard of flashes of light after earthquakes.'

"Well, it's true that we don't know what they were," said Renalyn Munz. "But we DO know that they were explosions."

"Nobody's goin' back to bed, that's for damned straight," added Bear.

People were mulling around as the dawn rose over them to the east. There seemed to be a red glow to the south.

"What's to be done?" said Garth, mostly to himself.

"People still need to eat. They still need to wash. Life must go on. We don't even know what happened," said Garth's mother. Somehow she had gotten up as well.

Garth noticed that Dove, Francesca, and Ophelia were hastening to the medical clinic. As though the explosions had somehow injured the patients.

'Who's on watch?" asked Garth.

"The young guns. Paolo, Beeston, Stan," responded Steve Sanchez.

"Ok, send in the girls to double that, especially Francesca, then let's break this up and make breakfast. Meeting after. Agree?" said Bat, loudly.

A chorus of agree's echoed from the group, and the remaining people began to scatter.

A small cluster, mostly of girls and women, clustered around Raley and Terp. Chuck the chorister among them.

Renalyn Munz walked over to Garth, Bear, Pike, Bat and Belinda as they walked back to their tents.

"I didn't want to say anything to the big group," she said quietly. "But you know I'm in medical logistics. All those medical supplies. I'm not really a nurse. Before that, I did my first enlistment in NBC."

"NBC?" asked Belinda.

"Nuclear, Biological, Chemical," said Renalyn. "We had training in how to recognize all the signs of different weapons, you know, the big weapons."

"Big weapons?" asked Belinda.

"Yes, you know, Nuclear, Biological, Chemical," replied Renalyn.

"What do you think?" replied Belinda.

"Of course I can't be sure," replied Renalyn.

"What's your best guess?" asked Garth.

"Well, those two flashes looked and behaved a lot like tactical nucs," said Renalyn.

Garth's blood froze. He focused on his breathing.

"You're right," he responded. "Big flash, big noise, ground wave."

"Tac nuc, not big. Far away," she said. "I've got an ambient radiation detector in the Humvee, remember?"

"Please go see what it recorded," said Garth.

"Meanwhile life will go on," commented Bat.

"We gotta go back out," said Pike. "The river fight was

rough, but it can't all be that bad. Meanwhile we don't know what's going on. It's damned time I did my job."

Salinas High School Football Stadium, Salinas, California

Wallace heard the helicopters before he saw them. The sun had set several hours ago. There was a natural lingering red light to the west, over the Pacific Ocean. The red sky meant there was a wildfire burning somewhere. Here in the Salinas High School football stadium, which was known as "the Pit" in the community, only a few lights were on to illuminate the field, so as not to blind the pilots. Now as the helicopters roared just overhead, Wallace could see them clearly. HH-60's, probably Air National Guard, bigger helicopters, more capacity. They circled. Surely in this small space they would land one at a time.

Wallace looked up into the high clouds in the darkness, no stars, and his hand reached instinctively for the bellows pocket of his utility pants. It was still there, a secret treasure. A burrito, handed to him by Katy just an hour ago, warm chili verde, although where they had gotten the meat was any-one's guess. Hunger was beginning to be a crisis. Hopefully these strike teams could help. Protect the burrito. It was still warm. Later when time permitted, he would savor it deeply. Something to anticipate.

The first helicopter came in to land, flared, set down. The rear doors slid open, and the strike team began to climb out of the passenger compartment. There were six of them, and they were young, very young, and nervous, and mostly Anglo, clothed in fresh green janitor clothes, cheap clothing, green ball caps, like a crew of kids picking up after a movie or a baseball game. They were armed, surprisingly. Why should they be armed? Alarming. Wallace noticed a variety of military weapons.

One young man, blonde, bearded, with a red beret, long unwashed honey-colored hair, seemed to be in charge. He directed the others to the far corner of the field, near the exit. Then he walked about thirty yards away from the helicopter, stood theatrically, lit up a cigarette and stared at Wallace in a commanding manner. Kid doesn't have a clue, thought Wallace. The boy was wearing a Makarov Soviet pistol in a military surplus holster and carrying an AK-47. Commie guns, thought Wallace. Now why would that be?

"I'm Fidel," pronounced the young man, with an artificially low voice. "Fidel Gutierrez. I am in charge here."

The helicopter's engine became louder as it began to take off.

"We need to protect the people," shouted Fidel, over the engine noise as the helicopter lifted off. It rose slowly into the darkness.

"Against what?" shouted Wallace into the noise.

There was a flash, as though someone had lit off a giant strobe light, to the north. Blindingly bright. In the instantaneous illumination, Wallace saw the helicopter, about one hundred yards into the sky, canted to fly forward. Above and behind it the other helicopter was turning to land. The flash was so bright. The helicopters seemed frozen in time.

A noise, a great bang, shocking, ear-splitting, and a sharp sudden wind from the north, and Wallace watched the scoreboard blow down, and he thought, tornado? Another earthquake? He looked up. The helicopter directly above them was on its side, impossibly, and the other helicopter was spinning into a sharp turn, and there was wind noise, and then silence, and then the helicopter above them plunged into the bleachers and exploded, and the rotors flew off and up and over and one blade...alarmingly bigger and bigger as it flew towards them...sliced Fidel Gutierrez in half not thirty feet from Wallace. In half. It embedded itself in the brand new expensive bright green artificial turf, like a new signpost. The tail rotor broke free and spun away, In the blazing tangle, someone shrieked in despair and pain, briefly, and was silent while the flames grew loud and the conflagration in the bleachers grew. There were shouts from the other members of the strike team, unseen in the darkness beyond the fire.

Wallace simply stood there, shocked, wanting to run, not wanting to show fear, and not knowing where to run in any case. Noise outside the stadium: the other helicopters engine grinding, uneven, then a crash somewhere beyond, and rising fireball somewhere over towards the community YMCA. Shock. But he must move. He turned on his headlamp.

He strode over where Fidel lay, literally cut in half, twenty feet of his small intestine snaking across the artificial turf from where his belt had been. Such a great length of intestine, steaming in the night. Wallace forced himself to kneel down. Fidel was trying to speak, staring straight up. Wallace leaned closer.

"Too soon. Too soon. Too soon," Fidel was whispering.

"Too soon?" said Wallace.

There was no use lying to this man, to tell him that all would be well. A fleeting image of standing up and loading his shotgun and ending Fidel's misery.

Fidel shifted his gaze and stared at him. Wallace reached down and took his hand and held it as Fidel quickly died.

Wallace stood up, fully erect, to find the other five members of the strike team gathered around him watching.

"What's too soon?" Wallace asked them.

"I.... I don't know," said a young woman. "I don't know what he meant. Perhaps we got here too soon. We didn't know it was going to be like this. We didn't know."

The girl had short purple and pink-dyed hair, black-framed glasses, early 20's, very European, and seemed in shock.

"We don't know what happened. Can you tell us?" she said, tentatively.

"I'm guessing a weapon. Perhaps someone blew up the mall," said Wallace. "Damn that was big. Too big. I think we've been attacked.

"Who would do that?" asked one of the strike team. "We don't have any enemies, do we?"

A young, red faced boy who seemed shocked as well. Heck, thought Wallace, they were all in shock. He was struggling to control his own shaking. He felt weak, somehow hungry, disoriented.

"I have no idea," said Wallace. "My orders are to get you to city hall."

One of the strike team looked at the remains of Fidel, turned pale, half turned away, and vomited. He was soon joined by another.

"What do we do about him?" asked the young woman, motioning at Fidel's remains.

"What do we do about em," the young woman with pink-purple hair corrected.

"We're out of body bags so we're using trash bags," replied Wallace. "You know, the extra-large lawn waste size. Or we use sheets. Anyway, I've got both, here on my motorcycle. We should roll him up. There's no real place to take dead now so we simply bury them where they fall. But this is Astroturf, and there's concrete underneath. Outside the stadium is the athletic field, with real dirt. And I've got a shovel here somewhere. Let's get this done. Follow me."

Wallace was aware that he smelled. Jet fuel and smoke from the helicopter, a disturbing aura of liver from the splattering dismemberment of Fidel. He had used a stick from the shattered fence to poke Fidel's still-warm viscera into a pile. Then Fidel received a trash bag burial, in parts, on the slopes of the stadium's backside, where the ground was softer, they didn't have to cut through grass, and the grave could remain undisturbed without cheerleaders dancing over it once the social recovery took place, and all this was a half-forgotten memory. Sometime in the distant future.

After the burial, the five remaining members of the strike

team, the survivors of the twelve originally sent from San Francisco, stumbled off to a meeting place selected by Gillian McTavish via walkie talkie. Wallace took a seat in the bleachers, far from the burning helicopter, and took the burrito from his pants bellows pocket. Ignoring the liver smell radiating from his hands, he took a bite. Delicious. The burrito was a banquet in foil. Disturbing feelings of affection for the person who had made this meal for him. Appetite reduction when he considered the concept of meat. Overwhelming thoughts of Katy. A recent widow, she was entirely off limits. But she had cared enough to give him this food, in a world of hunger. Chili verde. It was delicious. How he missed his family's food. His wife's food.

When he finished the burrito, he carefully deposited the folded foil wrapper in his pocket and walked to his dirt bike, reattaching the camp shovel to the cargo mount with bungee cords. Still shocked by the surreal image of Fidel coming apart, he found himself driving past the YMCA in the darkness. The other helicopter had missed the YMCA and hit the abandoned and looted liquor store across the street, where it now burned fiercely as firefighters attempted to quell the blaze, without water. Perhaps Richard Green was there. He should stop and help. Somehow his mind was numb. He let himself drive to where he had not been since the earthquake: home. He felt like he was going AWOL.

As he drove up in front of his home, his cell phone buzzed. That was very unexpected. There had been no cell service for days, weeks. His wife.

"Oh my God, dearest, how are you? I miss you!" he said, stifling the urge to sob.

"Oh," came his wife's voice, somehow reluctant. Subdued. "We've been trying to reach you all the time. We get the news. It is so terrible. That Candida, is it near you?"

"No, no. No cases yet near us, as far as I know," said Wallace. Our problem is that there was just a big blast, and we don't know what it is."

"Oh. You don't know? That was why we tried to call you. The children saw the news, they began to cry, so I called," said his wife's voice.

Her Danish accent was quite pronounced.

"What was the explosion?" said Wallace.

"There were two nuclear bombs. Small ones. San Francisco and Los Angeles," said the small voice on the phone. "We don't know much more than that."

"Oh, my fracking God," said Wallace. "We are at war. Who did this?"

"Oh, they don't know," said his wife's voice. "They don't know yet. And Candida is ripping the United States in half, and they are having denial of service attacks, and the cell phones and power are down. Your country is coming apart!"

"WHO IS DOING THIS TO US?" shouted Wallace into the blackness of the unlit night.

"Oh, it is the Nazis. The media here in Denmark is saying that you are doing it to yourselves, after the earthquake. They say it is the white supremacists."

"I... I didn't know that," said Wallace. "I haven't heard that."

"Here in Aabenraa the sun is shining, and it's lunchtime. I go outside and my mother is picking red currants from their berry field with our children, and the wheat is tall, and the life is good, and....

The phone went dead. Wallace stared at it, frustrated, enraged, curbing the urge to throw it onto the cement and smash it. Instead he forced himself to put it into a ballistic vest pocket. He could hear it there if it rang again. He stepped over a human turd on his front porch, unlocked his front door, and went inside.

Inside it smelled terrible. Total blackness. He switched on his headlamp, feeling remorseful. The batteries should be saved only for critical times. Just this once. The sliding glass window into the back yard had been broken open, and the food looted, with debris and glass fragments strewn across the kitchen floor. A bat or a bird flew past his face. The smell was apparently coming from the refrigerator. It was ajar, black maw of a door reeking from the unseen decayed food inside. Leave it. Instead he looked at his pantry. Completely cleaned out. Bottled water all gone.

Living room: fireplace had been used. Someone had been sleeping on the couch. The blankets were still there. Many bottles: all the alcohol in the home had evidently been consumed on-site. A used condom on the coffee table. Who was practicing safe sex now? He stifled a laugh. This did not feel like his home.

Children's bedrooms. The world must have enough stuffed animals and blankets, he thought, because these were all here. A large "BLM" had been spray-painted on the wall, over the children's wallpaper.

Gun safe in the den: intact. Large scratch marks where

someone had tried to chisel in. After a good night's sleep, he would retrieve his guns and take them back to the station, where they would be useful. After he boarded up the sliding glass door. Strange that the terrible smell would still be here, this far away from the kitchen.

The main hallway bathroom: someone had been using the bathtub as a toilet. Perhaps 20 human turds, and associated toilet paper, lay mildewing in a liquid pile. Damn. Who could live in a home, even temporarily, with poop marinating in the room next door? Yet someone had used the bathtub as a toilet many times. He stepped back into the hall, shut the door, moved on.

His bedroom: a rotting corpse laid out peacefully in the center of his bed. The bed where he and his wife had created their children. Their bed of sunlight and snuggling and laughing babies. The blue misshapen remains had once been a young man, weeks ago. The hypodermic was still in the corpse's bare and blackened arm. Intentional? Accidental? The room reeked, overwhelming, ammonia-pungent, and there were small white dots moving on the corpse. He looked again in the headlight beam. The corpse's skin seemed to be undulating. It all seemed too much. All too much.

He unslung his shotgun and rested it against the door, and gathered the bedspread over and around the corpse, and dragged it, limp, heavy, gaseous, and thumping, catching on the door frames, out into the front yard, smearing the porch turd as he went. The smells welled up through the fabric and Wallace gagged. To hell with all this. Too much. He dropped the sagging bundle on the front lawn, went back into his bedroom and gathered all the bedding, added it to the pile.

Into the garage for a hidden quart can of chainsaw oil, which he poured over the pile. Finished, he dropped the empty oil can onto the mounded fabric. Back to his bedroom, where he gathered up a small bag of flint and steel and tinder, fire starting tools from the old ways. He slung the shotgun and walked out into the darkness of the front yard. Unbundled the flint and steel. I'm supposed to pray, he thought. That's what my father does. Then he struck the flint, and the char took, and he placed it in a bird's nest of tinder, dry grass and Spanish moss, and blew it into flame. Then he dropped the burning tinder onto the oily pile of blankets, and it caught, and the flames rose, and Wallace thought of the prayers: accept stewardship. Warrior path. As we eat, so are we eaten. This man...this boy...goes on a journey. Journey well.

He watched as the flames rose, until the pile of blankets was blazing fully. Then he looked up. The stars were brilliant. Back in the former days we didn't have stars like this in Salinas, he thought. Back when we had light. There's got to be a blessing in all this. But this despoiled wreck of a building is not my home. Not my home anymore.

Suddenly he was hungry. Ravenous. Weak. Done. He hoped that Tiny and Mickey and their group might have some food to share. Screw sitting here in the dark. He turned on the dirt bike, the engine surged, and he drove away to find his friends, savoring a secret joy that his family was not here.

Nacimiento-Fergusson Road, at the Cone Peak Road turnoff, Los Padres National Forest, California

Garth, Bear, Tiger, Pike, and Hopi sat still on their horses under a giant bay tree and watched as the solitary two-person quad approached on the old Nacimiento Fergusson Road. The quake had broken the tarmac of the road in many places and gouts of dirt and roadway had slumped down into the deep canyons. Today, they were part of a Pike-suggested scouting party to see what was happening towards the ocean. Here, at the turnoff to Cone Peak, they could look down and see the distant smooth blue Pacific Ocean. The plan was to gather up another slow elk on the way home, if possible.

Now here was this red quad, about three hundred yards distant, bounding over the broken asphalt. Red, two people riding on it, pulling a small flat black trailer. Strangely silently propelled. It looked somewhat like a giant articulated crawfish, thought Garth. Unlit headlights for eyes. Garth felt a sudden surge of longing for his community. He wanted Dove to see this. He wanted his daughters Francesca and Akemi to witness this astonishing machine.

"Should we stop it?" asked Bear. His horse was watching the silent machine as well.

Garth looked down. As always, Dogfood was smelling the foliage. Bay leaf wasn't edible, really.

"Well I don't think we can just step out into the roadway when it gets to us and block it. I'm not sure that's legal and, anyway, why provoke a fight?" said Hopi Jack.

"I represent the Sheriff. No harm in asking what's going on," said Pike. Garth looked and remembered that yes, Pike was wearing his official uniform shirt, khaki, complete with bright golden sheriff's deputy badge. It occurred to Garth that Pike had always worn that shirt, daily, even in the hospital. Garth had simply gotten used to it. Garth looked more closely. The bullet holes had been embroidered shut with matching thread. Probably by Katrina Paxley, he guessed. She was always sewing.

"It's coming straight at us anyway. I suppose we can wave politely," responded Garth, "But Hopi and Tiger, why don't you gentlemen step behind that bay tree in case they aren't as friendly as we'd hoped?"

Silence. Garth turned in the saddle to see the back end of Hopi's horse moving behind an elderberry sapling. Tiger was well-hidden, his Garand already drawn from its saddle scabbard. Plenty of leaves there. A momentary thought: could Tiger stay calm? He had shot a man at the river, after all. After the Salinas River fight, they were all on edge. And, as the quad grew close, Bear pulled his horse apart...harder to hit them both...and looked over his shoulder.

"That quad looks like a June bug," said Bear. Pike spurred his horse slightly ahead of them all. Good. That was official.

The driver of the quad was a woman, a young woman, red plastic bike helmet with red short hair, attractive curves, wearing goggles, with a silver Remington 870 pump twelve-gauge shotgun slung over her shoulder.

"That riot gun will kick the snot out of such a small shooter," said Bear.

Exactly, thought Garth.

Meanwhile the person clutching the driver closely from behind was also wearing goggles and a helmet and seemed to be a young man, with a thick black braid of hair, with a bolt action rifle with a scope across his back. The machine whirred quietly as it approached and slowed to a stop. The rear rider dismounted, raised his goggles, smiled, and held up his hands. He was actually she, with curves, Garth guessed. Or something. Fit, though. Defined muscles in his/her arms. Confident. Healthy. Not a victim. Radiating comfortable command.

"You from the Mission?" asked the person, the braid swinging. Feminine voice. A woman.

"Yes," said Pike. "We're up here on a scout. We don't know what's happening over here, so we thought we'd look. I'm a Monterey County Sheriff's Deputy working out of San Antonio, just seeing what's going on after our big shake. How are you all, if I may ask?"

"And how does that machine work?" asked Garth, smiling despite himself.

"After our big blasts, you mean. I'm Pat, and this is my wife Glenda," responded the woman, gesturing to the driver. "I'm a retired inventor, and we live near here, and we were hosting a weaving conference when the quake hit."

"Everybody OK?" asked Pike.

"Shaken, not broken, thank God," responded Glenda, smiling, removing her bike helmet and shaking her short red hair. Auburn, really. Rather conservative. Beautiful small girl. "Happy to see you, actually."

"How did you know we were from the mission?" asked Bear.

"The old timey uniforms and the horses," replied Pat, pointing at them. "There are some people wandering around here starving and lost and there are a few...not so nice people. We met two of the monks a few days back walking back to the monastery, and we know the monastery, so we talked with them, shared a meal at our place. Monks with muskets, that's different."

"Ah! That would be Chuck and Hugh. They wanted to go back and check in. How are they?"

"They are a little shook up, and scared, after your big fight in the river," said Pat. "We know them well, especially Chuck. He's one of us."

"One of you?" asked Pike.

"Well, he likes green technology," said Pat. "He likes to sing and to cook and to make a homestead."

"Oh, yeah," said Bear.

"And he's gay," said Glenda, perched atop the quad elf-like, grinning broadly. "Don't tell the church."

Actually, she was pretty, thought Garth.

He laughed. "My lips are sealed."

"You had any trouble?" asked Bear.

"A little, looters, bandits, desperate people looking for food and shelter, up off the highway," replied Pat, more serious now. "No problems. We've been able to feed most people who come by. A few have stayed."

"How did you get that thing to go like that?" asked Tiger Tanaka. He had ridden out from behind the elderberry bush, sliding the Garand rifle back into its scabbard. "I'm a solar power engineer and I like what I see."

"Well, I am Pat Foreman."

"THE Pat Foreman? You invented the deca-panel?" replied Tiger.

"Deca-panel?" asked Bear.

"Just coming online now. Well, it WAS coming online. I can't say what the earthquake has done to production. We can't get complete comm up here," replied Pat. "The factory was in Sunnyvale. News isn't good from up there, and they don't answer the phone."

"Yes, but what's a deca-panel?" pressed Bear.

"It's a solar panel times ten," responded Tiger. "Astonishingly efficient solar power. It's going to change the world. My guess is that this is what is powering the quad. That's a deca-panel, right?"

He pointed at the trailer.

"Yep!" said Pat. The roof of the trailer is the fuel supply, and there's the Tesla battery Mark 52 in the compartment, along with storage space."

"You aren't just hauling around a big battery?" asked Tiger.

"Oh, no, look!" said Pat, raising the trailer's lid like a giant cigar box.

Garth started as he realized that there was a bloody cloth under the sheet metal spring loaded trailer lid. He saw Pike spur his horse forward and reach for his pistol.

"Chill out, Deputy Dawg, it's a beef," said Pat, looking up.

She...Garth thought of her as a she, actually a rather

attractive she...pulled back the sheet, revealing large red meaty ribs and carcass quarters.

Pike seemed to relax. "Ah...slow elk," he said.

"Slow elk? That's what you call it?" laughed Pat. "We call it 'Free Lunch' although of course it's not free. Someday we'll be able to pay the ranchers back."

She rearranged the sheet to cover the meat back up.

"Flies" she said absent-mindedly. "It's crude, really, but this meat is still better than what they're eating up the coast."

"What are they eating up the coast?" asked Pike.

"All we know are rumors," said Pat. "But we're hearing awful things. Probably bullshit."

"Such as?" asked Pike.

"Eat the rich," chirped Glenda. "We happen to be rich, so we're worried."

"Eat the rich?" asked Hopi, speaking from behind for the first time. "What does that mean?"

"Shouldn't someone be watching our ass?" said Bear to Hopi. As he spoke, he turned his horse to watch behind them.

The two women looked blankly at them.

"He's the law," Glenda finally said to Pat. "You said you wanted help."

Pat seemed to ponder for a moment, then looked up at Pike.

"You're not going to believe this," said Pat.

"Maybe not. Try me," said Pike.

"We had a Mercedes SUV, one of those lifted back country rigs, come into our compound last week. Somehow it got through to us from the north, before there were more slides on the road," said Pat.

"I think they came in through the Old Coast Road, then down from Los Burros. Cut the locks and went through the Army base a bit," added Glenda, looking disgusted.

"Yes," said Pat, looking at Glenda for confirmation.

"Anyway, there was one dead guy in the car, from up by Carmel Highlands, where the movie stars live, and there were two women. No guns, bad for them because that's how they got shot. No gun equals defenseless nowadays," continued Glenda. "Even a cowboy gun from 1870 is worth something."

"The women are still back at our place," said Pat. "Still all shook up. They say that some kind of gang has taken over up there."

"A gang?" asked Pike.

"You'll have to ask them yourselves," said Pat. "They were pretty incoherent, and they've been traumatized and silent since they've been with us. We've been guarding the place twenty-four seven anyway since the quake, but they're still scared witless."

"Of what?" asked Hopi.

"Eat the rich," said Glenda, "they said the gang eats the rich."

"They what?" asked Pike.

"The gang takes over a rich family's mansion, loots it, has a trial, condemns the family to death for being wealthy. One mansion at a time."

"Whole families?" asked Pike

"Whole families. Men, women, children," said Pat. "They

use them as slaves. They abuse them. They rape them, communally. They torture them into revealing everything hidden in the home.

"Then they eat them all," added Glenda.

The Salinas Public Library, Salinas, California

Wallace ducked as a bullet snapped over his head. High. Supersonic. Someone had a rifle. He felt a chill in his guts. This could get bad.

"Heads up, guys! This is the real deal," he said.

"Why are they just shooting out into the street?" asked Tiny.

"Guess it's just shoot up the street day," answered Mickey.

At that point a bullet from the library hit an old metal rubbish can. The half-rusted waste can was abandoned, laying on its side in the street, debris strewn around it. It boomed like a drum when the bullet hit.

"Dang!" shouted Tiny. "Stay away from the cans!"

Wallace had to chuckle, quietly.

They were sheltering behind the giant old palm trees of the Salinas Public Library. One officer per tree. More shots banged into the can. Apparently, it was time for target practice. Good for the shooters. Better than shooting at people.

These palm trees. His father had told him about them: once part of a wonderful old Victorian home which sprawled in the rural horse-drawn days across the entire city block. The palm trees had separated the barn, horse, and carriage areas from the more elegant home and gardens. Now, 120 years later, he was sheltering behind their giant knobby trunks, hopefully unseen, as bullets snapped past.

"Hey Sarge! Ain't responsibility wonderful? You get the joy! You get to find out what they want!" laughed Tiny, who barely fit behind the width of one of the thick trunks.

"Apparently they hate that can," replied Wallace.

"What did that old metal bin ever do to them?" said Mickey. "I mean, did it give them a load of garbage?"

"More likely it just talked trash," replied Tiny, on the other side of Wallace.

Laughter. God, he needed that. Wallace was shaking. Fear, exhaustion. Whatever. Think of his wife. Somehow the image was faded. Think of Katy. Heat. Energy. Katy was right about this.

I'm gonna shout at them, see what they want," said Wallace. "Maybe get to the building along the gutter and try to talk them out. Don't send in Diablo yet. Smoke the parking lot."

"You sure we should do this?" responded Mickey. "Aren't we supposed to stand down? Let the strike teams deal with this?"

Wallace answered, "These people aren't hitting anything except that receptacle. We wouldn't even be here if we hadn't blundered into this. If we can talk 'em down, we're doing our job as the city wants."

On the opposite side of the row of trees, towards the

USO building, Tiny was tossing smoke grenades, one after the other, multi-colored, filling the air with dense smoke. The rifles from the library increased their fire somewhat. In the opaque smoke, Hitting nowhere near them. Wallace crawled sideways, into the gutter, which he realized wasn't deep enough to protect him. Frighteningly not deep enough, and the bullets cracked overhead sporadically, terrifying. Wallace crawled faster. Behind him he heard panting, and turned cautiously and looked and there was Diablo, low crawling along behind him, with Mickey crawling behind the dog. Damn. Crawl faster. Someone was going to get shot. Tiny's smoke grenades were now flying over their heads, landing in Cayuga Street, so they were mostly obscured. That Samoan had a throwing arm on him.

When they got to the edge of the library building, Wallace stood up and rushed frantically for the windowless wall of the structure. Now he was near the opening from whence the shots had been fired. HIs shotgun was in his hands. The shotgun's side saddle ammo carrier was caught in his vest zipper. He fumbled with the tangle as Mickey came up alongside.

"Thought Diablo could help," said Mickey, panting. "Don't make me do a crawl like that again."

Occasional shots rang out from the broken full-length window, about five feet from them. Wallace could see the rifle barrel protruding from the opening. Tubular magazine, he realized. Old fashioned. Unthinking, he reached out with his gloved hand and pulled, and the rifle came away easily. Wallace threw it out into the parking lot with a clatter.

"Aw frack," came a man's voice from inside, sheepishly.

"ARE WE DONE NOW?" shouted Wallace.

"YOU DON'T GET NEAR US! WE STILL GOT GUNS!" another man's quavering voice responded.

"I got a Daisy! And it's loaded!" said another small voice inside.

"What the hell are you doing here?" asked Wallace. "We don't need to be doing this."

"We here to protect the WHITE PEOPLE, AND THE WHITE CULTURE!" came the first man's voice. "WE HERE IN THIS CITADEL! THIS FORTRESS OF WHITE MAN'S KNOWLEDGE! TO DEFEND AGAINST THE DEFAMING BY THE 'NOTHER RACES!"

"That makes about as much sense as roasting horse shit and calling it dinner," said Mickey. "HEY, WE LIKE THE LIBRARY TOO!"

"Well, it's like we forgot the library in recent years," said the voice, conversationally. "What with the homeless stealing everyone's val-ables here and all. It was like a vagrant campment."

The voice was turning maudlin. The speaker must be drunk or stoned.

Overhead there was a humming, and a small drone appeared. It flew directly overhead, then across the window, and circled. It sounded like a large mosquito. It appeared to be watching as it weaved in and out of the diminishing tendrils of colorful smoke. The smoke grenades were burning out.

"That your dragon fly?" said the voice.

"Not mine. Probably the Republic," replied Wallace. "Just watching. No problem. Let's get this done before they arrive, to make sure."

"Sure am thirsty. Oh so tired. Ready to return to the days when America was an English speakin' land. A proud land where a white man could stand tall and see only his kind."

"Which it never really was," said Wallace quietly to himself.

"Look at that rusty old beater," said Mickey, pointing out towards the rifle. "That old .30-30 was made back in the stone age. Feel kinda sorry for these racist fools, if that's what he's taking to a gunfight."

Mickey reached down and pulled out his canteen, reached around Wallace and chucked it into the open window.

"Oh!" there was a startled shout. "Oh. It's water. You poisonin' us?" came a man's weak voice.

"It's my own canteen. Unless you got problems drinking from a Hispanic's canteen," replied Mickey.

"Water's water," came the voice, "Got no problem with the Messicans, just want to hold my own head up. Thanks."

"We can get you more. How many of you are in there?" asked Wallace.

"Ah, so we can come out?" said the voice. "I reckon this demo-stratin' has gone on long enough."

"We want to end this right now just like you do," replied Mickey.

"There's a bunch in here. A goodly-size group," said the voice. "So we can all come out?"

"RPG! RPG! RPG!" shouted Tiny from across the parking lot, and a smoking projectile like a large spear shot into the side of the building with blinding speed, smashed through the doors on the other side of the building, and exploded with a rattling thump in the interior. The windows blew out and flaming pages of books billowed into the parking lot and the street. Wallace felt the blast wave pass through him, through his teeth, and he saw the glass falling from windows around him.

"YA DIDN'T HAF TA DO THAT!" screamed the voice. "We surrender! We surrender!" shouted the voice, and a skinny older man in a wife beater shirt with a small paunch leapt out of the smoking window, tripped over the broken glass still protruding from the frame, and sprawled into the parking lot. He was followed by a torrent of people, eight, Wallace counted, smoke-covered, coughing, mostly men, a few women and some young teenagers. All white.

"ROCKET!" shouted Tiny across the parking lot, as another missile, apparently fired from the parking structure across the street, smashed into the library and exploded somewhere inside.

Smoke and burning pages erupted onto the street and there were screams inside.

"TINY TELL THOSE PEOPLE TO STOP SHOOTING!" yelled Wallace.

"A few more in there," said the leader of the white supremacists. "Please...please help them."

"Diablo! Find! Secure!" said Mickey, and Diablo raced into the burning interior of the building. Wallace could hear barking.

Another rocket blasted through the doors into the burning library and exploded, pushing another gout of flames and paper out into the parking lot. The people were all standing over by the palm trees with their hands up. Mickey, covered in ash, ran into the building, and emerged a few seconds later with a man, who was wincing, holding his misshapen broken arm gingerly with his other arm. Another man followed, clothing smoking, carrying the limp form of Diablo.

"Too hot...too hot in there," the man gasped. "There's another guy in there, but he's past caring. He's dead. Rocket blew his head off. He's really dead. God almighty what am I going to tell his family?'

"Maybe he shoulda' stayed the frack away," Wallace was enraged now. "Play stupid games, win stupid prizes."

Wallace looked over at Mickey, who was on his knees in the parking lot. Mickey was bent over the limp form of Diablo, sobbing, fighting the tears.

The Mayor approached from the parking structure with a platoon of very young strike team members. He looked stern. He watched the library burning fiercely.

"Had to be done. Had to be done. Cruel necessity," he said. "Besides, nobody reads books anymore anyway. We're gonna get some great government funding and we'll build an internet center.

"WHY DID YOU DO THAT? WHY DID YOU DO THAT?" shouted Wallace, about to strike Happy Johnson. "Why by all that's holy did you DO THAT?"

"You shouldn't have been here," said the mayor. "You were ordered to stand down. These are racists, the worst subhumans you could find. They've been a plague for hundreds of years. And nits make lice."

"But the library? The library?" replied Wallace.

"Books, I mean the old-fashioned paper books, they're dangerous," said the mayor. "The forces of truth can manage the Internet. When the internet is restored it will be the bigliest internet ever. Better, and managed for truth and for the welfare of society. But a paper book? It can go anywhere, like a bacillus. Like Coronavirus. Like Candida. Dangerous."

Wallace turned to watch Mickey. Mickey was still kneeling over his dead dog, wiping his eyes, struggling to control himself.

"Redevelopment. Big dollars. Redevelopment," said the mayor, as though to himself, "Someday, a shining city, the new Silicon Valley. We aren't radioactive, like they are up north. The jobs and the people will come RIGHT HERE!"

The library was burning strongly now, and there was no fire department in sight. In the parking lot, the strike team, in their green janitorial coveralls, were roughly pushing the group of disheveled white supremacists into a column, to walk towards the courthouse. As Wallace watched, the leader, his sparse hair waving, looked at Mickey and his dog and shook his head sorrowfully.

"Officer," he said, "We screwed up. I got ratcheted inta' frenzy by some old videos of Fox News, an' a bottle of Jack Daniels. We all got crazy. This was wrong. This was evil. I... I so regretful."

A very young woman strike team member pushed him into walking after the rest of his group. She was carrying a submachine gun, which looked like an Ingram. Not a military gun.

"Officer," he shouted back, "I'm sorry...I'm really sorry, about your dog."

Near Los Burros Road, Big Sur, California

Yurts, large shining white lacquered cylindrical tents, gleaming in the sun, clustered around a stone-made central bathroom and a metal central cylindrical dining area, shaped from grooved sheet metal like a barn roof. Deca-panels were clustered on the roofs, and on the rocks on a nearby hillside, to provide solar energy. On an overlooking hill, a large metal lattice ham radio antenna rose upon a structure like a watchtower with a big water tank as its base. About 50 people. Vegetable gardens amidst the chemise brush. Tents...apparently refugee tents.... on leveled pads down to the ocean. Very well done. Of course, Garth didn't know these people, so he couldn't be sure of what was going on. And the people...at least twenty of them...were damned well armed: everyone with a slung long gun, even if that was a pump shotgun or a lever action carbine.

"We haven't been outgunned like this since the Soledad River fight," muttered Bear, riding alongside. "We should'a kept Tiger and Hopi. Tiger's our best shot."

"Yep. I see it," said Garth. "These people are gonna help us lots, if they don't kill us."

"And eat us?" added Pike, who was riding opposite. Quiet voice. He was spooked a bit as well. "I see several of the quads. I think that one belongs to Pat and Gretchen, that one, over by the kitchen. Don't see them."

"It's Glenda," said Garth. "Anyway, I don't see them."

"Indoors with the slow elk, maybe," said Bear. "Say how long do you think it's gonna take Hopi and Tiger to get back to the mission? I'm guessing they'll be there tonight. By dark."

"Unless they fetch some meat," replied Pike. "Someone had to tell the Mission what's goin' on over by the coast. Might be crazy and might be wrong but still they need to have their guard up."

"Amen," replied Bear. "This is getting bigger than just the ground shaking."

"Look at the bright side. We are pretending to be the U.S. cavalry and we were just rescued by billionaire lesbians," chuckled Garth. "Something to tell our grandkids. That was one fast and silent machine that Pat has invented."

"Fast trike. Hell of a trike. They got here hours before us," laughed Pike softly. "Besides they're hot. Beautiful and geniuses. Not a John Wayne movie, is it?"

"More like that anime that my daughter reads and watches," said Garth quietly. "And they have a hot tub. Check that out. This is glamping. These people know how to survive in an emergency."

"I'll bet Pat's been working on this place for a decade," said Bear. "Pat's laid this thing out to fill this small valley, but they control the high ground with the hill behind us, where they've got the antenna and the water tank. Look what's on top of that water tank."

"It's a control tower," said Pike, squinting up the mountainside.

"More like a small command post," said Garth.

"On a water tank," said Bear. "Roofed in deca-panels to keep the people and the water cool. As I said, well thought out."

"I got internet!" said Pike. He had removed his iPhone and was poking at it.

"God, don't tell Hillary," laughed Bear.

"YOU'RE HERE!" came a friendly shout.

Garth looked. Pat was striding assertively from the round metal central structure. "Welcome to my home!"

"I'm really impressed," said Garth. "Has this place got a name?"

"I like to call it Castillo de Suenos," replied Pat. "Castle of Dreams. So far so good. No nightmares yet. But the day's young."

She smiled engagingly. She really WAS quite attractive, thought Garth. Uniquely feminine with an aggressive masculine manner. Slender, fit, like a dancer, obviously brilliant. And she owned all this.

"It DOES look like a castle from a distance," said Garth. "A mostly canvas castle."

"OK to dismount? Where do you want the horses?" asked Bear.

"Down the hill, in the horse corral," replied Pat, smiling and pointing. "The Eagles Nest can watch the corral at night. Night vision."

"Eagle's Nest?" asked Bear.

"Up there," said Pat, and she pointed to the water tower. "Seven of us on duty, 24/7, and it's also where we keep our satellite com systems."

"Wow Dad this is the first time I've had a good look at you in months!" said Sarah.

She and her Norwegian husband Osten were clustered around their computer camera in Oslo, in Norway. Far away from this insanity, thought Garth. In the small dark room, apparently made out of a repurposed metal shipping container, the wall-mounted screen seemed vividly colorful and gigantic. He jiggled his belt so that his 1858 Remington revolver was free from the metal chair, and thus not digging into his side.

Another frame on the computer screen showed Ernst, crowding his computer camera, with what appeared to be a window-lit sunroom and, incongruously, a large blue macaw parrot in the background.

"Hey, I love you all. I only got a few minutes from our host. I'm at a converted resort at Big Sur, and we're visiting, and she was kind enough to give me a few minutes of satellite time. We're still mostly cut off. The rest of the family is well, they're over at the mission. We don't know much; we're still cut off from cell. We're living happily like it's 1850 with benefits. I love everybody deeply, and I miss you all, but frankly I'm glad you're not here. I love you. Please tell me what's happened. We literally have only about 5 minutes before the piggybacked satellite signal goes away. Apparently, it's not geosynchronous."

"Well, for one thing, I'm in Mexico City," blurted Ernst.

"What? Not Brooklyn? What the heck happened?" said Garth.

"You really don't know?" said Osten in Oslo. "America goes to shit! Ha! That idiot president of yours! And finally you shoot nuclear bombs upon yourself so you can sympathy have with the Japanese, finally."

He seemed to be pleased. Sarah scowled, then made

shushing noises and tried to nudge herself to occupy more of the computer camera's field of vision.

"Tell me more," said Garth, flatly. No time now to answer back with anger.

"Let me give it to you all in order," said Ernst. But first, are you OK after those nucs?"

"We saw distant blasts to the north and south of us, flashes in the night, and big bangs. Our current host here, Pat, told us they were tactical nuclear devices," answered Garth. "Are we in any danger? Pat's not recording any radioactivity. We didn't record any at the mission. We've got an ambient radioactivity counter there as well. I'm really curious and ready for some answers."

Garth pondered that he loved these young people, and he ached to be with them. He hungered for more discussion. But he was talking too much, and he needed to shut up and listen.

"Two tactical nucs, one at the Port of Oakland, one at the Port of Long Beach. Apparently suitcase nucs, Soviet, left over from the 1970's. Somebody added a little extra to make them dirty, intentionally, so it's going to take years to clean up, but not very big, so debris didn't go farther than the Los Angeles basin and the San Francisco Bay Area. They are betting on perimeter cleanup in three years, ground zero in a decade or more," said Ernst. "That means we get San Francisco and Santa Monica back in three to six years."

"We are at war," said Garth blankly, with a sinking feeling, as though his chair was collapsing. "Who with?"

"About 100,000 dead, a half million injured, and a million

or more homeless long term in each blast," continued Ernst. "Believe it or not we don't know who did it. Cameras got images of what are apparently the bombs embedded in cars. The media is saying white Christian nationalists but that hasn't been substantiated."

"So what are we doing?" replied Garth. "I mean as a nation."

"The military has mobilized but they don't yet have a clear target," continued Ernst, his serious face looming on the large computer screen. "Carriers are deploying to the California coast with guided missile cruisers, but the bombs seem to have been delivered by ground, of course. They were driven into position by people wearing those Anonymous masks."

"On the ground?" asked Garth, still stunned. "Who would do that?"

"Well President Price is blaming the North Koreans and the Iranians but the Defense Intelligence Agency broke with him when he tried for a counter strike. They said there was no evidence. Then a domestic group nobody's ever heard of claimed credit. Eagle Rising, a white supremacist group," said Ernst. "That's the media's story right now."

"Ha! See? You did it to yourselves!" came Osten's voice from Sarah's computer image.

The line was beginning to fuzz. The satellite would soon move out of position.

"We're losing the connection," said Garth. "I love you. Fill me in fast."

"California declared independence again right before

the bombs, they declared that they were going to be 'The Republic of California' and issued some big new laws. They instituted a wealth tax. Reparations to be paid by whites for the bombings. All churches lost their non-profit status, and all religious organization property will be confiscated by the Republic. Gun confiscation. Open borders. After the bombings, President Price told them they could handle it all without federal aid," rushed Sarah. "Instead, they'll get aid from China."

"Wow!" responded Garth.

"Then the Congress, which as you know is dominated by the opposing party, promptly passed a wealth tax, raised income taxes, and reinstituted an inheritance tax," added Ernst. "President Price has broken Twitter ranting about all that, when there's internet."

"Rich people are moving out," said Sarah, shaking her head.

"To Nevada?" asked Garth.

"US credit ratings have fallen, and Congress has also instituted that national wealth tax retroactively, so there's no place for rich people to hide in America," added Ernst quickly.

"About time! Serve them right!" came Osten's voice.

"Which is why Facebook is moving to Zurich," said Sarah. "And Apple to Mexico."

"Apple to Mexico?" asked Garth, dumbfounded.

"Yep, Mexico passed some emergency anti-corruption, tax reduction laws to attract Americans here, and it's working. After about the fifth denial of service, internet and power blackout in New York City, there were riots, people were running wild. My building in Brooklyn got ransacked, at least the bottom floors. Looters set fire to the trash in the bagel shop downstairs. My condo was on the fifth floor, but the smoke came up the stair wells and filled my home anyway. For a moment I thought the rioters were coming up the stairs, and I didn't even have tear gas. That was that. I just packed the computers, left the condo, wired all the money, and Ericson and Associates now has its central office in Mexico City operating under a complete provisional license," said Ernst.

"Some other countries are lowering taxes, streamlining regulations, working hard to capture American business," added Sarah. "I mean, the demand for Apple and Facebook products isn't going away."

"Norway! Norway rocks! And we have Tesla and Lindt and Becton Dickenson now!" shouted Osten, from offscreen.

"I don't understand. The United States isn't helping California?" asked Garth, ignoring the unseen baiting. "I mean, we haven't seen any aid on our end, and there's all kinds of rioting in the cities, we hear. The Army base down the road from us is shut tight."

"Well, the big news is the weaponized candida and the DOS," continued Sarah. Her image wavered on the screen.

Garth sighed deeply. "Tell me more. Hey, this connection is getting much worse, isn't it? If we get cut off, I love you all."

"We love you too, Dad!" said Ernst. "The Candida appears to have been released around Saint Louis and it has killed about one million, hospitalized about ten million, spread into Chicago and south to Denver, and cut the country in pieces. I mean, they have stopped air travel and they've installed border checkpoints. They ha...."

Ernst's image fluttered on the screen and froze.

"God almighty," said Garth, apparently to nobody.

"bout like the Spanish flu in 1918. Anyway, that's why I went to Mexico City as soon as Brooklyn shut down," continued Eric. "The broken internet has made it that much harder."

"That's likely to spread," said Garth. "How are you all?"

"Russians are making a noise about the Ukraine," said Sarah. "Also, they are picking a fight with Estonia. But the big news is that the Russians worked out a vaccine for the Candida. First vaccine for a yeast. Untested but they're going to use it."

"Mexico is actually very nice," said Ernst. "Getting better. I've met a very nice young woman."

"Oh!" said Garth, smiling. "A silver lining!"

"She's very different from American women. She's not angry about anything," said Ernst.

"Back to the Candida," said Garth. "They have a vaccine, so it's done, right? All that's left is the cleanup?"

"People are resisting the vaccine," said Sarah.

"Why?" stuttered Garth.

"Because there's an internet rumor going around that it makes you sterile. That the Candida epidemic was actually planted by the United States to sterilize people, especially in the flyover states. You know, reduce conservative populations. Some are avoiding it.

"Let me get this straight. They're avoiding the vaccine?" asked Garth.

"Yep. They duck out on the inoculation and try to run, and that spreads it," said Sarah. "Word is that the infection, the Candida, actually DOES make you sterile, so perhaps that's where that comes from. Anyway, it's still more of a mess than it needs to be."

"The big news is that we're both doing great and we're both not there," said Ernst.

"Wonderful!" said Garth. "Quickly, how are the clients? At least, how's their money?"

"Dollar's dropping like a rock. US stock markets are down about 78% from pre-quake, and remember we shorted that. Interest rates are rising sharply with gold as credit quality becomes an issue. Now we're in yuan," said Ernst. "So we're good."

"Yuan?" replied Garth, and the screen went black.

The satellite link had not been recoverable. The information had been emotionally crushing. The world was going insane. Now, here he was, sitting in the dirt on the mountain by the water tower, slightly downhill, on the gravel trail under a mid-sized live oak tree, feeling the spines of dead oak leaves on the ground spike through his pants, feeling the heat of the sunset on his face. Such a beautiful day. The sunset was absolutely spectacular. Smoke from distant wildfires was making the sunset red. A pang of longing for his family. All of them spread out all over the world. Garth pondered that he had never enjoyed deployments in the military. Now he was gone one night from his family, away from Mission San Antonio de Padua, and he missed them all so mightily. What was Dove doing now? What was his son, the police officer in Salinas, and his family, doing while this sunset was happening? All of them, everywhere. His mother. Ah, well, it was just for a short time. All would be well. They would all be together again soon.

He moved the .45-70 Marlin rifle so that it rested across his lap. A quick mental check: yes, it was unloaded. More comfortable. Unearthly quiet, even compared to the mission, where there was always some loud voice. Or bagpipes. Here, there was the sound of a dove, cooing in the branches in the new darkness, and beyond that overhead oak branch, so leafy and green and geometric, the black night sky, vastly full of stars, and beyond that, as he lowered his vision, the very calm Pacific ocean out there in the growing darkness. Out there was an underwater wilderness, and a myriad ecosystem in which all this chaos did not exist. All this chaos. Damn.

Garth was aware that he was stressed, more stressed even than he had been before. Slow deep breaths. Count them. Listen to that jay. Feel the light wind off the ocean. It's all good.

"Ah! There you are!" a bright, cheerful, energetic voice. Pat.

Garth opened his eyes.

"I brought you a relative," said Pat.

Garth turned his head and looked at her in the dim light of a nearby solar-powered lantern affixed to the water tower.

How strange, he thought. She's so attractive as a PERSON and she's feminine but she's not...well, what is she not? She's all woman, in her own way. I'm deeply relieved to have her here.

There was an old man with her, an old cowboy, weather-beaten and gray, angular in the shadows. Cowboy hat. Jean jacket, faded. A slung rifle. He recognized the rifle. Then he recognized the man, a memory from early years, now astonishingly aged. Behind them stood Pike.

"Kiffin Rockwell Ericson, JUNIOR!" Garth said as he stood up. "Cousin!"

"Damn, Garth, you've gotten old," said the man. "¡No te he visto en mucho tiempo!"

"How are you related?" asked Pike, smiling.

"Kiffin's the son of my father's cousin, from my grandfather's brother," replied Garth. "We share a great-grandfather, a mighty rancher."

"Clear as mud, right?" said Kiffin.

Turning to Garth he said, "I haven't seen you in forty years. I've been hearing all sorts of things. Sorry about your family losing your ranch. Sorry about your father's death. Both a'those happened about thirty years ago, right? You know I didn't know what to say."

"I didn't know what to say either," said Garth. "I guess I just wanted to hide."

"Ah.... well. That's that," said Kiffin, reaching out and patting Garth on the shoulder. "We're still on the goat patch. Rancho Las Cabras. We never left. Best not to stick your head up, you know?"

"Goat patch?" asked Pike.

"Oh, it's his ranch, it's just inland from here. He's our neighbor," replied Pat. "Although it's quite nice, actually."

"No goats," laughed Kiffin. "The last time I checked."

"I recognized the rifle, speaking of memories," said Garth.

"Ah, well, if it ain't broke, don't fix it," smiled Kiffin.

Pat cut in. "How was the call?"

"Overwhelming," said Garth. "I'm guessing you know all the big stuff."

"We just got briefed," said Pike. "And here's the thing: we got email contact with Monterey County Sheriff. It's gone to hell out there."

"I can guess," said Garth.

"All I know is what they tell me," responded Kiffin.

"Anyway, the Sheriff told me that I'm the law enforcement here in Big Sur. The state...or the Republic, whatever the frack it is. They're up to their ass in chaos in the cities. The Sheriff's trying to get a grip on the towns. Rural areas are..."

"Shit out'a luck, I'm guessing," said Kiffin.

"Yep. They want me to go north to check out the "Eat The Rich" rumor, visit the monastery, and Kiffin and his son Kiffin the third have offered to guide. Can you and Bear go with us, please?" asked Pike.

"We call him "Tres", added Kiffin. "Just Tres. Like three."

"On this expedition, there's going to be you, Kiffin...and Tres," responded Garth, carefully stating the names, "and Bear and me."

There was a distant jet roar in the sky, to the south, in the darkness, and the blinking lights of a fast-moving aircraft appeared out over the sea, flying north along the coast.

"You don't see those much anymore," said Pat. "Flying this low, anyway. To continue, let's plan on taking Glenda, and two others...I'll introduce you to them later, and there's me," said Pat. "I need to take a look around, and we can bring a few quads to back you up, in case we need..."

There was a flash of light from the distant aircraft, like a camera flash, and a growing flame and the jet veered abruptly, a trailing comet of fire curving across the heavens, burning bits detaching as it slowed, still at least two thousand feet high, and there was a faraway pop and a separate upward flame like a firework going up.

"No kidding. Ejection seat," said Pike.

"No shucks," said Bear. "At least it's over land, barely."

The flaming comet began to break up and plummet, finally arching down until there was a bright flash of billowing light against a nearby tall mountain, and a few seconds later a thumping boom filled the night.

"You guys show up and everything goes to shit," said Kiffin.

"I hope everyone got to safety," said Bear.

"We'll find out soon enough," responded Garth.

"Every time I think I've seen it all, it gets crazier," said Pat.

"Can I go with you, when you check it out?" piped the young Tres from the darkness.

The pilot was middle aged, slender, European. Graying black hair. The drones had found him quickly with their infrared, and he seemed dazed now, in the lights of the Castillo, facing a ring of people. He was wearing a green flight suit, with a built-in holster. Garth noticed that the plastic pistol was still in place. A moment of unease. Should they remove it? The man had just survived an ejection from a burning jet, at night, and had barely managed to parachute into the redwoods, as opposed to the rocky shoreline or the depths of the Pacific Ocean. There was a Mexican Air Force triangle patch, red, white, and green, on the man's shoulder. He didn't seem agitated. And removing the gun would be a form of surrender. Better to wait.

"Hi!" said Glenda, all friendship, extending her hand to the man. "I'm Glenda"

The man stared at her blankly for a few seconds, then broke into a large smile. Great teeth, thought Garth. A real chick magnet. He seems nice.

"Why hello! I'm Ramon Urrea! Mucho gusto!" said the man in unaccented English.

The man extended his hand and shook Glenda's warmly.

"I didn't expect to make my visit here on the ground," he added, still smiling.

"What happened? Obviously, you are Mexican Air Force, and this is California. What brings you up this far north?" said Glenda.

"Oh, we were asked to do a nuclear scan by the United States government. Of course, we're watching very carefully. Someone just exploded two nuclear devices just north of Mexico, so of course we want to go see. It's all with permission. We are to share the results."

"Reconnaissance?" asked Garth.

"Yes, no guns. Rigged up on the spur of the moment. I was called out of retirement and they told me to fly over Oakland and Long Beach. I'm a retired Colonel, and there I was enjoying my life on my small rancho when poof! I am here. Life is strange," replied Ramon Urrea expressively. "By the way this is an exquisite Cabernet wine. Who made it?"

"I did," responded Kiffin. "I live next door."

Kiffin makes wine? Garth considered that.

"My compliments. Very excellent complexity and range," said the Colonel. "I've struggled with it a bit myself. I graduated from the University of California at Davis, with a degree in viticulture. However, I spent the next thirty-plus years flying and now I struggle with the enology of actually making the wine."

"What kind of aircraft was that?" asked Bear. "It seemed like a fighter, from the way it flew."

"It was a fighter, but from the 1950's. A great old vintage aircraft. They brought it out of retirement just for this mission. A T-33, which is like a P-80 with two seats. It has... it had....extra-large reconnaissance gas tanks, since we can't aerial refuel. And it fits a 1970's nuclear radiation sensor. I think that's why it caught fire. Just old, and it hadn't been used much. I'm lucky the ejection seat worked."

"Wow! Yes you are!" said Bear. "Imagine that. A World War II aircraft."

"Well, not quite," replied Colonel Urrea. "My father flew P-47's for the Mexican Air Force in the Philippines in '44 and '45, against the Japanese. Now THAT was a World War II aircraft. This airplane was made in 1959, so...it's not so much World War II"

"Still amazing," said Pike, standing behind them. "Can you tell us anything about what's going on out there?"

"Well there was the Mexicali Massacre," said Colonel Urrea, shaking his head.

"Wasn't that fake?" asked Pike.

"Oh, yes, very fake," answered Colonel Urrea. "But it means that someone wants us to fight. Our two nations at war because of lies. Then the cities in the United States began to break down and the riots happened. There's a lot of Mexican nationals involved in all that. The U.S. government shifted military assets out to deal with Taiwan, and California declared independence. Then the nucs."

"Lots happening," said Glenda

"So the U.S. asked us to do a flyover, and here I am. California didn't want any U.S. Air Force, I guess."

"How's the border?" asked Pat. She had just stepped into the empty dining room.

"It's a mess. We native Mexicans don't know what to do down in Mexico. Suddenly everyone wants to go there. Did you hear that many of your corporations are moving there?"

Garth nodded his head. "Yes, my son is living down there now. He moved our financial business there. He says it's great."

The Colonel seemed to brighten. "Ah, so you may be Mexican too, soon. Where is he living?" he asked.

"Mexico City."

"Big, beautiful, smoggy, and crowded," answered the

Colonel. "You know, like a beautiful large woman after a fast dance, at 2 AM, when the night is warm. You should visit when this is over. Perhaps you will live there."

"Meanwhile we're here," said Pat. "Our comms are down temporarily. We can get you in contact with anyone on the next satellite. For now, you may as well make yourself at home. We're about to have a late dinner. Can you join us?"

"I thought you'd never ask," responded the Colonel, smiling.

North of Los Burros Road, Big Sur, California

"Well that was something!" said Bear. "I haven't had a feast like that since before the shake. At least I haven't had that many vegetables since before the shake."

They were sitting on their horses looking down at Highway One along the ocean, in the bright morning sunlight. The usual. A beautiful clear day. Whales spouting unseen in the distance, thought Garth. Birds singing in the trees. Unreal. The Mexican Air Force Colonel was sitting on the horse alongside. Unreal.

Garth looked at Bear, sitting on his horse. Bear was wearing the same blue cavalry uniform, 1860's to 1870's, 1860 Henry rifle slung over his shoulder, a touch sunburned, modern sunglasses, broad blue campaign hat on his head, like Garth. The Mexican Colonel was sitting his horse slender and straight, still wearing his olive flight suit, pistol still in its built-in chest holster, wearing aviator sunglass and a "Hooter's" ball cap. Where had THAT hat come from, thought Garth. Best to ignore it.

"One doesn't really miss cabbage until one is denied it," answered Garth.

Below them on the coastal highway was a column of six vehicles, stopped before a giant chasm in the road. The chasm was spectacular, thought Garth. The fill in a natural ravine, about 100 yards across and thirty yards deep, had slumped into the sea below, taking the roadbed with it. There was a light track across the disturbed dirt of the chasm where people and animals had walked since the slide. There was a soil slump along the track where some 4x4 vehicles had attempted to force their way across. In the bottom were two vehicles, a red jeep and, incongruously, a white sedan of some sort, which had not been able to get across.

It looked like a sinkhole, thought Garth.

There were three large farm trucks, now carrying supplies, which would return empty to the Castillo with refugees, if any were encountered. Undoubtedly, they would now stay here at the slump as a forward base. There were about a dozen people on horseback with the trucks. There were several free-roaming quads, each with a small flat deca-panel trailer, each with two people. And, finally, there was a quad pulling a slender roofed metal trailer with about five people seated in it. Dark gray deca-panels comprised the slanted roof of the trailer, which appeared to be infested with large lumpy brown crabs, several on each side, about the size of boot boxes. Or perhaps those drones were giant water bugs, thought Garth. The people under that trailer roof were intently looking at laptops.

"Looks like a hayride, don't it?" commented Bear.

"Looks like genius to me," said the Mexican Colonel.

Hearing the sound of breaking foliage, Garth looked behind them. There were Tres and Kiffin, on horses. Both had rifles and pistols. Garth noticed that Tres was remarkably handsome, about the same age as Terp, blond, blue eyed, robust. Intelligent, smiling, like his father wearing a cowboy hat and dressed in old denim.

"Looks like genius to me too," commented Kiffin, motioning towards the column of vehicles down the mountainside.

"How many drones are they managing?" asked Bear.

"Hello Mr. Ericson. Hello Mr. Singleton, and hello Colonel," said Tres.

"Call me Ramon," said the Mexican Colonel. "Thanks for picking me out of that tree last night, thanks for your hospitality, and thanks for letting me come along this morning. I've been thinking about last night's satellite call with my Mexican Air Force amigos, they can't get me out of here. They're quite busy. And I don't want to sit back in some yurt while this is happening."

"To be expected, that they are busy," said Kiffin, "Still, I never thought I'd be sitting on a horse right here with a pilot from the Mexican Air Force watchin' the world fall apart."

Ramon shifted in his saddle and winced.

"What's up? You OK? Feeling last night's ejection?" asked Bear.

"I know I'd feel it, if it happened to me. Like being shot 300 feet in the air on a bungee cord," said Garth.

"Well, yes, you know I've never been shot out of an airplane before," replied Ramon. "I was hoping to avoid that sort of amusement."

"Good for you," said Bear. "I share those sentiments exactly."

"But it's not that," responded Ramon. "You know, it's the cabbage. So so so much cabbage."

He laughed. "I'm trying not to...you know..."

"Fart?" suggested Kiffin.

"Head for those redwoods behind us. We'll try not to listen," said Tres.

"I have to ask, why are the rich folk in California obsessed with fiber?" said Bear. "And what is this quinoa? And wheat berries? And jeweled millet? Doesn't anyone eat a tortilla around here?"

Laughter.

"Thank you for saying that," replied Ramon. "I was thinking about it myself."

"But you were too polite to ask," added Kiffin. "Well we gotta admit that Pat and Glenda have created a paradise and they're saving our collective asses. Your collective asses, I mean. I'm good with my wine, my bees, and my corn up at my place."

"You gotta admit, we're in the twilight zone," said Bear. "Earthquake, social unrest, disease, riots, secession, and quinoa. I can't believe we're here."

More soft laughter. Their drowsy horses shifted beneath them.

"Perhaps it would be better if I persisted for a short time, and you explained what I'm seeing," said Ramon. "Consider me a visitor, and you will help me think of other things."

"Well that there, that wagon which looks like a hayride, that's a drone management unit which Pat put together," said Tres, pointing enthusiastically. "Four operators. They are each managing up to six drones, but the drones are autonomous, each following a map-programmed surveillance pattern until it spots something. Then the operator is notified and engages."

As Tres spoke, one of the lumps on the roof appeared to come to life; it silently shook itself as propellers extended and began whirring. Then the drone pulled itself up to level, detached, and flew straight up, then turned and passed over them, heading north. Another drone appeared in the sky, flew silently from the seaward side, hovered, attached itself, and then allowed itself to hang motionless on the slanted roof as the propellers retracted and folded flat.

"See, now that one's recharging. They do that automatically," added Tres.

"Damn she's good," said Bear. "That Pat's a genius."

"Actually, Glenda thought this one up," said Kiffin. "Glenda's the software. She's into AI. Pat's the hardware. Kind of like their relationship."

Garth had to smile at that. "Anyone else got this? The military?"

Ramon was quietly easing his horse backwards. As Garth watched he turned his mount into the trees behind them.

"That's who the end user was supposed to be, but Glenda added a few extra touches," said Kiffin. "These drones have the ability to be passive rather than active, so they can turn off their signatures. They do that with independent terrain following mapping software rather than using GPS. They also are quite small, like ducks, really, so hard to spot. They can see thermal and at night. And in addition to cameras she put a Glock nine-millimeter pistol in each one. Mounted sideways. Just a store-bought pistol with an extended 20 shot magazine in each."

"Isn't that illegal?" asked Garth. "The twenty-shot magazine?"

"Yep," answered Kiffin. "But ya know, Pat 'n Glenda 're rich. They got connections."

"Damn they're good," repeated Bear.

Garth's black plastic walkie talkie radio came to life on his belt. "Hey Garth, this is Pat. You up there?"

"Roger that," responded Garth, careful to hold down the transmit button.

"Drones are seeing several people hiding in the chemise up the canyon to your north. We got them on thermals. They seem to be trying to remain fully concealed. As you know we are still about two miles south of the monastery, so we aren't sure who these people are. Can you check them out, please?"

"Surely," responded Garth.

"Vital signs say they are terrified and dehydrated. Body posture indicates a family unit. Heads up, but be kind," said the voice. "Pike's on the way up behind you, with two other riders. After all, it's a law enforcement issue."

"Damn she's good," said Bear.

Monterey County Courthouse, Alisal Street, Salinas, California

The crowd below them in the street was moaning. A thousand people in the street. What a field day for the heat, thought Wallace. Men, women, children, dressed in all sorts of garments. From Hawaiian shirts to workout clothes to what seemed to be underwear. The crowd was gathered in front of the county courthouse. It looked like an impromptu concert venue, with trash blowing and broken windows.

Wallace stood on the nearby rooftop terrace of the old Californian newspaper building which had withstood the earthquake almost undamaged. 1950's bunker architecture.

"I guess I'm your babysitter," said Chief Jefferson. "Damn you guys screwed the pooch at the library."

"Is that why we're up here?" asked Mickey.

"Mayor Happy says that we are to stand down during this public meeting," said Chief Jefferson. "I figure that won't last long. These strike teams are all college kids. They don't have a clue. We'll be back in the game soon enough. If you guys are still on the playing field by then. That's the key, I think. Keeping you guys here until you're appreciated, and you're needed."

"I still don't get why we are here at this demonstration in the first place, if we don't have a mission," said Tiny. "I mean, I don't even know why these people are here."

"No tienen agua," said Katy. "No water. None."

"Not for three days." said Mickey. "That's what this meeting is about, according to this here paper."

He waved a printed notice.

"Apparently there's some water here, and the city's agreed to hand it out."

On the stairs of the courthouse, where the water distribution was scheduled to take place, a few government employees were speaking with the crowd. Wallace recognized Causwell Dubbers.

"WE DON'T HAVE WATER AGAIN TODAY! I APOLOGIZE. WE APOLOGIZE. BUT THE FEDERAL GOVERNMENT AND THE OPPRESSORS KEEP THE WATER FROM US!" said the loudspeaker voice of Happy Johnson.

Happy Johnson was really taking sides these days, thought Wallace. Mayor Johnson was following the money, as always.

A box-sized drone buzzed down the street at their level, over the crowd, with a camera slung underneath. It began circling. Wallace eyed it evenly. He moved his shotgun from one shoulder to another.

"You've got your shotgun. Feel lucky?" said Mickey, pointing at the drone.

"Don't I wish?" answered Wallace.

He was keeping the shotgun with the chamber empty these days, and the magazine loaded with buckshot. Not expecting to use it. The gun felt sleek since El Tigre had removed the sidesaddle magazine on the firearm's receiver, added sights, and spray painted the gun brown.

Someone unexpected was now on the courthouse steps. She was a young Hispanic woman, and she was shouting, leading the crowd in both Spanish and English.

"Where is our promised water?" she yelled up at the small group of politicians.

Happy Johnson, Gillian McTavish, Causwell Dubbers, and a gaggle of the strike team stood together at the top of the stairs, by the microphones.

"¿Dónde está el agua que prometiste?" shouted the crowd.

"¿Dónde está el agua que prometiste?" they chanted.

"¿Dónde está el agua que prometiste?" again.

The politicians looked at the woman and the crowd blankly.

"Isn't it supposed to be la agua?" said Wallace to himself.

"THE FEDERAL GOVERNMENT! MONTANA, TEXAS, IDAHO, NEVADA, THE FLYOVER STATES, THOSE YOKEL BIGOTS DID THIS TO YOU BECAUSE WE, THE PEOPLE, CANCELLED THEIR ELECTORAL COLLEGE LAST YEAR! WE TOOK AWAY THEIR CONTROL AND NOW THEY ARE PUNISHING US! THEY DON'T CARE ABOUT OUR THIRST!" said Gillian McTavish into the microphone.

"True?" asked Wallace.

"Lies," responded Katy. "The information I'm getting is that the wells have sea water intrusion so they can't be used for drinking water, and the strike teams are keeping water from coming in. Diverting it to the blast zone, up at the port of Oakland."

"You better be sure of your information, girl," said Chief Jefferson. "You could start a war with information like that."

"I'm also hearing that the Oakland bomb wasn't nu-clear. It was an entire container ship of ammonium nitrate, docked next to a liquid propane tanker. The biggest conven-tional blast in history," added Katy. "With a little medical radioactive material thrown in to make the detectors go off and the cleanup more difficult."

The crowd was growing more and more stormy, loud, and now small objects began to fly through the air. Wallace saw that the people were throwing bricks they had pried from nearby planters.

"THE OPPRESSORS KEEP THEIR KNEE ON OUR NECKS!" shouted Happy Johnson into the microphone. "WE DIDN'T CAUSE THIS! FREEDOM! FREEDOM! THE CAPITALISTS, THE ONE PERCENT, DID THIS TO US! THE POLICE DEFEND ONLY THE ONE PERCENT!"

"WHAT?" said Mickey. "What does the police have to do with water?"

"AGUA! WATER! AGUA! WATER!" roared the crowd, now surging up the steps of the courthouse towards the politicians. "LIBERTAD! LIBERTAD!"

A brick narrowly missed the group of leaders as they retreated from the wave of angry citizens into the courthouse and shut the doors. The crowd pressed against the doors, pounding. Wallace could see the strike team members through the windows, looking confused, raising their firearms.

"See what I mean?" said Chief Jefferson. "No evidence of any authority, organization, or control,"

"It's like they want a crisis," said Tiny.

The crowd fell back, then surged up the steps in a wave, smashed in the door in several lunges, and poured into the building, roaring, scattering into the offices and courtrooms by the hundreds. Some of the lower story windows were broken already, and boarded over, but now the remaining windows were shattering. Wallace looked down and saw a pale young white woman in the mob, purple-pink short hair, black-framed glasses and dark clothing, pick up a brick, scream something, and throw the brick through a courthouse window as she exhorted the people near her. She seemed to be the strike team member he had seen at the stadium, but here she was, in civilian clothes, rioting. Couldn't be the same person. Wallace watched as she ran through the crowd into the courthouse.

"Should we get involved?" asked Tiny.

"Let's wait to be invited," said Wallace. "We are still in the doghouse over the library incident."

"After the fracking strike teams killed Diablo," muttered Mickey.

The rioting was growing angrier, and louder. A car's hubcap, probably from one of the several cars abandoned nearby, flew high into the air like a frisbee and banged against the wall of the abandoned Californian building.

"We gotta do something. Why did they tell us to get up here if we aren't allowed to intervene?" said Wallace.

"I think they want you on the news," said Katy. "The police, standing here with their thumbs up their butts. That way they have it on film that what happens is legal."

A surge of adrenalin hit Wallace, and he said, "Chief, we gotta get into this. It's out of hand," he spoke. "Katy's right. We're gonna be the fall guys on this."

Chief Jefferson appeared to be grinding her teeth as she looked down on the crowd. "Good point," she said quietly.

She keyed the mike on her shoulder. They had been cautioned to wait for orders, and to save the precious batteries, so to call was to violate standing instructions. The noise was growing, and Wallace could not hear what she said.

Wallace looked down on the crowd, which was now turning upon itself in anger, now destroying buildings near the courthouse, people fighting each other. There were two drones circling. One was filming and the other dipped lower into the street.

There was a flash and a smashing blast in the street below, and the concussion rocked Wallace off balance. Deafening, the blast wave pounding him, and he wondered if the building was going down beneath him, everything shaking, then he saw the dust rising from the street, and Chief Jefferson was on the ground, blood on her head, Tiny was down, and Mickey was staggering, and Wallace's ears were ringing from the blast, and he struggled to remember where he was and what had happened, and then Katy was looking in his face and she said something and then she motioned, look, look.

Wallace turned. The dust from the blast clouded his vision, but he could see that the courthouse was still standing, some pillars cracked, but still standing. Bodies everywhere. Katy turned him, to look down towards Main Street, and there were two more pillars of smoke rising into the sky. She pulled his face to hers, and spoke,

"Adelante! The people need us!"

When they got to the street, it was absurdly quiet. A window breaking. A lone voice shrieking atonally. Inert dead or injured people close together, some moving, some still. Some obviously dead, a few decapitated, many torn into parts. Blood covered by dust. A smell of burning.

Then more sounds as some people rose up. Dusty air, dust on everything, people covered in dust, several abandoned cars burning street side. More people, more screaming, then angry tones, and Chief Jefferson motioned and said, "Triage. Work the program, as we've been taught. If you've got your felt pens, mark foreheads, move fast, so when the fire department gets here, they don't have to spend time on assessment. Spread out and stay focused."

"YOU DID THIS!!!" a woman's voice screamed "YOU MURDERED US!"

Wallace turned and looked, and there was the young woman, purple-pink hair, black rimmed plastic glasses, shouting.

"Ah, no, we're just respon..."

"YOU DID THIS!" shrieked the girl, and she threw a brick piece at Wallace. "THE POLICE ARE MURDERING US! ¡La policía nos está asesinando!"

More people were coming out of the courthouse, and from elsewhere, swarming onto the street, others who had not been near the blast. Where had they been before?

"Take back the street! Take back the street! Take back our republic! The police are trying to kill us!" came voices from the crowd.

None of the police were now trying to assess any of the casualties. All the police were watching the mobs coming towards them from both directions.

"Into the courthouse, now," said Chief Jefferson. "Move!"

Tiny led the way, pushing through the dust-covered survivors standing stunned in the street, across the broad low stone stairs to a large ground-floor window which had been blown in, the frame bent. He picked up a dust-covered pair of pants.... a pair of pants, thought Wallace....and wrapped them around the window frame and pulled the gap wider. "In here, fast!" he said.

Wallace unslung his shotgun and watched the oncoming mobs as they converged from both directions. Don't chamber a round yet, he thought. Don't signal combative intent. He looked over his shoulder. Mickey, Katy, Chief Jefferson, were all through the opening, and now Tiny was attempting to get his massive form through the gaping broken window, and Wallace had to laugh, had to smile, and then he followed, and for him the opening was wide.

Down the darkened hall. There was no electricity, Mickey in front with his pistol drawn, people giving way before him. To the conference room where the mayor and the strike teams and Gillian McTavish stood, huddled in discussion, a platoon of strike team security eyeing the police warily, long guns pointed at the police as they entered the room.

"Time for you to leave, I think," said Gillian McTavish, glaring at the police officers and Katy with scorn. "Chief Jefferson, you stay here and help us discuss how to get a handle on what's going on out there. Sargent Ericson, you take your two stooges and your pocha and see what you can do about Main Street. The people are seeking justice down there, and sometimes justice is harsh."

"Cruel necessity," intoned Happy Johnson.

"Any more professional police down here?" said Wallace.

"You don't trouble your pretty little head about that," said a strike team leader. "We are in charge now."

The strike team leader was a well-muscled young man, taller and bigger than Wallace, with a tattooed neck and a shaved head. The young man looked squeezed into his green janitorial uniform and carried an AKM. A new AKM assault rifle, thought Wallace. Illegal in California. Where had that come from? Anyway, the kid could probably kick Wallace's ass. Two junkyard dogs and one junkyard. Better to defuse.

"On our way," said Wallace, and led Tiny, Mickey, and Katy from the room.

Katy turned and faced Gillian McTavish as they left.

"Tu follas por poder, yo follo por amor," Katy said to Gillian McTavish. "¿Cuál de nosotras es más honorable?"

"What she say?" Mickey called back. "Not sure I understood that."

"Keep moving," replied Wallace.

Out the back of the building, where there were few people, across the alley to Howard Street, past the abandoned National Guard armory which had been used as a shelter after the earthquake. The eye-watering ammoniac stench was intense: barrels of human waste had been stored alongside the building, and rioters had spilled these over onto the brown dead lawns. Looking through the gaping shattered front door, Wallace could see people moving inside the large central gymnasium, in the gloom.

"It's a mess in here, guys," called Tiny from the darkness. "You name it, you got it. Rape, theft, battery. The mob came through here earlier."

"Ok, we can help out," replied Wallace. "Let's see what we can do."

"SARGENT ERICSON? IS THAT YOU?" echoed a voice from the far end of the room.

Wallace was puzzled. Who was that?

"HOW CAN I HELP YOU?" he shouted back.

Causwell Dubbers came scuttling into the light beams of the high windows. As Wallace watched Dubbers' small stooped grey mottled form and disheveled thin gray hair come towards him from the shadows, he was reminded of a pet rat from his childhood, who had once escaped and found refuge in the dusty storage boxes under Wallace's bed.

"Oh, my God, thank God you are here," said Dubbers. "They are trying to kill me."

"Who is trying to kill you?" replied Mickey.

"The mob. The rioters. They are trying to kill me. They haven't found me, but when they do, they'll kill me for sure," said Causwell Dubbers.

The little man was shaking, thought Wallace. The little functionary was genuinely terrified.

"Well, jeez, Old Causwell, they're trying to kill us all," replied Mickey. "Don't shit yourself over it."

Wallace looked around the shadows of the large gymnasium, high and low. Katy had disappeared into the shadows with Tiny. Subdued sobbing, of a woman or girl. Small noises of movement. Awful stench. Causwell Dubbers smelled terrible.

"Are they trying to kill you in particular?" asked Wallace "Or do they just hate everyone on principle?"

"Oh, me. It's me they're after, for sure," said Causwell Dubbers. "The mob came, and I knew they had instructions, and I hid...I hid in the waste...the sewage barrels...they turned them all over but I was in...I was in the fresh one. The woman's sewage barrel."

"In the lady's room?" asked Mickey. "You hid in the girl's room? You're shitting me."

"No...no, that's why I'm alive," said Causwell Dubbers, softly.

"But why were they trying to kill you?" asked Wallace.

"Because I knew...I know.... I know what the plan is," replied Causwell. "This is planned. Of course, the earthquake wasn't planned. But a lot of this is planned. The explosions were a surprise to me. But the strike teams, the power shutdowns, the internet monitoring...definitely planned."

"You knew, and you didn't tell us? We're the police," replied Mickey.

"No, you aren't," replied Causwell Dubbers. "You're the enemy. You're the enemy to THEM, anyway. That's why they are trying to wipe you out. After the first strike team attack didn't kill you all, I thought we should ask the survivors... you..to join the plan. Join us. That's not what they want. That's why they want me dead."

Near Highway One, Big Sur, California

"I tell you, kind sir, they kill and they kill. They kill and...and I think they eat. The gods be kind, but I think surely they eat the people."

The words rushed out of the nervous East Indian man, perhaps about 50. He was paunchy, or perhaps, given his sagging features, formerly fat, and he was small, with stubby fingers, and his black, graying hair was thinning almost entirely. Garth watched him carefully. Yes, the man had been searched repeatedly, as had his wife, his two children, and a younger woman, all East Indians. The man sat trembling, his expensive dress shirt filthy, perspiration stained, his formerly dress shoes entirely worn of polish. The man reeked of old sweat and fear and feces. Yet he was so nervous, so panicked, that he might be capable of acting out. Meanwhile his family sat cowering against the oak tree trunk, as though they might blend into the bark.

"You say that's your car down there in the ravine?" asked Pike, again. Slowly. Perhaps even tiredly, thought Garth.

"Oh, yes, when they came, they made us work. They came to our home at night, and they surrounded, and then they came in. Oh, God," said the man, and he began to hyperventilate.

His entire family began to cringe, and tears appeared. Garth studied the family. There was the wife: East Indian, she was about 50 as well, and had apparently been heavy in the past also, given the lines and folds in her face. She had a proud, contemptuous expression. The boy seemed about ten years old...possibly a good playmate for his daughter Akemi, if they ever met. He seemed entirely subdued, yet hypervigilant, a frightened ferret. The daughter was younger, perhaps about six, and she seemed slenderer, not the same genetically, and Garth mulled over that for a moment. She looked more like the apparent older daughter, who seemed to be about twenty: slender and attractive and haunted. Garth wondered at what they had seen. All of them now were dirty and sweaty and terrified, sitting as close together as was humanly possible.

Pat and two helpers appeared with a basket. The basket had what seemed to be home-sliced French bread, with plastic containers containing sliced cheese and sliced tomatoes. Damn they grew superb tomatoes here, thought Garth. But this was food for the family.

"Garth, eat, you, Pike, eat," urged Pat, waving at them.

"We're good," said Pike.

"Look at them," said Pat. "They are afraid to eat our food. So you had better eat."

"Will do," said Bear, and he reached into the basket, carefully arranged a sandwich, stood up, and gave it a healthy bite. He stood chewing in front of everyone with a smile of great satisfaction on his face.

Garth, Ramon, and Pike both made their own sandwiches and began to eat.

Finally, the young woman, the attractive one, thought Garth, reached into the basket. The older woman scolded her in a foreign language. The younger woman paused, glared at her, and assembled a sandwich carefully.

"See? No meat," she said to the older woman, and passed her the meal. "Only bread and tomatoes."

The man looked at them submissively. "You see, before we knew, we ate...we ate their food. We ate what they gave us as they looted our home. Now we know...we think we know. That was not good. Oh, it was horrible, now that we know."

"Now we wonder if we will ever be clean again," said the older woman. "We wonder if we should die. We live only for him," and she motioned at the boy.

Garth pondered that. They hadn't mentioned either of the girls.

"Tell us please what you know," said Pike patiently, inspecting his cheese and tomato sandwich. "Please tell us from the beginning."

The man seemed to curl up and stare at his feet.

"My husband and I, we own a CAD company in Oakland," said the older woman quietly. "Together with my brother. We are very successful. You wouldn't know us, here in the farmlands. In the...how you say...flyover places."

Maybe you own a company, maybe you don't, thought Garth. Oakland's probably a bit different now.

"Cad?" asked Pike.

"Computer Assisted Design," answered the woman. "Clearly you are not one of the people who understand. We make the software for people who create and invent complex devices. Do you understand software? They use our software to design them. With built in pricing of components, it has an algorithm which, let me tell you, is the best at..."

"So there you were in Carmel Highlands," interrupted Pike.

The woman paused, gathered herself as if slapped.

"Yes, yes," she said, apparently offended.

"Please continue. My apologies, Ma'am," answered Pike. "I just gotta understand the threat as soon as possible."

"Oh, yes, oh they are coming to kill us," said the boy, his voice rising shrilly. "To kill us! To kill us!"

"We got security, right?" said Pike to Pat.

"Drones and three horse uphill. We're on full alert. Also, the people down on the road have continued on to the monastery. They're almost there. Trucks and drone base are staying put on this side of the ravine," replied Pat.

"OK, so ma'am, sir, you are all as safe as we can make you. Meanwhile we still need to know what happened. Please continue," said Pike.

"My brother and I, and our spouses, we own an estate in Carmel Highlands. It is an estate, really," continued the woman. "We have two groundskeepers, two Mexicans who live on the property, and we bring two security guards with us when we come from Oakland."

"Is the security armed?" asked Ramon.

"They...they have pistols, I think," said the man.

"Excuse me, but what is your name, Sir? Please? I'm Pat. We're going to need to talk for a while and it would be better if we knew everyone's name."

Pike stared at Pat when she finished speaking. Apparently, he hadn't thought of that, thought Garth.

"Oh, oh yes, I am Salman Singh, everybody calls me Sal, this is my son Shahid, my wife Sobhita," said the man.

"I am to be called Mrs. Singh," said the wife.

"And these ladies are?" said Pike.

"Oh, she is my brother's.... plaything. Girlfriend. Nobody to worry about," said Sobhita, her mouth twisting.

"I am Priyanka Kapoor, and this is my daughter, Radhika Khan," said the young lady, emphatically.

"Well, technically, not really Khan," said Sobhita. "Priyanka is not my brother's wife. The child is, you know..."

"Pistols," Pike interrupted. "What kind of pistols?"

"I don't know. It is not our problem. Security is for the hired men to consider," said Sal.

"Where are they now?" asked Pat, kindly.

Good cop, bad cop, thought Garth.

"They went to get help just after the earthquake. They never came back," said Priyanka.

"Where's your brother?" Pike said to Sobhita.

"Oh, he went out to face the people, when they came. They, they, they killed him," said Sal. He seemed to shake.

"Can you tell me about them, please?" asked Pike.

"There were ten," said Sobhita. "At least ten, a mob. All Mexicans. MEXICANS!"

Garth saw Ramon wince slightly but remain silent.

"There were five, at first" said Priyanka. "Three men, two women, three dirt bikes, like little light motorcycles. All white."

"First they knocked on the door, politely, then my brother went to talk with them and there was shouting, then we saw him being struck down with a kathir," said Sobhita, sobbing. "So disgusting for a man of his class to be killed by the foul peasants."

"A kathir?" asked Bear, gently.

"It was a machete, you know, a long knife. I took the children and ran out the back door quietly, quickly, and we hid then in the trees up the hill while the people were there," said Priyanka. "Until the night."

"Then they came into the house, and they were yelling, and threatening," said Sobhita.

"Five people?" asked Pike.

"Quickly there were more," said Sal. "They blew a horn, like a hunting horn. Like the Vikings used, you know. More people came in a truck."

"They were chanting, 'Eat The Rich', said Priyanka. "I could hear it all the way up the hill. I could see them making Salman show them the house, take the valuables, while with Sobhita they..."

"I was forced, and you will NOT speak of it," interrupted Sobhita, her voice rising. "They would have killed me. They took me to the pool area where they...."

"Yes," said Pike, interrupting her loudly. "We'll get back to that, please. What else?"

"I could see them cutting up my brother," sobbed Sobhita. "In front of me, while they were on me."

"What do you mean, cutting him up. Wasn't he dead already?" asked Pike.

"They butchered him like a sheep, into parts. I saw it

too," said Priyanka. "They chanted as they did it. 'Eat The Rich.' I would not let the children watch."

"When they were finished with me, they put me in the living room with my husband. I was allowed then to dress. They made so many jokes. They were cooking...they were cooking my brother's meat in a large pot they had...outside by the pool."

"Men and women?" asked Pike.

"Yes, all young, mostly white. A few Hispanics. They said that they would eat us the next day. Or at least one of us a day," cried Sobhita.

"Guns?" asked Ramon.

"What about guns?" said Sal.

"Did they have guns?" asked Pike.

"Oh, I don't know. A few, I guess," replied Sal.

"Only a few?" asked Pike.

"Perhaps two long guns, how do you say it?" said Priyanka, spreading her arms apart. "Also of course machetes."

"They made us eat," wailed Sobhita.

"Didn't the women help you?" asked Pat.

"Oh, no, they watched while the men...and they made jokes. They said I deserved it, that I was rich, that it was my turn now," cried Sobhita.

"How did you get out? How did you escape?" asked Bear.

Priyanka answered, "In the night, when it became dark, I crept down and set fire to the house. They had left the cooking fire untended by the pool and I left the children in the trees and came down and pushed the coals into the grass next to the garage. Then I went to the back room where they had Sal and Mrs. Singh and I broke the glass in the window, and they came out, and we went away together. The others were too drunk and too stoned to chase, I think. Then we got in the white BMW."

"I still had the keys in my pocket," added Sal.

"Oh, they saw and they chased us," said Sobhita.

"I drove as fast as I could. I turned off the headlights in case there were more," said Sal.

"They chased us but on the highway they couldn't keep up. We went south and we stayed fast," said the boy, Shahid.

"We hit a person, I think," said Sal. "Or a deer. I don't know. My headlights were off."

"Did you stop to help?" asked Tres, who had been listening from behind.

"Oh, no, they were right behind us," said Sal, shaking his head negatively.

"I think only one motorcycle When we hit the person in the dark there was nobody chasing us," said Priyanka wearily.

Mrs. Singh erupted in a loud foreign language, took off her shoe, which was more like a cloth slipper, and attempted to hit Priyanka, who leaned out from the older woman's blows. Bear stepped in and pulled Mrs. Singh back. More foreign language from the entire family. They resumed their seats.

"Then we drove into the hole. The big hole," said Sal.

"We got air! We really got air! And we rolled all the way over, upside down," said the little girl, suddenly, excitedly. Garth struggled to remember her name.

"Then we crawled out," said the boy, Shahid. "My father had shit himself."

Involuntary laughter from Bear, "Hey, be nice, I might'a shat myself after an adventure like that."

Sal was curling down, mortified, and Sobhita, the wife, was glaring at her son.

"Indeed yes," said Ramon.

"Then we crawled up into the trees, where you found us," said Sal, looking at the ground.

"You must get our car out of that hole this morning," said Sobhita. "It's a BMW 760i, and it's very rare. It is my brother's car. I demand that you call a tow truck and have it removed at once."

Pike reached down and picked up a cell phone from the belongings at his feet.

"Here ya go, Ma'am. Go for it. It might take awhile, though. I'm guessing Triple A is a bit busy," the young man added.

"Meanwhile we thank you for everything," said Priyanka. "Please let me know how I can care for these children, and help you as much as possible."

"I'll show you," said Pat, and she led them down the hill.

Beyond the landslide, scouts on the road and trails and the drones indicated that the monastery was undamaged, although replete with refugees, so Pike, Pat, and Glenda made the decision to move past it and continue north to the Singh mansion. Now they were up the ridge and about three quarters of a mile from the home, at around four AM or so, in a dense wet coastal fog, and they were watching laptop computer screens showing the thermal imagery feed from the drones over the Singh building. They were under a hastily assembled roof of tarps to prevent putting out light. Inside the canvas, the body heat and the computers made the dark space comfortably warm, thought Garth.

"I count five people, three apparent men, two apparent women," said Glenda.

"One couple, one threesome," added Bear. "Dang."

"Nice beds. Might as well use them," said Kiffin. "Better than the ground."

Where are all those other people that Priyanka reported?" said Pike. "By the way, this is astonishingly good imagery."

"Great. We can watch people having sex through walls," replied Bear gruffly.

"I miss that," said Glenda, wistfully.

"Looking through walls?" laughed Pike.

"Those other people are down here, down by the highway, with the truck,' said Pat, waving another computer screen at them.

"They will come running up the access road as soon as they hear shots," said Ramon.

"Yep," said Pike. "But look at them now, look at how they are deployed."

Garth studied the scattered red forms. "It's an ambush. They are spread across the road to ambush people on Highway One."

"That's one interpretation," said Kiffin. "Maybe it's just proactive security."

"Could be, but they are there on the road to encounter people somehow. Not just let them pass. Otherwise they would simply be on one side of the road, watching," added Pike.

"Does anyone see any other security? I know there are security cameras at the Singh home, but other than the ambush at the road and the people sleeping in the beds, anyone else?" asked Glenda. "Pretty self-confident, if that's true."

"Could it be that they don't know we're here?" asked Garth.

"They aren't acting like they know about us," said Glenda. "I was in the Air Force drone program for a few years, and they aren't acting like the Taliban. They are acting like looters."

Pat reached out to Glenda and stroked her head in the darkness. An act of love, thought Garth. He thought of his wife, Dove. So long since they had been together. Months since they had been close. Deep longing. He missed his wife, missed her deeply.

"Let's go get them," said Pike.

"We don't have to do this," said Kiffin. "We got enough problems of our own. We can just head back to the Castillo and let someone else deal with this."

"I'm deputizing anyone who comes with me. Anyone who wants to go. The Sheriff told me to go check this out, and I'm here, and now it's too late to pretend I'm not," said Pike.

"Well. I'm out. This is too big for me," said Kiffin.

"I'm in," said Tres. "I figure you'll need the help."

"The heck you are," said Kiffin. "You're my son, and you

-321-

are only 18. Guess that makes you a man, but that don't make you wise. This "eat the rich" cult is evil, Tres. This is the kind of thing you will never unsee, if those Pakis aren't fakin' it."

"I don't think they're Pakistanis," said Glenda, evenly. "I think they're Indians. Sikhs, to be precise."

"We are a warrior culture," said a woman's voice from the back. Garth turned and looked, and in the light of the computer screens he could see the haggard face of Mrs. Singh. "Make no mistake, we are powerful."

Oh, damn, he thought, more arrogance and drama.

But the woman's face, so deeply lined in the flickering light, seemed calm and resolute.

"Priyanka and I are going with you," she announced to Pike. "Your fight is our fight. Tell us what you need."

"Where's your husband?" asked Pike.

"He washed himself, and now he is ah, indisposed," said Mrs. Singh. "Meanwhile we are ready to assist you in your recovery of our home, Sheriff."

"Deputy," replied Pike.

"Well I guess that puts THAT cat in the bag," said Kiffin, apparently to himself. "You don't need us since you got the iron lady here. She's just gonna glare them to death."

"Kiffin, you always did hate hard work," replied Garth.

Inside, Garth was feeling terrified again, and he focused his mind on not shaking. Don't show them. He forced himself to turn to Kiffin and say, "Even with the Iron Lady, I still have to go along to keep Pike safe. He attracts bullets."

"And I can't stay back while Garth goes and gets himself into another mess again," said Bear.

"I'm not letting you Gringos walk into a trap," added Ramon, behind them. "It is OK if I come along? Pike you can deputize the Mexican Airforce?"

"Adelante! You got it," said Pike, smiling, "Beggars can't be choosers, and we need the help."

"Whatever you heroes want to do, do it fast," said Glenda. "It's dark, it's foggy, those beds are warm, and that ambush team is likely cold and stiff. They are blind and dumb right now."

"I'm out," said Kiffin. "This isn't Tres' fight, and it's not my fight, and I think the whole cannibalism myth is a fairy tale and Pike is playing God. Not our place. We need to wait for the government.

"I AM the government. At least I'm law enforcement. Doesn't seem to be anyone other than me," said Pike.

"You don't know that," replied Kiffin. "If you want to send anything back to the Castillo, I'll take it. Otherwise this is your problem."

Glenda spoke to Pike, "I'll support whatever you decide, with the drones. Meanwhile they are out there blind, cold, dumb, and stiff."

"Let's do it," said Pike.

"Blind, dumb, cold, and stiff," quipped Bear. "Sounds like me on Monday morning. Pike, you better tell us the plan."

South of Carmel Highlands, California

Garth did not see the bone pile before he slipped on it. His right foot went skidding out downhill from him within 20 yards of the looming mansion, and he felt his groin muscles strain ominously as he slid into an involuntary split. Trying not to make more noise, trying not to cry out, he fell over sideways into a nearby Monterey pine tree, making only a moderate crunch.

There in the green glow of the night vision monocular, with no depth perception, he could see the skull, the green-white bubble of the cranium, and he reached down without thinking and touched it. Slick, a bit slimy. Cold. Fresh. Apparently, they had boiled it for some reason.

That was the trouble with this night vision monocular, he thought with one part of his mind while the rest of his mind grappled with the urge to vomit explosively. No depth perception. He focused on that thought. No depth perception. And no lateral vision. That was why he had tripped. Then he realized. Yes, these were cannibals. Yes, he and Pike and the others were right to be here. The cannibalism was not just a story.

Against his will his mind wandered into just how these bones had been prepared, and stacked, a few yards from the house. Boiling. Had to be. Who had this skeleton once been?

Fighting his spasming stomach, he forced himself to keep moving towards the giant house, over the short stone wall marking the pool area. There, a bloom of light showed him the lingering coals of the fire which had been lit on the tiles. A large pot, with tubes, apparently from a brewery or a commercial cannery or some industrial kitchen, was raised up on bricks over the fire. Garth did not look in. A smell of boiling meat, garlic, spices. Against his own awareness, Garth thought of chili verde. He was hungry. He was aware that Bear was on his left, duck-walking like a SWAT officer with an 1860 Henry rifle. He, himself, carried his .45-70 Marlin in a very similar position.

Skidding sounds, and a small crash, and Garth worked the lever, chambered a round and braced himself for imminent shooting. A cat, apparently feral, came skidding around the corner of the house, and someone let out a small yelp, and then there was the flashbulb burst of light from the second floor of the mansion, a blast with the flash, and a crack as a bullet hit the pavement. They had guns, apparently. Without thinking, Garth raised his rifle just below the source of the light, now in blackness, and fired, and was instantly blind as the flash filled his night vision. He twisted the optic up from his face in time to see a dark form smack limply into the pavement a few feet away. Reaching into his pocket he felt a large .45-70 cartridge with his fingers and shoved it into the loading gate of the rifle. Until he knew what was going on, he would leave the chamber empty.

"Superb shooting. Just like Hollywood," said a crisp voice behind him in the darkness. Ramon.

Ramon did not have night vision, Garth remembered.

"Hope it's a bad guy," said another voice, and Garth was gripped by fear. Could he have just killed one of their own?

Killed a hostage? He reached up and pulled down the night vision optic, which by now had returned to normal. As had his own eyes.

Through the optic he saw three other men surrounding the downed body. Yes, there was Bear, there was Pike, and there was one of Pat and Glenda's security, a Castillo person. Garth didn't know his name. Behind them came Ramon, who reached out decisively and rolled over the body, and the dead person was clearly a man, Caucasian, with a beard and curly long hair, eyes half shut, face crushed and misshapen by the fall. Then Mrs. Singh pushed her way into the group, looked down, and muttered some foreign words. "Yes, he is one of the men. He is one who did things."

She spat on the corpse. Garth noticed the dark spot, where the bullet had apparently entered, at center chest. Solid hit.

"Keep moving, we're not done yet," whispered Pike. "Let's get into the building and beyond."

There was a click on Pike's cell phone, which was operating under a local internet umbrella. He looked at it.

"Glenda. Her drones say the other four people in the house are bolting and the bad guys at the roadblock are coming up here.

There was a buzz in the darkness above them, and a loud snapping sound on the other side of the house.

"Nine millimeter. Those are Glenda's drones. Move it."

Through the living room, a cavernous expanse of sprawling couches, a high ceiling, the power out, total

blackness. A shriek and a woman, a slender seemingly attractive young woman, came running at the them from the
entry hallway, a machete held high, wild screaming, and a
firearm's crash, utterly ear-splitting and a fireball flash of
Pike's shotgun and the girl, machete tossing straight up,
flung away as though by a rope, flipped backwards to slide
on the slick polished marble floor. The night vision monocular bloomed white again, partially blinding Garth, and
he missed a step down into the living room and almost fell
over. Behind him, Ramon reached out and steadied Garth,
and Garth realized that at the moment Ramon could see
better than he.

"They're all downstairs, all trying to go out the front
door!" said Pike, and the sound of his pump shotgun racking
was loud, through Garth's angry tinnitus.

"We surrender! We surrender!" came a young woman's
voice, and a young shapely woman without a shirt appeared
in the doorway in the light of a fire in the front yard. Her waist
was slender, and her stomach was smooth and her breasts
were solid, and she looked like fertility itself.

"Cabron!" whispered Ramon.

"Head's up!" said Pike. "She's naked for a reason, and
there's two more out there."

Garth forced his eyes away from the woman and saw that
there was light...firelight...reflecting off the garage windows
across the lawn.

"Bear," he said.

"I see it," replied Bear steadily.

As Garth watched, Bear moved stealthily to the right, out

of the doorway, to windows facing the garage. Bear raised his rifle and fired once.

There was a scream, out of Garth's vision, and a man completely engulfed in fire came running around the side of the building, wailing, the young topless woman screaming and pulling back in horror, and then a shot from Ramon's pistol and the burning man collapsed into a flaming, writhing pile. The young shirtless woman was so overwhelmed that her keening became one long shriek, interrupted only by sobbing breaths, and Garth saw Mrs. Singh leap forward, the dead girl's machete held high, shouting, "YOU WATCHED! YOU WATCHED US BEFORE AND YOU LAUGHED!!!!"

All chaos, and loud. Garth heard Pike yell, "STOP THAT NOW! LET HER SURRENDER!" but Garth's eyes were transfixed on that raised machete, and then there was Priyanka, behind Mrs Singh, pulling Mrs. Singh back with all her strength, and her words, loud and firm, "We don't want any more. We don't want any more. WE ARE NOT THEM!"

Mrs. Singh just let the machete fall gently from her grasp, the young topless woman still screaming and sobbing and cowering against the wall while the dead flame-covered man burned on the cement deck, and then the security man from El Castillo grunted, like a loud belch, so incongruous, and Garth turned, and the man had an arrow through him, a broadhead arrow, the large steel broadhead protruding from his back.

From the angle, it had been fired from a dark upstairs window, and the El Castillo man fell over as they all watched, and Garth heard Pike yell "Hey! Hey! Stop!" and there was the young topless woman...so beautiful, calm now...walking towards them, bending down, picking up the machete, raising it, looking at Mrs. Singh and Priyanka so close, so calm, as though she was posing, then a shot from Bear, and she fell limply, a large hole in her forehead, and her eyes staring.

"Enough of this," said Pike. "We can't let them hurt any more of us. Let's finish it."

Alisal Street, in front of the Monterey County Courthouse, Salinas, California

Wallace looked up at the still, swinging form of Chief Jefferson. She had been hanged by the mob. Alongside her remains were the hanged remains of Officer Mendoza. Hanging from a light post in old town Main Street. Both were nude, and large cuts and bruises scored their bodies. Chief Jefferson's eyes were swollen shut. She had been beaten before her death.

'HOLYJESUSMOTHEROFGOD!" shouted Tiny, looking up. "I'M GONNA BEAT DUBBERS TO DEATH RIGHT HERE!"

Wallace could smell Dubbers behind them. He could feel the little man cringing without looking.

"'LIL GOLLUM HERE COULD'A WARNED US!" shouted Mickey, cuffing the odiferous cowering man.

Katy pulled Dubbers back and stepped forward.

"Think with the front part of your brains, gentlemen," she said. "This man is the key to getting through this. The key to our survival and the key to our families' survival. All we have to do is sit him down and get him to tell us what he knows."

"Cut them down," said Wallace. "Katy's right. Keep our little shitbunny alive and we'll squeeze him until he bleeds."

Mickey climbed on Tiny's shoulders, and one at a time the dead forms fell into Wallace's arms. Wallace felt crushed and confused as he laid them down. Nothing was whole anymore. Nothing was true. All was corrupted and covered in sewage, like Causwell Dubbers standing behind Katy.

"Give me a rope," said Katy quietly.

It was hard to remove the ropes from the corpses' necks. The cords had locked down, dug deep into the flesh. Wallace worked them loose, threw one aside, and handed one to Katy. Quickly she looped it around Causwell Dubbers' neck and cinched it tighter.

"NO! NO! DON'T KILL ME! NO!" shouted Causwell, pulling back against the rope.

Katy held it firmly.

"Listen up, and listen well, hormiga. You don't deserve to live. You DON'T deserve to live. But we will let you live. I will PERSONALLY protect you, as long as you help us and tell us what we need to know. Lie to me and this rope goes into a tree and you swing. For now, it stays around your neck. Take your hands away from it. It stays around your neck, until we know that you deserve to live," said Katy. "Screw me over and you swing. Try to escape and you swing. Scream for help and you swing. Any questions?"

"I say he hangs now," said Tiny.

"No, she's right," said Mickey. "We can always kill him later."

"Meanwhile we need to cover these two," said Wallace. "They didn't deserve this."

He searched the vicinity, and found a downed tarp, a banner for the Republic of California. Covered in dust, and torn, it was still strong enough to carry both cadavers if all four men carried the corners. Wallace turned the banner over and shook it, raising a small plume of dust. The dust caught the light of the setting sun, and shimmered golden as it settled.

The front was painted with a mural of happy families, smiling, marching together in solidarity. A woman at the head of the group carried the new Republic of California flag, pointed and smiled back at the people following her. "Adelante hacia un futuro brillante" was painted across their feet in red.

"Forward into a brilliant future," translated Katy.

"They look kinda Asian," said Tiny.

"Not such a brilliant future if you are these two," said Mickey, gesturing at the corpses.

Wallace turned to Causwell Dubbers.

"Hormiga. Ant," he said. "It suits you, Causwell. Now take a corner of this tarp, and let's carry it somewhere to give these people a proper burial."

"Oh, God, please, no," said Causwell Dubbers. "I can't do that. I'm exhausted."

Katy jerked on the rope, lightly.

"You're not as tired as these two, are you?" she said. "Now we'll all take a corner, including you, and we'll all go adelante into the brilliant future that you helped create. PICK IT UP!"

South of Carmel Highlands, California

It really WAS a very nice house, thought Garth, letting the sunlight play on his face. Eyes shut. Such a nice warm day. He sat on the retaining wall by the pool, the cement deck still blackened where the burning man had lain. The inflamed tinnitus of the night's shooting still sang in his ears. They had literally shoveled the burned man away, in slimy cooked chunks. The remains of the El Castillo man, who had apparently been named Juan Portilla, a trained chef from New York, were covered by a blanket on the nearby green lawn. They had scooped up the smooth white previously cooked human bones into a large trash bag for later identification. Several individuals there, apparently. All mixed together. The forensics people would piece the remains back together whenever such a forensics team would be available, at some point. Meanwhile, for want of any other place, they would be buried with the remains of Juan Portilla beyond the driveway. Not a bad grave, thought Garth. Great views. Historic.

But what about the cannibals? Too many of the cannibals to bury. Perhaps eight. After the fight, after the ambush of the road team at the garage, the shooting, the scuttling in the dark, the final obvious decision that surrender was not going to happen, there were eight. Eight bodies. Mostly white people. Young adults. "Eat the rich" slogans spray painted all over the house. On the walls. In the bedrooms. Worse yet, the cooked remains actually smelled good. Damn. They were planning to pour the leftover stew into the graves. After all, they were remains, weren't they?

And that young woman. Model-beautiful. How was she mixed up in such a travesty? Three other young women as well, now all dead. Truly, truly, truly, the world was insane.

Garth counted in his mind. He had killed at least two, himself, with his .45-70 Marlin. At least. Perhaps wounded a few others who were killed by others later. Up close and in the dark, but good instinct, good hits. 12 shots. He remembered stoking rounds into the loading gate of his rifle, hands trembling, terrified yet determined, there in the dark. One way or the other, we lost one man, what was his name? Oh, yes, Juan Portilla. And there's eight dead of them. Were any of them innocent? Oh, Christ, what if some of the people we killed were innocent, just forced to go along?

A wave of nihilistic bleakness washed over Garth like a physical blow. He forced himself to remain still, face to the early morning sun. Tired on a cellular level. That was it. He felt ill. Nauseated. His arms, legs, and back ached. Had to be the stress.

He forced his mind away from the events of the night and focused on a condo on Maui. Napili Shores. Probably untouched by anything, perfect even now. Where they had visited last year. A certain day, the day they had watched the sunset over Molokai. Such a bright perfect day that had been. Think of his wife, Dove. So beautiful in that bikini. So beautiful. Look at her, he told himself. Ahhhh, they should have made a baby on that trip. A baby. Smiling, joyful, life-creating, all things good. Visions of closeness. Lovemaking. Nudity. The memories brought a sense of calm to Garth. Focus on the beauty. Dove. Maui. Bikini. Just like that.... remember when she was sitting on the beach, in the water only a little, little wavelets dancing around her crossed legs. In that bikini. Orange.

"Hey Garth? You woke?" came a tired voice. Bear.

"Ah, I was ever thus," replied Garth sadly.

"OK, Shakespeare, here's the commander in chief and she brung the planning committee," came Bear's voice.

Garth opened his eyes. Bear. Pike. Priyanka. Glenda. Ramon. They all looked exhausted. Bear and Pike looked filthy dirty, as well.

"Well ain't we having fun now?" responded Garth. "It's a pool party."

Ramon looked at the others. "Actually, you know, we SHOULD wash while we're here."

"Mrs. Singh is doing that now," replied Priyanka. "She wants to scrub down the whole house, but I told her it's too soon. We can't guard this place, can we?"

Garth noticed a spark of appreciation pass between Priyanka and Pike. In the sunlight, Priyanka was disheveled, but beautiful. Why was Garth's mind on sex, romance, and babies, after such a horrendous night?

"No, we can't spare the people to guard it, unfortunately," replied Pike. "No power anyway. And I know it's got to be awful up north, up by Carmel."

"Didn't these crazies come from up north?" asked Glenda.

"Santa Cruz or someplace near. Inspired by Toltecs and Aztecs, the whole "man corn" thing," replied Priyanka.

'Man corn?" asked Glenda.

"Yep. We found some pamphlets when we went through their stuff. The bags on their motorcycles. It's a progressive thing. The rich have wronged them, they think, so they claim the right of tlacat-laolli as the Aztecs called it, the right to eat the rich to gain their power," replied Priyanka.

"Well that's just polecat crazy!" said Bear. "Who'd think up such lunacy?"

"Apparently the "Eat The Rich" movement was a club at University of California at Santa Cruz. Led by a charismatic archaeology teaching assistant. They tried out all the old Aztec recipes, on pork, before the earthquake. Kind of a dark political satire thing," replied Priyanka.

"Kinda like Charles Manson," said Bear.

"It started out as a living history satire thing," Priyanka said. "Reliving the Aztec experience."

"In Mexico this would be so crazy that we couldn't even put it in fiction," said Ramon. "I still don't believe it."

"And yet I saw it all," replied Priyanka.

Garth watched her. Priyanka's boyfriend had been devoured by these maniacs. The father of her daughter. Yet she seemed hardly moved. Or perhaps, he pondered, she was so shocked that it was all theoretical. She was remarkably well spoken.

"First came the quake," said Glenda.

"The quake was inevitable," said Priyanka. "It seems like a hundred years ago."

Silence.

"Are there any more of them?" asked Pike.

"I don't know," answered Priyanka. "If there are, they are probably up north. All the cannibals here are dead so we couldn't ask. Amazing that they all preferred to die fighting."

"Where's the teaching assistant who started all this?" asked Glenda.

"Oh, he's rotting in the sagebrush with the rest of 'em," replied Bear.

More silence.

"Even if there ARE more of them, that's not our job. Our job was to take this group out, and we did that, and so long as I'm not seeing any other criminal activity, my thought is to head back to El Castillo, report in, and await further word. From my point of view, task accomplished," said Pike.

"I disagree," said Pat. "If it's this bad here, it's likely to get worse the farther north we go. We should keep going all the way to Carmel."

"All the way to Carmel? What if it's crazies and cannibals all the way up?" said Pike. "Besides, am I exceeding my authority?"

"Carmel. They were already nuts before the quake. And now this. If this is any indication, it's gonna be like the battle of Okinawa," said Bear. "One damned fight after another."

"One casualty after another," said Ramon, quietly. "But they probably need us up there, if it's that bad."

"We should get back to the homestead, back to San

Antonio de Padua." said Bear abruptly. "Castillo for communication, then home."

"Home?" asked Priyanka.

"Home is now Mission San Antonio de Padua," said Garth, a sudden feeling of awe and loss sweeping over him. Had it been that long? So much had changed.

"Ok, let's clean up, then decide later," said Pat. "This decision can wait for tomorrow. Let's decide in the morning."

"Carmel won't change by morning. But the world has changed. Everything has changed in just a little time. I don't think I'll ever look at meat the same way again," said Pike.

"I could use a salad, now that you mention it," said Bear, turning to Pat. "Did you bring any quinoa?"

San Antonio Mission, California

It was a misshapen battered little yellow bus, with monster truck all-terrain tires. A school bus for freaks. Like nothing she had ever seen before. A franken-bus. For a moment Raley wondered if the world outside had returned to normal and now they were starting school field trips again. She had a brief flash of the joyful field trips in her own childhood. Those memories seemed like another world.

Where was the security team? Raley thought. Then she realized: her grandpa Bear was off with Garth Ericson and Pike, chasing god-knows-what in Big Sur. Terp was off with his father, his grandpa, Tiger, Dove, Gritz and Randall and all the other shooters, fetching "slow elk". Most of the other women and the lancers were out reaping the remains of the barley fields towards Jolon.

Raley realized with growing fear that there was only as much security as the geezers...the true geezers....and the young people who did the electric grid...could offer. That derringer pistol between her legs. Not much good.

The bus pulled to a stop, and the folding panel door inverted, and a little cheerful plump woman jumped down. Curly hair. About forty years old. Janitor clothing. Smiling brightly. She saw Raley immediately.

"Well hello there! We're from the government! We're here to help!" the woman said buoyantly.

"Which government?" said Merry Thomas, standing behind Raley.

Raley turned and behind her, she saw the people of the camp, turning from their work at the horno, from the kitchen, from the tents. She saw Fred Paxley emerging from the privy. He was strong willed. He could help.

Poppy Roswell stepped up, and asked again, "Which government?"

"Oh, don't be afraid, citizens. The new government, the government of the people. The new Republic," said the woman, cheerily.

"Well," said Poppy, "If it's a government of the people then it's OK."

And he stepped back, just one step.

Raley's heart sank.

"How are you here to help us?" said Mrs. Ericson. There

she stood, with her walker, next to Larry. Larry was carrying a trapdoor carbine in one hand, down by his side, Raley saw. Some help in that.

Raley found herself pining for Terp. His solidity. His common sense. And wishing for Francesca. Francesca was strong. Neither was here.

It was a sunny day. For a moment, nobody said anything.

"Oh, I'm here because the State has decided that rural living will no longer be supported by the urban masses who toil on your behalf. I'm here to bring you all to the relocation center for processing," said the woman. "You'll like it. It's better than this in many ways."

"We like it here," said Samantha Roswell.

"When you're enlightened, you'll understand. You may love it here, but the state can't afford to take care of you here. It's time to move to a place where you are less of a burden on society," said the curly-haired lady.

"And here we were, making our own food, living our own lives. Clueless of our parasitic ways," said Mrs. Ericson.

"You'll come to understand," said the woman. "You'll be educated."

"I'm sure that's part of your plan," said Mrs. Ericson.

"Hey, do you have internet?" asked Hillary.

"All the internet you want. In fact, universal internet is one of our Republic-wide pledges," said the woman, smiling. "You'll love it. Lots of games. New clothing, new everything."

"I'm ready to go now," said Hillary, turning to the group. "Everyone, tell Poppa Bear I went, and divide up my stuff. I don't want it."

"Not so fast, young lady," said Belinda Jefferson. "You are leaving everything you know. You are leaving everyone who loves you. Why do you want to do that?"

"Reality sucks," replied Hillary, her voice breaking. "It sucks. The cloud is much better."

Hillary turned and climbed on the bus without so much as her water bottle. Raley felt a sob rise in her throat. The awareness swelled up in Raley's soul, how much she loved her sister Hillary, how much she loved them all. She restrained herself from shouting.

As Hillary climbed the high steps of the modified bus, two janitor-clad young people stepped down. They had military rifles. One young man, one young woman, Raley noted. Oh if only Terp, or Francesca or Dove were here.

"So? Who's next? Let's get everyone on board and get back to our station!" said the short woman cheerfully. "Internet! Hot showers!"

"I'll go later," said Katrina Paxley. "I'm making bread right now."

"But we have all the bread you'll ever be able to eat, and someone else will make it for you!" said the cheerful woman. "It's VEGAN bread!"

"This is MY bread," said Katrina Paxley.

"Your bread ain't that great," said Fred Paxley. "Besides, it IS the government, and they ARE here to help. "So let's get on the frakin' bus!"

"After the bread," said Katrina.

"Well hell, I'm not gonna be shamed by goin' without my wife," said Fred Paxley.

"We HAVE to take someone!" said the woman. "And we have to take all your guns. You'll only hurt yourselves with those."

She motioned at the two young people with the rifles, standing behind her."

"Get these people," she said to the young people. "Leave their trash."

The young janitor-clad people moved forward into the tents, holding their rifles at the ready.

"Now hold on!" said Beeston Bragg. He was one of the few young people left behind at the mission. "Just stop!"

Beeston reached out and gripped the young woman by the shoulder, and the young man lifted his rifle, and fired a burst of automatic shots into Beeston's back. Beeston tensed, stood tall in his 1873 cavalry uniform, and then collapsed, completely still in the dirt. His pistol was still in its holster.

The young green-clad man stood staring down at the still form of Beeston with his assault rifle held hot in his hands. Paolo Archuleta was standing nearby, and instinctively he raised the shovel he was carrying and brought it down hard. The shovel struck the young man in the head, and there was a crack, and the young man went down.

The young woman raised her M-4 and fired a burst into Paolo, and Paolo collapsed backwards. Oh, please, no, thought Raley, and someone grab his rifle, you're close enough.

Nobody moved.

There was a shout on the bus, "Go go go!" and there

were three more people in janitor clothing tumbling down the steps of the vehicle, with M-4 assault rifles, and they pointed their guns at Raley's people, and Raley thought to herself, we're all going to die here, all of us, and my baby, and suddenly she didn't want to die and more than anything she wanted her baby to live and she wanted Terp. She wanted Terp. These people from the bus were the enemy, thought Raley. She felt horror, shock, and anger. Rage.

Silence.

"Hey, he's still alive, his skull isn't even fractured," said one of the young janitor-men, looking up, lifting his fallen compatriot.

"Get him on the bus and then we'll deal with the rest," said the woman.

"I guess we know what your goals are, after you murdered our sweet young boys," said Mrs. Ericson.

Mrs. Ericson was holding a .45-70 trapdoor carbine at waist-level, and she was pointing it directly at the small woman. The large hammer was cocked back. The carbine was ready to fire.

"That young man was a criminal. He was wearing a pistol. All guns are outlawed, except for strike teams. Oh my!" the curly haired woman sighed. "You have a lot to learn. I imagine you still eat meat. And you, poor old dear, on the wrong side of history. Ready for processing."

"Can't see anything, so I may need to kill you twice. Or you can leave."" said Mrs. Ericson in a quavering voice.

Raley looked at the bus. She could see Hillary's shocked

face looking through the window glass. Hillary probably hadn't expected the shooting.

"There's no afterlife, you know. There's nothing more," said the woman, swinging her arm in an encompassing arc. "All this is a monument to an imaginary vengeful playmate. The Republic will rightfully end the farce."

"Maybe so. You'll still be dead," said Mrs. Ericson.

"A truce then?" said the woman, "Rather than a big gun battle in which many....many...will die, and rather than calling for assistance, I'll go now. I'll be back. My name is Mrs. Chesbrough. Remember my name."

"Take Raley! Take her! She's pregnant anyway. Teenage girl shouldn't be havin' babies," said Fred Paxley, motioning at Raley. "Maybe you can give her an attitude adjustment."

"Fred, you shut your mouth!" said Katrina Paxley.

Raley looked at Mrs. Ericson. How long could a 102 year-old woman hold up a trapdoor carbine, she wondered. Once Mrs. Ericson let that gun down, the young janitor-people would start shooting. The young janitor-people had machine guns.

"Well, folks, she IS from the government," said Poppy to the group. "Terrible...terrible...about young Beeston and Paolo. But everyone makes mistakes. Governments make mistakes. Mrs. Cheese bureau IS from the government! We should do what she says. They've got experts in the government, so...so I figure they know the right thing to do."

"It's Mrs. Chesbrough," said the woman fastidiously.

Raley was going through a quick calculation. She was angry and terrified. For herself. More for her baby. And even more for all these people. The horror of Beeston and Paolo's slaughter enveloped her. Courage, she thought. As brave as that Sioux at the Battle of the Rosebud, Buffalo Calf Road Woman. Don't show them.

"What will happen to me?" she asked,

"Teenagers, especially European teenagers, aren't allowed to have babies," said the woman. "But there's internet! Lots of games! And we serve HUMANITY!"

"I'll go, if the others can stay," said Raley. "That way you can avoid bein' dead."

South Carmel Highlands, California

After a breakfast of oats and ground walnuts...lacking the quinoa which they had eaten last night...Garth stood by Dogfood. Dogfood the horse was saddled, ready to go, looking tired and unkempt, as tired and unkempt as Garth felt. Garth missed his family. He missed the mission. He missed Dove more than ever. And last night he had been unable to sleep in the house. The bed had been oh so soft. Perfect. But it had too many possible memories. Too much had happened there. Perhaps, thought Garth, they should simply tear this house down and start over. So now he stood there, clean from last night's cold shower but unshaven, exhausted, wondering when they would head north.

North to more "Eat The Rich". Bear was right, it was going to be like Iwo Jima.

Across the driveway, beyond the giant glass windows of the entry, Garth could see Salman Singh, and his wife, incongruously scrubbing the poolside deck where the burning man had cremated. The burning cannibal, Garth thought. So many memories. Dogfood rolled his bit in his mouth. The day was getting hotter.

Salman and his wife would be staying here. Rebuilding. Burying the eight corpses in the bushes beyond the driveway. Amazing that they would want to stay here after all that had happened. They would be keeping some of the cannibal's guns, a .30-30 lever action rifle and a .357 revolver, but still. Insane.

Visible in the giant foyer windows, Priyanka came down the stairs in a new set of jeans and a safari shirt, and a jean jacket. She looked rested, put together, sexy. She walked to Ramon, who was seated on his horse waiting next to Garth.

"I will go with you all, go north," she said.

"What about your daughter?" responded Ramon.

Clearly there was some chemistry between them.

"We know there are no enemies to the south. They are all to the north. So she will stay with the Singhs until I return here."

"Hmmmm," said Ramon. "What...."

"I've already cleared it with Pike," interrupted Priyanka. "I can handle a horse, and a gun, and I'll spend most of my time with the drone wagon anyway."

Garth saw a movement beyond the house, through the windows, and his adrenaline surged. Something on the trail up the hill, from whence they had attacked this house last night. He reached for the Marlin rifle in its saddle scabbard, then relaxed as he recognized the mounted rider. It was Tres, and he looked battered and horrified.

"He's dead. He's dead. They shot him dead. His own friends," said Tres, and he began to sob.

They gathered around him in the driveway, all appalled.

"Kiffin's dead?" asked Bear. "How did it happen?"

"They've taken over the Castillo," moaned Tres.

"What?" said Glenda? "Who?"

"Some of the refugees. They said that all property belongs to the people now, and the Castillo is the property of the people. They had already killed the foreman and a few others."

"Hold on. These are refugees?"

"Yes, and also some of the employees. There's also some new people there, from the California Republic, and they say that all private property is now the property of the Republic. They say that everything Pat owns is now confiscated. She's a billionaire, and her corporation is now the property of the republic."

"Well that's just a couple of hotheads," replied Bear. "What happened?"

"They told my father to give them his rifle and his ranch, for the good of the people. My father said, "Not my rifle and not my ranch, you gooseshit eating cretin!" and one of them just pulled out a pistol and shot him through the head," answered Tres. "That was it! No discussion! And I just backed away! I was a coward! I just turned and snuck out and rode here! I know that some of the people...our long-term neighbors...must have covered for me."

"Better a live donkey than a dead lion," said Ramon. "You've been wise, not cowardly. Now you can fight again."

"Where's Pat?" asked Glenda. "She was here this morning. She should be hearing this."

"I met her on the trail," answered Tres. When I told her she just revved up her quad and headed down to the highway. She said to follow as soon as possible. She was in a terrific hurry."

"Oh damn it!" replied Glenda. "She's used to being in charge. She's friends with Governor Grantham. She's head of the LGBQ Commission for the state, for God's sake. Why would she put herself at risk by a couple of crazies?"

"I'm sure she'll be fine," said Pike. "She's going to be respected by the new government. After all, her friend is the new premier, or president, or whatever. But let's saddle up right now and head south. South, not north. Let's ride."

"The Battle of Okinawa appears to be postponed," whispered Bear to Garth, as they reined into line.

"Not so sure," replied Garth, in a low tone.

South Salinas, California

Happy Johnson set down his fork in the brilliant electric light of his large, well-appointed dining room. Beyond him at the table, Gillian McTavish sat next to Pastor Paco, who looked recently showered, and six strike team leaders. They were all apparently stunned by Wallace's unplanned arrival. The food smelled wonderful. Apparently, some sort of chicken cacciatore.

There was wine on the table, and water. Precious water. Wallace stifled his intense desire to shoot them all, right now, and end this. He raised his shotgun to port arms. How gratifying to see a look of horror spread across the face of Gillian McTavish.

Beside Wallace stood Causwell Dubbers, newly washed, vastly less pungent, yet still with the noose around his neck, held by Katy. Behind Causwell stood Katy, and with her were Dina Montero and Mike Rogers. Tiny and Mickey were providing security in the doorways.

"So you talked your way in here with dear Causwell?" said Happy.

"Actually, Causwell is a well-known bandit chieftain now. His name is El Hormiga," replied Katy. "And it's the other way round. He talked his way in with us."

"Hir new name is El Hormiga," said Gillian McTavish. "Use the correct terminology."

"Ahhhh," replied Happy. "A misunderstanding, I see. Hormiga. What does that mean?"

"Dragon of freedom," replied Katy.

"An apt name, certainly," chuckled Gillian McTavish.

The strike team members laughed into their hands, chuckled silently.

"What happened back there?" asked Wallace, barely curbing his anger. "Why were the police set up? Why were the Chief and Mendoza lynched?"

"Beyond your pay grade, I'm afraid," smirked one of the strike team members.

Wallace loudly worked the action of his shotgun, chambered a round. Frack them all. Pastor Paco and Gillian McTavish visibly jumped at the sound.

"Now, now, don't be too fast. We have your families," said Happy Johnson. "Rashness now will have unpleasant results. Calm down. Breath through your nose."

"You don't have my family," replied Wallace.

Happy Johnson gazed calmly at Wallace. "Oh, but we have Officer Ramirez' family. Do you want to call him...ah, em...over here and tell em you want them...hmmm, em...oh, heck, them... all to fall victim to our current social unrest? After all, it's a mob. You never know quite where they will go, or what they will do.

Gasps and muttering from the people around Wallace.

"Do you mean to say...," said Dina Montero, but Wallace quickly raised a hand, and she was silent.

"And, as if you really cared, we have the late Officer Mendoza' family. Imagine the loss. A wife. Two very young children. I understand one is still in diapers," said Happy Johnson.

"If you think we're gonna...," began Dina Montero again, and Wallace squeezed her shoulder hard, painfully hard, until she again was quiet.

"Oh, and we have Lacy Rogers," said Gillian McTavish.

A sharp intake of breath from Mike Rogers. "You mean... you mean she's still alive?"

"Ze is alive, but not well, not yet," said Happy Johnson.

"Zer health remains precarious. You remember ze was very badly stabbed."

"And a person of our community was murdered as well, with NO prosecutions," added Pastor Paco.

"Yet Lacy's health remains precarious," continued Happy Johnson. "I would guess you wish to help in her recovery."

"Why wasn't I told?" demanded Mike Rogers.

"We've been waiting for the right time to share the good news. Now seems to be especially apt," said Happy Johnson.

He took a sip of his red wine.

"Why?" asked Dina Montero. "I accept that you control these police officers, but why make them the enemy?"

"Cruel necessity, Mix Dina," said Happy Johnson. "The people need someone to hate, and the Republic needs to destabilize society, dislodge the holders of power and wealth. Two birds with one stone, if we take out the police. Chaos begets transformation, transformation begets a vacuum, and in that vacuum, a little something by us goes a long way."

"Why kill them? Why kill the Chief? Why kill Mendoza?" asked Wallace.

"Cruel necessity again, my knuckle dragging friend. Not a deep thinker, are you? The mob needs to see we're serious, the world needs to see we're serious, and both of them were never going to get on board. Especially the Chief. No, ze was incorruptible. Now, presto, ze's corrupting anyway."

"Scares the shit out of people," added Pastor Paco. "A little social justice goes a long way. Everybody falls right into line."

"Like xou, as of tonight," said Gillian McTavish.

"I think a lot of people aren't going to be happy about this. A lot of people are going to see through the social unrest you are creating. And as for the upper class, color them gone. What will you do when everyone who matters has left?" said Dina.

"That's kind of the point," answered Pastor Paco.

"For every two who leave, there are five who want to come here, mostly from far away," said Gillian McTavish. "We've learned there's political power and economic benefit from simply putting occupancy in this great republic up for bid. Yep, the people who have to stay here will serve, and the people who can afford to come here, and pay for the luxury, will do just that."

"Who was it who said, ah, money talks and bullshit walks?" said Pastor Paco. He laughed. "Oh, it was that comedian, Richard Pryor. Yep, like the rest of them, killed by his needs."

"If that's true, then you'll sign up with us quite soon, if not tonight," said Happy Johnson. After all, the Republic of California now controls your pensions too. Isn't that all you police care about? Pensions?"

"Doughnuts," chortled Pastor Paco. "Let them eat... doughnuts."

Pastor Paco chuckled and squirmed in his chair.

Wallace fought back an urge to reply with defiance, a shout, brave words. He looked at Katy. She was telling him with her eyes: don't say anything. A look at Dina: she was ready to burst. Mike, eyes popping, seemed angry enough to bite a chair in half.

"What do you want us to do?" asked Wallace.

"Well, you're the police, so right now we want you to appear uncaring," replied Happy Johnson. "Disinterested. We want the people to see you...ah, excuse me, xou, castrated. Powerless. Effete. Get them to make us some living space for newcomers."

"Oh, oh, we want you to be bumbling, even," laughed Pastor Paco. "We've been looking forward to this for years."

"But the people are SUFFERING!" blurted Dina Montero. "This isn't pretend. The criminals are looting. There is no water. There is no power. There is no food."

Ah, well, I learned about that as a pastor, watching over my church. You WANT them to be suffering," said Pastor Paco. "There's big money in pain."

Near Los Burros Road, Big Sur, California

Glenda's atonal wordless shrieks filled Garth's ears. So loud. So unending. One would think that a person so cerebral would not be so emotive. But there was Pat's body, laid out before them next to several of the Castillo residents.... Garth recognized the riddled corpse of one of the farming staff,, and Kiffin Senior as well. All shot in the head. Pat had been shot in the eye, a very ugly wound. The eye itself had exploded by the bullet, and death had been instantaneous, so far as Garth could see, looking down at her. Her remaining eye was open. She looked surprised.

Pat's executioner, a bearded young man with a definite Che Guevara vibe, complete with beret and an olive-drab military surplus shirt, also seemed surprised. The retaking of El Castillo had been relatively simple: Glenda had used the drones for a rapid reconnaissance, none of the new arrivals seemed to know much about long range shooting, or basic military tactics for that matter. One sweep: long range takedown of the inattentive strike team security and a quick rush. None of the new strike team arrivals seemed to know much about guns, and except for Che, none of them seemed very eager. Che had surrendered his Glock quickly after Pike had shotgunned his two pistol-waving protectors.

Buckshot, thought Garth. Double-ought buckshot. Amazingly effective.

"You are GOING TO LISTEN TO ME! YOU ARE GOING TO FOLLOW MY INSTRUCTIONS! I REPRESENT THE NEW REPUBLIC OF CALIFORNIA! I REPRESENT <u>FREEDOM</u>!" Che shouted, gesturing to all around, perhaps two dozen people. Bear was guarding him and three other captives with his Henry rifle. Two of the other captives had come with Che. The other was a woman, a longtime employee who had somehow sided with Che. Garth wasn't entirely sure. She looked afraid. Bear looked sullen and murderous.

Glenda was quieting now. Garth looked up by the yurts, where she was standing, and saw young Tres hugging her. He was wearing Kiffin's .300 H&H Magnum rifle slung diagonally across his back. It had been recovered during the raid. The invaders hadn't even tried to use it. Lucky for us.

"This is a manifesto, it is certain," said Ramon. He was holding the man's documents which identified him as a District

Administrator of the new Republic of California, authorized to do whatever was necessary to bring power to the people and carry out "Restorative Justice" after centuries of oppression. He was authorized to "bring justice summarily wherever such action is necessary for the welfare of the people."

The documents were printed in three languages. English, Spanish, and Chinese. And they were all signed by President Grantham.

"This is like the Twilight Zone," said Garth to himself.

"I agree," replied Ramon, standing close to him. "We aren't in Kansas anymore."

"All in all, I'd rather be in Kansas," said Garth.

"You know my parents fled this kind of insanity in India in 1948." said Priyanka.

Garth spoke to the Che-like man, loudly. "You've murdered five people here. Why?"

"Because I CAN!" shouted Che. "Two of the people I processed would not tell me where this lady was! They were her downtrodden SERFS, yet they refused the hand of liberation."

He motioned down at Pat.

"Why her?" said Garth.

"Because she was a pig-tyrant billionaire who owned the people's wealth! A yapping puppet of the oligopoly. When the state attempted to claim her corporation, she transferred it to Mexico via the internet. Except for this fortress. This palace, this monument to excess," he gestured around him.

"Seems like a buncha tents to me," said Bear. Bear still had his rifle pointed at the man, and he spoke through clenched teeth.

"You don't get it, rural meat-eater," said Che. "She possessed it, but she didn't build it. Yet she had billions of dollars. And the people did not."

"How does her death enrich the people?" asked Ramon. "Are they richer now?"

"Well, yes, actually, "said Che. "The people will sell this place to fund the rebuilding and the government."

"Who makes that decision?" asked Priyanka.

"Actually, I do," replied Che. "This is my district. I will make this my headquarters when all my command team arrives. I've already selected my yurt. There is some discussion that we will make this a tourist destination. Like Hearst Castle."

"YOU MURDERED MY WIFE TO SEIZE HER PROPERTY?" yelled Glenda.

"I will tell you again. She didn't build it. She had only the miniscule concepts for her corporation. Consider: if I think of something, is it real? If I think of a child in you, are you pregnant? No. The ideas do not matter TO THE PEOPLE! The tiny droplets of her ideas were made real by the oceans of sweat of the millions," answered Che.

"That is one way to see it," said Ramon quietly. "Granted that the corporation has removed itself to Mexico City, you are left only with her personal property, such as this place. Glenda here is her wife. Does she inherit? According to you, who now owns this place?"

"The new elites of the proletariat," responded Che. "The people."

"And who will those be?" asked Ramon. "We had this in Mexico. Revolution. Suffering. Murder. The new elites replaced the old elites, who had replaced the older elites, who had in turn replaced the Aztec elites who were before. Revolution. The elites always look after themselves."

"Our elites will be wiser. There will be wealth sharing," responded Che. "We of the revolution are wiser."

"That's what they told us too," replied Ramon. "That's what they always say."

"This time is different," said Che. "I am one of the elites."

"For that, you murdered these people," said Ramon.

"To make an omelet, it is necessary to break eggs," said Che. "You will see. The new Republic will offer freedom for..."

There was a blast. Che stepped back as though he had been punched, and a large bloody hole about four inches wide appeared in his sternum. He tried to breathe, and as he realized that he could not, his eyes opened wide. He stared around the group, walleyed, stricken, his chest heaving, imploring silently. Then he simply fell over.

Pike stood beside Ramon with his shotgun raised, the barrel smoking.

"We don't have time for this," he said. "We got lots to do."

"AAAAHHHHH!" shrieked one of the prisoners, falling to his knees. He had been standing next to Che. "DON'T KILL ME! DON'T KILL ME!"

"We gotta get up the hill," said Pike to the others, ignoring the prisoners. "If they did this here, then I'm guessing they've also been to the mission."

"The mission? The mission?" replied the groveling man desperately. "Yes, yes, there's a team going to the mission too. They should be there now."

Garth's heart leapt in his chest.

"What's happening at the mission?" snarled Bear.

"It's a place of religion, and the Republic has banned those places of hatred and anti-LGBQ intolerance," replied the woman prisoner, calmer now, prouder now.

She reached down sympathetically and helped the groveling man rise up. He stood up hunched and shaking, a Chihuahua in jeans. "It is better to die on your feet than to live on your knees," she told the man, dusting him off.

"It is better not to die at all," said Priyanka. "It is better not to envy, not to hate, not to covet."

"Easy to say when you are beautiful, and rich, as you are," said the woman. "But I lived as a campesino. I did not own. I am proud to say that I own nothing."

Garth pondered that word, "campesino". The woman had pale skin and red hair.

"But you lived here?" asked Ramon, gesturing around.

"Yes, but it was never mine," the woman replied.

"I've never owned anything either, really," replied Priyanka. "Except my intellect and my self-esteem. And my values, whatever they are."

"Those are all obsolete concepts, in the new century," said one of the prisoners, a small, runty man, with tortoise shelled glasses, speaking for the first time, and standing taller. "All swept away in the new era. You'll learn, citizen. Guillotine 2022!"

"We don't have time for this," repeated Pike. "Who's gonna be in charge here?"

"I'm going with you, and I'm taking the drone team," replied Glenda.

A gray-headed African American man stepped up from behind Glenda. "I'm Mick. I guess that leaves me in charge."

"Who's Mick?" Pike asked Glenda.

"I'm a facilities manager, and I own, or I guess I SHOULD say I OWNED a facilities service business as an independent contractor. My firm kept this place running and managed about five enclaves and hotels along the coast here. You know, change the sheets. Restock the soap. Polish the floors."

"Mick, why didn't you put a stop to this madness?" asked Pike, angrily.

"She...she brought them," said Mick, motioning to the red-haired woman captive. "She snuck them in. Said they were her friends and got them past security. First I heard of it was when that beret guy on the ground there shot Pat. Pat was angry, and he just shot her right there. Then the killing started. That was that."

"Who's she?" asked Pike to anyone.

"She's my cousin," responded Glenda. "We grew up together. I got her this job, gardening. We grew up together in Berkeley and she's struggled with addictions and failed relationships and anger all her life, and so I gave her a home here. A home here." Her voice trailed off and her face grew hard.

"If you are taught anger and hatred, it's what you know," said Priyanka quietly.

"OK Mick, you're in charge," said Pike. "Do whatever you want. Please give these people a fair trial when you have the time. Do whatever you want. Be wise. Be just. I gotta go."

"Mick, Pat always loved that hill behind the water tank," said Glenda. "Please dig the grave there. Oh, might as well dig graves for all of the...the dead. It's wonderful up there. Oak trees."

She began to sob, and turned to her quad with the deca-panel trailer.

"We wanted children. We wanted children for this wonderful place," sobbed Glenda.

"My wife died...breast cancer...nine months ago," said Ramon, behind her. "I know how very terrible it is right now. I will support you in any way."

"Oh, oh, and Mick, if I don't come back, it's all yours. Until of course I DO come back," Glenda sobbed a little and laughed. "God damn it was a beautiful life here."

Garth looked around. It was a beautiful sunny day. In the distance he could hear the descending notes of a canyon wren, somewhere out in the chemise brush. The ocean glittered down the hill.

"Saddle up!" said Pike. "Ten minutes."

"Oh Pike?" added Mick

"Yep?"

"I was 82nd Airborne, Afghanistan and Iraq. When you meet the enemy, give 'em hell from me."

King City, renamed "Libertad", Republic of California

The young people in the janitor clothing roughly pushed Raley from the back of the military truck, hustled her into a dark room, and shut the door. Dim lighting. This must have been a school, she thought. Grass lawn in front, now dead from lack of watering. Institutional look, and there were students' desks, all pushed into the center of the room. A table at the head of the class. A chalkboard. And in each corner, a young woman, eyes white in the semi darkness. Three young women, she thought. They all seemed to be about her age.

"Where am I?" Raley asked quietly.

"Reeducation," said a young red-haired girl from the far corner. "You pregnant like the rest of us?"

"Yep," said Raley.

"Re-education is one name for it," came the sneering voice of the last girl, blond hair so evident in the half light. "You're under eighteen, right?"

"That's me, blondie," replied Raley. "Were there any other women here before?"

"Yep, two others but they got taken away. Never came back," said the blonde girl.

"Damn," said another voice, a black haired pale skinned woman in another corner. "Before that happens, the guards get to play with us. They play rough."

"Doesn't the Republic protect you?" asked Raley, aghast.

"Maybe they don't know, maybe they don't care, maybe this is part of re-education," said a voice.

"Anyone fight back? Anyone go out those windows?" said Raley, pointing to the windows on the side of the classroom.

"They have tasers, and there's too many of them," said the red-haired girl. "The girls before us said they tried."

"Have any of you tried?" asked Raley.

"Gonna shame us because we don't fight back?" said the dark-haired girl. "They came through my town, Gonzales, like a flood, and they shot my father in front of me. You gonna shame me now because that took the fight out of me? I spent my whole life being told to be peaceful, and now this. This."

The girl's voice broke, and she sobbed.

"No...no," said Raley. "This is all so overwhelming."

Raley was acutely aware that she had not been searched. Not really. A little groping. A diffident patting. But they hadn't found Poppy's gift, in a napkin in her panties. The Republic people had just grabbed her out of the franken-bus and put her in the truck. They had had a gun pointed at her the entire time or she would have escaped before. And probably she would have died. Well frack it.

"My grandpa Bear, he was in Vietnam, and the Viet Cong got him, and he says that the best time to escape is as soon as possible, before a routine sets in. And before we get weak." said Raley.

"Your funeral," said the red-haired girl. "Just don't expect our help, OK? They'll be coming any minute. Can't guess what you got up your sleeve, though."

"It's what's in our panties, ladies. It's our superpower," said Raley. "That's what my mom said, anyway."

There was masculine laughter in the outside hallway and the door opened. A shaft of the bright hallway light poured into the dark room. A young man stood silhouetted. Light brown hair. Sparse beard. Pale. Pimples. M-16 slung over his shoulder.

"No, my turn, my turn," he laughed to the young men behind him. "You got the last one."

Another voice, "You might as well, before the big cheese get their turn."

"Those old goats," laughed the young man, and he turned and entered the room. The glass paned door rattled shut behind him.

Total surging fear swept through Raley. She thought she might faint. What to do. Always do the unexpected, her grandpa had said. Unexpected. Do it. Push through the fear.

"You're the new trainee. Blonde, small, slender, Bourgeoisie, and soon to be re-educated. Just how I like 'em", the young man said quietly. "I'm gonna take you down the hall for an interview. Just don't make a fuss and you won't be hurt."

"How ya gonna hurt me?" asked Raley, forcing herself to act slightly seductive.

"I'm gentle. Some of the others aren't. I don't have to be gentle. After all, this is generations of payback in fifteen minutes. You and your family brought this upon yourselves," said the young man. "You deserve this."

He was wearing those green janitor clothes like the others, Raley realized.

"You know my family?" asked Raley."

"No, but you are like all the other white oppressors in this room," said the young man. "You brought this upon yourselves."

Impulsively, she moved backwards, away from him, towards the teacher's table. He followed her.

"No need to move away. Let's just go down the hall and

do this. You'll probably like it. First time with a liberator," said the young man. "Too bad it's too late."

She leaned back with the table behind her, and the young man reached for her. She reached out and pulled him to her.

"Hey, save it for the interview!" laughed the young man.

Then his eyes widened as he felt her hand groping down by her groin, pulling her heavy antique dress up, and he said more emphatically, "Not here. Not in front of the others."

"They've seen it before," she said as she felt for the handgun in her underwear.

The thick fabric was making it hard to find.

"Ah...you want it, don't you? Can't wait?" said the young man. "Let me unbuckle."

He reached for his pants.

Raley jammed the derringer into the boy's manhood. He tried to pull back as his pants fell down around his ankles. She held him against her.

"I know what you're thinkin', Festus," whispered Raley into his ear aggressively. "Is she pressing a .44 Magnum derringer into my tender parts, or is it an iPhone ten?"

The young man seemed to shiver.

"I'm not Festus," he gasped. ".44 Magnum? I dunno. Maybe a phone."

"It's OK, Festus. I get so excited I forget my own name sometimes too," said Raley. "And to tell you the truth in all this excitement I'm not entirely sure myself. I mean, we haven't had cell service in months. So what did I grab out of my panties? Was it my cell phone, or was it my .44 magnum derringer? Can you tell me?"

".44 Magnum?" he repeated.

"Ya know, we "booj wa jee", we like it as big as possible," she whispered. "What do you think? iPhone or gun? Wanna guess? Maybe wait for it to vibrate?"

A wave of anger swept through her. She cocked the gun, and he felt it.

"I...I can't tell," he responded. "Might be either. Either way, you're givin' me shrinkage."

"I understand, Festus. After all, I'm Bourgeoisie," whispered Raley. "'Seeing as how this might be a .44 magnum derringer...you know, the .44 Magnum, it's...bigly...it's powerful...and it would blow your man-parts clean off, you might want to be careful...and quiet."

"Careful. Yes. Careful. Yea. I agree. I might want to be careful."

She felt the power now, and the anger, and the exultant rage that nobody, nobody, nobody, would kill her baby. She would die before they took her baby. She could squeeze the trigger now, and they would both die. Not a solution. How to get out of this?

"I mean, do you feel lucky? Do ya Festus?" whispered Raley.

The young man squirmed as she pressed the derringer into him.

"I'm...I'm not Festus," he stuttered.

"Oh, but you ARE Festus. Now don't back away. This is kinda comfortable. Do you feel lucky, Festus?"

"No...no I do not feel lucky."

"Now give me that carbine," said Raley. "Nice. Nice little commie. Now say, 'I'm Festus'"

"Ah....Ah, don't feel lucky. No sirree. Here's the carbine. I...I'm Festus."

The blonde girl chimed in, whispering, "For God's sake just shoot him. He's had his way with three of us."

The red haired girl added, "I wanna see you blow his junk into the hallway!"

"He's got his pants down, so he'll bleed all over me," said Raley. "It won't get the Good Housekeeping Seal of Approval. That's not good, right, Festus?"

"Let's cut his gonads off with the ruler. There's a ruler in the desks," said the black-haired girl. "Metal edge. They hit me with it."

"Quiet, ladies," said Raley. "We just gonna take a little re-education vacation day with Festus here. School's out. Now come over here and let's take a walk on the wild side.

"I gots to know," said Festus. "iPhone or gun?"

"Patience, Festus," said Raley. "Later on, you'll know."

Salinas, Republic of California

"Happy Johnson says that bad things are bound to happen in the creation of a new Hispanic nation. It's Reconquista," slurred Mickey. "I think he's frackin' right. Like Mao said, power grows out of the barrel of a gun, and we just gotta accept it. Takes breakin' eggs to make an omelet. They've got my family, and I put my family into their clutches. God it sucks."

Wallace watched Mickey evenly across the firepit's flames. During their confrontation with Happy Johnson and his people, Katy's entire clan had moved suddenly, mysteriously, and quietly to an abandoned carpet wholesale warehouse in East Salinas. They had left their homes in an instant to avoid retribution, and to protect the police who lived with them. The camp had produced a bottle of tequila, a rare event, and Mickey had consumed about half. Now Mickey struggled to stifle a sob.

"Frackin' people get what they want. OK, they want a new way of livin'? Let 'em have it and good frackin' luck. Here's to Mayor Happy! Here's to the frackin' pension and the frackin' doughnuts. Where do I sign up?"

"Well, I'm up for the doughnuts. The rest.... just not me," said Tiny. "Remember they murdered Chief Jefferson. That mob got stirred up by someone."

"Looked an awful lot like a lynchin' to me," said Mike Rogers.

He had joined the group at the fire and had mostly been lost in somber thought.

"Mickey, I don't think you get it," said Katy, across the flames of the firepit.

Wallace watched her. Tonight, after the backyard secret burials of Chief Jefferson and Officer Mendoza, everyone was disturbed. A lynching. A lynching had taken place, and the government...whatever government THAT was...had done it.

"I think the people who are taking power are killing anyone who opposes them, who might oppose them. I think we, the police, were set up to take the fall for that bombing," said Tiny. "I think we're next."

"Gotta agree," said Wallace. "Gillian McTavish and Happy Johnson have been targeting the police since this all started. Now I think we know why. But I don't understand.... I don't get the morality of it. Life was bad enough after that earthquake. Why make it worse?"

"Because people of color were being held down. We've been suppressed for generations, and this is our home. It's high time we got what we deserve," said Margarita.

Tiny looked down at her, surprised.

"I'm a person of color, too, Babe," he said.

"But you're not Hispanic. You don't know what it's been like. It's time we had rights," said Margarita. "California is our state."

"I think I heard that Hispanic people gonna get the boot too, honey," said Tiny. "They're gonna sell the place to the highest bidder.

"This isn't really about California, or Hispanic rights. This is about the entire concept of the United States," said Katy.

"I mean, what's in it for whoever is creating all this?" asked Wallace. "Personally, I mean."

"What's in it for them? Seems pretty obvious to me," said Mike Rogers. "Money, power, riches. The United States is a spent force, and the state's got the power, so they're in charge. And they're using race as a tool to get what they want."

"Just like every other failed nation in history," replied Katy. "Make one group hate another group. It works until the demographics change. Then who invades or overwhelms next? Be careful what you wish for."

"I don't get it," said Margarita. "Why shouldn't the Hispanics be in charge? It's way overdue."

"Because the elites are once again playing us to make themselves the beneficiaries," said Katy. "Besides, the core promise of the United States was that it evolved to avoid the tyranny of the majority."

"People should be empowered because they are people, not because of their race," said Tiny. "Pacific Islanders will never be a majority anywhere in the United States, so the less racial preference the better, from my perspective."

"I know some of my ancestors were slaves," replied Mike Rogers. "That feels like the tyranny of the majority to me."

"That's right, and the entire evolution of American history has been liberation from that, hasn't it?" said Katy. "Painful, fitful, messed up at times, but still the United States has evolved to defend the rights of the minority, whatever that is."

"But black people still get murdered by the police," said Mike Rogers, shaking his head.

"And when that happens, what takes place?" said Katy.

"Government tries to cover it up, press exposes it, and people demand change," said Mickey, newly sober. "It's part of the evolution. I see your point."

"Only conservative governments try to cover it up, right?" said Margarita. "Progressive governments are on our side."

"ALL governments make use of ANY crisis," said Katy. "It's what governments do. The elites always look after themselves. HOW they make use of a crisis depends upon the government."

"I'm still not getting this," said Wallace. "Why is what we are experiencing now 'un-American'? And why does that matter?"

"What we're facing now is about determinism," said Katy. "Born white, you stay white. Born black, you stay black. Born Hispanic, you stay Hispanic. That's as enlightened as saying that when you're born a serf, serving the nobility, you stay a serf to the ruling class all your life."

"Letting Hispanics have the power is un-American?" said Margarita. "Jees, Sis, we finally got a chance at life where we want it."

"Letting Hispanics have power because they are a certain dominant race IS un-American. Also, the concept that the government 'lets' anyone have power."

"OK, I'm sober," said Mickey. "I'd thank you except I'd rather be drunk. Just tell me why THIS is happening now?"

"Weakness," said Katy. "Both major political parties have served the elites instead of the middle class for decades. And we're all being played and manipulated by the internet."

"Isn't this payback? Years of being held down?" said Margarita. "Seems like justice to me."

"Was it justice for Chief Jefferson? How about Officer Mendoza?" replied Tiny.

Silence.

"It just seems that if Hispanics are the majority, and we've been held down, then we should rule. It's about time," said Margarita. "Like you said about the United States, bad things are sure to happen in the process."

"That's what Hitler told the Germans. After the Versailles

Treaty crushed the German people," replied Katy. "And he was Austrian."

"Essentially what Happy Johnson told us was that the Republic has a unique right to lynch people," said Tiny.

"Good point," said Margarita. "But we've still been held down too long."

"What do we do now?" said Wallace.

"We fight back," said Katy. "Carefully."

"How do we do that? We are mice facing an angry elephant," said Mickey. "They have my family. I have no desire to be one of their jackbooted thugs."

"Hey, free doughnuts," said Wallace.

"No such thing," replied Mickey.

"First we have to get your family out of THERE, then we have to get them away from HERE," replied Katy.

"Count me in," said Mike Rogers, holding a sleeping child in the firelight. "Gotta get Lacy out of there too."

On the Nacimiento-Ferguson Road, near the Mission San Antonio de Padua, Republic of California

In the half-light of the hastily erected pup tent, which they had pulled up to hide the light from the monitors, Glenda wiped away her tears, and muttered "I still can't believe it, I still can't believe it," to nobody in particular.

Then she refocused her attention on the iPad screens

relaying the drone-generated images of San Antonio de Padua. Images from above, and from the side.

It was 5 AM. Garth felt exhausted. He wondered how Glenda must be doing, inside, after a day in which her wife was murdered and her home invaded. Garth felt his fingertips. Numb. Stay hydrated. Glenda had to be feeling much worse.

My God, he thought, that's my family at that mission. Prayers that they were OK, alive, safe. Prayers that the 'team' which Che had mentioned had only been imaginary, a ploy to save his own life.

"Bingo," said Glenda quietly. The camp at the mission was mostly asleep. There was an unknown person who appeared to be standing guard in front of the kitchen. Another in the back of the mission. Both seemingly anxious, with frequent small movements. They might be friendly. Or not.

There was also a person who was laying flat on the hill above the mission with a long gun. Whoever it was, was not moving much. And, finally, there were two heat signatures of people with long guns laying uphill from the road to the outside world, about two kilometers from the mission. A team. Waiting for something.

Another drone was watching the heat signatures of Bear and Pike. They were in the earthquake-created ravine about two hundred yards away from the mission, towards the Army base, on their horses. Otherwise silence.

"I'm guessing it's a go to approach," said Garth. "Those two are probably people we know."

"I'm seeing some fresh graves," said Glenda into her

walkie talkie. "Something has happened. Get down there with the dawn. In the daylight they won't shoot you by accident."

"Roger," came Pike's voice. "Daylight."

To the southeast the sun was rising. Pink light was gradually filling the sky beyond the mountains, over beyond King City. Cool night. Warm morning. Brown grass, with dew. Winter was coming. The warmth of his expected homecoming purged the chill of the dawn from Garth's mind. Soon it will rain again. He gripped the saddle horn and swung into the saddle atop Dogfood. Dogfood stepped slightly away, and Garth's holster slipped down his leg. He adjusted it so that he wasn't sitting on it and realized that he hadn't changed the load in it for a week. An 1858 Remington cap and ball .44. The powder might be damp. The thought nagged him.

"Hey, hold on, I'm seeing something," said Glenda from inside the tent.

Garth sat on Dogfood as Ramon rushed out of the tent and climbed atop his own horse.

"El baile cominza," said Ramon hastily. "Someone goes like a rushing bat towards the mission in a jeep. He is chased."

Ramon put the spurs to his horse and careened precariously down the hill, frighteningly fast. Garth followed, lagging as Ramon dodged around an oak tree...a live oak tree. The spiny leaves scored Garth's face as they plunged ahead. Oh where did that fool learn to ride? Somehow Garth remembered that Ramon had played polo back in Mexico City.

"The people who chase are in a truck," yelled Ramon over his shoulder. They bounced across a modest crevasse from the earthquake, Garth scarcely remaining mounted. Dogfood seemed to sense the urgency and raced to catch Ramon and the horse ahead.

Dawn. Dust. Motion. A distant helicopter in the sky. To help whom? Dots racing overhead. Drones, flying from behind them towards the rushing jeep in the distance. The helicopter over the rushing jeep. A loudspeaker. Unintelligible. The jeep hit a small crevasse from the earthquake, went airborne, crashed back to earth and tipped sideways. Dust.

The driver's door banged open on the top of the tipped jeep, and the driver leapt down to the ground like an acrobat.

Garth was barely staying in his seat as Dogfood raced forward behind Ramon on his horse, and he had the astonishing recognition that the driver was Raley...long blonde hair and antique powder blue dress...she raised an M-4 military rifle and began snapping shots at the helicopter, and she fired shot after shot. The helicopter turned sideways, exposing a door gunner, who began to aim a large machine gun.

Dust, motion as Garth chased after Ramon. He could see Bear and Pike, to the left, both mounted and riding as fast as Ramon, Bear with his Henry rifle. Garth drew Marlin rifle out as Dogfood raced onwards, focusing on the act to quell his terror, and then he heard the first firecracker sound of the drones firing...those little nine millimeter Glocks. And then the door gunner slumping and recoiling, still moving, trying to avoid the shots, and the helicopter spinning in retreat and flying away, and below the truck in the distance, braking, and turning and retreating as well.

And there was Bear, leaping from the saddle like a

teenager, hugging Raley, and Raley was saying, "Calm down, Poppa. I HAD to shoot. Nobody gonna murder my baby."

Garth sat on his horse as they both gulped air and wondered if his family was safe, and what had happened. He had the thought as he watched Raley that she looked to be about fourteen years old, and she scarcely looked pregnant at all.

"I brung friends!" said Raley, smiling, and she climbed up the axle of the tipped over jeep and hollered down into the interior.

"C'mon, girls! We got BEEF," said Raley, down into the passenger compartment.

Then she turned and smiled down at Bear.

"I brought three friends! And we're ALL PREGNANT!"

Garth sat next to Dove and looked down at the metal plate of food she had brought him. She was watching him expectantly, smiling slightly. What he really needed was sleep, thought Garth. Sleep. His mind was wandering now, dreaming while awake. Focus. It's food. I should eat.

"Wow that looks great!" said Garth. No quinoa, no mustard greens. A large piece of stewed meat. "Looks delicious! What kind of meat?"

Deep thoughts.

"Oh, it is beef, I think. Terry shot it yesterday," said Hopi Jack, across the table.

Garth looked at Terry Taylor. As always, Terry was immaculately dressed in his cavalry uniform. Looking at Terry's pristine appearance, Garth was aware that he himself was unshaven. He wondered if perhaps he might smell. No washing since the mansion, yesterday morning. He wondered how they were doing there. Possibly sleeping. Sleep seemed very attractive at this moment. He had slept last.... three days ago, he thought.

"Thank you, Terry," said Garth, and looked down the table at Ramon and Bear and Glenda. They were poking at their meals.

Oh, why the hell not? He thought and took a large forkful.

"Least I think it's beef," said Terry quietly.

Garth's fork stalled. Then hunger overcame him, and he ate. It was delicious. He should eat before he fell asleep over his plate. Suddenly he was gripped by fear: was Dogfood eating? Was he OK? Memories returning...yes, yes, that nice young man, Steve Sanchez's son, was taking care of him.

"Try the bread," said Dove. "Completely hand-ground from the wheat in that field in Jolon. Merry Thomas and Francesca and Akemi and I made it. The horno was in use, so we steamed it in woven cattail baskets, like in the Philippines"

It really WAS delicious. Yet somehow it felt to Garth like they were all regressing into a past primitive era. El Castillo, he realized. He had become used to marvels.

How long had he been away? Perhaps five days? Dove was noticeably different. Not angry, not agitated, just silently different. Something had happened. Dove was wearing modern clothing. Alongside her sat Akemi, who seemed content and quiet, dressed in her 1860's pinafore. On his other side sat his daughter Francesca, in a high-waisted feminine Victorian riding dress. That seemed new. Were they sewing here now? Anyway, she had plenty to say, and was laughing and talking deeply with her friends.

The young people, thought Garth. A whole different world to them. And about to be even more different, with four girls pregnant, and that whole marry-and-baby mood inevitably to sweep through all of them, perhaps four to six years early but inevitable nonetheless.

They have no idea, thought Garth.

The Salinas River, Monterey County, California

The moon was half-up, but Wallace could see well enough. He was standing on a small mud beach at the Salinas River estuary, where the Salinas River met the ocean. The river was much stronger this year, probably because there was much less irrigation going on. Along the banks were rows of what looked like trash bags. Many, swollen, pushed by the muddy current up against the shore, shining in the frail moonlight.

"How many?" whispered Wallace to Causwell. He couldn't decide if he was going to vomit, scream, or faint. He could hear Mike Rogers over in the reeds, trying to vomit as quietly as possible. The smell of decay was horrendous.

"Hun...hundreds," Causwell whispered back. "I know there are hundreds. At least."

"Lacy's not here yet, right?" said Mike Rogers behind them, fiercely. "You haven't killed her?"

"Not that I know of," replied Causwell.

"You knew! You knew and you did NOTHING!!!" snarled Katy from behind.

Causwell's head snapped back and Wallace knew that Katy had jerked on his rope.

"Katy, keep it quiet. They catch us here and it's a shoot-out for sure," whispered Wallace. "I'll fight before I'll let them do this to any of us."

"Most people don't fight, though," whispered Causwell, as though to himself. "Especially the gun owners. It amazes me, really. They just surrender when the strike teams go door to door. The old people too. Especially the white people. They never fight back."

As they stepped down closer to the water, Wallace was looking more closely. He could see that some of the heads were above the water, the plastic bags carried off somehow, the flesh partially eaten. Some still with hair. A few bobbed in the current. Floating volleyballs came to mind. Lots of white hair. Lots of empty eye sockets. The corpses seemed to be linked to each other in some manner. Hugging in the water. Unwilling to separate, even in death.

"How did you kill them? I'm not seeing bullet holes," he whispered.

"They tell them they're being sedated for long term transport, up to Redding, then they give them shots of animal tranquilizer, then put trash bags over their heads so they suffocate," said Causwell. "If an elderly person goes to the hospital, this is almost automatic."

"What age is considered elderly?" asked Tiny. He had come up behind them in the dark.

"Sixty. It depends. We've got a whole stadium full of them at the rodeo grounds. They're the people with relatives outside. Gillian's afraid to euthanize the..."

"Murder them, you mean. Say it," snapped Katy. "Say it, damn you, or I'll drown you right here."

"We want Causwell alive. He's the only witness we've got," said Wallace. "But you can kick him around a little, if you like."

"...Murder them because she's afraid of the people outside. We haven't got all the guns from the community yet," said Causwell Dubbers. "But nobody's fighting back. Not many, anyway."

"What happens to the gun owners?" asked Tiny.

"This, unless they surrender everything they have," replied Causwell. "In fact, if anyone hides anything, including wealth or an old person, they end up here. Family. Kids. No witnesses, of course. That's why the jail isn't in use anymore."

"I thought it was because of Candida," said Tiny.

"Seen any Candida? Really?" whispered Causwell.

"Why? Why not just slave labor, why not just reeducation?" said Wallace, watching the heads floating in the current. He was trying not to scream.

In the night there was the sound of a helicopter flying in the night. Instinctively, everyone stepped into the reeds, and followed a trail until they were under the low hanging branches of a battered willow. Wallace felt the soft leaves brush his face as he walked into the deep darkness under the tree. Out the other side, and there was the riverbank, and more bodies, floating bunched, apparently tied, together. One corpse floated face up. Empty eye sockets, face partially consumed. Wallace recognized one of the white supremacists from the library.

"Holy shit," he said, under his breath.

"I agree. What a stench," said Mike Rogers. "Horrible. These poor people."

"To answer your question," said Causwell, "Social Security is shot, pensions are shot, there is no water, no food, no medical care, no law enforcement, no judicial system, and all these elderly people will do is suffer, and take food from those who produce. If we admit any of this, we're going to lose political power, and the Republic of California will fail. We're being flooded with refugees from up north, and some of them have radiation sickness or other diseases, and our casualty center at Carr Lake is overwhelmed. Even though we're processing them as fast as we humanly can. And as for the criminals, well, we don't have the resources to house them. And, of course, there's global warming. The planet is overpopulated."

He was speaking more strongly now.

"So this was considered the most humane solution," he concluded.

Silence. Everyone listened to the helicopter in the distance. In the area enclosed by the dense willow foliage and the riverbank, the smell of unwashed live human bodies mixed with the smell of the dead.

"Think the helicopter will see the motorbikes? By the heat signatures?" asked Tiny.

"Most of the helicopters don't have infrared. No

heat-tracking ability. Heck, most don't even have night vision goggles," said Causwell. "That's all being used up north in the big cities."

"Think Mickey's OK with the motorbikes?" repeated Tiny.

"He's cool, Tiny. He won't panic," replied Wallace.

"So why not just bury these poor people? Why just dump them in the river?" asked Mike Rogers.

"We don't have the manpower, and we want to keep this secret to avoid panic," said Causwell. "Eventually, you know...the sea and the sand will take them all. In a few hundred years the archaeologists will find the remains, and nobody will care. They'll build beach houses over them. This is California. Look how we treat Native American remains."

"Got a point," said Katy.

Causwell scoffed. "Meanwhile we're trying to avoid unfortunate...social unrest."

"Revolution, you mean," said Katy. "If people knew, you'd all be dead already."

"People don't want to know," said Causwell. "You saw that with the mob."

"I think we're in a revolution already," said Tiny.

Wallace was lost in thought.

"You said there's a whole stadium of people at the rodeo grounds? What's the plan for them?" asked Wallace.

"Well.... this, eventually," said Causwell. "We just can't figure out how to process them without angering the community."

"Process them...." said Katy.

She gave the noose around his neck a gentle tug.

"Kill them," replied Causwell Dubbers shortly.

"Wait a minute, are the rodeo grounds where Lacy is being held?" asked Mike Rogers.

"Yes, yes," replied Causwell. "That's where all the police families are being held as well."

"Like Mickey's family?" asked Wallace.

"Yes. The plan is that holding them there will keep you all in line, and Lacy will keep Mike in line. Et cetera," Causwell responded. "They stay there while others pass through and move on to be processed."

"So they don't murder the people there?" asked Katy. "They don't kill them at the rodeo grounds?"

"No," whispered Causwell Dubbers, "They load them on buses, tranquilize them, tell them it's to keep them asleep for such a long journey without food or water. Then the facilitators...they're called facilitators...put plastic bags over the peoples' heads, and the strike teams bring them here. By the time they arrive, they're all suffocated. Almost all of them, anyway."

San Antonio Mission, California

Garth awoke with a start with his head resting on the table. He sat up straight. His body ached. It was darker outside. What had awakened him? Adrenalin. Another earthquake? No, bagpipes. Bagpipes. Yes, as was their habit, Poppy Roswell and Gritz Garwood were playing their bagpipes for taps, for the sunset, on the front steps of the sanctuary. He remembered now, and he felt much better. Much more rested. All the food and all the clutter of the meal had been removed, and the darkening room was clean and welcoming and serene, and the bagpipes were playing outside. Bear was stirring on the floor in the corner. Apparently, he had fallen asleep as well. Oh, they should have been preparing, should have been planning. But planning for what?

Garth stood up. This was his home now, he felt, and these were his people. That other life, that other time, seemed like one of his vivid dreams, something unreal yet always lingering. He didn't know anything, he realized. Something big had happened in the past few days. He realized that he hadn't seen Fred Paxley or heard him whining for that matter, since he got back. Katrina, Fred's wife, had seemed wilted, in the background. Gritz had apparently been sober all day. They had all been here for the meal, but much had changed. Something had happened.

He needed to ask someone. He could hear talking through the open door of the kitchen and the light was on as the daylight dwindled outside. He would ask.

He saw Bear go to the outside door and open it. There was more light out there than here in this dark quiet room.

"Listen. Listen to those bagpipes. And now, listen, there's the taps on the Army base. Someone's still there," said Bear.

"Someone to keep the flag flying," said Ramon, behind them.

"Hey, Ramon, what's happening?" asked Bear.

"Apparently this is your ritual, is it not?" replied Ramon.

The sound of the bagpipes ended, and the music in the distance from the Army base faded. Then they could hear another tune from the distant military loudspeakers. Ramon stared into the distance.

"¡Imposible!" he muttered. "Impossible."

"Impossiblay what?" asked Bear.

"It's El Deguello," responded Ramon.

"El Armadillo?" said Bear.

"Nope. El Deguello," said Hopi Jack, standing behind them. "It's the song the Mexican Army played at the Alamo, the night before the big attack."

"It is the sound of no quarter, no prisoners," explained Ramon. "They used to play it, right before they slaughtered everyone. Someone is sending a message. When they get done, not even the perros will be alive."

* * *

Main Street, Salinas, California

"I smell something," said Dina Montero.

"I took a bath two days ago," responded Wallace. "Cold water, but I did it anyway."

"I smell news. I still print the newspaper, you know. Three pages front and back. Word is you've been looking for Jesus Garcia," said Dina.

"We've just been laying low," said Wallace. "Aside from groveling to Happy Johnson, all we've been doing is working security for city hall food supplies. What there is of it."

"So after they hanged Chief Johnson and Mendoza you still gonna kiss their ass?" said Dina Montero. "You went crawling back?"

Silence. Wallace looked at her steadily.

"They really got to you, didn't they?" said Dina.

"I don't want any trouble," said Wallace. "I'm just trying to avoid another riot."

"And avoid being blamed for it," said Dina. "You guys are like hunted squirrels. Happy's got you right where he wants you. Has he asked you to kill anyone yet? Strong arm anyone? He will."

"Ah well," said Wallace. "The bookstore looks good, considering."

He looked around. The windows had been replaced with translucent construction plastic and were almost opaque. There were perhaps 200 used books in the store, on mostly empty shelves. In the back of the room there were stacked, broken bookcases. No dust, he noticed.

"Considering it's been looted twice, blown up once," replied Dina. "The last open retail store in Old Town. Word is that Happy's sold us out to the big boxes, when this whole thing settles down. He comes in here and tells me that he's going to get big redevelopment dollars to put a great big mall right here, with thousands of new residents making this 'San Jose South'."

"He say where the new residents will come from?" said Wallace.

"No, I'm guessing they'll relocate people from up where the bomb went off," said Dina.

The prospect of a new mall in this treasured part of town made Wallace's stomach clench. He shifted in his seat.

"Is the mob still looting up at Northridge?" asked Wallace.

"Nothing left to steal," said Dina. "Now the mobs just loot homes. Mostly South Salinas and North Salinas. The strike teams and the mobs are working together, I think. The strike teams target a specific house for the mob. Searches, then they hold political struggle sessions out on the street, followed by looting. Abuse or lynching when the people aren't politically correct enough. It's becoming a sport."

"How about East Salinas?" asked Wallace, glad to shift the topic.

"Even the strike teams don't touch that," said Dina. "That's Jesus Garcia's turf. He DOES protect his own. Any mob goes in there, it's like a roach motel. They go in but they don't come out. So Jesus is risen. I'm hearing he's moving up in the world."

Wallace perked up. "How's that happening?" he asked.

"Medical supplies, mostly. Insulin. Antibiotics. Essentials. Plus the standard criminal stuff. Apparently they have the mother of all marijuana grows going on in the old salad plant on East Market Street. And here's the kicker. There's a big market in SPAM. Like as in, the lunch meat. It's the delicacy of choice in New Salinas."

"Why can't people get these things through normal channels?" asked Wallace.

"Oh, it's all controlled by the Republic. To get anything, people have to grovel and serve. Sex is a good way to get rations from the strike teams. They're young, they're horny.

It's the same as it ever was," replied Dina. "The whole 'Me Too' campaign turned out to be a passing phase, didn't it? Nobody's complaining now."

"That work for you?" asked Wallace.

Dina laughed.

"Seems rather hypocritical to me. Nothing surprises me anymore. I'm happily married, and they've got my husband over at the rodeo grounds. Apparently at his age he's at high risk for Candida."

Wallace said nothing. He tried to keep his face impassive.

"I'm over 40," replied Dina. "Promiscuity works better if you're slender and 19 and have the brains of a turnip."

"Do you talk to Jesus?" said Wallace.

"I don't talk to Jesus. At least the Jesus we're discussing. But he talks about you. He said you're a very good marksman with that shotgun," said Dina.

Wallace unslung his 870 pump shotgun, held it out, and looked at it. "Just lucky, I guess. Haven't used it much," he said. "Actually, you know, us police folks are supposed to lay low. We're trying to stay out of sight. Like Jesus, I guess. Where would one find him?"

"Many seek Jesus, but few find him," Dina smiled. "He was wondering when you'd ask. One would find him at the Foster's Freeze on South Main, across from Salinas High School, tomorrow night at 7 PM."

"Hmmm. But Foster's is closed, right?" said Wallace. "No food means no restaurants. And all restaurants are closed because of Candida."

"Well, Officer, don't tell anyone, but Foster's is gonna

reopen," replied Dina. "One night only. SPAM sandwiches. The newest food sensation. On white bread, with Foster's sauce. $20 in coins, no paper money, or a reasonable barter."

"Expensive," said Wallace.

"At least it's not dog," replied Dina. "You want a used copy of 'The Winter Of Our Discontent?' John Steinbeck's last novel. He was born and raised here, you know."

"No, thanks, I've read it before," said Wallace. "A stale message, and not his best. Do you have anything by Louis L'Amour?"

San Antonio Mission, California

After taps, after the rush to finish evening chores in the disappearing light, after darkness had fully descended, everyone naturally congregated in the chapel, as always. The great hall was lit only by candles and a flickering dim electric bulb, running off the battery from solar power. The three monks were preparing the evening religious service which would take place immediately after the evening meeting, and before the communal meal. All eyes were to the front when a man's voice sounded from the back of the room.

They're back," said the voice. Garth turned and looked. One of the lancers...the man who had been shot in the river fight, still limping, Garth saw...Paul Desault. The man reached down and picked his miquelet escopeta front-loader, incongruous in an age of nine millimeter pistol-mounted drones, and strode outside. Garth noticed that Dove reached over and picked up the short double barreled shotgun from the serving table, opened the action for loading, and paced wordlessly outside, looking resolute, followed by Tiger Tanaka and his Garand rifle, and most of the people. Renalyn Munz, still in her Army camouflage uniform, quickly exited the back door with her three other military women.

"They got the Humvee hidden out back in a dugout by the septic tank," said Poppy Roswell, across the pew. Garth noticed he seemed to be sinking into his seat, in distress. Next to him Hero the Service Dog lay sprawled across the ancient tile floor, sleeping. Hero seemed to be getting fatter, Garth noticed.

"That Humvee belongs to the government. It doesn't belong to us. We need to give it back," muttered Poppy. "Please, please, let's just do what they want this time. It's the government. It's the government."

His wife...Garth remembered her name was Samantha... stood next to him, her hand soothingly on his shoulder.

"Somebody shut him up," said Gritz Garwood, following the others out the door.

Garth watched the small convoy approach. In the lead was a bizarre little rural school bus, on giant all-terrain tires. Behind the bus was the largest quad Garth had ever seen, with six wheels, and they had a white flag, and they drove up in the gathering darkness with their headlights blinding. Garth thought about Tiger Tanaka, out there in the dark somewhere with his Garand, and hopefully others. These

Republic people would expect drones now, and, if they had the resources and the awareness, would have infrared resources watching everyone.

Garth looked around. Glenda was missing. So Glenda probably was manning her own drones, right now. The thought was comforting. Garth missed his night vision monocular, which was laying uselessly back on his bunk in his tent. As was his .45-70 Marlin. If this went down right now, his only firearm would be his pistol, and he wasn't even sure that the powder would ignite.

A small stern-faced heavy-set woman exited the quad. She had very curly short hair, reflecting red in the waning sunset. Five other people got out of the quad after her, all with belted pistols, two military plastic AR long guns. All in cheap green clothing, like school custodians, all with green cloth military billed caps. The clothing was ill-fitting, wrinkled. And, Garth noted, they were wearing some sort of athletic shoes. Each of them wore a nametag, and Republic of California patches on breast and shoulder.

The small portly woman raised an electronic loudspeaker to her lips, even though the two groups were only about ten feet apart.

"It has been decided by the Republic of California," said the woman, her amplified voice deafeningly loud, "that wilderness areas are to be closed and given back to nature. With that in mind, you were commanded to report to a collection center for reassignment based on your racial and social credits. We regret your earlier deplorable decision to not comply."

The woman lowered the megaphone and stood there scowling.

"Where's my sister?" said Raley, quietly.

"Oh, she's moved on. Wherever she is, I'm sure she's happier than she was here," said the woman. "I'm sure you regret not staying at our re-education camp at Libertad."

"I'm happy to be home," said Raley quietly.

Raley stood in front of the other girls, arms folded, that M-4 military rifle slung over her shoulder, dressed in her 1860's style dress with a military cloth cap identical to that which the man wore. Sullen youth personified.

Garth sent a silent wish that Raley would not reach for the firearm she was carrying. Tiger and Gritz and a few others were out in the dark, on the flanks, but surely the woman in green had allies in the darkness as well. Surely they had night vision. A spasm of fear coursed through Garth as he thought again of his own night vision monocle, sitting on the bunk of his tent. He watched as Hero the Service Dog ambled between the green-dressed people in the quad and the mission inhabitants. The dog plopped down and slumped into a dozing posture. Most people were looking at Hero. Good. A distraction.

"Cheese-borrow ain't it?" said Raley with a sneer.

"I am Mrs. Chesbrough. Say it correctly," said the woman, reddening.

"Cheese-brewski," said a black-haired young woman who had arrived with Raley in the jeep.

The woman from the quad was perhaps forty years old. Her new green clothes were baggy. Despite the rising coolness of the evening the woman was now red-faced, sweating profusely. She looked back at Raley with contempt on her face, and she looked over the group and she raised the megaphone back to her mouth, and she spoke, deafeningly, distastefully, as though the act of communication was repellant.

"Listen you people. These girls made the unfortunate decision to resist reassignment and resettlement. With that in mind, all parental rights are terminated, and these girls will undergo reeducation. You WILL surrender them immediately."

"I don't think so," came a voice, clearly. Patty Martin.

"Parental rights are terminated," repeated the woman, not raising the megaphone, apparently tired of explaining this.

Patty Martin replied, "I'm a psychologist. I'm familiar with parental rights. I'm also supportive of the law which allows parents and child to make a decision about a teen abortion. The right to a juvenile hearing. And a choice of how to form a family unit,"

The woman raised the megaphone to her mouth and spoke, her voice echoing off the walls of the mission.

"That was then, in the old time. Now is the new Republic. That was then. This is now. The habits you speak of are now outdated. Quaint. The government, as always, knows a better way. You must trust the Republic of California in all things."

The woman motioned to the girls, sweeping her arms and pointing, and spoke to them through the loudspeaker, "You will come with me now."

"I'm not a juvenile," said Raley, "And I'll make my own choices about my own baby."

"Legally, yes, you ARE a juvenile," said the woman in green without her megaphone. "The Republic makes the choices about your pregnancy. We will not allow you to ruin your future. You will come with us."

"No," said Katrina Paxley.

The woman in green shook her head, as though disappointed. She raised the megaphone back to her mouth, and her voice boomed with the artificial amplification.

"You are bad people who have made bad life decisions. Deplorable, deplorable. Clutching your guns and Bibles in this dirt. You are not pro-city as you should be, you are ignorant of the blessings of efficient truthful living for the good of all, and your lifestyles are primitive. You CAN'T be trusted to make good choices."

"I don't feel primitive. What you are doing scares me more. We're happier here," said Katrina. "We want to stay here, at the mission, until we can clear all this up. Trust us to work something out."

The woman looked at Katrina and at her 18th century Spanish working dress and she sneered.

Hero the Service Dog sat up between the two groups and began to scratch.

The woman raised the megaphone to her mouth and her voice boomed mechanically. The intensity of the noise was making Garth's tinnitus roar and he struggled to hear.

"The Republic of California will not support your bigoted religious fantasies. The Republic of California will not subsidize your bad choices. The Republic of California will not tolerate your abuse of the wilderness. Bad, bad, bad," said the woman in green in her amplified voice, "The Candida pandemic has spread to California, and you must be re-housed."

"We are going nowhere tonight. Give us the evening to organize this, and let's talk again tomorrow," said Hopi Jack. "I'm an attorney. We'll work all this out somehow."

At this point, Hero the Service Dog ambled over and urinated on the woman's leg, panting happily. The woman shrieked, recoiled, shaking her pants.

"God, that's SO disgusting!" said a girl's voice, and Ophelia rushed out, grabbed Hero, and pulled him reluctantly through the crowd.

"Goddamned fleabag starting to grow on me," whispered Bear, standing alongside Garth.

The five people with the woman in green stepped forward from the quad now. Garth saw that they were all armed, all with belted pistols, two at the rear with military long guns. Garth could see the muzzles. He thought to himself that the shooting would start at any time. Here he was, with a cap and ball revolver, and he was uncertain that it would fire.

Two small flashlight beams shone down from above, and descended, with a slight whirring noise, and Garth could barely see two of Glenda's armed drones hovering above them.

"Deus ex machina," said Hopi Jack. "Surprise. We are not so primitive after all."

The woman in green glared at the drones, and glared at Hopi, and at them all, then she raised her hand and motioned her people to step back. She raised her megaphone and spoke, deafeningly.

"Cruel necessity, then. You who are elderly have been declared non-essential anyway. We will return tomorrow at 7 AM to collect all of you. All possessions are contraband. Complete surrender to the will of the people is your only choice, regrettably. Reeducation will be uncomfortable. Only by hardship, reassignment apart from each other, and by the conscientious practice of intense struggle sessions can you be saved. We will return tomorrow at 7AM!"

The artificial voice echoed off the walls of the old adobe.

Silence.

"See ya later, Mizzuss Cheesewhizzy!" came a girl's voice from behind Raley.

"They are such children," said Dove, standing behind Garth with her shotgun.

Salinas, California

Jesus Garcia gently put the SPAM sandwich back on the plate as he chewed. Across the booth, Wallace was having a hard time restraining himself. The sandwich he was eating was exquisite, a communion on toast, a symphony of meaty flavor. He felt like shouting.

"I treasure its saltiness," said Jesus quietly.

"And the crunch," replied Wallace.

"The softness of the white bread," said Jesus. "It is as though I have found God."

"And the sauce," replied Wallace.

"I see that you are a gourmet," said Jesus. "The sauce I have resurrected myself. We made it from memory. Next we will reconstruct the deep fat cooker from scratch. This place...this Foster's Freeze...will come back to life. As it was, so shall it be. Fries without end."

"Where did you get the bread?" asked Wallace.

"Oh, one of the women makes it here. Before things changed, she worked in that French bakery. Now she is here," replied Jesus.

"Tell her this bread is world-class," said Wallace.

"Oh, I will," said Jesus.

Silence. They ate and savored.

"I see you still have your big gun," said Jesus.

"Yes," said Wallace.

"Good. Mira... mira...I know that this won't last. I know what is happening. I know all our days are numbered," said Jesus.

"As ever they were," replied Wallace.

"No, no, I'm serious. And there are no chinchas...no listening devices...here. Let us talk."

"Thank you for having me," said Wallace.

"Yes.... now tell me, how are you getting out?" said Jesus.

"Getting out?" said Wallace.

"Let us not be tontos," said Jesus. "This cesspit is no place for either of us. I stay here only because of my community."

"Get out? How?" responded Wallace.

"Stop fracking with me," said Jesus.

"How do I get everyone held at the rodeo grounds across the border?" asked Wallace.

"Ah. There it is," said Jesus. "I knew you weren't going to just roll over after they murdered your jefe. Good for you. I was surprised you didn't disembowel that Johnson."

"I honestly don't know how to get them all out," said Wallace.

"Well you know they have buses," said Jesus.

"You know what they use them for," said Wallace.

"Yes, but still, they have a lot of buses," said Jesus.

"True," replied Wallace. "How can we make a plan with this?"

"I would need to pay my people," said Jesus. "I would have to pay for supplies. Gasoline. What would I use for money?"

"They have lots of anesthesia. You can sell that. It's good medical grade. And guns," said Wallace. "Let's not forget the buses themselves."

"I could just take all those things myself," said Jesus. "I could just take those things for myself and not worry about your people."

"Ellos son los viejos. Ellos son los pobres," said Wallace. "They are the people we defend. We are warriors, right?"

"Am I still? Now I just feel like a cockroach. I take what is unnoticed," replied Jesus.

"As long as we are unnoticed, where's the border now? Where does the United States begin?" asked Wallace.

"You don't know?" asked Jesus. "I mean, you're the police."

"I haven't gotten news of anything for months. I have no idea what's happening. No phone, no internet," replied

Wallace. "Of course I don't know what to believe from the Republic. Dina's newspaper is censored, all three pages of it. I haven't spoken with my wife in months, so she hasn't told me anything either"

"Yes, I remember, your wife and children are in Germany," said Jesus.

"Denmark," replied Wallace.

Wallace pondered how Jesus had learned about his family.

"The thing is, with the Republic I get a fresh start. A clean slate, as you say. A chance to start over, as an insect this time, like your famous writer."

"Kafka."

"Whoever he was, he knew something. To the people in charge, we are always the insects. We've always been insects," said Jesus. "Awareness is knowing that we are insects."

"You learn that in prison?" asked Wallace.

"Oh, that, and more," said Jesus.

"More? I'm beginning to think you are right," said Wallace.

"If the people wanted something different, the people would focus on education and stability, but we don't. We want to stay insects. We let the professional educators make money while our children can't read, and we let the elites help us by keeping us down. But we don't insist on real education and the habits that make success. We blame others instead, and we watch a woman internet celebrity put baby oil on her backside. Therefore, I have decided, we want to be insects, and live in a world of insects," said Jesus.

"So here we are in the world of bugs," replied Wallace. "What do we do about that?"

"I'm not sure. You come here telling me that I don't have to be an insect. I can live differently, you say. I don't really know what to do with that opportunity. So far, nothing you've offered makes me want to take the big risk of change. You want to leave, which will disrupt life under our rock, life in our rotten log, but I may wish to live here in this decaying compost pile when you are desaparecido. Gone away."

Wallace pondered that.

"Do you really?" asked Wallace

"Really what?" replied Jesus.

"Do you really have to live here?" said Wallace. "Do you really choose to be a cockroach?"

"Nobody's forcing me out of here. It's my home, this rotten log. Es mi tierra," said Jesus. "I am accustomed to it. But I am not happy that my children live in this alcantarilla. This sewer."

"You have children. I didn't realize that. Well, what about your legacy for them?" said Wallace, desperately.

"What do you mean?" asked Jesus. "And yes, I've got children. The oldest is 23 and the youngest is six months. Total of seven children. So what?"

"What do they think of you?" said Wallace.

"Of course, they think good things," said Jesus. "They say only good things. They do, I know. I do not beat them as my parents beat me. Damn, what a couple of drunks they were. Always shrieking. Always hitting. I'm not like that. I know my children think good of me."

"Honestly? No bullshit? You were always gone. Always in

the slam. What do they really think? What will they really say about you when you are dead?" said Wallace.

"They would say..." Jesus began.

"Be honest," interrupted Wallace.

"Hmmmm," replied Jesus. "You know, you're right. I wasn't around much. I was in prison. Perhaps they don't think so good of me."

"Here's your chance," said Wallace. "Your chance to write them a legend. Be a hero for the United States. It's a chance to save people. You can make them proud of you, at last."

"A cucaracha as a hero. Imagine that," said Jesus.

San Antonio Mission, California

As the quad and the bus drove away, there was consternation in the milling group, until Bat Jefferson shouted, "Meeting in the church." The swarming, gabbling people moved into the mission. A few electric lights, mostly candles. People filled the pews. As before, several women sat before them, as leaders. Belinda Jefferson obviously in charge.

"For those of us who have been gone, we need a recap. Then we need to decide what we are going to do. I know we all have a lot to say, but we have a lot to do. So, please, let's keep this organized, and keep this goal-oriented. First, for those of you who were over on the coast, this is not our first meeting with Mrs. Chesbrough."

"Missus Cheese-bro?" asked Bear. "As in, my sister who art in Cheddar?"

"Mrs. Chesbrough," said Belinda Jefferson. "She spelled it for us during her first visit. She came and got the girls. When the girls wouldn't go, she killed two of us. Paolo Archuleta and Beeston Bragg."

"Well, Paolo and Beeston asked for it," said Poppy Roswell. "They shouldn't have fought the government."

"Fred Paxley ratted us out," said Raley.

"Then he drowned in shit," said Gritz. "We found him the next morning with his head in one of the outhouses, only his feet sticking out through one of the holes. Apparently, he just dived in there and strangled on turds."

"Think of it as pearl diving," said Francesca.

"He must have been really drunk," said Sally Beth, from alongside Gritz. "Anyway, he was right. He WAS fracked, after all."

Sally Beth seemed happier and more confident. But somehow Gritz had given up drinking. Perhaps that was it. Garth's mind was boggling from this overload of news.

"Let's get back on topic," said Belinda Jefferson. "The bottom line is that they came...she came...and after some discussion they took the girls by force."

"Then we got away," said one of the new girls.

"Freddy Desault and the other children were able to hide," said Patty Martin. "Thank God."

"Thank Mrs. Ericson and God," said Martin. "Sometimes God is an antique carbine."

"Bad, bad, bad," said one of the Caballero Vistadores.

"You should have done whatever they asked. You got two wonderful young men killed for no reason."

Garth didn't know the man's name yet. He realized that he should have learned it.

"They wanted to make me have an abortion, and I didn't WANT an abortion," replied Raley hotly. "This is my baby with Terp, and I'm gonna keep it. To hell with everyone."

Belinda Jefferson interrupted. "Back on track! What happened over by the coast?"

Priyanka and Ramon and Glenda and the two others were quickly introduced, and the adventure was related.

"Well, that sounds like that Che fellow was rogue," said Samantha Roswell, as Poppy nodded his agreement. "Surely no government would allow such a thing."

"Well, God damn it, they DID allow such a thing," said Glenda, beginning to cry.

"Oh, it has happened all the time," said Garth's mother. All eyes turned to her.

"Build up enough hatred and a government can use chaos to do the brutal work, then get what it wants by cleaning up the mess afterwards. World history is full of it. Race riots. The Armenian massacre by the Turks. Anti-Jewish pogroms by the Russian government. The Trail of Tears in American history. Use the radicals to break the status quo and then inflame the populace with the media and clean up the mess to get what you want afterwards. It's a time-honored method of governance," she said.

"Add the Mexican Revolution to that list," said Ramon. "The Yucatan Caste War. The people bled and they butchered the elites, then the new elites who were waiting moved in and took over."

"No, no. no," said the young woman journalist. "That can't happen here. Our government cares for us. Our government is a democracy, of the people, by the people, for the people."

Garth considered that the young woman journalist had become elfin, reclusive. She looked furtive, frightened, hunted.

"Sorry but we don't have a lot of time. 7 AM will soon be upon us. We must move on," said Belinda. "What's going on in the outside world? Pike? Did you get a drone connection to the outside world as you hoped?"

"OK, here's the scoop, people!" said Pike, in a stentorian voice.

"I was able to contact the Sheriff with one of Glenda's drones as a radio relay, and it's all messed up out there. The riots in the cities are burning out mostly because there's nothing left to burn or loot. The nuclear blast areas are dead zones. Governor Grantham, now Chairman Grantham, has declared a new Republic of California and has allied this..." here he paused and looked at the floor.

"...allied this nation state with China and with Cuba. Apparently, these 'social justice committees' are the real deal, authorized by the new Republic. They are authorized to enact social change, totally and randomly, and without any restraints. Some are relatively moderate, and some aren't."

"It's like the Soviets, in 1917," said Garth's mother. "Terror, disruption, economic collapse first, then when they bring order out of the chaos they have created, they will seem to be heroes."

"Or, in the face of all this chaos, they are just doing what they think is best," replied Patty Martin.

"So you've got Mrs. Chesbrough deciding that all minors need abortion and all of the elderly should be euthanized to save resources in this time of crisis, and you've got others who aren't so radical. It's all gone nuts," said Chuck, the priest.

"They created the insanity, whoever they are," said Garth's mom. "At this point the Republic of California is forced by its own actions to declare independence, otherwise they lose the future possible benefits of what has happened, and what they've done."

"What they've done? WHAT THEY'VE DONE? This was an act of God!" yelled Chuck.

Garth startled. That was the first time Chuck had spoken up like this.

"It was an earthquake," said Garth's mom, looking at Chuck steadily. "We've had plenty of earthquakes. Governments and people made the outcome different."

"It's still the government!" said Poppy Roswell. "It's still the government, and if that's what the government is right now, then we should obey now and vote something better in later."

"Kill my baby so you can feel good about yourself?" said Raley sharply.

"Blind obedience is not what the sheriff is saying. I am instructed by the Sheriff to do what is best right here, right

now, in the moment. The Republic of California was not created by popular vote, it was created by a midnight session
of the California legislature without even a quorum. Most
members couldn't get to the chambers because of the emergency. It may not be legal," said Pike.

"But it's still the government," said Samantha Roswell.
"It's still OUR government!"

"The United States hasn't recognized it," said Pike.

"If President Price is the face of the American government, then it's better we aren't recognized," said the young
newswoman. "It's better for us to be independent than har-
nessed to THAT idiot."

"I've got a feeling that it's better to stay in the United
States," said Garth's mother. "There are many who will be
hurt from a breakup. We'll all be worse off."

Sounds of scoffing. Voices raised in anger.

"See? They've got us divided," muttered Garth's mother.

Finally Terp shouted above them all, "OK! WE DON'T
AGREE! So where's the border? Where's the border between
the Republic of California and the United States? I don't want
my baby born in a place that tried to murder him."

"Or her," piped Raley from alongside. "Maybe I'm gonna
have a little asskicker like me."

"Abort. Not murder," said Samantha Roswell primly.
"There's a difference. Children shouldn't have children."

"The border is the San Joaquin River," replied Pike quickly.
"If we want to go to the United States, now, we have to go
there. Tonight."

There was silence.

"That seems like a good plan for a person of my age," said Garth's mother. "I don't have much of a future anyway, but what there is, I would like to embrace. Better than the needle."

Renalyn spoke up from the side of the group, towards Garth's mother, "You can ride in a Humvee. We have room."

"We're going," said Raley.

Bear turned to Garth and spoke loudly. "I guess we just got marching orders!"

"But we aren't supposed to go," said Merry Thomas. "We are supposed to wait and let them tell us where to go tomorrow at 7 AM. We shouldn't let anyone go. It would get the rest of us in trouble."

"Aren't we already in trouble?" asked Katrina Paxley.

Tres spoke up, "My father spent his whole life trying to avoid trouble, and trouble killed him anyway."

"Oh, heck, in a couple of years nobody's going to care about us at all. It doesn't matter what we decide. All your heroics of fleeing to the new United States won't matter," said Steve Sanchez. "Better to stay here and let the government decide. What we are doing doesn't matter and running away will probably just kill us faster."

The talk dragged on. Garth felt immensely better after his sleep. He watched the candles make the shadows flicker on the wall. Debate. Disagreement. Argument. Telling of life stories. Oh God, the boredom of recited wrongs.

"Well then, some of us will go, and some of us will stay," said Belinda Jefferson. "All those who are leaving, gather around Pike and prepare for your departure. All those who will stay, gather around Poppy Roswell. Any further business?"

Silence. For once, Garth thought.

Then Terp raised his hand, tentatively.

"Yes?" said Belinda.

"We don't know when we'll be back, right?" asked Terp, rather shyly.

"You're right. We're splitting up. It's hard to believe, after we've been through so much together, but you are right. We can't say what will happen," said Belinda.

"Well then, please...please...can Chuck please marry Raley and me right now? We've been living in sin long enough."

"I thought you'd never ask," beamed Chuck, as Bear reached over and slapped him on the back, smiling. "Right now. No time. Let's just do it now, here."

The Roswells departed, shaking their heads. Katrina Paxley left with them but then quickly returned. She never could resist anything aesthetic, thought Garth. Dove and the girls were rushing in and out, gathering the sparse attributes of a hurried wedding.

Tres, Steve Sanchez' son, Pike, and Randall Smith had a quick conference in the back of the church with Ramon, and they all left hurriedly. Damned rude of them, thought Garth. He wondered if they were perhaps jealous of Terp, or perhaps angry because a time-diverting wedding was happening at this critical time. Garth noticed other people leaving as well. All the lancers. Now perhaps there was only a third of the people left in the church. The others were probably out there preparing to leave. They wouldn't want to take much. They'd want to travel very light.

Garth was a bit bemused. Emotionally drifting. The

electric light bulbs were quite dim, and there were moths fluttering around them. One, a large sphinx moth, kept battering itself uselessly against a light bulb. It spun suddenly into a nearby candle and fell to the floor, scorched, wings burned. All this time it thought it was flying around the moon, thought Garth. It fluttered helplessly on the old tiles of the floor. Garth felt an urge to go pick it up, put it outside. But he did not move.

Terry Taylor and Bear reached forward to Terp. Garth could hear them talking, "This ring was your grandfather's" and "This is my ring," from Bear. Katrina stepped over to Raley, reached out her hand, and said, emphatically, "This is my wedding ring, please, please use it," and Raley smiled graciously, like a debutant, and said, "Oh, please give it to me when Chuck asks for it." and thus Katrina joined the young girls clustered around Raley, smiling sheepishly, caught up in it now.

The chorister was speaking now, in Latin, as Raley had requested. The couple was kneeling before the priest. Then there was Hero the Service Dog, off his leash again. Had Poppy ever bothered to leash him? Then there was Terry Taylor, dragging the drooling slack-jawed dog away, toenails skidding on the tile floor. Garth looked at Dove, and saw she was stony-faced, as the bridesmaids, Francesca among them, quietly covered their faces and shook with laughter. Behind him, he heard Glenda whisper, "This is normal here?"

"It's a madhouse, routinely," whispered Dove, as the priest chanted in Latin. The candles threw his giant shadow across the altar and across the shelved wooden icons at the head of the church. So old, Garth thought. To think those statues were painted over two hundred years ago and now they were witnessing this.

Chuck the priest continued to speak and to interact with Terp and Raley. He was preparing communion now. Should I take communion, thought Garth. So many sins in my life. Yet tomorrow...tonight...we face something which we may not survive. God will forgive me. I hope.

Glenda whispered again, unseen behind Garth, "When all this is over I want a baby. Hell, I want two. Pat wanted to wait, and now I know life's too short for that."

Another woman's voice, whispering, "You'll need a man for that."

Glenda, whispering: "Pike or Ramon? I can't decide."

Woman's whispered voice: "Hmmmm Both are delectable, aren't they? I think they'll have a choice in the matter. And for God's sake, wait till we're safe!"

Glenda, whispered: "What are you going to do when this is over?"

Woman's voice, whispered: "Oh, I love it here. If it all recovers I'd love to live here again. I'm going to miss this. It's been wonderful and terrible at the same time. I mean, look at us, at a wedding."

Garth was startled to hear his wife Dove, whispering now: "I want to go back to the Philippines, to Mindanao with our daughter Akemi, away from this craziness."

Woman's voice, tentatively now: "Oh, we've done OK. We'll all be OK. This is a beautiful country. Just a disruption."

Dove's whispered harsher voice: "So many here are like

spoiled children who have no idea how blessed their lives have been. Instead you hate imaginary enemies. I don't want to be here for that."

Silence.

Garth looked at the burned moth on the ancient tiles. The flickering lights scarcely provided enough light. During the wedding, someone had smashed it flat.

The taste of the communion wine was still in Garth's mouth, and he was looking at the stars as the oncoming evening fog overtook them. So clear, so bright, and always always there. He was standing next to the walled old cemetery alongside the mission. So many new graves since the earthquake. Those people in the crushed car, on the first day. At least they had known what they were doing when they died, thought Garth. Where are you, God? What are you? Have you looked down on all this chaos the whole time? There are corpses here who were our enemies in life, and in two hundred years the archaeologists won't be able to tell who was who. Do we really write our own sagas? I hope.

Suddenly, deeply, he wanted to cry. He wanted to scream. He felt weak. He missed Ernst and Sarah and Wallace, and he had no idea what was happening to anyone. How had this happened? A giant cavern of grief. A tug on his sleeve.

He turned suddenly, startled, and there was his mother, all of 102 years old. Soon to be 103, with her walker. One of the young women soldiers was helping her, Garth saw. Garth's mother looked up at him with calm, steadfast tortoise eyes, glittering in the starlight.

She spoke, "You have a lot to do, I know. I just wanted to tell you that I'm too old to be on a horse when we go out to-night. These gracious ladies," here she gestured at the young woman. Garth recognized her as the young woman soldier who had been uncontrollably sobbing in the river fight.

"They've offered to take me out in the Humvee like a sack of potatoes. I'd rather go out in Jonathon Sanchez' truck, but a ground squirrel ate the battery cables. It's the Humvee for me. I may not see you tomorrow. Remember I love you always."

Garth felt tears springing to his eyes. "I wish it was eas-ier," he responded.

"Well, my son, remember that all of us are descended from people who faced big challenges, over hundreds of years, yet they found their courage and they were lucky."

She reached out and took the young soldier woman's hand, then reached out and held Garth's hand as well.

"I'm a long way from the Chickasaws," said Garth's mother. "But I still believe the ancestors are here. They can see us. Let us make them proud. Now leave. I will watch the moon, if the fog lets me."

Eyes wet, Garth heard a scraping sound from the creek bed, beyond, in the fog. He turned to look. Out of the fog rode Ramon and Tres, and behind them was a burgeoning herd of cattle ambling in the darkness.

"Buenas noches," spoke Ramon from atop his horse. "We brought some heat sources."

"Heat sources?" asked the young woman soldier.

"Targets for their infrared to watch while we get out of

here," said Ramon. "If the Republic wants something warm to watch, here they are."

East Salinas, California

The entire community had moved again, to a tin-roofed warehouse on the outskirts of Boronda.

Wallace woke up sharply, shaking with adrenaline. It was a hot night, unusually humid, and he had sweated so much in his sleep that the sleeping bag was steaming and sodden. Images from his dream: Chief Jefferson and Officer Mendoza, nude, the crowd beating them as they dragged the two, stumbling, terrified, to the steps of the courthouse where the ropes waited. The ropes.

He lay there alone for a short time, consumed by the horror and then the anger, and he felt for the shotgun, and he realized that sleep was done for the night. He had no idea what time it was. Pulling on his pants, still wet and overheated, he unzipped the door to his tent and stepped out into the night. So dark.

He walked carefully to the communal campfire, now almost entirely embers. In the darkness, he could see a person wrapped in a blanket hunched in one of the folding sports chairs, lost in thought. Slinging his shotgun, he approached. The person saw him, appeared to startle, and a hank of hair fell free of the blanket. Katy, he realized. A surge of feelings.

"Hey there. Sorry to scare you," he said.

"Couldn't sleep?" came her small voice.

"Oh. Nightmares. Again. You know," he answered.

"You see them again?" she asked.

"Dragged to the ropes, as always," he responded. "In the dreams, I feel them."

Silence.

"You think she was terrified?" asked Katy, after a time.

"In my dreams she is," said Wallace. "But she doesn't show it. She was tough like that. I'm not sure how tough I'd be."

"Damn," she said. "I don't know about myself either."

"Why are you up? Same old story?" asked Wallace.

"Same old story. I close my eyes, and there is my husband, and life is good, and we're in our home, and the kids are with us, and it's all so wonderful," she replied. "Then he's dead and I can't bring him back to life, and the kids are screaming and the house is burning...."

Her voice trailed off.

"I'm sorry," said Wallace. "I wish I could fix it."

"I know I have to go forward, but I'm stuck," she said. "I'm not sure how to get my head out of it. You know we'll be dragging ass again today. I'm always tired. So are you."

Wallace gave a small laugh. "Too true. I'll walk five miles to get there, show up with Tiny and Mickey, and Happy Johnson will have us guarding the toilet paper supplies again, like they did yesterday."

"Just don't let them know where we live," said Katy. "We've moved all over but you know they want to find out where we sleep. When we aren't armed or prepared."

"If they get us, you know we have to fight," said Wallace.
He looked up at the stars.

"I think we don't have a choice," replied Katy softly.

"I wish it was different," said Wallace, matching her quietness.

"Is it OK if we sat together? Can you move your chair?" asked Katy.

Wallace moved his chair and sat back down, deeply conscious of her nearness. Silence. Quiet. He looked into the night sky, as did she.

"Look at those stars," she said quietly.

"We didn't have stars like this before," he said quietly.

"Oh I think we did. Perhaps back then there was too much light, or we were too busy to notice," replied Katy, almost whispering.

Wallace felt her hand questing for his.

"Go ahead and take it. Just this once. Just once. You know I still love my husband. I know you still love your wife. But here we are, and we're alive. Just this once," she said. "After all, we've been true to them, haven't we?"

Wallace gripped her hand. It was callused and worn. Dry. It was wonderful. New sensation.

"Really magnificent stars," he said. "You can see the Milky Way."

"Do you think anyone up there cares?" she asked. "Is God up there looking down?"

"I honestly don't know," he replied. "My father would probably discuss his Christian God about now, but I don't know. All I know of church is that they kept asking me for money and the assistant pastor ran off with the secretary. I think the kids liked it though."

"This isn't about religion. This is about God," replied Katy.

She sounded sleepy.

There was a small scuffing sound in the darkness behind them, and Wallace turned to look, one hand gripping his shotgun. El Tigre emerged in the night, looking skinnier than ever. Katy pulled her hand away from Wallace's hand abruptly, furtively. Wallace stood up and faced the young man, who was scarcely visible in the blackness.

"I have massage," said El Tigre, passing a thick envelope to Wallace. "From Jefe Jesus."

"Well. A massage. I could do with a massage," said Wallace.

Katy was standing as well. She turned on her headlamp, which was temporarily blinding, reached for the envelope, and ripped it open.

"Greetings Señor Ericson. Or should I say, Sargento Ericson. I write this with memories of delicious Spam in the forefront of my mind. Distressingly, I have not found more, or I would invite you to partake.

"I am told that there will be a big thunderstorm which will come here tonight. The weatherman whom I consult...that hairless man previously from the TV station...tells me that it will arrive this evening around 10 PM and bring thirty mile per hour winds and great rain.

"This is important because it will keep the strike teams

from employing drones to seek anyone should they attempt to flee.

"Should you wish to take advantage of this opportunity, I will have an assortment of vehicles, perhaps twenty, gathered at 7 PM in front of Salinas High School for an emergency transshipment of the refugees and families at the Rodeo Grounds. My sources tell me that if you do not move the internees, special strike teams are coming to take them for their final journey tomorrow. So this is very fortunate for us.

"Please come prepared for a journey as these vehicles will be entirely at your disposal. Aside from drivers, you must provide all personnel for this expedition. Also, given the infectious climate, my family will be going with you. They will be in the vehicles, with the weatherman and his family, Dina Montero, who will retrieve her husband, and others. I will meet you with my friends at 8 PM at the Rodeo arena. It's likely to be quite the hoe down tonight. A true bronco ride.

"Please send any response with this young gentleman, give him food, and I will feed him again. He looks as if more good food will help him.

"Thinking of the special sauce.

"Jesus

"El Jefe de las cucarachas".

Wallace forced himself to continue breathing.

"Can we do this?" he asked Katy.

"Si, se puede," she replied. "I can. You need to show up at work. You three go act like nothing's different. Grovel extra. Kiss their boots. The ladies here will get this done.

MAKE SURE you are at the Salinas High School at 6:30 tonight. Go pack your gear now. I'll make sure it is with us when we move."

"What do we tell Jesus?" he said.

"We tell him yes," Katy replied.

Katy stood bathed in light at the entrance to the rodeo ground, showing the guards the fake orders for evacuation of the facility. Her coat's hood obscured her appearance. Can they sense my fear, wondered Wallace. Can they hear my heart racing, see the sweat on my face? He said nothing. He did nothing. He simply stood stolidly behind Katy, his shotgun slung, feeling the slightly crisp wind on his cheeks and watching as the guards examined the papers.

Fake as hell, those papers. The County Medical Officer whom Katy had been cultivating for days with food and attention had written those papers, with Causwell's help. Emergency evacuation and processing of all the detainees due to Candida. All the correct stamps, in reality quite bogus, which were added by El Tigre, especially the much-coveted Republic of California central government stamp, a highly stylized eagle with outstretched wings gripping a single star.

In return for his signature and endorsements, the County Medical Officer and his family were in a VW van in the parking lot, waiting to convoy out with them. It was possibly the newest car in the collection.

Katy had been very busy today, as had they all. So many people were going with them. Their entire community, in addition to the detainees.

That thought caused Wallace to turn and look into the darkness at the gathering of vehicles on the tarmac. About twenty-five vehicles. Including a dump truck. That itself would be enough to alert the guards, if they had any awareness. Wallace wondered at Katy's calmness as she stepped back from the guard office. Tiny, Mickey, Causwell, the noose around his neck hidden by a coat, several other women, and Mike clustered around her.

"They accepted the papers, but something's not right," said Katy.

"What do you mean?" asked Mickey. What do you mean? What's wrong?"

"This is a clown show, and it's obvious. I mean, a burrito coach for an evacuation? Look at this gaggle," she said, motioning with her arm. "They should be noticing this and asking."

The wind blew her hood away and she pulled it back. Wallace looked across the parking lot and there in the congregation of vehicles was that large food truck reflecting the streetlamps in the dark, with the bright orange lettering "El Platinum Platano" curving across the sides. Nothing suspicious there.

"But the guards aren't asking enough questions. They are just saying yes. My first guess would be that they are on our side, they know what's happening and they're with us," she added.

"But these guards are strike teams," said Mike Rogers.

"Exactly. The strike teams aren't our friends, but these individuals are all friendly now. Like they were expecting this. Something's up."

"We have security on the perimeter," said Wallace. "Jesus' people are out there somewhere. Not much else we can do except play this out."

Security, he thought. El Tigre and a bunch of civilians with slingshots. Sporter .22 rifles. Good luck with that.

A young guard was motioning now. Come in, he was waving. A young white man in his green janitor clothes, with a civilian blue peacoat over them, and a pullover watch cap. He must be cold, thought Wallace. Cold and bored. The entire group followed him from the gate in the chain link fence, into the tunnel of the sheet metal stadium.

"Please come in and help organize the detainees," said the young man. "You brought your own medical supplies for the processing, right? The normal teams bring theirs. We don't have any of that stuff here."

"Yes, yes," said Katy deferentially, nodding to the man. "We have all our own supplies."

"Damn I'm glad I don't have your job," said the young man. "I've gotten a little attached to this bunch. Especially the kids. I understand when we have to process the children, but when we do that, it's always hard for me. Pretending, and all. Although it's for the good of the Republic."

You've processed children, thought Wallace.

"Yes, yes, it's hard for us too. Especially rushed like this," replied Katy, as they walked towards the tunnels into the stadium.

"You police have to leave your guns behind, sorry," said the young man, motioning at MIckey, Mike, Tiny, and Wallace.

Katy pulled her hood back and flashed a radiant smile at

the young man, "Oh you know, the police nowadays. Their guns aren't even loaded. All show. Just this once, OK? Show him, Sargent Ericson."

She flipped her hair attractively and blinked.

The young man turned slightly red.

Wallace cracked open the action of his shotgun and showed him the empty chamber. Hope he doesn't ask to see my pistol, under my coat. Chamber's not empty on that one, he thought.

"Oh," said the evidently befuddled young man, "I guess, just this once."

There was a shot behind them, in the parking area, and the young man tensed. Then he looked at them both sternly and said, "Oh, well, surprise." and reached out and grabbed for Wallace's shotgun. He tugged. Wallace did not let go. Wallace was contemplating chambering a round when Katy pulled a small pistol from her coat and shot the young man in the chest.

The sound was deafening in the metal tunnel, and then Wallace heard the brass cartridge case tinkle as it hit the ground, and as he worked the pump action on his shotgun. Loaded now, he thought. The young man stumbled backwards, until he thumped into the sheet metal tunnel wall behind him. Then he slid to the ground in a sitting position, hand to his breast pocket. Hopefully he's not fatally injured, thought Wallace. That's a thick coat and that's a peashooter pistol. Has Katy been carrying that pistol the entire time?

"You! You in there! Ollie ollie oxen-free," came an amplified familiar voice, from inside the stadium.

"Shit! Did Jesus rat us out?" said Katy.

There were several more shots behind them, outside in the parking area. Some screams.

"It's me! Your pal! Happy! And look who's here! With your main squeeze, Tiny Tupuola! We have your inamorata Margarita! We've been waiting for you," came the voice.

"What?" said Tiny, in the darkness. He came up like a bull towards the inside of the stadium.

The lights came on inside the tunnel, making them all blink, illuminating Mickey in the process of searching and disarming the injured young strike team member sitting against the wall. He had removed the young man's AR-15 and passed it to one of the women.

"Get security behind us," Wallace said to Mickey.

"I got that," muttered Mike Rogers as he turned to face back towards the parking lot, "You just get us out of here, Einstein. You got us in here."

"Any side doors here?" Wallace said to Causwell.

Causwell pointed at the young man. "Ask him."

"WE HAVE YOUR MAN HERE. ONE OF YOUR GUARDS," shouted Katy.

"Oh, you can EAT the guard if you get hungry. We don't care. Besides, we don't recognize gender. So you have IT," came Happy's cheerful voice.

"Access panel. In the ceiling. Gets under the bleachers," said the young man, grimacing.

"Keep them talking," Katy said to Wallace. "You, unscrew the light bulbs. We want to be in the dark. Oh, heck with it, just break them."

"MARGARITA! HONEY! WHAT ARE YOU DOING WITH THAT GUY?" shouted Tiny.

Tiny seemed crushed.

"Darling...Darling," came Margarita's voice. "They have all your people here. They're safe here. Really, they are."

A flurry of shots came from the parking lot behind them. Shouts. Engine noises. The light bulbs in the tunnel went out one by one.

"That's our strike teams cleaning up outside!" said Happy's voice.

The lights came on in the stadium. Brilliant light.

"Oh, you poor dears. You can't hide in the dark like that," said Happy's voice. "Besides we have your families, don't we?"

"MARGARITA, DIDN'T YOU HEAR WHAT I TOLD YOU ABOUT THE MURDERING? THE BODIES AT THE SALINAS RIVER?" shouted Tiny. "THAT'S WHAT THEY PLAN TO DO TO EVERYONE HERE! THEY WILL KILL US TOO!"

"Oh, Darling," came Margarita's voice. "They're just killing just old people. They're just killing gun owners. The government is on OUR side for once! We have our whole lives to lead, and Mayor Johnson and Commissioner McTavish tell me that we're special because we're people of color! This is our time!"

Wallace heard a shuffling and dimly saw a woman's feet go up through the open panel in the ceiling. Tiny had boosted the woman through the panel. Wallace stepped closer and peered through the darkness. The young strike team soldier looked back at him painfully. Saying nothing. Looking around in the darkness, Wallace couldn't tell who was in the tunnel and who had gone through the hatch above them.

"HONEY YOU CAN'T BELIEVE THAT," shouted Tiny. "THEY'VE BEEN LYING ALL ALONG."

"Aren't you angry? Aren't you finally fed up? I am! I'm mad as hell! This is OUR chance to grind the heel!" came Margarita's voice. "You've deceived yourself. Remember what President Obama said a few years back, how we've all been hated and hated and hated. Black Americans chained and whipped and hanged. Spit on for trying to sit at lunch counters. Beaten for trying to vote. It's always been like this. We've always been oppressed."

"No we haven't," replied Tiny softly. "Yes there's been some bad bad bad times. Yes there's been oppression. But the path has been upwards. It's been a better and better life."

He looked through the dark at Wallace, tears in his eyes, then he turned and shouted.

"HONEY, YOU'VE BEEN PLAYED!"

There was a surge of automatic rifle fire out in the parking lot, and Happy shouted, "What? What?" and a large boxy roaring form, a vehicle, headlights blazing, appeared silhouetted in the tunnel from the parking lot, and Wallace yelled, "Run! Run into the stadium! And bring that guard!"

Brilliant stadium lights. Running into the arena, and a sudden stop. There was a small group of people standing in the plowed dirt expanse. There was Happy. There was Margarita. There was Gillian McTavish with about six strike team fighters. Then Wallace focused on his footing on the uneven ground as he rushed sideways out of the way of the vehicle charging through the tunnel.

It was a tank, a little World War II tank, from the monument at the cemetery. And now, here it was, fully operational, and it clanked and churned out into the open light and the turret swiveled and there on top, his upper body protruding from the commander's hatch, was Jesus Garcia, wearing an old leather football helmet, smiling broadly. The tank approached Happy Johnson's group and throttled to a stop with a jerk. The small cannon in the turret depressed and swiveled, squeaking shrilly, until it was pointing directly at Happy.

Beside Wallace, Tiny dropped the injured tunnel guard into the dirt. The young guard looked up curiously from where he lay.

"Ah. Forgive my rudeness," said Jesus down to Happy Johnson. "You see, it was an ambush within an ambush. A trap within a trap."

Jesus turned to Wallace. "Sorry Amigo, I couldn't tell you until now. You see, we knew that someone would talk."

Jesus looked at Margarita, who cringed slightly.

"Oh, and the tank is for panache," added Jesus. "I like the effect. Don't you?"

"Darling, darling, mi Querida," Margarita said to Tiny. "You know I was right, don't you?"

"We don't need this Quisling's approval. The Republic is still right," said Gillian McTavish, standing next to Mayor Johnson. "Yes, the people will throw off the chains of oppression and liberate themselves. You!" she pointed angrily at Mike Rogers, then Wallace, then finally at Jesus.

"Enemies of the state. You will be processed. Families too. Deluded monkeys," she continued.

Wallace was aware of movement above them in the stadium bleachers. He looked up and saw hundreds of people coming up from the rooms below. High in the stands, Katy was waving. Success.

Gillian McTavish continued, "The day of righteousness is nigh. You cannot run from the wrath of the pee..."

There was a shocking boom, a stunning blast wave, and Gillian McTavish exploded. Wallace saw her head, hair streaming, sail at least one hundred yards high in the air, so slowly, shadowed in the brilliant stadium lights before it arched back down like a plumed lawn dart. The head bounced when it landed on its face.

Powder smoke curled up from the tank's cannon barrel, as people brushed off the viscera, blood, and body parts which had struck them. Wallace gently dislodged a large piece of liver which had covered his boot.

"Missed," said Jesus Garcia.

It began to rain.

To the east of San Antonio Mission

5 AM and dawn was lighting the distant horizon. Garth could now clearly see Dogfood's ears as he sat atop the horse, on

the hill overlooking the mission. Oh, it was such a beautiful dawn. A little steam rose from Dogfood's breathing. Directly west was the sparkling planet Mars, about to set behind the western coastal mountains, with fog on either side. And overhead, in a fissure in the overcast, was Orion's belt.

Garth felt in his vest pocket, and there was the arrowhead. He had planned on performing a traditional Native American point ceremony, as his grandmother had taught him, but that hadn't been possible. There had simply been too much to do. Too many interruptions.

"Do you think Roswell ever came back from informing on us?" whispered Bear, beside him on his own horse.

"I don't know. After we realized he was gone last night, I was too busy," replied Garth softly. "And I don't think we need to whisper."

"He wouldn't really rat us out, would he?" said Hopi Jack, mounted alongside them.

"Can't say. He seemed to feel strongly about our discussion last night. And he didn't like the fact that some of us were leaving." answered Bear. "I didn't see him or Samantha after the meeting. They weren't at the wedding."

"Let's see," said Hopi Jack, "We left at 2:30 AM and the gas-powered vehicles were due to leave at 4:30 AM. But I didn't hear anything, and I can see some cars down there. I see people. Can't tell who they are, though."

"Well, what? About half decided to stay and accept relocation. So those could be their cars and that could be them, packing," said Bear.

Garth felt the obsidian spearhead again in his vest

pocket. He was worrying. Francesca and Dove were on horseback, with the cattle, moving hidden in the thermal images of the herd. Across the Salinas River, perhaps, by now. But his mother and Akemi were in the Humvee, and they hadn't linked up as scheduled where the Salinas River met the Arroyo Seco. Anything might have happened, of course. It didn't have to be bad news.

The prevailing thought was that the vehicles had bogged down in the sand of the river bed, but nobody really knew, and the quick search by the drones from the electric deca-quads hadn't found them. So this small scouting party had doubled back. But the double back hadn't revealed anything. Mystery. Worry. Now the question he was asking himself: for some reason were they still down there at the Mission?

"Should we go down?" asked Hopi Jack.

Garth fumbled in his saddlebags for his night vision monocular and realized that soon it would be too light to use it anyway. Better to save the batteries.

"I'm not seeing any of the vehicles which were scheduled to leave," said Bear. "Maybe our group is already gone."

"I don't know, Merry Thomas, you would think after all she'd been through that she would have gone with us. I'm still surprised that she decided to stay. She can be pretty persuasive. Maybe she convinced our group of vehicles to stay. Maybe we should go down and un-convince 'em."

"Or Poppy ratted us out and the Republic arrived early."

Tiger Tanaka: "If the Republic at the mission already, there would be lights and chaos. None of their vehicles are down there."

"OK, then, let's circle around up canyon and pay them a visit, and see what's up," Bear.

"Adelante, as Chuck would say," replied Hopi Jack.

"Huh?" responded Bear.

"Chuck said that his church is the people, and so he's leaving," said Hopi Jack. "Always onwards, like Junipero Serra."

"We can't just sit here. Let's get back down to the mission and find out what's really going on," responded Garth. "Daylight's burning."

Before anyone could act, their soft discussion was interrupted by the rising sound of helicopters coming over the hills from the Salinas Valley. More than one. The four horsemen moved their mounts more deeply into the oak trees as the two helicopters swept over them unseen in the fog, emerging brilliantly into the clear air over the mission. The two relatively antique two-engine Huey's, high visibility green and orange, circled cantilevered over the mission in the tunnel of light through the clouds, blades whopping, apparently observing. Garth felt fear: perhaps they could see him under the oak tree, perhaps a bit of his equipment might be reflecting the rising sunlight. The helicopters circled slowly, and dropped lower.

"Repurposed California Division of Forestry birds. They got door gunners," whispered Bear. "Look, they even got missiles."

"Hour early," muttered Hopi Jack.

"They start to chase us and we're in trouble," said Tiger

Tanaka, behind them. "Don't move. Just stay still under this tree. It's becoming daytime, so they can't use infrared."

"Yep," said Garth, thinking that this was insanity, insanity on top of insanity, capped by madness. That they should be hiding. What would happen if they just rode out into plain sight?

The first missile flew straight through the open doors of the church, and instantly the windows blew out with blasts of flame, shards of glass glittering in the light. The second missile hit the front of the church, and the front of the mission collapsed and slowly, like an elephant laying down, the entire great ancient structure began to fall, billowing smoke and flames.

They heard a screaming, a long drawn out wailing, and out of the inferno of the main door ran Hero the Service Dog, on fire, blazing fur, racing arrow-straight past the graveyard, past the fresh graves, and Garth watched him until the light of his burning was concealed by the weed patch beyond. In a few seconds a small column of smoke began to rise there, from the dry mustard.

"200 years. 200 years," whispered Bear. "200 years."

"Now we know that Poppy and Samantha came back," spoke Hopi softly.

"So much for the promises of the Republic," said Tiger Tanaka, emphatically. "No internment camp for me. My great grandparents and my grandparents did that. Not so good."

"Why would the Republic DO that? Wasn't everyone in there?" asked Bear, mostly to himself. "Weren't the people in the church?"

At this point the entire central mission building was collapsing and in flames, but the quadrangle behind it had not yet ignited. The helicopters began firing their door mounted machine guns as they circled. Two small figures who ran out of the buildings were quickly gunned down.

"That's Merry Thomas. The little one must be Tabetha," said Hopi.

"No time to find out. We still have the other horse group heading out, and we need to think of them," replied Tiger. "We gotta move before the last of this fog lifts. Stay strong, guys. Right now, that means that we back down this canyon and head for the Salinas River while these two choppers are preoccupied."

Garth, stunned beyond words, reached for his walkie talkie. He had to know who was there.

"Don't use that! It's an open channel! They'll track us for sure! Get the rest of us killed," hissed Tiger Tanaka.

The words felt like a slap. Garth considered a harsh, angry retort. They...his own people...were down there, dying. People he loved.

"We have to do something," he hissed back.

"Live. Right now, the best plan is to live, and keep our families alive if we can," whispered Hopi. "We need to get out of here."

Garth wrestled the turmoil which threatened to overwhelm him, as the others silently maneuvered their horses into the fog behind. Then, wordless but shaking, he reined Dogfood behind the group as they rode back into the fog, single file, heading east. Oh God, Oh God, Oh God, he prayed.

Let my family be alive. Let them live through this. As the gray closed over him, he could hear the helicopters circling and machine guns, and once, a single loud boom. A musket. Someone was fighting back.

Later that morning, they crested the mountains on the western side of the Salinas Valley in brilliant sunlight and saw the fog laid out below them like a white quilt, covering the valley floor. Bright blue sky. A few contrails overhead. Below them, in the distance, a few very distant green and orange helicopters. Quietly they followed the trail downslope, past fields of dry ungrazed wild oats and brome, sheltering as much as possible in the gray pines and the oak trees, always on the alert, Garth numb with fear about the fate of his family. All silent with shock. There was a spring, fresh water, a horse trough. They watered the horses, refilled their water bottles, and rode on.

At around noon, as they dropped down into the blanket of fog, they found the tracks of the other horse riders and the solar-powered quads on the western side of the Salinas Valley, where the vineyards crept up the slopes, the grape vines now dead and dying from lack of irrigation, choking with dead brown weeds between the plants. These were the tracks from before, when they had all been together. Silently Garth took comfort in the fact that at least he was able to follow the tracks, that now they had not become lost in their emotionally distracted wanderings.

At sunset, following the tracks, they carefully crossed the Salinas River at the collapsed bridges below Soledad, where the Arroyo Seco River met the Salinas River, where they had left the others on horses before. The tracks indicated that the other horse group was still pushing cattle with them, still seeking to hide from any infrared detection. That was a good sign. A very good sign. The other group wasn't in full-blown flight. They were still operating deliberately. Hope. Dear sweet hope.

They crossed the dry Salinas River single file in the dwindling light of the blessed fog. Not a living person. Coyotes. A few squirrels. Vultures. Near Highway 101, close to the riverbed, there were corpses in piles, everywhere. Many of the corpses had plastic laundry bags over their heads. Men, women, children. Sometimes animals and people mixed together, with vehicle tracks. Apparently, the corpses had been dumped there. Others in groups, where they had apparently been herded and killed at the site. Some chewed and dismembered. Wild pig tracks. Stench, bloating, clothing and trash bags and other garbage blowing in the soft cool dark breeze. Praise God, none of the corpses were from the mission. None were fresh. None were people they knew.

Follow the tracks. As the darkness fell, they rose once again out of the fog, and the half-moon lit the path before them. They quietly rode single file up a trail beside a dry creek south of Pinnacles National Monument. Once, they saw a light in a window of a ranch house, a single light in the darkness, and Garth pondered how much he would love to be there, inside that ranch house, in another world, a peaceful, sane world with his family, and food, and rest. And books. Oh dear memories. How did we not appreciate it? And how deeply naive and blind we had been before. On they rode. Garth was aware of his exhaustion, but heedless of it.

Follow the tracks. Garth watched the dirt whenever the limited light allowed and studied the tracks of the electric quads with their battery trailers: they were apparently still moving with the horses and the cattle. A steep ravine of a creek...this with water. They did not stop. Ride with the North Star on the left shoulder, riding east. Finally, in the dark, an immense flatness in the dark light of the early dawn. Ahead, the Central Valley. And below them, in the vestiges of the hills, the tracks led down to another ranch house, a Spanish-style quadrangle smaller than the mission. Hidden from the Central Valley by several small ridges of dry mountains and sparse orchards. One dirt road heading towards Coalinga.

There were the dark shapes of cattle grazing on the hills around the ranch house. Until now, they hadn't seen cattle. All uniform in size, like the cattle the main group had taken from the mission.

"Hold up," said Garth quietly.

He reached back and pulled his night vision monocular from his saddle bags.

"Good thought. They wouldn't want to cross the Central Valley to the San Joaquin River in daylight. Too easy to be spotted," said Hopi Jack. "They'd rest up someplace like that for the day, and head across at sunset."

"Dove would know that," replied Garth.

Hopi Jack raised his ancient binoculars to his eyes. "So would Ramon. So would Terp. So would Terry," he said.

"There aren't any lights down yonder," said Bear.

Garth adjusted his monocular over his glasses, and the greenish artificially lit images became clearer.

"If they're smart, they aren't using lights," said Tiger.

"They're smart," said Bear. "Raley's smart as a coon at midnight in a campground."

"I'm seeing some movement," said Hopi Jack.

"I see a quad, hidden under a bush across the way. It's one of ours," said Garth.

West of Coalinga, now renamed Justicia Republic of California

The beef was as tasty as any Garth had ever eaten. It had been barbecued yesterday, then stewed during the night in brown mole sauce in a wood-fired horno, with shucked corn. His kind of people. They who lived here...those who survived... couldn't speak much English. Mostly they spoke Oaxacan with some Spanish. But they were very kind, and most spoke enough of whatever language was needed.

The sun was up brightly now, and the late fall dew was evaporating off the brown grass on the hillsides, along with the last coolness. Soon it would be furnace-hot. He could hear the trickle of water in a nearby green-mossed horse trough. So beautiful a sound.

"This place looks like a shithole from the outside, doesn't it?" said Randall.

He had organized the security here and had helped everyone get hidden.

"Especially on the road in from Coalinga. That's the beauty of it," said Ramon. Once again, Ramon had been priceless in communicating with the residents and in keeping the main group of people organized during their flight across the mountains.

Garth looked out from the shade of the porch. The place looked quiet, abandoned, ramshackle. In the sycamore tree opposite, across the yard of creek cobbles in the bright sunlight, acorn woodpeckers were chattering and fluttering. Everyone was well-concealed.

"What's the story here?" asked Hopi Jack.

"Con permiso, I introduce to you Alanza, who is one of the people who are living here," said Ramon. "She will help me explain."

The woman was about 50, tall as Ramon, slender and stern, unsmiling, strong, businesslike, black hair half gray, dressed in a man's farm laborer clothes. Worn leather work boots, Garth noticed. She seemed formidable.

Greetings all around.

"I speak only little English. But Ramon, he help," said Alanza. "The people come, and we are working down the road, and they come here, to this house, and they kill the owners, and they take things. They take what they want."

"Republic?" asked Dove, from behind. Garth had not spoken with her before now. His own wife and he had not had a word. Just wrong.

"She says she does not know," said Ramon. "People

came in a vehicle...they saw the tracks later, and they lined up the owners and shot them, and took what they wanted. They don't know who did it."

There was a burst of Spanish from Alanza, directed at Ramon. Garth understood most of it. They had buried the wonderful owners, who were their relatives, in the back, in unmarked graves behind the barn. The graves were unmarked because there were fears that others would come and loot the corpses. The survivors had been afraid to leave this place because the owners had warned them before the home invasion that they would be deported. Also there was a video of the Border Patrol executing Mexican refugee children, which the owners had watched with everyone on television before their deaths.

Bear shook his head and was silent.

"How long ago did the killings here happen?" asked Dove, who was shorter than Alanza by about a foot.

Alanza puzzled over the words. "We are here five years," she finally replied.

Spanish from Ramon.

"Oh, they die three months ago," said Alanza in English.

Ramon asked Alanza in Spanish, "You have been hiding here the entire time?"

Alanza in Spanish: "Our cousins who owned this place told us to always hide. No lights or fires at night. It was just like the hard times at home. We are used to hiding. In the cabins, in the barns, under the trees. We grow our own food and we don't go to town, so when the earthquake came, we were ready."

"You've done a superb job," said Ramon. "How many are you?"

"Twenty-six," replied Alanza. "Four are Chinese people who found us, like you. Children of God. Six in total are children."

Astonishing, thought Garth, that they should hide twenty-six people here.

"How many cars and how many horses?" asked Pike, in Spanish. "If you want to go with us."

"The people who came and killed our cousins took one car," said Alanza. "When the Republic people came in an SUV...that was after the other people killed the owners....another time, later...we all hid and they took another car. But there was an old work truck in the barn, with chicken nests in the back, covered in pigeon droppings. This we have cleaned up and repaired, and we had some gasoline as well. You know, in cans."

She said this with some pride, motioning and pointing with her hands. Indeed, thought Garth, it was impressive.

"So one truck," said Ramon in Spanish.

"No, there is another car, a Honda, which we hid in a hay barn, and another off-road truck. The four Chino brought it when they found us. And we have the gasoline for both," replied Alanza.

"Wonderful," said Glenda, who had entered the porch. "And horses?"

"We have veintiseis, twenty-six," replied Alanza. "Ten are foals or can't be ridden."

"And who will inherit this place?" asked Dove. "Who owns it now?"

"I...I do not know," replied Alanza. "I think perhaps I will own."

"Hmmm," said Dove, and gazed up at Alanza speculatively.

The planning and discussion continued in several languages. People joined them. Garth was delighted to see Terry and Barry Taylor and his own daughter Francesca. He met the "Chinese", actually Koreans, with names he immediately forgot in the rush of the moment. An older man, and a younger man, his son, and the son's young wife and near-infant baby.

The plan: They would stay here and rest during the heat of the day. An hour before sunset, which would be around 7 PM, they would leave to cross the Central Valley in darkness, to reach the San Joaquin River and the new border before dawn. A few would stay here, including Alanza, and hope for the mercy of the Republic. Alanza repeated that she thought she might inherit. That was probably wishful thinking, thought Garth. The Republic would take everything.

The travelers would cross the remaining open valley in the cool nighttime darkness with the cattle as thermal decoys, and then would cope with the actual river border crossing in the rising light of tomorrow's sunrise. They would hope to link up with the Humvees, who were not here, and Garth's mom and Akemi and the others, across the border. For now, nobody knew where the Humvees were, and they were unwilling to ask on the walkie-talkies, or to send up a drone, for fear of being discovered. For now, they lived in ignorance.

That not knowing ate at Garth, filled him with apprehension. If they are caught, we will never see them again, he thought. If WE are caught. Francesca, and Dove, caught. The concept gave him a surge of adrenaline, which made him dizzy. He reached out for a beautiful natural wooden porch beam for support. Beautiful grain in the wood, he noticed. Gotta hydrate, and eat a bit more, and sit down, he thought.

For now, they would all rest in the shade, and prepare, sleep as much as possible, and stay out of sight from any prying eyes. God bless these people...even the people who died... for this sanctuary, Garth thought.

After the meeting Garth turned to Dove and hugged her. She resisted his embrace, slightly, then her arms were around him as well, gently, lovingly but without passion.

Well, Garth considered, she's coped with a lot and we don't know where Akemi is. Then there was another pair of arms around him, and he shifted so that he could continue to hug Dove, and there was his daughter Francesca, hugging him.

"Dad, it's great to see you. I've missed you a lot," said Francesca. "It was hard being separated. And those girls, so hard to make them shut up."

"Since we don't have phones anymore, all we CAN do is talk, chatterbox!" Ophelia said from a distance.

"I missed you too, lots," Garth said, hugging her back.

"You gotta see this," Francesca said, after a minute. "Dove, you too."

They went through a passage into the adobe structure and stepped into a small quadrangle, much smaller than the quadrangle of the mission but nevertheless a beautiful garden. Roses. An orange tree. A patch of blooming milkweed.

All carefully tended. Open to the sky in the central atrium, otherwise under eaves.

Around the eves were many of their own people, in the quiet hot shade of a fall morning. Garth brightened to see them, most asleep. A few of the luckiest had commandeered hammocks suspended from the wooden roof supports. Smiles. Chuck the chorister shook his hand. Then Terp and Raley, down from their security post on the hill, silently waved, grinning. Garth noticed that Katrina Paxley was sleeping. Garth looked around the beautiful quiet enclosed quadrangle, as monarch butterflies fluttered, and it came to him that this was an historic moment. Right here, right now, history was being made in this flight, either to safety or folly, he could not tell.

At the Border of the Republic of California, North of Fresno at the San Joaquin River.

They were riding wordlessly through an orchard...apparently almond trees. In the chill predawn darkness, the orchard seemed untended for months. There were weeds to the horses' knees between the trees, scarcely visible in the shadows. The trees seemed to be dead or dying from lack of irrigation, the dry leaves falling from the branches and crackling under the horses' walking hooves. Few nuts. The San Joaquin River should be nearby.

Dogfood's head was drooping. In the last couple of days, the horse had come very far, very fast, without a chance to rest for more than a few hours. Now here they were, mixed in with the traveling cattle herd, and these orchards, dry as they were, had been a blessing, providing cover from any infrared observation. They were almost to the border, and they were exhausted. As Dogfood looked, so Garth felt. It must be much harder for the others. Terry Taylor, more than 80 years old, must be suffering. They had been in the saddle for ten hours, with few pauses.

The vehicles, the quads and the trucks and a Honda Accord filled with Oaxacans, were now traveling separately from the horses and the cattle, but often within eyesight of each other. Because of the occasional rough ground, with canals, ditches, fences, orchards, and roads, they had been zig zagging, essentially two different groups, barely staying in visual contact. But in the moonlight, Tiger and Bear and Hopi had picked up dim Humvee tracks, perhaps their own Humvee, several days old, and they were now following those through the orchard while the vehicles stayed on the nearest smallest road.

Garth felt exhaustion and nervous fear. They would not get to the river in darkness. In the east, beyond the distant Sierras, the sky was lightening. In that increasing dawn light, down the tree rows, Garth could now see a black ribbon of riparian trees which marked the river, with about a half mile of weedy cotton field between them and the boundary. The cotton was in bloom. It must have been planted before the disaster. In the rising light, it looked to Garth like a white blanket laying along the ground, gently sloping downhill to the trees of the river. To the left was another ordered stand of trees, an abandoned orchard of some kind. Just this big expanse of open ground between them and the trees of the river.

"Hold up," he said. But the cattle could smell what must be water in the San Joaquin River bed, even if it was mostly dry, and they began to bolt. Garth had to saw at Dogfood's reins to keep him from joining the herd.

"Hold up!" he repeated more loudly as the cattle jogged around him. "We need to check out the crossing first."

The riders behind them worked to corral the remaining steers, who milled about in the orchard, longing to move forward.

Hopi Jack pulled up alongside and watched the cattle who had escaped. "Hard to watch them beeves scatter to the trees like that, after all the miles we've done together," he said as he pulled his old binoculars up to his eyes.

"Hey," said Hopi. "I can see something off to the left, up the hill, get your thermal on it."

Garth pulled his night vision monocular over his eye. After all these hours the strap under his cavalry hat was hurting his head. There was a heat signature. Square. The Humvee was only a few hundred yards up the hill, slightly behind them to their left, looking down at what should be the river. The beginning dawn was cancelling the night vision effect and so Garth took off his hat, pulled off his monocular strap and all, and reached back to stow it in his saddlebags.

"Let's let the girls go make contact with the Humvee. Be

careful. As the sun rises we'll cross the river together," he said. "So glad this is over."

"Me too," said Terry Taylor behind him. "I'm about ready to retire from the cavalry."

Quiet voices as the girls got the word, and Garth saw them moving off, across the cotton to the trees, uphill to the right. There went Francesca, with Sarah's rifle slung across her back as always. No more need for that, once they were across.

Raley led the way, feeling relieved. Almost done. She was a married woman. She and Terp would have a wonderful proper honeymoon, on the other side. She missed him already, and they were only three hundred yards apart.

Francesca quietly called out as they approached the orchard, "Hey, watch out, don't skyline. Just in case the Republic is down there by the river. In the trees."

"Why would they be down there?" said Ophelia. "Why would they want to keep us from leaving? They wanted to kill us anyway."

"Opie's got a point, Moonpie," said Raley to Francesca, as she slowed her horse and they drew abreast of each other.

"It's like the song," said Francesca.

"What?" said Ophelia.

"You can check out any time you like but you can't leave," said Francesca. "Remember East Germany? Heads on a swivel!"

As they rode up to the Humvee they saw Mrs. Ericson, Francesca's grandmother, smiling out the open right side front passenger window. Renalyn was standing up in the gunner's hatch, in her digicam army uniform complete with Kevlar helmet, looking down at the tree-filled riparian channel with her binoculars. She passed the binoculars down to the young girl driver, who was also in full field uniform, and smiled at them broadly.

"Hey ladies," Renalyn said quietly. "Great to see you. I'm not seeing any movement between us and the good ol' USA. I'm seeing some US forces across the river, complete with flags, which I can't fully make out. But between us and the river, nothing. So I guess it's time to cross."

It was much colder than she had realized, thought Raley. Renalyn's breath was steaming.

"How are you, girls?" asked Mrs. Ericson from the front seat's open window.

"Francesca's got the heeby jeebies," said Raley.

"No call for that," said Renalyn, standing tall behind the big fifty caliber machine gun. "It's all good."

"If there's anyone off to our left, they can see you," said Francesca cautiously.

"If there was anyone there, but I don't think so," said Renalyn.

Akemi was waving happily from the back seat, around Renalyn's legs.

The sunrise was a bit cloudy, a bit red from a late fall wildfire burning somewhere. From here Raley could look back to the right downhill at the horse riders, and beyond them she could see the Koreans, the Oaxacans, and their cars on a parallel dirt road. This should be easy.

"I think I see something," said Francesca, unslinging her rifle. "Down in the trees."

Garth was sitting on Dogfood. They had lost control of most of the cattle, who could smell the stagnant water of the river before them. Not much of a river. The fall rains hadn't really increased the flow. In fact it seemed to be pooled in places, with gaps, not flowing. The sun was rising over there in the United States.

The lost cattle were jogging across the cotton field now, down towards the dry river, spreading out, lowing.

"Lookee on the right, there's the vehicles, ready to cross too. Everyone's there," said Bear.

Then one of the cattle exploded, a roar of explosive as the animal was lifted off the ground, dismembered, shrieking indescribably, from the force of the detonation. It fell to earth with a crunching of dry cotton stems and began moaning loudly.

"Oh my God," said Priyanka. She had rode up behind them. "Somebody shoot it. For God's sake put it out of its misery."

"Shoot it and they know we're here," said Bear.

"They already know we're here, I'm guessing," said Pike, behind them.

The cotton near the steer was smoldering and the dust was rising as the animal thrashed. Garth hoped the cotton field would catch fire. Smoke. That would hide them, and give them time, and if it alerted Republic forces, they would probably arrive here too late. But the field wasn't burning. Probably too much dew in the night.

"We got bigger issues," said Hopi Jack. "That's a mine, that means that someone doesn't want us to cross. There's probably guns covering that field as well. That's what I would do, back in Vietnam. What good are mines without guns coverin' 'em?"

Off to the right, about a hundred yards, there was a whooping and cheering as the Oaxacans drove their old ranch truck straight down a dirt road towards the river, between the cotton fields, apparently unaware of the danger of the mines. Garth keyed his walkie talkie.

"Hold it up! Hold it up!" he shouted as he keyed the device.

No answer.

There was a rattle of shots. In the distant riparian trees, someone began firing a machine gun. A banging sound as the shots hit the metal of the truck's body. The truck swerved sharply into the cotton, flipped, and rolled over on its side in a cloud of dust.

"Oh! Oh my God I hope they are OK!" said Priyanka.

"What are we gonna do?" said a voice. Barry Taylor.

"The Crow at the Rosebud," said Terry Taylor.

"The Crow at the Rosebud?" repeated Terp, his horse skittering behind them from the sounds of the distant machine gun, stark in the distance.

"Countercharge fast, from the flank," said Terry.

A machine gun...firing alone, individual shots clearly audible in the clear dawn air, began shooting non-stop, and they turned to watch. Someone didn't know how to shoot a machine gun, and it wasn't theirs anyway.

The Oaxacan's Honda Accord was racing along the track through the cotton field where the old ranch truck had gone, slightly to the left, so that it would slightly pass the overturned truck without striking it. The sun was higher now, and the rising sun shone through the windows of the car from behind.

"They are insane," said Dove, behind them.

"There's nobody in the car," said Hopi Jack. "Someone has weighed the gas pedal and tied the steering wheel and turned it loose."

The plan came together in Garth's mind suddenly. What Terry had said. He spoke into his walkie talkie.

"Base of fire, on the left, Tiger and Tres, get with the girls, on the left, suppress that machine gun, when you find it. Just keep their heads down. Horses, follow the cars on the right. That's where the mines aren't. Go fast or they'll catch us in the open."

Traveling fast now, the Honda Accord smashed into the riparian trees on the far side of the cotton field and was enveloped in the dense green willows.

"No mines over yonder," said Bear, swiveling his horse. "They've set them all off by drivin' over 'em."

"The Crows at the Rosebud! Imagine!" said Terry Taylor to himself.

Garth noticed that Terry was dressed as always in the blue uniform of the cavalry. The octogenarian pulled his .45-70 military issue carbine from its carrying boot and flipped open the trap door to load it.

Bat Jefferson pulled around them to the right and began to gallop inside the orchard. Always in front. Always impatient.

"Oh, the hell with him going first," said one of the lancers, who incongruously had brought his lance and was now carrying it straight up, as he allowed his horse to follow Bat. Three other lancers joined in, including Randall.

As he rode past, without his lance, Randall smiled at Garth in the half-light, and commented, "Hell I can run that in three minutes. We're here, dude. Chill!"

Garth noticed that Randall was carrying Poppy Roswell's blunderbuss across his back.

"I wish we could put a drone up," said Belinda, who had ridden up behind them. "Get a look around."

"Where is Glenda, anyway?" said Priyanka, on a horse behind Belinda. "If we don't know what is going on, we shouldn't rush."

There was a snapping sound as a shot came from the river trees to the left.

"Oh man, that sounds like we just kicked the alligator," said Bear. "That's from a new friend. We gotta get around behind them."

Without a pause the riders began to gallop their horses onto the trail of flattened cotton created by the cars, crowding in their haste. Garth pulled back. Not enough dispersion. He looked back and saw Ramon pulling his horse in front of Dove and the others, causing them to pause. Oh, good man.

From the left came a swelling of shooting, the base of fire with the fifty-caliber machine gun going into action. That would be Tiger Tanaka and his straight-shooting Garand, and the girls and the Humvee's machine gun, and anyone else they could collect. Keep that Republic machine gun down.

Already in the open, Garth turned Dogfood and spurred him into a gallop, chasing after the first cluster of riders who were now at full tilt racing across the open ground. Suddenly there was a ripping sound as a new, larger gun opened up somewhere beyond the base of fire, and the first group of riders went down like bowling pins. One of the lancers tumbled out of the saddle, lance spinning, the point gleaming as it turned. Then another rider fell into the cotton, and one of the horses screamed and went down kicking. There was a boom and an explosion. Artillery? Garth thought of turning Dogfood around and realized instantly that his greatest safety lay in getting to the trees beyond. So loud now. So much shooting. So much was happening so quickly over-whelming noise and chaos. Then it seemed that time slowed down. He put the spurs to Dogfood to make him go faster, to get to the trees, to safety. Faster.

Then an explosion, smashing him, smashing his head, blinding him, lifting him up, waves of brilliance and burning flame and darkness and the sky below him and the ground above, and the smashing, crunching, into the flesh-piercing spines of the dead brown cotton, now the cotton stalks rising from all around him, deafness, tinnitus, glasses still on his head, thank God for his glasses strap, pain all over, still mov-ing, Dogfood down flat, looking at him through the cotton stalks like an intelligent sentient human, eyes blinking and wide. Bullets snapping and cracking overhead, Oh God don't stand up, crawl. Dizziness, nausea. I've been slammed hard, thought Garth. Again he felt his arms and legs for injuries. Just pain, just bruising. It seemed to be snowing, thought

Garth. Warm snow. No. It was cotton which had been shot or blown off the plants.

So loud, shots and screaming and his tinnitus roaring and Dogfood raised his head and tried to stand, and a machine gun stitched him with little black dots and the bullets made snapping noises as they hit the saddle and dust came off Dogfood's side in a puff and the horse fell back down, and lowered his head flat in the cotton, looked at Garth, two feet away, and said, clearly, with a groan, "They've killed me," and a torrent of blood came out of Dogfood's mouth, and the horse's eyes glassed over in death. Garth turned his head to the side and screamed.

It was a big machine gun, fired from somewhere on the left. Renalyn died instantly as she stood in the gunner's hatch of the Humvee. She grunted as the five bullets hit her and smashed through her body armor, and she fell from the Humvee roof into the dirt alongside the vehicle. Akemi in the backseat wailed.

Raley turned, stunned, as her horse took a bullet in the flank. It screamed, jerked the reins out of Raley's hands, and went galloping off without a rider to join the other horses downhill.

Francesca's horse pulled free moments later and raced after it, saddle empty.

Raley looked behind her and saw Tiger Tanaka and Tres Ericson in good sitting positions, with their horse tied solidly to trees. Tiger was peering through the sights of his M-1 Garand, but apparently, he hadn't fired yet. As she watched,

Tres looked through the scope of his long rifle and fired a shot. There was the blast of another shot from the other side of the Humvee. That was Francesca, working the bolt of her rifle.

"It's some sort of armored vehicle, like a tank, and it's got a machine gun and a bigger gun, like a cannon," said Francesca. "I just drilled the officer. He was standing up like Renalyn. Tres, aim for anyone in command."

"I already did that," said Tres. "Frackin' greenies."

Raley felt terror. A tank. Their plan was completely unraveling.

"It's gonna cross our front between us and the river and rip into our people," said Francesca. "Tres, aim for that vehicle's vision ports! You've got a magnum!"

There was the ear-splitting sound of the big fifty caliber machine gun firing. Akemi was in the hatch, and she was shooting down at the armored vehicle. There was a snapping and pranging of bullets hitting all around them. Akemi ducked back down to the safety of the interior of the Humvee.

Behind them, Tiger Tanaka began shooting, slowly. Methodically. There was a ping as his clip ejected from the M-1 Garand rifle, and Raley saw him quickly reload.

Francesca hadn't budged. She was still peering through the scope of her rifle. She fired a shot and worked the bolt.

"There went the replacement commander," muttered Francesca, then she looked up and said to Raley, "The fifty isn't even getting through the skin of that thing. We need a bigger gun."

"There's your bigger gun," said Mrs. Ericson.

Raley looked and saw that Mrs. Ericson was looking through Renalyn's binoculars and pointing across the river, where a square little tank on wheels was sitting in the shade of a windbreak of eucalyptus trees. The little tank had a great big cannon which stuck far out in front. The sun was behind it. Hard to hit from here, thought Raley. If that thing opens up on us, we're screwed. But it's on the United States side.

Fear. Oh, what to do. Do something.

"Why isn't it shooting?" asked Raley.

"That's the United States. This is the Republic," said Mrs. Ericson.

"They're gonna let us die?" said Raley.

She ducked involuntarily as a stream of machine gun shots went over them from the left.

"With nobody in charge down there, they're not so accurate," said Francesca.

"Unless the Republic shoots at them, the United States forces probably aren't going to shoot back," said Mrs. Ericson.

"So what the Republic needs to see is bait," said Raley. "And we're it."

Garth saw his Marlin rifle where it had fallen a few feet away, and he low crawled through the dusty field, crushing the dry cotton stalks, cotton snowing down upon him. Look back at Dogfood. Oh God. Laying there still as a rock, eyes opaque. Oh God. Then Garth reached a hand to the Marlin, staying down, time going so slowly, and he thought, I wish I had brought an M-203 grenade launcher instead. Crawl, crawl to the others. There was Randall, dead with a hole the size of grapefruit in his chest. A wave of nausea. Randall looked startled. Chill, dude. There was that blunderbuss. Incoherent thoughts. Gotta give it back to Poppy. Never leave a gun, Garth thought, and he slung it over his back, stunned. Crawl around. Bullets snapping overhead, then thumping loudly into the guts of the dead horse beside Randall. Randall surely did love that horse, thought Garth.

Crawl. Another blast, somewhere. The cotton snow. There was Bear, laying on his back, with his Henry, eyes wild, and Terry, Terp, and Barry on the other side of him, laying behind a row of dead horses.

"Crow at the Rosebud. More like the Little Bighorn," muttered Bear. "Hope the girls are OK."

There was a blast of firing to the left, beyond the base of fire, and Barry said "That's the nine millimeters in the drones. Glenda's got 'em up."

"Well God bless Glenda," said Garth. Astonished he could talk. His jaws hurt terribly when he moved them. Everything hurt.

The firing was slackening over them now as the noise of incessant firing increased to their left. Then the "bang bang bang" of a fifty caliber machine gun. "That's the Humvee!" said Terp. "God I hope Raley's OK. Oh God, Oh God."

"Finally showed up. Like Crook at the Rosebud." said Terry Taylor. "History doesn't repeat, but it DOES rhyme!"

There was a ripping sound like a giant machine gun, even louder than the fifty. "That's a chain gun," said Garth. "And it's not ours. We're in trouble now."

There was shouting from up the trail, from the other band of horses, and looking back down the trail of crushed cotton, Garth saw smoke...someone had gotten something burning, at any rate, and out of the smoke galloped his wife, Dove, with Ramon, Hopi, Priyanka, and Belinda galloping close behind. So slow, so slow, their horses flat out. Somehow time was standing still. Cotton blowing in the wind. Like snow.

"We gotta give those riders a base of fire," said Bear. "Gotta cover them."

Bear rose to a kneeling position. They all pulled themselves up alongside him.

"Shoot at anything you can see as a target," said Garth.

A shot from the nearby trees, and Terry swiveled and fired his .45-70 trapdoor single shot towards the source, then methodically looked down to reload. Garth turned and blasted two shots towards the willows as well, and looked back at the riders, only to see Belinda career from the saddle, shot, as the rest came on and passed them and disappeared into the trees.

Dove reined her horse to a sliding, cutting-horse stop as bullets began to snap around them. "Run to the trees now! There is a tank...an enemy tank over there. Go!"

Looking up at Dove, his wife, stern faced, mounted on her nervous prancing horse, so high up. Garth had a quick image of her as Boudica, a horse-borne goddess of war, so formidable and so calm and yet so small, and she reached down without another word and pulled him into the saddle behind her. He seemed to leap up there and the horse's rump came up and slapped into his backside as she spurred the horse into a gallop, the double barreled shotgun on its sling slapping into his face as she rode. Wind. The day was cool, he realized.

Straight into the dense green of the willows, the branches clawing at him, and they slowed and twisted down an animal path, deeply, deeply, slower and slower, the noise of battle farther and farther away. Garth began to become alarmed, they had no idea where they were in relation to anyone, then suddenly into a small clearing on the edge of the trees and Garth saw, horrified, that they had come up behind a machine gun crew in the act of firing. All wearing green. All wearing body armor. Republic?

One of them...a shaved-head man in a green ball cap... saw them behind, and shouted, and another raised his military rifle and Garth leaned around Dove and shot him quickly...hardly aiming...with the Marlin, piercing the body armor through the chest, and as the man sprawled down backwards, the horse bucking now, Dove struggling to control, Garth fell off carefully, tripped, sprawled, the blunderbuss slung diagonally behind smashing into his back, getting away from the horse, and the two others were trying to turn the entire machine gun, tripod and all, and Garth pulled himself to kneeling in the tangle of willows and shot both with the Marlin, as fast as he could work the lever. Tinnitus screaming.

Two others in green ran away, out into the open cotton field where bullets quickly cut them down. Garth looked at the machine gun. It was undamaged. A swarm of bullets snapped through the trees overhead and there was the loudness...the fifty, and that chain gun, and smaller guns, and Garth was terrified that Francesca and Akemi would be caught, would be killed, would be wounded. Should he have killed these people? Had he just killed friendlies?

There was a terrific boom, and Garth jerked around, Marlin raised, and saw Dove on her shivering, bucking horse, holding her double barreled shotgun, and below her was a woman, green janitor uniform and body armor, bloodied and dead, and Garth thought, body armor doesn't protect your face, and then he focused on the trail, the cramped, low-grown trail to the left. The woman had come from the trail to the left, where the fighting was happening. He had possession of the enemy's machine gun, laying there surrounded by dead fighters whom he had just killed, and the enemy didn't know that. The enemy were at the other end of that trail.

Noise. So distracted. Aching all over. Garth forced himself to stand close to Dove, focus, and speak clearly and loudly.

"I'm gonna take the machine gun up that tunnel," Garth pointed at the overgrown trail. "Please go get the others. I don't think you can take a horse there. Get Bear, and Terry, and Terp, and Barry, please. Tell them to bring up the tripod and the ammo cans, fast."

Shooting, out there. The girls were at risk.

Dove looked down at him calmly. Her horse was calming down. "I understand. Hurry. Come quick. Bring packs."

"And the tripod," Garth added.

Dove turned her horse. "And the tripod!" she shouted. "I love you, husband!" and she galloped back down the path whence they had come.

Alone. Stunned. Grab the machine gun. Marlin slung over the front, machine gun over the shoulder. Crawl and kneel and duck into the overgrown maze. Bullets and shooting and noise, somewhere else. Hands bruising on the path, rocks, and a slight cut on a broken bottle on the trail. Faster. Faster.

"Amigo!" a shout behind him, in the leaf-wrapped trail, startled Garth, and he turned on his knees, let the machine gun drop, grabbed for his rifle slung in front. He recognized Ramon, pushing two cans of ammunition in front of him. Relief.

"Go fast," said Ramon. "I met Dove on the trail. There's a bunch of us lost in the trees behind."

Garth turned, pulled the machine gun, and began pushing his way through the branches in the emerald foliage, bent low. Now he could see daylight. Now he could see the edge of the cotton field, where it met the trees. The trail opened. Garth stood up straight, hefted the machine gun. An old M-60, Garth realized. An M-60 machine gun. Where the hell had that come from?

"I'm gonna get hats for everybody," said Ramon, coming up behind him.

"Hats?" asked Garth. He worked the action of the machine gun. A live cartridge ejected. The gun was ready to go.

"Three Amigos Hats," said Ramon. "What the hell, we live through this, we all get hats. Do we have a plan?"

"No plan," said Garth.

"A person cannot overthink these things," said Ramon, calmly.

A feeling of immense relief, of a weight removed.

"Just stay away from the cans," said Ramon.

Ahead, in the daylight, there was the roar of the fifty-caliber machine gun, and that chain gun, whatever it was. Ahead they could see green-clothed figures at the edge of the trees, static, obvious, untrained. They were shooting at a twinkling machine gun: the girls, about 100 yards away. As Garth watched the orchard, where he had come from before, he saw one of the Koreans with his telltale SKS carbine move from tree to tree. Thank God the Republic fighters weren't skilled shooters.

Garth silently pointed the targets out to Ramon, and motioned with his hands: get around the trees for a clear shot from the side. If they fired from here, they WOULD catch the targets mostly from behind, but they wouldn't get them all, and the survivors could get into the trees and create a toe-to-toe slugfest. Better to move a bit out into the open along the cotton field, into the bright sunlight. The Republic troops seemed to be preoccupied with the base of fire: Renalyn, the Humvee, the girls and the machine gun, and Tiger. Tiger had to be killing many. Garth felt a surge of hope as he realized that whatever that chain gun was shooting at, it couldn't be the girls, because the girls must be still alive. Oh God let that be true.

Ramon nodded his agreement. Behind them crowded others: Bear, Terp, Barry, and Terry, still clutching his .45-70 trapdoor. They began to move out to the edge of the trees, to a large thick downed willow trunk laying in the cotton field, big around as a barrel, where they could see all the green clad targets. To shoot from here, they would be exposed. But they could also see, both here and across the river behind them. They had to take the pressure off that Humvee.

"Hey look, the promised land!" said Barry, pointing away from the gun fight, down the willows to the bluffs on the opposite bank of the river. High ground.

"Focus," said Terry to his adult son, pointing back down the face of the trees to the Republic forces, who at that moment seemed to notice them. Faces turning. Garth rested the M-60 machine gun over a downed willow tree trunk, aimed at the green-clad figures, and began to fire. Short, steady bursts. Walking them into the clustered groups of people. The tree trunk had been down for some years, and the recoiling machine gun was polishing off the bark, which tumbled down around their feet with the brass.

Garth was aware that Ramon was expertly feeding the ammunition belt into the M-60. The others were firing. And the targets were wilting, going down, or running. Keep it up, he thought. Keep firing. Small, aimed bursts. Like back in the Marines, almost fifty years ago. So loud. Deafening. He was aware that the others were shooting as well. Bear with his Henry. Terry with his .45-70 trapdoor. Terp, shouting with enthusiasm. And the target...the target was gone, or down. Garth stopped firing.

Tinnitus roaring. Otherwise Garth couldn't hear anything. Someone...a girl...was waving from the orchard on the other side of the cotton field, up the hill. Not even the fifty or the chain gun was shooting. A few shots far off, but that was it. He could see the Humvee vaguely through the trees.

Terp stepped out into the field a few paces and waved across the cotton field with both arms. Holding his trapdoor carbine. Sunlight on his blue cavalry uniform. White cotton fluff and the brown stalks up to his knees. Garth could see Raley stand up across the cotton field and up the hill in the trees and wave back energetically, pointing down at the river. So good. So beautiful. She seemed happy, joyful.

Garth forced himself to look at the smoking M-60 machine gun, radiating heat and smelling of burning lubricant and gun powder. He looked at Ramon. Ramon grinned back. Garth realized that he now had two guns slung across his back: his Marlin .45-70 and the blunderbuss.

Blunderbuss. Cursed demon weapon, thought Garth, laughing to himself. Such relief.

"We've WON," shouted Terp, still standing in the field.

"The goal isn't to win, the goal is to retreat across that river," said Terry, "The Nez Perce and the retreat through Idaho. And we're not done yet."

Garth let the M-60 rest balanced on the willow log, and looked across the cotton field, and down towards the Republic forces he had decimated. There was movement there, but nobody seemed to want to fight. It was time to move across that river, move across that river to safety, as fast as possible.

Across the cotton field, to the right of the orchard, about 300 yards away, there was a loud grinding engine noise, like a bulldozer, startling Garth, and suddenly he saw a tank...a military tank...no, a Bradley fighting vehicle, Garth recognized, an armored personnel carrier, emerging along the orchard to face them. The Humvee had fled, thank God. There was a large flag flying, a California state flag, now changed. Smaller bear, big red star moved to the high center of the flag. The armored vehicle moved slowly along the edge of the far orchard, towards where the girls and the Humvee had been.

Then Garth saw two men, two Asian men, the Koreans, running at the Bradley from the far side, through the orchard, bottles with flaming rags in their hands. Where had they gotten the gasoline? Garth wondered for an instant, then realized they had drained it from the Honda before launching it across the field. Time seemed to be slowing down.

Something kicked Garth hard in the rump, with a crack, and his right leg gave way, and he stumbled, knocked forwards, spinning, seeing the young green clad girl with bright dyed purple-pink hair and black-framed glasses crouched in the foliage tunnel behind them, her look of fear and hatred in her face as she aimed for another shot with her military rifle. She fired, and there was a shout, Terp....Terp was down, and then someone else, and Garth groped for his Marlin but the Marlin's stock came away, broken by that first shot, and there was the blunderbuss in his hand behind his back, and he thought, as he spun the flintlock around, I should have gone for the pistol, the pistol, and then Barry stepped forward, close on his right, and there was a shot from the girl in green, so inexperienced that she closed her eyes as she fired, and Barry went down with a grunt, knocking down Ramon beneath him, and the blunderbuss came up, as though on its own, and Garth cocked the hammer, full cock, get it to full cock, and the gun went off in a giant cloud of white black powder smoke, and the recoil punching Garth in the shoulder, and then explosions all around, deafening, and he fell down as flat as he could make himself. Flat. Noise. Explosions.

When Garth looked again, the girl was laying still in the willow bower, in a mass of rags, white flesh, broken black-framed glasses, dyed purple-pink hair, and blood. The M-60, perched on the log, blew apart as a bullet from somewhere else hit it. So loud. Barry, wounded, was creeping towards Terp, reaching to pull him from the cotton field, where Terp was laying flat, grimacing, but still alive and still exposed. There was the sudden new roar of firing all around them.

The trees above them shattered and shredded and the cotton in the field blew apart, and the torn leaves fell down in the cacophony and the cotton floated in the air. The Bradley fighting vehicle must be shooting at them with its automatic cannon. Thank God not very good shots, thank God for this willow trunk, Garth thought, and in the distance behind him, across, on the United States side of the river, on the opposite side of the field from the Bradley, he saw a strange little tank, a wheeled tank, with a little square body and a small turret and a great big cannon sticking out in front. It drove along the ridgeline, across the river, and stopped like a prehistoric cricket. We are dead now, thought Garth. Trapped. Hoka hey. He wondered how Dove was doing, if she was still alive, and he wondered if Francesca and Akemi and his mother could somehow survive. I still have this projectile point here in my pocket, he thought. I wish I had done a point ceremony.

Terp was moaning and trying to crawl back to shelter be-hind the willow log. Slim protection. Terry and Barry were reaching out to him. Garth peeked around the willow log.

The Bradley was moving at about 3 miles an hour towards them, partially in flames but still rolling resolutely along the face of the orchard. No sign of the Koreans, but at least they had delayed the monster and disrupted its aim. The gun was pointing right at them. The muzzle sparkled and there was a loud explosive bang in front of the log.

Garth looked around. As he watched, an explosive cannon shell from the Bradley's main gun hit Terry and Barry together, through the body, and dismembered them, blew them apart, as they were reaching for Terp. Blood and parts and bits of cotton and vegetation peppered them all.

Terp wailed as cannon shells from the Bradley fighting vehicle exploded all around him. Time was so slow. Garth knew that the next shots from the Bradley would blast that willow log to hell, and him with it, and he wondered if it would hurt, and then he saw Bear, crawling along the ground, reach out to Terp and half the extended hand suddenly vanish, several fingers and all, and the horror of it all seemed to enfold Garth in a smothering paralysis, and then, looking behind, down across the river, at the border, he saw a Humvee, what seemed to be their own Humvee, pull across on the near side of the river.

The Humvee had moved. It was no longer on the hill. It had driven around the entire battlefield. Now it was down by the river, and it was driving across the cotton field like a carnival shooting gallery target, dumb as a mudhen. Right out in the open. The Bradley was sure to see it, and it was only a few feet from the border.

He saw a blonde-haired girl standing in the Humvee's

turret aim the fifty-caliber machine gun, and fire at the Bradley. Wap wap wap wap! The tracers flashed the length of the cotton field, pranged off the Bradley fighting vehicle impotently, and bounced off into the sky and the trees. Behind her, only fifty yards behind the Humvee, across the river on the far bank, the United States side, the small square wheeled tank with its giant cannon sat there stolidly, watching, the gun pointed down and towards the Bradley. A small pennant fluttered from its deck.

The Bradley fighting vehicle ceased firing at Garth.

Oh, my God, thought Garth, Francesca's gotten herself killed. the Bradley will kill them all and then drive over here and crush us.

A moment of quiet. The Humvee ceased firing and raced forward to hide in the riverside trees. Nearby, Bear was laying with Terry's cavalry bandana, completely blood soaked, wrapped around what remained of his injured hand. Ramon was pulling a wailing Terp over the parts of his father and grandfather to the ephemeral shelter of the willow log.

Garth peeked again around the side of the willow log. The Bradley seemed puzzled. The turret moved towards the little tank on the bluffs. It fired a few tentative shots in that direction. The shots hit the slope below the tank. Small explosions.

From the small tank came an loudspeakered voice: "THIS IS THE UNITED STATES ALLIED TASK FORCE! REPUBLIC OF CALIFORNIA FORCES ARE COMMANDED TO CEASE FIRE AND WITHDRAW IMMEDIATELY."

The Bradley seemed confused. It sat for a time. Then it

fired another string of automatic cannon shots at the small tank on the ridgeline. They all hit far from the tank.

Holding his injured bloody hand, Bear rolled over on his back and looked through the cotton at the Bradley. It was still smoldering from the firebombs. "It don't know what to do," he said.

Silence. Then there was a giant boom from the small tank, and the Bradley exploded. Flames erupted from the engine compartment, and then a second internal blast blew the turret about fifteen feet in the air. Flames, smoke, pops and cracks as ammunition burned in the fire.

Alongside Garth, Terp was sobbing uncontrollably, with his eyes screwed shut. Blood and bits and chopped plants all over everything. Terp looked, and he spoke quietly, "I'm sorry. I'm sorry. I'm sorry."

Garth followed Terp's gaze. There was Barry's wide-eyed head and upper torso staring back sightlessly a few feet away. And beyond that, Terry's cavalry boot-clad legs, disconnected from the rest of him. The boots were shined.

Roaring tinnitus. In the silence, Garth dimly heard the call of a red wing blackbird, guarding his territory, in the willow trees.

Bear was sitting up now as well, looking at the little tank on the ridge with Terry's binoculars, with one hand. His bloody wrapped left hand was now squeezed under his right armpit.

"Well, this takes all," he muttered.

"I recognize the vehicle," said Ramon. "I don't believe it either."

"Ya know that tank what saved us?" said Bear. "It's flyin' the Mexican flag."

Garth leaned back against the willow log. God let my family be alive, he thought. And bless this willow log, which kept me alive. He allowed his head to fall back, and he looked at the sky. Bright blue sky. Some smoke from the burning Bradley. It was going to be another long day.

Oakhurst, in the new state of East California. United States.

"So you left her?" asked the intelligence officer. "You left Margarita Sanchez there?"

Wallace wrestled his mind back to the discussion. Of course this florid faced gentleman might be trying to entrap him, attempting to ensnare him in the confusing politics of the moment. The shower and the food had left Wallace incapable of much emotion. The clean clothes. A fresh sleeping bag. All part of a trap? The bright Sierra Nevada sunlight slashed across the room, here in this manufactured cubicle, illuminated the man's pink, well-fleshed face, his camouflaged battle dress. 'Stendhal' and 'US Army' on his shirt. A Captain. Ah the hell with it. Answer the question.

"I know you've been interviewed before," continued the intelligence officer. "We're just trying to fill in the details."

"Margarita Sanchez seemed to want to live there, so we

left her. Actually Tiny...ah, that's Hugh, Hugh Tupuola, her boyfriend, he didn't want her to come along.

"He didn't want her to come along?" asked the intelligence officer.

"Tiny threw her off the bus. Quite the scene. She was begging," said Wallace.

"But all the other strike team members wanted to go?" said the intelligence officer.

"We only took a few," said Wallace. "The ones who knew what was going on. The wounded guy. Katerina Sanchez shot him so she felt that she owed him."

"And Mayor...ex Mayor....Johnson?" asked Captain Stendhal, his full face crinkling.

"He didn't want to go," said Wallace. "We took him anyway. Later he was helpful getting across the border. How's he doing?"

"Faced with genocide as he is, he's singing like a bird. He's charming everyone he meets. He wants money," replied the intelligence officer, smiling. "Believe it or not, he wants his pension restored, and he wants a job. He claims he can build a new city. He'll get a job all right: as compost, after he's processed. There are enough people here from your rodeo grounds to convict him, and then there's a rope with his name on it."

"Processed, you say?" asked Wallace, subdued.

"Yep, processed. That's the new term. And your friend Happy is a sure bet. But we're still negotiating with the Republic, so we might make some kind of deal.

"Some kind of deal?"

"Yes...you know, we might trade him from some of their prisoners whom we want, if they haven't been processed yet. The east coast is coming apart as well. We're not sure yet what's going to happen. The vote is next week. Meanwhile the capitol is still in Washington DC, and Congress and the new administration are very divided about what to do. Some factions are saying that the processing you describe isn't really happening. They're saying that the mass killing is fake news."

"I saw the processing. The mass killing. Hell, I smelled it," said Wallace.

"Well. Others disagree. They say you saw Candida victims. In a few weeks the capitol may be in St. Louis. Or Omaha. then there'll be a different point of view, perhaps," said Captain Stendhal. "Meanwhile it's very possible that Happy Johnson will go build his city in the Republic of California after all, as a goodwill gesture. A trade."

"But he MURDERED people!" said Wallace.

"Officially, we're saying we aren't sure. Officially, the United States isn't sure if the processing is happening or not. It may be caused simply by Candida."

"You may not be sure, but I am!" replied Wallace.

"Oh, personally, I'm sure. I feel for you. I hear this every day. But you might want to keep your opinions to yourself, for the time being. You see, the Republic is also asking for extradition of anyone who leaves them. Says it's about stolen intellectual property," said Captain Stendhal. "They've been asking lots lately. I'm imagining they'll be asking for you soon, probably by name."

"Why isn't the United States doing more?" asked Wallace. "You aren't protecting me. You aren't protecting anyone."

"I'm not sure the United States CAN protect anyone," said Captain Stendhal. "We're pretty preoccupied. Then there's Casawal, how do you say that name?"

"Causwell. Causwell Dubbers," replied Wallace. "How's he doin'?"

"He's found religion. Can't help us enough. Filled with guilt. It seems he wants revenge," said the intelligence officer.

"Did you take the noose off?" said Wallace quietly. "The noose seemed to motivate him."

"Oh, yes, it's off. Who was it who said that the prospect of being hung clarifies the mind wonderfully?"

"Some British guy, long ago," replied Wallace. "Anyway Causwell....can't really be so angry at Causwell. Happy is a different story."

"What about Jesus Garcia?" said the intelligence officer.

"He saved us all," said Wallace. "I bet we are the first group of refugees with its own tank."

Captain Stendhal laughed.

"You got that right. The tank seemed to be important to Mr. Garcia. Says its his heritage."

"Most people in Salinas don't remember. But heritage it is," said Wallace. "Now can you please answer some of my questions?"

"Fire away," said the man. "If I shouldn't answer, I won't."

"We went out over Gloria Road...a dirt road, then Panoche Road, and both roads were passable. They told us in Salinas that all roads were down. But we just drove right out. If we could get out, why can't you get in? Why didn't you come save us?"

"You know the President is dead, right?" said the intelligence officer, seriously.

"Yep, they told us," replied Wallace. "Along with a big chunk of the government."

"You also know that after they repealed the electoral college last year, the interior states lost most of their national political power," said the intelligence officer.

"Yes."

"And the United States overspent, overspent by a lot, debt up to our frackin' eyeballs, in the past few decades to bail out the financial system, to rescue ourselves from 2008 and from COVID a few years back. So, no money," added Captain Stendhal. "We sure lived large before all the troubles, didn't we?"

"So we're broke," said Wallace.

"Hell of a party, while it lasted," said Captain Stendhal. "Then there was Candida, which by the way is weaponized. We don't know who did that but it's definitely a supernatural bug with some extra manufactured tricks."

"We don't know who did that?"

"No, but whoever did that kicked our asses," replied the intelligence officer. "Plus the internet and cyber-attacks and the fake news, and more. Personally, I think it was a collection of nations. China, Russia, Iran, and perhaps a few more. They just got sick of seeing our face."

"So we're divided, sick, and broke," said Wallace. "And we hate each other."

"Plus we've had several nucs in California and that attempted coup d'état in Washington DC," added Captain Stendhal. "After all that, and after the coastal cities spent years politically attacking the interior, why would anyone want to rescue the coasts? It's like Margarita Sanchez, the coasts seem to want to live in their own messes, so why not let them?"

"Most people on the coasts don't want what's happening," snapped Wallace. "They didn't vote for this. It's not really constitutional."

"Perhaps, but you didn't really do anything to stop it. The people who didn't like it just got up and left," said the intelligence officer. "They left a while back."

"You're going to have to have some coastal access, aren't you?" asked Wallace, calming now. No sense antagonizing this man.

"We'll negotiate some access, probably at San Diego and Humboldt, but right now we just CAN'T do anything more. The Republic of California is going to collapse on its own, anyway."

"Speaking of which, who were those people at the border? At Firebaugh?" asked Wallace. "They looked Asian. Black uniforms. Not strike team. After they talked to Happy, who had my shotgun up his ass, they let us right through."

"Ah. Good observation. Chinese Special Forces. They're advising the Republic," said Captain Stendhal.

"And you are tolerating that? The Chinese are already invading Taiwan. When you add up the evidence, you'll probably find they created Candida," said Wallace. "What about the Monroe Doctrine?"

"Don't forget, they also tanked our international Treasury market. Ruined our economy. I mean, it'll take decades to recover, if ever," replied Captain Stendhal. "All of that was perfectly legal. Right now China is the number one economy in the world. And they're polluting the snot out of it."

"So why don't we admit they're the enemy?" demanded Wallace. "Them. Russia. Whatever."

Captain Stendhal sighed. He looked out the window. He looked at Wallace.

"Perhaps someday. Right now, are you ready for a war? A big nuclear war?" he replied. "Most of the genuine warriors come from the interior states, and we've got our hands full. I know. I'm from Texas, and right now...it's hard. I know I'm not ready to bleed for the coasts. After everything is divided up, they can bleed for themselves, if they wish."

"Seems to me that someone just knocked the United States out of the ring, in terms of the global economy, and in terms of history. I mean, whoever did this to us has lost maybe thirty people to pull this off."

"If that," replied Captain Stendhal. "Most of all, we did this to ourselves. We literally spent ourselves into poverty and we hated ourselves to death."

Wallace stood up and turned. He picked up his shotgun, now fully unloaded, which had been leaning against a chair. The brown finish was wearing off and the shiny metal gleamed in the sunlight.

"You're going to be asked to go back in," said Captain Stendhal.

"Kill one and run? Isn't that what they're saying?" replied

Wallace. "That's the plan, right? Kill just one strike team member, kill just one Republic representative."

"We don't have money for an army. We can't invade," replied Captain Stendhal. "So we have a new plan. Everyone kills one, then lies low for the rest of their lives or flees. Imagine if you're on a strike team or in the new Republic government, and every time you go out someone takes a crack at you. That's our plan. The gun owners should have been doing that already."

"But they didn't," said Wallace, "Because they didn't think things were bad enough yet. Until it was too late."

"That's why the Republic is processing as many gun owners as possible. Not even taking the chance that people might have hidden firearms or fight back. They're using computer-driven algorithms and removing anyone who might create a problem."

"And you won't admit that it's really happening?" said Wallace.

"Not publicly," said Captain Stendhal. "The United States...what's left of us...doesn't need a full-on fight, especially with the Chinese. But think about it: there's millions of unregistered guns out there. Hell, you could kill one, then run with water bottles filled with gasoline. Light up the enemy, wherever they are."

Wallace., looked down at his feet. He was quiet for a time.

"Seems like it just goes on and on," he said, finally.

"Well," said Captain Stendhal, "We didn't start the fire."

"Seems to me that if we all just took a step back, we might come to some sort of truce, at least," said Wallace.

"That's what their plan is. They want to just outlast us while they drive away and process anyone who might fight back. All the while confiscating wealth."

"We just keep to the plan? Kill one and run? For how long?" said Wallace.

"Relax, Mr. Ericson, that plan is just for normal people. You'd be on an extended mission. You're.... abnormal."

"I'd like a little time first," said Wallace. "Before I decide."

"Jesus Garcia says he'll go back," said the intelligence officer.

Wallace laughed. "Jesus Garcia is crazy," he said.

"My guess is that you'll get a choice. Go back for us, or go back when the Republic asks for you, extradited back to them with your family, if you have any, without the assistance of the United States."

Wallace looked at him stonily.

"By the way, here are your cell phones, and your electronics. Sorry we collected them, but we had to scan them for bugs."

Captain Stendhal hefted a large cardboard box, and passed it to Wallace, who slung his shotgun and accepted the large rattling container.

"We've actually got cell service here, so you can catch up with your family," said Captain Stendhal. "Let us know if we can help. The computer says that the postal service has a package from Denmark for you as well. I'll get that to you as soon as I can. It's being held in Elko right now."

"If you send me back into California, you're not helping," said Wallace.

"I wish I could do more. Alaska's going alone, and they

don't want us. Canada's closed. Europe is closed, in fact they are deporting anyone with a US passport."

"I have a wife in Denmark," said Wallace. "She's a Danish citizen. So are my kids."

"In that case, if she sponsors you, you can go there," said Captain Stendhal. "Hurry. We expect the extradition demand for you any day now."

"I'll call her today."

"Oh, and pass the word to anyone of Mexican heritage in your group," said Captain Stendhal. "The Mexican government doesn't want any more non-Mexican refugees without assets, but they will accept anyone with Mexican heritage. Or anyone married to a person of Mexican ancestry. And family, of course."

"What are you saying?" asked Wallace.

"It's hell in the Republic, and likely to get worse. If anyone who isn't Mexican in your traveling circus has the opportunity, tell them to marry a Mexican. That will give them a coveted Mexican green card and squelch extradition. Especially, DO NOT let them take YOU back to California. All you have waiting for you there is an injection of horse tranquilizer and a plastic bag over your head."

Wallace strained to listen as he heard the ring tones. One after another. Outside the tent children were playing, laughing, shouting in Spanish. A thump. Something impacted the canvas tent wall. Soccer. There was a click.

"Hello," came his wife's voice. She sounded reluctant, guarded.

"Hey Babe.... I'm out of California. I'm in the United States. I'm free," said Wallace into the phone.

He closed his eyes, trying not to cry, trying to visualize Aabenraa at night. So peaceful there. So green.

"Oh.... Wallace. What a surprise. I'm...I'm happy for you," said his wife's voice. Sullen.

"How are the kids? I've missed you all so much," said Wallace.

He felt like he was finally deflating after months of pressure.

"Oh, they are well enough. They are learning to be Danish," said his wife's voice, formally.

"What do we do now?" asked Wallace, filled with dread from the distant tone in her voice. "I've missed you. I've missed all of you. I'd like to come to you as soon as I can. There are flights, I understand. I'll get the money somehow. The thing is, I... I think I'm going to need you to sponsor me. No US passports to Europe without an invitation. Can you get me a sponsorship?"

"Wallace...Wallace," came his wife's voice.

There was the sound of a man's sleepy voice, in Danish. It didn't sound like Wallace's in-laws. He couldn't recognize the voice.

"Who is that?" he asked gently, adrenaline filling his body.

"Oh. Wallace, there is no use in lying, and no use in hiding. He is my new man," said Wallace's wife.

Wallace felt a crushing loss, but also something else. What was he feeling? A need to cry...a shocking blow...but also a strange desire to laugh. What was that something else?

"Wallace, I'm sorry. I'm so sorry. But I have a new man now. I don't want anything to do with the chaos of America. I'm just done," said his wife's voice. "You are all so hateful. All of you. It's an embarrassment to say I was ever there. I've moved on. Therefore, we are done, OK?"

"I want my family," said Wallace, his voice cracking. Laugh or cry? Strange divisions inside him. But also a genuine hunger. "I want my kids. God almighty, I've stayed alive and I've done so much just to be back with you all."

"Wallace, now, I'm sorry, but you know you brought this upon yourself. All your American obsession with guns and fighting. Always roaming the world, looking for a fight. Well now your fight has come to you. How does it feel? Now it's all gone, isn't it? All that American bullshit. I will never come back to the United States. That's gone."

Behind his wife's voice there was the sound of other voices. Waking up. An angry older voice. His father in law, Wallace guessed. Probably his father in law supported Wallace and was none too happy with the situation. He had always been good with Wallace.

"I've already filed for the divorce here in Denmark and it has been approved," his wife's voice continued.

"I'll do anything. I'll get to you somehow. I'll find the money," said Wallace, voice cracking, pleading.

"No," said his wife's voice. "They aren't letting American refugees come here anyway, and I won't sponsor you. Don't come here. I've moved on, Wallace. The world has moved on. Past you. Past America. The kids won't miss you. They already call Alva their far."

There was a click. Wallace called back. The phone went to his wife's message. It was in Danish.

Outside, a group of adults were singing. Wallace tried to compose himself. He listened. They were singing a theme song from an old TV show from the 1960's. Farm Acres. The place to be.

Cathey's Valley, East California, United States

Garth stepped off the air-conditioned bus into a cool evening with a slight breeze. Very like San Antonio Mission, which evoked a pang of homesickness. As he descended the stairs, he noticed with a shock his eldest son Wallace, whom he had not seen since weeks before the earthquake, in those timeless long-ago days when they lived in peace and bliss in Salinas. Wallace, dressed in jeans and a long sleeve western jacket and cowboy hat, was standing next to a heavy-set pale hatless man in a black windbreaker coat, who seemed to be in charge. And, to Garth's surprise, there was a young woman whom Garth had never seen before standing next to Wallace, arm in arm.

As Garth put his own 1850's hat on his head he looked at the group as they descended behind him from the bus. There came Terp and Raley down the metal stairs, Raley now looking radiant but genuinely pregnant, then Tres. Tres was glum. He must be hurting inside. Apparently, according to witnesses, Tres had been absolutely lethal at the San Joaquin crossing with his father's .300 H&H Magnum rifle. Good for him.

Garth pondered that. Anger had hardened within Tres, sharp as obsidian.

"OK everyone! Gather round for a second," said the man. "I'm Hector Gomez, and I'm your representative for the State of East California. Not the Republic. That's those people, over there towards the coast. I represent the government of the part of the state which did NOT engage in secession. More on that later. The new administration, with the new president...."

"It's not an election year. Did something happen?" asked Katrina Paxley.

"You don't know?" asked Hector Gomez, looking genuinely stunned. "Oh, Jeez."

While Hector Gomez was talking, Wallace began to walk inconspicuously around the group.

"Not a clue," said Hopi Jack. "We've been out of touch for a while. Since April."

"Well," Hector Gomez stumbled, "They shot him. Four months after President Price was killed, they shot President Parsons. Close range, with cut down shotguns. They killed his wife and son, too. The internet's full of joy about that."

"Joy about that?" said Hopi Jack.

"You know this kind of hatred has been building for decades. Now there's a large faction on the internet which is advocating nonstop impeachment, obstruction, and assassination. Just chaos," said Hector Gomez.

"We're familiar with non-stop hatred," said Garth.

"We arrested the perpetrators. Then the opposition tried to take over by impeaching the Vice President. That didn't work because the California representatives are currently not considered voting members."

"Holy smokes," said Bear. "Two presidential assassinations in four months. Are we in a Civil War deux here? One was enough for this possum."

"On the internet, the opposition is posting 'Assassinate, assassinate, keep on assassinating.' That's their mantra. New York, Washington D.C, and most of New England is holding a secession ballot next month. The current Supreme Court opinion is that secession is legal if it takes place through a public vote. California didn't do that," said Hector Gomez.

"We kinda guessed the California secession wasn't legal, since they were trying to kill us most of the time," said Gritz.

"The California secession was a coup. The elites took advantage of the earthquake to consolidate power, and most people were too scared to fight back."

At this point, Wallace had crept around to Garth, and the two hugged energetically. It felt wonderful, Garth thought. Then hugs with Dove, Francesca, and Akemi. Quiet introductions while Hector Gomez was speaking to the group. Trying not to be rude. Through the din of his tinnitus, and Hector Gomez' presentation, Garth learned that the woman with Wallace was apparently named Lacy. Or Macy. Or something like that. She seemed intelligent, very attractive, very young, and very connected to Wallace. Yet Wallace was married, happily married the last time they had met, almost nine months ago. Something had changed.

"Who's the president now?" Katrina Paxley asked Hector Gomez.

"Oh, Willard Montgomery, the former Speaker of the House and the former Vice President," answered Hector Gomez. "But politically he's in a storm. Unsuccessfully trying to keep the northeast in the United States, battling Candida, dealing with the Republic of California, the difficulties in Taiwan, Saudi Arabia, the Philippines, the Baltics. All the people who ever wanted to see America defeated or to beat up their neighbor are in motion now. The list is ENDLESS! That's why the Mexican Army is generously helping us with this. Our own military has its hands full."

"Is there gonna be a draft?" asked Ophelia.

Hector Gomez seemed about to answer, then he shook his head. "Look, we got a lot to cover. Let's get you settled in your FEMA tents, get some dinner, and handle those questions at the campfire later tonight."

Dove looked up at Garth, Wallace, and Katy and muttered, "You Americans are so crazy."

Wallace looked down and whispered loudly, "Can't argue with you there."

"I want to go back to the Philippines," muttered Dove.

"Why are we being kept separate?" Katrina Paxley asked Hector Gomez.

"I'm sure you've heard of our Candida pandemic," answered Hector Gomez. "The inoculation is rushed, and we know it, but Candida IS lethal, and you all aren't inoculated.

Candida is just beating the stuffing out of places like San Francisco, New York, and Denver. We also want to keep you here to decompress a bit. Yes, before you ask, you'll keep your guns and belongings. Just obey the law. Use common sense. And we'll get you inoculated in the next couple of days, and then YOU will decide where you go next."

"Ahhhh! Hold on! What's happening in the Philippines?" asked Dove, as the news impacted.

She pushed through the crowd and stood before Hector Gomez.

"Well, I'll tell you more tonight after dinner, OK? Short answer: Chinese troops have invaded Taiwan. They say it's a Reconquista. The Taiwanese and American forces trapped there are hitting back pretty hard, and the Chinese have taken the Spratlys, you know, those little islands."

"But what about the Philippines?" Dove repeated.

"Essentially the Chinese have strongarmed the Philippines by loaning them money the Philippines couldn't pay back, and in payment for that debt, they are claiming that they can foreclose on Davao, in southern Mindanao, as a colony. They did the same in Panama and Bangladesh. The UN agreed with all the purchases. Anyway in the Philippines, the Chinese own Davao now, their troops have taken control, and they're announcing a new 'East Asia Co-Prosperity Sphere', and moving up the island to quell what they say is armed terrorism."

Dove stepped back as if slapped. "But I have family in Mindanao."

"Well, if you do," said Hector Gomez, "They are about to be Chinese. Martial Law. Nobody gets in or out. And no internet."

After the comfort of the tents, and the showers, and a good dinner, and a campfire with Hector Gomez, late in the evening, Garth couldn't help himself. He couldn't sleep on that nice cot, even with his own sleeping bag, so he wandered out under the stars. At times like this at the mission, he thought, he would have walked out to check the horses, or visited the cemetery. Tonight, though, the stars were brilliant, and everything was different, and in the starlight he carefully walked down to the creek, with his 1858 revolver newly reloaded and comfortably in its holster.

I wonder if I will ever again feel safe without a gun, he wondered.

He looked up at the stars. Orion. Three quarters of a moon. More rains would come soon, and the world would cool and turn green again. Unless the weather had changed permanently as well.

"The same stars are shining down on the mission tonight," said Dove's voice behind him. He turned and saw her shadow in the darkness.

The whiteness of her eyes. Beautiful. She had her shotgun slung across her back.

"I wonder what it's like there now, with the damage," he said quietly. "I wonder if anyone is still at the mission. Even in the rubble."

"Who knows?" she answered. "I wonder about our home in Salinas, too. These stars shine there as well."

"Salinas. That seems like a million years ago, doesn't it?" he said quietly. "I still can't believe all this has happened. We were supposed to be at the mission for one weekend."

Silence. They watched the stars.

"From what Wallace is saying we were lucky to be stuck at the Mission," said Dove.

"Still want to go to the Philippines?" asked Garth.

"My husband, we haven't really spoken in months. I understand, it's been busy. But we have to face that things have changed in me. You know that don't you?" said Dove.

Garth shook his head affirmatively then realized that she probably couldn't see in the dark. He felt dread. Yet he also understood that Dove was being correct, and honest, and he was filled with sorrow.

"Yes," he said.

"My passion has died somehow. We can have respect, and we can have friendship," said Dove, quietly.

"Let's see what will happen." said Garth. "I feel...."

He stopped talking abruptly when they heard sounds of quiet laughter and approaching footsteps. Dove turned to the noise.

Out of the darkness loomed the shapes of a group of people.

"I tell ya, the Vienna sausages gave me gas. Stand back, I'm gonna blow," came Raley's voice.

Laughter.

"It comes with pregnancy, my dear," came the voice of Garth's mother. "Just stand over there. About ten yards away, that's it."

Laughter. Garth and Dove were silent.

The obvious silhouettes of Ramon and Glenda appeared.

"Anyone ever told you that Gringos are nuts?" said Ramon to Dove and Garth, laughing gently.

"Do we still get hats?" asked Garth.

"Oh, si, big sombreros," responded Ramon. "Better if you come to my home in Mexico to get them, though. This place is gonna be rough for a while."

"Ernst is already there," said Wallace, behind them. "He got a rancho for us. He says to tell you that it has an horno oven, like our place here. I suppose I'm about to become a Mexican citizen, if you'll have us."

Wallace was carrying his shotgun.

"Ernst will sponsor you," said Ramon. "You'll love Mexico. And you will already have friends there."

"It's tempting to go visit Sarah and her husband Osten in Norway for a while, if we can get an invitation," said Garth.

"Sarah?" said Ramon.

"My oldest daughter. She's in her thirties, living with her Norwegian husband in Oslo," replied Garth.

"Oh," said Ramon.

He looked carefully at Dove, a Filipina who seemed to be in her early 40's.

"Remarriage," said Garth.

"Oh, well, the Russians are in Estonia and I couldn't get an invitation to Denmark, so that's not likely," said Wallace. "I just want my children out of there."

Silence.

"My grandchildren. Maybe first we should just go set up a safe place in Mexico," said Garth.

"I'm sure the Russians won't go as far as Norway," said

Glenda. "That's a bridge too far. They would have to get through Finland first."

"I have to come back to California someday. Come back and see what survived. If anything. The Republic and I have unfinished business," said Garth.

"First get the family to safety," said Dove. "Rest and re-cover a bit."

"I'll be going back as soon as I can," said a voice. Tres. "The Republic can eat shit and die in its own vomit. I'm go-ing back to remind them of how they executed my father. They'll wish..."

"Better to not let people know," said Wallace. "Just keep your own council, and act with your mind, not your anger."

"And in the meantime, load up about three hundred rounds, at least. They don't sell that .300 H&H cartridge anywhere," said Bear. "Don't think you need to load copper-only to protect the condors, though."

Glenda's voice: "Tres, I gotta tell you, it's healthy to be angry, but making a good life is the best revenge. I'm gonna remember Pat by moving the business to Mexico or wher-ever is best, and then I'm going to have babies. Babies, and peace, and sunshine, and flowers."

"We'd love to have you and your corporation," said Ramon. "Speaking for Mexico."

"You got a baby daddy picked out?" said Bear. "A husband?"

"I still prefer women," said Glenda.

"Surprise!" joked Bear, and they laughed.

"For the glory and honor of Mexico, Ramon," answered Glenda. "Our baby would be an instant Mexican citizen."

"Would there be sombreros for that, too?" asked Garth.

More laughter. Garth heard his mother's voice nearby, talking with Francesca and Raley and Terp. He couldn't make out what they were saying.

"Babies," said Dove. "I can't think of a better way of remembering everyone we left behind."

"The people we lost," interrupted Terp. "My family."

Silence.

"They trusted governments," said Dove.

"Hopefully we'll learn," added Katy.

"So many," said Tres.

Silence.

"Speakin' of babies, Terp and Raley want to try Idaho, and I'm goin' up there with the entire herd. Takin' Ophelia," said Bear, brightly. "A great new start."

"I just want to start over. Let all these haters do their thing. I won't go back to California, and I don't want to be in the United States. Too much hate," said Katy, alongside Wallace. She was smiling.

Garth tried to accept that his son was divorced, as he had learned at tonight's campfire. And apparently this new woman was his ticket to freedom. Hard to believe.

The voice of Garth's mother: "We are still blessed."

A thought came suddenly to Garth, with a ripple of fear. "Security. Who's got security?"

"Tiger's taking care of that with the Mexican Army. They're very impressed with his antique M-1 Garand rifle," answered

Ramon. "It doesn't have a magazine, you know. He's with Hopi. They are hoping Pike will show up."

"Pike. I wonder what the heck happened to him," said Tres. "He was there one instant and gone the next."

Silence. Everyone studied the night sky.

"Will we ever get over this?" asked Dove quietly. "I wonder if I'll ever sleep again."

"Oh, yes, Dove. Look at the stars," said Garth's mother. "We'll still make something beautiful."

Garth looked up. Somewhere out there, he thought, these stars are shining on our home, our mission. The ruins, I mean. The unburied dead at the San Joaquin River. The ruins of our home in Salinas. In their memory, I have to go on. These same stars are shining down on Ernst, safe in Mexico and making us a new home. Shining down on Sarah, safe in Norway. My mother is right. We can do this. And tomorrow is another day.

Carson Valley, Nevada, United States

"Does this make us trailer trash?" Katy asked.

"We're married," Wallace replied. "We don't qualify."

"That is one overworked priest. Maybe Chuck is fake, you know, some tourist who was visiting the monastery in Big Sur when the quake went down. For a priest, he's enjoying life too much. A normal priest would have marriage burnout."

"I still can't believe this is happening," said Wallace.

I gotta say, it's your ex's loss. There she is, out there in Europe eating cheese and butter with some puffy pallid sheep-boy. I got the real man."

"I'm sure he's quite civilized," said Wallace. "She was always admiring scientists."

"So we're just Visigoths pretending to be civilized?" she said, laughing.

"Barbarians with clean flush toilets and showers. At least for now," he laughed.

"I hope I'm a pregnant barbarian. Barbarians are breeders, aren't they? It's the effete urban masses who don't have kids. The sheep-boys and the inbred ewes, all flocking around while the wolves eat them. Baaaa."

She reached up over their heads from the bed and made a swirling motion with her hands.

"One night? Our first night? You hope you're pregnant?" asked Wallace.

"It was the kind of night they make sagas about. 'On this night, King Arthur was created by Uther, King of all England, and Igraine, and the bed split in two from their coupling.'"

Wallace laughed.

"Besides, you've been storing it up for months," said Katy, rolling onto him and softly biting his chin. "Hmmmm. You need a shave, Tiger."

Wallace said nothing. The bright Carson Valley light was flooding through the windows despite the blinds.

"What about the children?" asked Wallace softly.

"The children are being well cared for. You saw that Mickey got a new puppy, so they're busy. Everybody had a family sleepover with Jesus and his family. Jesus promised to show them the tank again."

"An ex-felon teaching the kids to drive an armored vehicle with a cannon. What could go wrong?" replied Wallace.

"It's 90 years old," she said quietly, kissing him. "It's an antique."

"Oh, so it's an obsolete wreck of an armored vehicle with a can..."

She kissed him.

"You've waited a month since you made that phone call."

"Six weeks. It's been six weeks," said Wallace.

"I can't believe the Republic asked for you by name," said Katy. "Anyway that's stalled."

"My children are in Denmark," replied Wallace. "Hard to get over that,"

"And still, here it is, a wonderful new life, if you act now." said Katy. "Show them, even at a distance."

"I love you," said Wallace.

"I love you too," said Katy.

"Say, were you carrying that miserable little pistol the whole time?" asked Wallace.

"Since before you met me," she replied. "It didn't even get through his rib cage, you know."

"Ah well, it did the job. Still got it?"

"I'll keep it always. That's one of the lessons of this whole mess. Stay armed."

"You're not wearing it now?"

"You should examine me. Find out."

"You're naked," said Wallace.

"Still, one never knows," said Katy.

That thought made Wallace smile, as a joyful energy surged through him.

"Then a shower, a cleanup, then back to our tents and our people. Let someone else have this conjugal trailer," she added.

"They really call this the conjugal trailer?"

"Yep, and it's more than we've got. Aside from tents, guns, and children, we've got zip."

"At least we're free," said Wallace.

"Oh, we're never free. Someone's always out there to mess with us," said Katy. "Besides, we're all hostages to life. Prisoners of the sperm and the egg."

"Speaking of the sperm and the egg," said Wallace, kissing her nose.

"Speaking of tomorrow, we're going to live with your family, and all of them. Your father, his wife, your younger sisters. How do you think we'll get along?"

"Well, there's about thirty of us, and we're going to be in Mexico. Lots to like.

"Yes, but about me. How will they get along with me?"

"They'll love you. They treasure courage."

At the Finnish/Russian/Norwegian border

In northern Norway, the sun was rising. Dressed in thermal-dampening snow camouflage, Sarah inspected the rifle.

It was a Tikka, a Finnish 7.62 not unlike the guns she had used at the Swiss Rifle Club, back near Gonzales, at home in California. This gun was painted mottled cream and white, and had a suppressor, and a bipod, although Sarah had not extended the legs.

The snow tunnel was deep enough to keep Sarah in the shadows. She had dug it at night during a snowfall, partially behind a tree and up a cornice, so that the opening would be shielded from view. She had learned most of this from her father, Garth, back in the high Sierras in her teens. Back then it had been pretend, indulging a father's PTSD from his days in the Marine Corps. Now this was not pretend at all. Sarah adjusted the rifle so that it rested more easily on her backpack and peered through the twenty power scope. The Russians were moving very slowly down in the valley.

She didn't want to shoot just anyone. It must be an officer. To make them pay for Osten. A question came to her mind: out there in the rising sunlight, was the heat creating an updraft? That would shift the point of impact for a 7.62 at 1000 yards. She checked the range again. 938 yards. Hopefully the Russians didn't have IR detection deployed. Still, she chewed some snow to cool her breath.

She had competed in 1,000 yard F-TR class matches in the United States, and in Scandinavian long range matches at Haparanda, Talvisota, and elsewhere. This was going to be a lot like that, she hoped. Hunger. Ignore it. The snow-breeze was cold on her face, here in the shadows. Must keep the mittens on until the last instant.

Osten. My dear Osten. My lovable, caring, compassionate

Osten. She wondered if the snow of last night had fallen at his grave, or only here in the north.

When the Russians had occupied Latvia, Lithuania, and Estonia, a sudden rushed invasion to "protect ethnic Russians in the near abroad", she had warned her husband. He had assured her that the Russians had only intended to recapture what they had lost when the Soviet Union was demolished. Besides, he had reasoned, the ethnic Russians WERE the subject of discrimination. Then the overnight occupation of Denmark and a host of demands by the Russians against Norway. Sudden brutal demands, and Osten had suddenly become a patriot.

"We are NOT craven Americans," he had shouted at the protest at the Russian Embassy. Then the firing by the Russian guards, and Osten on the ground, choking on his own blood from a lung shot, and then the ambulance, and the sorrowful doctor. Dead on arrival. Poor naive bovine-stupid Osten, she thought as her anger grew. She was shaking, from the cold and from memories. She must calm down.

The next day: Russians pushing across the top of Finland, unable to crack through the Finnish defense to Helsinki farther south, unable to get their Russian Marines landed across the Swedish peninsula, the bombing of Oslo, and in the flight to safety, to Osten's family cabin in the Jotunheimen, a crashed military truck, hard men, Finns, a sniper team, and one of them injured.

She had taken the injured man's gear and sent him on to the cabin.

Now the Finns were in the adjoining canyon, and she was

waiting. Waiting for a Russian officer. And there he was. Adjust the scope for parallax. Yes. Nice bright shoulder boards. Photographers. Even better. The officer was waving his arms at the truck convoy which had just crossed the Norwegian border. Soft ushanka. No helmet. The photographers meant that he was important.

She removed her right mitten, checked the range, looked for any wind indications, saw the trees shiver. Five miles per hour from the right. Adjust. Now she would wait for the Finns to shoot first. At any moment they would open fire, and she would shoot, her noise covered by their firing. Any moment now.

Osten.

The End

"The Pyre" Afterword: Author's Notes and Comments.

Optional Reading For A Deeper Dive

WHY I WROTE THIS BOOK

"Don't quit your day job!"

That's the best advice anyone ever gave me as an author. Since I've been a fee-only investment advisor for 32 years, I have another wonderful professional life to enjoy. But that experience has developed the ability to identify long term trends. What I'm seeing now is not good news. I could either worry or write. So I wrote. Mostly at 4 AM and 8 PM, during 2019 and early 2020.

My last novel, "Honor", was my attempt to turn my insomnia into Steinbeck. It has sold perhaps 300 copies. Having come to the realization that I won't be Steinbeck and this book is very unlikely to sell much, I wrote The Pyre for my family, and for myself, to record the absurdities of social and political discourse in our present era. It's an extrapolation of current political trends and social behaviors. All the bizarre comments and suggestions across the political and social spectrum have intentionally been brought to realization in these pages. "Eat The Rich", for example, is a popular saying in certain circles. Consider what is being said. Likewise, "Cancel the Police" has deeper consequences than might be imagined in the heat of the moment.

When the grand experiment which is the United States of America comes to an end, as I perceive it will, individuals will ponder how such a wonderful invention could fail. This book is about that failure.

The United States will end because we, as individuals, did not have the self-discipline necessary to sustain it. There's a lot of political commentary afoot about how "they" are ruining the country. "They." The Republicans. The Democrats. The illegal immigrants. The rich. The reality is that few are looking in the mirror to see how they, themselves, might alter their lives for their own benefit, and for the benefit of their communities, and ultimately for the enhancement of their nation. We have lost self-discipline. How Roman of us.

It's so much easier, and in the end so much less effective, to blame someone or something else. Politicians know this, which is why self-determination is never a topic for them.

Many novels about the demolition of the United States take refuge in catastrophes and wars which are too huge, too apocalyptic, and too innovative to be resisted. That's not the story here. Everything I've written is far below the intensity and the scale of what is unwinnable. Instead, though, people will fail, and the nation will fail, because we simply don't have the political will. We've lost the understanding of why the states are better united than apart.

Novels have astonishingly predicted the future before. The great (and extremely financially successful) author Tom Clancy's novel "Debt of Honor" is not usually regarded as his best. Most often that accolade goes to his novel "Red Storm Rising". Yet in his 1994 work "Debt of Honor", Tom Clancy did something remarkable. He predicted 9/11.

Unfortunately, few people in the American team were paying attention.

I deeply hope I am not predicting anything with my own fiction. Yet I'm unable to resist the question of "what if" in our current era.

The City of Salinas and the State of California, in my opinion, have a history of pandering to the homeless virtue signaling industry, carrying out band aid projects which perpetuate but do not solve the issues of homelessness. The state of California has genuinely surrendered itself to the exaltation of social anarchy. Go to San Francisco and you'll see this novel brought to life. All the governmental and societal wailing has done nothing except enrich those who, like Pastor Paco, have found that there's big money in pain.

At the same time state and local governments give lip service to environmental issues while ravaging wilderness, such as the development of the North Pacheco Creek Dam for supplying water to the sprawling megalopolis of Silicon Valley, or not dealing with critical water shortfalls, and, for example, encouraging 1950's-style energy-inefficient development in fire and flood zones here in Monterey County.

Then there's the "self-canceling" of the Los Angeles

County Museum of Art. The roster of self-indulgent insanity across the political spectrum is a long read.

In fact, local governments, and the State of California, while successful in some ways, have a rather devastating history of hypocrisy, minor tyranny, and virtue signaling concerning just about everything. Of course, the elites of both parties have almost always looked after themselves first. Salinas is notorious for its self-oriented government. That's why I wrote this book. It's a form of protest against our nullification of culture and ethics.

This book also contains manipulation by foreign powers. In the story, none of them overtly attack the United States. It's all done rather neatly with false news and "soft force." NO flags flying. My thought is that historically our enemies have intruded or attacked when we are weak. Study history and you will note that wars usually have followed the downsizing of the United States military. Political interference by foreign nations usually has trailed periods of American political decadence.

In the 21st Century, the United States unfortunately has a plethora of weaknesses. Most of them are self-inflicted. The question posed by this novel is, what would happen if an external political power, driven by its own internal crises, decided to take advantage of a natural disaster to deliver repeated small covert attacks on a politically divided United States? What would happen if the enemies kept piling on, using disinformation and the standoff capabilities created by modern technology?

My guess is that in the fictional scenario of the novel, the enemy would lose about 20 personnel killed at most in order to incite us to rip ourselves to shreds. That's the point: in this disaster novel, we are our own worst enemies. We are the disaster.

Witness our recent COVID-19 self-destruction, and 2020's Black Lives Matter protests, and the challenges of maintaining a relatively free multicultural society become more obvious.

We have learned that factions in the media, some government-sponsored, some corporate-sponsored, and some simply trolls, are manipulating, modifying, and shaping our attitudes and behaviors. Our essential history and self-image are being rewritten by unseen advocates.

Regrettably, without the examples of history, many Americans don't handle sacrifice or responsibility well these days. Instead, governments seduce us with the "we'll do it all for you," siren song, which in the long run seldom works well. Government involvement always comes with a price tag.

THE DETAILS

The earthquake: I obviously set the date as the same day as the great San Francisco earthquake of 1906. On the Richter scale, that was apparently a 7.9. According to the very informative July 20th 2015 article in the New Yorker by Kathryn Schulz, "The Really Big One", the 1989 Loma Prieta earthquake was 6.9. The Richter is apparently logarithmic, and somewhat dependent upon earthquake duration, so I made this one about an 8, lasting 4 minutes, and it's a real ripper, the REALLY REALLY big one, you might say, reaching from San Diego all the way up to Vancouver. The San Andreas and the Cascadia all rip loose. My thought is that this is in reality very unlikely. But I wanted to create a situation which pushed our emergency response system to the breaking point.

On the other hand, I wanted to avoid the ludicrous overkill of movies such as "San Andreas" in which buildings fall like dominos and giant grand canyons open in the Salinas Valley. That's so unlikely as to be impossible. One other feature of the movie San Andreas that I have to mention is that apparently to survive a giant California earthquake, at least from that movie's perspective, you have to be very muscular or you have to be a woman with a very small waist and a very large chest. Watch the movie again and check it out: beautiful people live, and ugly people die. I didn't do that in this novel.

But what about tsunamis? Frankly that's a bit of a push around Monterey Bay, but it IS possible, and to the degree I described in the novel. Here's a great map of tsunami risk in California: http://maps.conservation.ca.gov/cgs/informationwarehouse/index.html?map=tsunami

To follow up the science of what the next big quake will look like, here are more California earthquake ideas: https://www.smithsonianmag.com/science-nature/what-will-really-happen-california-when-san-andreas-unleashes-big-one-180955432/

In a real earthquake would a tsunami hit central California? It could happen, but probabilities are moderate.

Again, I threw this in to provide a situation where the system was mildly overwhelmed. I've imagined a fifteen-foot (five meter) tsunami which would be caused by a disruption of the ocean floor, probably caused by fault action under the sea. Something like the Fukushima tsunami, which is well within the range of reality. Locals will remember that we DID have a tsunami which was underwhelming to watch but nevertheless did surprising damage. My tsunami damage model was essentially derived not only from the above data but also from Monterey Bay Area Research Institute's sea level rise studies.

I've also altered geography as well. The beautiful San Antonio Mission is in reality surrounded by the US Army base of Hunter Liggett, which encompasses thousands of acres of national park-worthy meadows. I'm praying they don't build houses all over it. In the novel I've moved the mission farther back into the National Forest, and Hunter Liggett is smaller and miles away. I did this to create isolation for the group.

Likewise, I moved the Jolon road up towards Soledad to make the prison closer. I'm sure that the residents of Soledad Correctional are better behaved than that. I altered Salinas Valley geography. Forgive me, but this is a novel.

SOME BOOKS AND LINKS FOR ADDITIONAL READING

Debt Of Honor by Tom Clancy. This isn't really a disaster novel. It's more of an adventure novel which ends badly. But it gets credit for inspiring Pyre: it seems to have genuinely predicted 9/11. A good disaster novel should be usable, and should change the way we see reality.

Failures of Imagination by U.S. Congressman Michael McCaul, Crown Forum, 2016. This is an interesting, fictionalized synopsis of various scenarios envisioned by congressional study groups. Individuals within the Federal Government are aware of the risks we face, and some of those scenarios are pretty ruthless. One of the scenarios is China buying the White House. Another is a pandemic of a weaponized agent released at an amusement park. All rather relevant. My novel is more realistic than we might wish to accept.

Rigged: America, Russia, and One Hundred Years of Covert Electoral Interference by David Shimer, published by Alfred A. Knopf, 2020. Countries messing with each other's elections and internal politics is not a new phenomenon. It's been a feature since the invention of voting. The relationship between the United States and Russia is particularly rich in covert political action, and Putin's Russia is only the latest player. Yes, the Commies have been after us since they began, as we have been after them. Including external political intervention in my novel is thus a realistic feature, and sensible for the external agency. In the novel, it's mostly China, which can't really be blamed for intervening. If the Republic of California is dumb enough to join the Belt and Road initiative, that's their problem.

The Crack At The Edge Of The World: America And The Great California Earthquake of 1906 by Simon Winchester, Harper Torch Publishing, 2005. This is history, yet it reads like a novel. This was one of the primary influences of what the earthquake in my novel might be like. The experience of a great shake is something I don't wish to have, yet I wanted it to be as realistic as possible. While construction techniques have changed since 1906, the ground and its behaviors have not. At some point we'll have another great quake here in California. I hope I'm in Maui when it happens. This book gives us some insight into both the earth moving and peoples' behavior.

This Nonviolent Stuff'll Get You Killed: How Guns Made The Civil Rights Movement Possible by Charles E. Cobb Jr., Duke University Press, 2016. Tyranny seems to happen whenever one side has all the power and the other side does not. Genocide sometimes follows thereafter. Part of the campaign of those who would be tyrants is to convince potential victims to disarm themselves. As this book points out, suppression of African American gun ownership was a precursor to lynching and bigotry. Freedom for repressed minorities came with greater gun ownership and the courage for self defense. Thus, in my novel, firearms are outlawed quickly when California becomes a fascist state. The Republic's rationale is very seductive.

Drone Warrior by Brett Velecovich and Christopher S. Stewart, published by William Morrow, 2017. Oh, yes, the drones invented by my fictional characters Pat and Glenda are quite real. I actually used less of them in my novel than would probably be present in reality, because I didn't want the novel to be about drones and technology. It seems reasonable, though, that in a relatively isolated place like the San Antonio de Padua Mission, precious drone resources would be lightly used. This book is a gripping description of what is really going on. It's more like the Terminator than Les Misérables.

Lights Out by Ted Koppel, published by Crown Publishers, 2015. A look at the realities of our power grid vulnerabilities. The outages described in my novel would be normal, even expected, especially if an external political agency decided to create a deniable, untraceable, break in our power supplies. Given political realities, my expectation is that perhaps even a slight version of what is discussed in this book is quite possible.

The Great Deluge: Hurricane Katrina, New Orleans, and the Mississippi Gulf Coast by Douglas Brinkley, published by William Morrow, 2006. Since Hurricane Katrina is a recent example of a large-scale disaster in the United States, it serves as a reasonable case study for another large scale disaster elsewhere, such as the earthquake I envision in this novel. This well-written history provides us some lessons: Help may be at least a week away. You can sit in the rubble or you can do something about it. The police and other emergency services may be completely overwhelmed, so you may REALLY be on your own for at least a week. This is yet another reason why you don't want to disarm, and another reason to have adequate toilet paper, food, medical supplies, and survival gear, as we discovered again in 2020. It helps to have links to a place outside the area affected by the disaster.

Also, a small yet surprising percentage of the population will become brutal thugs. Rape, unpleasant as it is, apparently quickly becomes more common in times of civil unrest. That's why it's in my novel.

When Money Dies by Adam Fergusson, published by Public Affairs, 1975. At some point, perhaps relatively soon, the United States will cross the tipping point where excessive debt begins to reduce the growth potential of the American economy. Perhaps we're already there, especially in terms of our overcommitted defined benefit pensions. In my novel, I try to bring that out front and center, because it's potentially going to be a major feature of any coming disaster. If the rapacious advocates for increased taxes on the wealthy continue their antics, other nations are going to get wise and money is going to do what it does: move. Moderation in all things. This history recounts what happens when the government doesn't work, in this case in 1920's Germany. Does anyone remember what happened next?

Trade Wars Are Class Wars: How Rising Inequality Distorts The Global Economy And Threatens World Peace by Matthew C. Klein and Michael Pettis, Yale University Press, 2020. What if all the laborers of the world are one big labor pool, including those in the United States and China. What if all the elites of the world are implicitly working together to maximize their wealth? What if, in fact, we are ruled by a "Uniparty" of elites and their bought minions in both parties who rely on media and hype to keep citizens across the globe focused on less important issues and divisions while they grow affluence? This is not fiction. It makes one think. Thus, in my novel, the elites of the Republic of California evoke the various politically correct issues while seeking to grow their own abundance. Patriots they are most assuredly not, yet patriotism is their first justification.

One Second After by William R. Forstchen. Tom Doherty Associates, 2009. This is the first book of the John Matherson trilogy, and all are great case studies concerning the real-world threat of electromagnetic pulse. I decided not to include an EMP in my novel because Mr. Forstchen has pounded the topic to death, and his description of the event is unbeatable. We must content ourselves in Pyre with mere hacking and denial of service. Read this book to behold a more catastrophic alternative future.

One Year After by William R. Forstchen. Tom Doherty Associates, 2015. The second of three books in the invaluable John Matherson trilogy, this is a ripping good read. Intentionally, I decided to NOT make the disasters as apocalyptic as this because reality favors a lesser catastrophe, and because I feel that international political actors would rise up sooner and more emphatically.

The Final Day by William R. Forstchen. Tom Doherty Associates, 2016. The third of the gold-standard John Matherson trilogy, and profoundly the most far-reaching. How do I communicate the story I'm trying to express in

Pyre? One way is to spread out the family geographically, which is what I did.

However, as great a game-changer as an EMP or series of EMP's would be, I decided not to include them in Pyre simply because to do so would ensnare the entire plot line in a traditional all-out thermonuclear war. That is utterly horrendous but not the theme of the book. The basic thread of Pyre is that natural disasters and external forces give California and the United States slight blows and both self-destruct like France in 1940. See here for more discussion: https://nationalinterest. org/blog/the-buzz/would-90-percent-americans-really-die-emp-attack-some-think-24005.

And here: http://www.thespacereview.com/article/1549/1

Much easier (and realistic) to have the power grid destroyed by cyber war, which we know is already in the realm of reality.

And then a few small tactical nukes smuggled into ports in fishing vessels: https://www.sciencemag.org/news/2017/02/test-blasts-simulate-nuclear-attack-us-port

Blackout by James Goodman. North Point Press, 2003. Nonfiction! On the hot summer evening of July 13th, 1977, New York suffered a catastrophic power failure. Almost all people behaved wonderfully. But a criminal minority created absolute havoc. Cities still won't or can't admit that some citizens take terrible advantage of any disaster. So, let's take the July 13th, 1977 power outage, and recreate it in a city already seething with political divisions and false news. Make the cause a mild cyberattack. Sprinkle some racial rumors over the whole mess. There you have it.

This book was full of ideas. I might add that this book provides more confirmation that you really want to know how to use a firearm in a safe, legal manner because the New York City police department was apparently completely overwhelmed during the July 13th, 1977 blackout, and surprisingly many people became criminals when the opportunity presented itself.

What would make the State of California's government respond to its citizens like that? Elite politicians dictating policies in the midst of crisis are actually rather normal, as we saw during the COVID-19 pandemic. "Defunding" the police has already happened in some communities, and citizens have been left to defend themselves.

A less dramatic example was when France tried its gasoline tax in 2018 which resulted in riots in November and December 2018. That also resulted in some looting.

Patriots: The Men Who Started The American Revolution, by AJ Langguth, Simon & Shuster 1988. What does a book about the American Revolution have to do with a book about the collapse of the United States in 2022? My perception is that within the US, people are cultivating contempt for each other, and in my book that contempt leads to both violence and abandonment. Its worth wondering why, only a few years after the successful conclusion of the global Seven Years War, known in North America as the French & Indian War, the most powerful nation in the world, Great Britain, would go to war with its own North American colonies. In short, misunderstanding, poor information, disinformation, and contempt.

One could say that the American Revolution began by accident, created by a tiny minority of radicals. A similar condition exists today between the coasts and the interior states of the United States. In this novel, that cultivated contempt leads to disaster.

1861: The Civil War Awakening by Adam Goodheart, published by Alfred A. Knopf, 2011. Likewise, this fascinating history deals with the great contempt and the many illusions which ravaged American society on both sides prior to our Civil War. Disinformation, hatred, and romanticism led us to our greatest national self-immolation thus far. There are many similarities with our modern era. Hint: Trump was not a cause; he was a symptom. Also interesting is the concept that secession is LEGAL if it is carried out by a vote of the people. That didn't happen in 1861, hence Abraham Lincoln was able to claim that the Confederacy was illegal. What would happen if states could come and go at will? If secession was carried out on a county by county basis, my guess is that California would divide at the San Joaquin River, creating the independent Republic of California, and the state of East California.

The Coming American Civil War by Tom Kawezynski, 2018. Let's try to calm our national dialogue down a notch. As this book demonstrates, civil war is being actively discussed, sometimes with romanticized images which downplay the true catastrophe of a real conflict. Remember, we're all being played.

Cyber War by Matthew Mather brilliantly read for Audible by Tom Taylorson. Great fiction written about a nest of yuppies who freeze to death and eat each other while they can't find their butts with both hands. Seriously: The New Yorkers in this novel are startlingly incompetent. The challenge, a cyber-attack in the middle of a snowstorm, is stunningly realistic. This book colored how I presented our own protagonists, and also how extreme their challenges would be. After all, what I'm writing is really about how the United States comes apart because people are filled with hate. In my own novel, the disasters are just catalysts for human actions.

The Winds Of War by Herman Wouk, Little, Brown, and Company, 1971. One of the best novels of all time, ever, this novel helped me understand how to fictionally place a family in several places at once. It also wonderfully depicted a family caught up in onrushing evil. Some family members can see what's coming, and some can't. **War and Remembrance,** the sequel, is also a stupendous read. Of course, the premise is fictional to the point of absurd fantasy: a family can't be in all those places at exactly the crucial times. Yet novels such as these often do a better job than most histories at depicting the avoidable carnage of World War II, and the astonishing self-delusion of many of those who were caught up in it.

Hitler's Willing Executioners: Ordinary Germans And The Holocaust by Daniel Jonah Goldhagen, Vintage Books, 1996. What screams at you in the pages of this frightening history is that the war criminals of the German Nazi Reich were...

well, they were us. They were ordinary people twisted into doing dreadful unspeakable crimes. This book helped me to see that there is a hidden demon in all of us. Do we feed it with disinformation and hatred, or do we put it as far away from us as we can? In the novel, this reality makes some of the bizarre manias in the plot quite possible.

In The Garden Of Beasts: Love, Terror, and an American Family In Hitler's Berlin by Erik Larson, published by Broadway Books, 2011. Envision 1933, Berlin, Germany. Hitler is clearly bent on murder and expansion. Surely the world will stop him. Well, no. In fact, as this history details, Hitler and his banal gaggle of political gangsters faced few barriers in taking over the nation and creating the Holocaust. While the ambassador's daughter flirted with Nazis and Soviets, the anti-Nazi ambassador faced almost as much opposition from President Roosevelt's government as he did in Germany. A fascinating read about how evil exists because people don't care to act. I incorporated this concept in my novel.

Shake Hands With The Devil: The Failure Of Humanity In Rwanda by Lt. General Romeo Dallaire, published by Random House Canada, 2003. One dangerous emphasis of political virtue signaling, both in 1933 and today, is that somehow we've all grown up, we've grown beyond evil. The fraudulent message is that we should all turn in our firearms and our warrior pretenses and join the peaceful community of man. Just follow the government and all will be well.

The reality is brutally different: in all of human history,

my studies suggest that pacifism and individual disarming has always led to violence, and sometimes it has been catastrophic and genocidal. The global community routinely enables recurrent genocide by international thugs with hand-wringing, thoughts and prayers. Usually that's about it. Any genuine armed response to mass murder is usually derided as war-like.

It seems that the propensity towards genocide is a 'normal' human trait: when one side has all the power and the other side is utterly helpless, genocide and abuse are historically frequent, as we saw with California Native Americans in the mid-19th Century.

This book's history is horrific: in the early 1990's the UN forces in Rwanda, commanded by Lt. General Dallaire of Canada, were forbidden from intervening in the Rwandan Civil War by their desk-bound superiors thousands of miles away. While the UN security forces stood by, over 800,000 Rwandans were murdered, including over 300,000 children. Rape, wholesale banditry, and starvation were commonplace. The entire event took about 100 days. This book cemented my perception that the world will usually stand by when bad things happen, until it's too late, unless there is compelling national interest.

Faced with the looming cataclysm of Rwanda, the responses at the time by the chinless prevaricating weasels of the U.N. and its craven member nations were the normal responses of functionary governments. It's happened before, and it's happened since. Ethiopia. The Gulags. The Rape Of Nanking. The Holocaust. Tibet. The Cultural Revolution.

The Congo. Cambodia. Bosnia. The Uighurs. Genocide is normal. Government virtue signaling and inaction is routine.

That's why the sight of American Congressional leaders kneeling with Ghanaian prayer shawls draped around their necks after creating decades of oppressive legislation, and with most of these individuals having consciously chosen to neglect the slaughter of innocents such as occurred in Rwanda, leaves me undecided to vomit, cry, or laugh hysterically. Virtue signaling while doing nothing is normal. Selfless statesmanship is actually quite rare. If we teach our children otherwise, we are lying.

I must note the special moral heroism of General Dallaire. Everybody involved now wants to cover up the quagmire of intentional neglect which was the Rwandan Genocide. It takes special courage to drag it back to the light of public scrutiny.

Total Resistance by H. Von Dach, Snowball Publishing, 1958. This was written by a member of the Swiss military to prepare the Swiss nation for invasion by the Soviets. It is now standard reading by people who expect a civil war to erupt here. It was a great source of ideas for the novel, but also a stunning indication of how utterly vicious another American Civil War might be.

The Great Degeneration: How Institutions Decay and Economies Die by Niall Ferguson, published by Penguin Press, 2013. This is a great short read about how robust cultures and economies fade and devolve into squalor. Packed with statistics and details to document that the core success-oriented values of the western world are slipping away. This is a must-read to face reality before we alter our personal behaviors to make things better. Best in small doses, since it is quite sobering. I can't read this stuff and sleep soundly afterwards, which is perhaps why I have insomnia. Nevertheless, this is reality.

Man Corn: Cannibalism and Violence In The Prehistoric American Southwest, by Christy G. Turner II and Jacqueline A. Turner, published by The University of Utah Press, 1999. Let me present a paradigm: whenever there is utopia, either barbarians or a government will come to try to destroy it. Utopia attracts destruction. That's what seems to have happened in the Anasazi Culture in the American Southwest before the Europeans could get in on the looting. Even more disturbing, there seems to have been an abundance of ritual cannibalism, perhaps not by the Anasazi but by some yet-unknown group which invaded them. I read this book, which is large and emphatic and even more frightful than any horror film I've ever seen, to determine if the "Eat The Rich" movement could ever get hysterical enough to commit actual cannibalism. Answer, reluctantly, yes. Scary as hell. The need for defense of a well-functioning society is ubiquitous and multi-dimensional.

The authors get creds for vast scientific courage, in an academic and socio-political climate which has adopted the mythology of the peaceful pre-European Native American wonderland (never mind them Aztecs), it requires tremendous moral bravery to stand up and disagree, especially when the subject matter is this...gross.

Upheaval: Turning Points For Nations In Crisis by Jared Diamond, published by Little, Brown, and Company, 2019. Any good books list for the breakdown of societies has to finish with the compiled works of Jared Diamond. His ***Collapse: How Societies Choose To Fail Or Succeed***, Penguin Books, 2005, is also a superlative read. I'm left with the impression that many Americans think "it can't happen here", and this novel is my response. Yes, it CAN happen here, and the path to avoiding societal breakdown will lead us back to personal responsibility. This book will get you down in the weeds, in the details, where reality truly resides. Yet my book is a novel. It's all made up.

RESEARCH, TRAVEL, AND PLACES TO SEE

Now for something much much happier.

Nobody in this novel is real. Everybody is fake, imaginary, untrue. I was especially cautious about accidentally depicting the motives or actions of someone in reality in this novel. So, if you see yourself, calm down. It's all completely made up. Unless you see yourself as a vaquero with a blunderbuss. If that is the case, we should talk.

I used real places in this novel so that readers can, where possible, visit. My perspective is that this makes the book more enjoyable. Here's a few ideas for visiting the settings in this novel. I'm going to explore some if not all of these on YouTube as well.

San Antonio de Padua Mission. By all that is holy, and I mean that literally, you should visit this beautiful place, preferably the first Saturday of April during the celebration of Mission Days. In 2019, I was there as a volunteer living history person, completely dressed in 1840's attire, when someone made the comment, "Gosh, I wonder what would happen if we had an earthquake right now?" That's when the idea for this novel entered my mind.

If you can't be there during Mission Days, consider a visit in spring when the wildflowers are blooming. It's a spectacularly welcoming place, replete with genuine history, and you'll see the giant fences of the Army base looming nearby. Get there early enough and you'll hear reveille. Ask about the famous cat. Visualize, if you can, the events of the novel taking place right there. The Mission's phone number is 831-385-4478. They also have a great website.

If you contact the mission, it may be possible to arrange a genuine group religious retreat to the San Antonio Mission de Padua and stay overnight in the monks' bedrooms. I don't know anywhere else where it is possible to sleep at a genuine mission. This is for genuine religious retreats: it's not a hotel. If you are lucky enough to be there in the fall when it rains, you are blessed indeed.

For a special treat, research The Hacienda at Fort Hunter Liggett, which IS a hotel. Unlike our protagonists, you may actually be able to sleep inside the wire of the Army base.

Nacimiento-Ferguson Road: Here's a great outing: when you visit the mission, drive over the road to Big Sur on the path of Bear, Garth, Tiger, and Hopi. Stop at the turnout to Cone Peak. Drive down to the beautiful, world class Highway One, and head north to Carmel. You'll need to reserve lodging or a camping space months in advance, but if possible, stay the night in Big Sur, so that you can see the stars I mentioned in the novel. Perhaps you'll see the Mexican Air Force fly by.

Bonus hints: there IS a place with yurts, Treebones, near Los Burros Road, although I didn't consult with them at all during the creation of this novel. They often have quinoa. And yes, there's a monastery to the north. I didn't consult with them either when I wrote this, but I hear the fruitcake is excellent.

Nope, no cannibals. Yet.

Old Town Salinas: I did not consult with Salinas City government, Salinas business owners, or Salinas property owners while making this book. As a lifetime resident I've learned how the system works by living within it.

For some reason the City of Salinas routinely tears down the oldest and most beautiful buildings it can find. My experience is that this is a common behavior of many city managers, who wish to aspire to making whatever town which hires them into another Silicon Valley. Also, there's a lot of money in redevelopment, and the developers are usually very connected politically. There's always intense pressure to destroy, rebuild, and expand. Apparently, empire building is not limited to the Caesars.

Few of Salinas' older monuments have survived, although these are always in danger from zealous pencil pushers and eager developer elites. Some of these classic buildings are to be found on Main Street in Salinas. When I wrote the novel,

I figured I would let the Salinas City government have what they really want, to get those redevelopment dollars which are apparently more precious than the quality of life of its citizens.

If the city and property owners haven't yet been pressured by elites into destroying them, some places to see on Main Street are **Downtown Book And Sound,** which was the fictional location of Dina Montero's bookstore and newspaper headquarters, **Patria,** which is one of the hideouts in the book, and also **Monterey Coast Brewing.** Both provide superb meals, as does **Tico's Tacos,** which is the source of inspiration for Katy's superb cuisine. **Salinas High School** is nearby, although it requires a permit to visit. In reality there are no strike team personnel entombed near the stadium.

The **Steinbeck Center,** the home of a delightful small John Steinbeck museum, became a reeducation/processing receiving center in my fictional world, where they took people before sending them to the larger facility at the **Salinas Rodeo Grounds.** The Salinas Rodeo Grounds WERE used as a collection point in 1942, for Japanese American citizens who were interned in World War II by the very eager Warren California government and the Federal Roosevelt Administration. I must recommend attending the Salinas California Rodeo at least once. Come hungry because the food served during the event is epic.

The Salinas Public Library has now become a gathering place for the homeless and a venue for petty crime, largely neglected by people with families who dislike feces, pandering, and purse-stealing. Go there and you can walk the fight with the white supremacists (they aren't really there) and visit the palm trees. Bring any belongings with care.

Steinbeck House is the author John Steinbeck's childhood home. Make reservations and enjoy a superb lunch. I've waited to see John's ghost, but it's never happened. This place is roughly where Katy and her family lived. Walk over by Roosevelt school to read the flagpole monument to Salinas' World War I dead, and you'll be able to see the county offices which tilted in this fictional novel. Look down Capitol Street and you can see the filled-in slough which awaits our next big shake.

Further afield, if you go to **Seacliff Beach**, one of the most beautiful places on earth, you will see an old cement ship, the SS Palo Alto, with a fascinating story of its own. Look north and you will see those expensive beach houses which must someday fall prey to sea level rise or, yes, a tsunami.

EQUIPMENT, MATERIAL CULTURE, AND GUNS!

I researched these issues a lot.

The highly efficient deca-panels are already invented as we speak, and electric quads are already with us. As these get more available and cheaper, they will remake the wilderness experience. The days of loud engine bullies who race their off-road vehicles past our campsites will happily be mostly behind us.

The "1858" Remington cap and ball revolver, often called the Remington Beals or the Remington New Model Army, was a primary handgun of the Civil War which saw use through the 1870's. Garth has one of these because his unit is portraying 1860's to 1870's. This was my own first pistol, which I acquired with lettuce picking money when I was 14. During my studies I was surprised at how GOOD a firearm this is. Check out my YouTube videos about my research. According to **Percussion Revolvers, A Guide To Their History, Performance, and Use, by Mike Cumpston and Johnny Bates,** page 121, the fully-loaded Remington produces energy levels about on par with the .45 ACP. So Garth isn't under gunned. I fired about 300 rounds in researching this book.

The cavalry troops of the 1870's were mostly equipped with the Springfield trapdoor carbine, which frankly was a cost-saving effort after the Civil War and was obsolete when it was created. They were also armed with the Colt Single Action Army pistol with a long barrel. Both of these were featured in the novel, but I haven't yet had time to study them.

The Marlin 1895 .45-70 rifle is a go-to gun for me, a relic of my ranch days. Garth had it during my novel "Honor". It's back because I needed an "old timey" gun with enough energy to stop a vehicle. Part of my research for this novel was to take an 1895 Marlin on a pig hunt. The .45-70 Barnes 300 grain bullet went from one end of the pig to the other. So, yes, it CAN stop a bison, or a "slow elk". Again, check my YouTube.

I gave Bear a Henry rifle when, to be historically accurate, he might have had a Spencer. Henry rifles were rare, trea-sured, and weak during the Civil War. They fired a cartridge with only 25 grains of black powder, which is about what a pistol of the era would shoot. Underpowered. But that brass frame films well, and Spencers are scarce and expensive. Plus, a Henry allows him to shoot a lot, so I put it in.

A blunderbuss? I put that in because I've never fired one, and it seems like it could be dramatic on film, especially the 4 gauge behemoth marketed by Sitting Fox Muzzleloaders. It also highlights that in this era of obsession of modernity by gun writers, the gun you've got is better than no gun at all. Plus if this novel ever gets filmed, a blunderbuss is going to make the world's biggest shoulder-fired explosion.

Finally, I have Raley use a .44 Magnum derringer because such an absurdity really exists. The gun I fired in my research for this novel was dreadfully inaccurate, with the bullets producing a group about 8 feet across at 25 yards. Bullets which actually hit the target, a rare event indeed, tended to go in sideways. That's why I have Raley jam the miserable little gat into the guard's gonads, and not shoot. She might have missed.

Thank you to....

My wife, **Karen Andresen,** who tolerated my 4 AM wakeup. Writing this book was like running an ultramarathon, and sometimes very emotionally painful. Thanks to my family who tolerated my studies and obsessions about something which was art for art's sake.

Alan Maxwell provided great and plot-altering feedback early in the process of writing. Thank you! See the difference?

Peter G. Andresen

Exceptional complete detailed line-editing was provided by **Dan Mason.** Thank you and Semper Fi! I gotta come see those elk.

Peter Garin...how do I describe this? **Peter Garin** was way far ahead in the disaster Olympics. He was a doomscroller before doomscrolling was cool. Imagine sitting around the pool at a remote wilderness cabin discussing the ten most likely ways society will collapse. If possible I'm going to create some YouTube of our musings over a bottle of local red.

Jack Swallow is one of the living history gurus at San Juan Bautista State Historic Park. COVID permitting, **San Juan Bautista State Historic Park** offers a living history program on the first Saturday of every month. He provided a great deal of feedback about what would be present at a living history encampment and what would be absent.

Chris Bunn was another early proofreader who suggested plot changes which are now baked in. He's also a sci-fi Fantasy author under his own name and possesses one of the most effective and unusual senses of humor I've ever known.

My mother, **Ruth Andresen,** is now 100 years old, and she is wise enough to see the parallels between this era and that of the 1920's. Her ability to provide long term historical insights for comparison with current events has been a core feature of this book.

Patricia Sullivan has the moral courage to confront the self-created bizarre behavior of Salinas City government, and thus served as an inspiration for this novel. And yes, she owns a genuine bookstore. That takes monumental courage right there. All those dangerous paper books. They aren't even registered.

Mike Middaugh was the source of many of my research materials, which provided the depth in this tale, as well as some sleepless nights when I couldn't stop reading.

The staff at San Antonio Mission de Padua deserves thanks for hosting Mission Days and providing an exceptional venue to understand original mission culture as it was before urban congestion.

Next...

If **"The Pyre"** is at all popular, I intend to do a sequel. If not, I face a decision. I have created about twenty partially written historical novels. Do I start with the first in chronological order, which begins in the year 1588, or do I leap ahead to the middle of the timestream? All these novels are connected. Eventually, all these families have descendants who are connected to each other and who are alive in the 21st Century in Monterey County, California. My effort is to capture the incredible struggles of all our ancestors and how, in a very real sense, we ARE all related. Every person, and every family, has within them the stuff of legends.

Here's the tentative opening from the unfinished outline of my 1897, **"Ventana,"** set in Monterey County.

"Just as I told you. These bones are from the Digger cem'tery by the San Juan Bautista mission. We dug 'em up a few nights back for you museum types. Big business in bones. For yur feenology."

"Phrenology"

"That's how you use science to prove dark people aren't as good ez us, right?"

"Unfortunate. Still, it's science, so it must be correct."

"You got an accent. You an immigrant, right?"

"Yes, but she wasn't."

"Yeah. How do you know she was a she?"

"The bones look polished"

"Museums like 'em like that. You said you was from a museum,"

"Ah. Well, there are museums and museums. Notice anything odd about this?"

The tall slender gray haired man with glasses pointed to the glistening skull, at the teeth.

"A fillin'. What's a fillin' doin' there? Hey, I KNOW this is a digger gal. I got her from Mission San Juan Bautista. Anyway she was a digger. A Mission digger. That's why she's for sale. Don't know who she was. Don't care."

"Oh, I know who she was. She was my wife."

"Now put that pistol away. Damn it's an old horse pistol. Put it away. No cause to be angry."

The gaunt gray haired man shot the bone salesman twice,

and watched wordlessly in the stench of the swirling black powder smoke as the man slumped back against the bookcase and died.

"Ah. Well, yes, it's a horse pistol," said the gray haired man softly with a slight accent. He put the large revolver on the counter on the table next to the bone-filled wooden box, calmly sat down, and waited for the Salinas City Police to arrive. This was Main Street, in the center of town. Surely someone had heard the shots.

He looked at the wooden box. It read, 'Ivory Soap, Proctor and Gamble'. It looked new.

"We had a wonderful life together, didn't we, Maisy?" he said, quietly.

Contact me...

With comments, feedback, or suggestions. I'm at peter-gandresen@gmail.com, and at "Pete Andresen, Writer" on Facebook. Advice welcome.

Made in the USA
Middletown, DE
18 February 2021